PRAISE FOR GRAHAM BARTLETT

'*City on Fire* is such a thrilling instalment . . . like being given secret access into an incident room'
Araminta Hall

'An immersive, gripping and tightly plotted thriller'
Nadine Matheson

'Enthralling . . . told with the confidence and verve that you'd expect from a writer who's been there and seen it for real'
Neil Lancaster

'Authentic, pacy, gripping and first-class characters'
Steve Cavanagh

'An absolutely electrifying read'
Imran Mahmood

'Bartlett has set a new standard for the police procedural'
Kia Abdullah

'A brilliantly gritty slice of British crime'
T. M. Logan

'Explosive'
Vaseem Khan

'A fast-paced, just-one-more-chapter thriller'
Clare Mackintosh

'This one's a cracker!'
John Sutherland

'If you want to walk on the wild side, read *City on Fire*'
P. D. Viner

By Graham Bartlett

Bad for Good
Force of Hate
City on Fire

CITY ON FIRE

GRAHAM BARTLETT

Allison & Busby Limited
11 Wardour Mews
London W1F 8AN
allisonandbusby.com

First published in Great Britain by Allison & Busby in 2024.

A CIP catalogue record for this book is available from the British Library.

First Edition

ISBN 978-0-7490-3051-3

Typeset in 11.5/16.5 pt Adobe Garamond Pro by Allison & Busby Ltd.

By choosing this product, you help take care of the world's forests. Learn more: www.fsc.org.

FSC
www.fsc.org
MIX
Paper | Supporting responsible forestry
FSC® C171272

Printed and bound by
CPI Group (UK) Ltd, Croydon, CR0 4YY

For Julie, Conall, Niamh and Deaglan
who believe in me even when I do not.

I always tell authors that the story and characters must come first. With that in mind, this is a work of fiction, hence some structures, titles, locations, even some police procedures, have been modified to serve the story and the characters for your enjoyment.

1

'I said strip,' boomed the voice from behind the pistol, which was trained rigidly between Ged's eyes.

'Jesus. Fucking calm down mate,' said Ged, trying to steady the wobble from his voice. 'What is this? I thought we were sweet.'

'You're either a grass or a fed,' the man said as a statement, not a question, in the faux-patois lilt that without the barrel so close, Ged would have mocked.

He glanced around, weighing up his chances of flight or fight. The basement looked – and smelt – like a disused beer cellar. The reek of stale yeast and the chill suggested that it was months, maybe years, since a jolly publican had scurried down here to change the lager.

The only door was guarded by a masked-up meathead who, by the way he held his Glock pistol across his chest, had clearly watched too many episodes of *Narcos*. Surrounding Ged were three others, all of whom looked desperate to rip his head off should he try to escape. There was even one stood under the beer-drop hatch as if, even at his most athletic, he could possibly scale the clammy bricks to launch himself out of that.

His only option was to style it out.

'Let's not get excited,' he said. 'I know you have to be careful, but we're all in this game together and you seeing my todger, such as it is in these temperatures, might scar you for life.'

'Fam, if you don't strip now I swear to God, I'm going to plug a bullet right through your brain.'

Ged couldn't allow the gunman's anxiety to become contagious. There was no telling what the other numpties would do if a drop of adrenaline found its way into their bloodstreams.

'OK, but bear in mind what I said about it being cold down here.'

First he unzipped, then slowly removed, his grey hoodie. He was about to drop it on the floor when a girl's voice to his right snapped, 'Chuck it here.'

Ged looked round, genuinely shocked. He turned back to the mouthpiece with the gun. 'Really? Does she need to see this?'

'You ain't shy boy, are you?' the gunman sniggered.

Ged shrugged. No point arguing, but to be called boy by a scrote young enough to be his son was taking the piss. He launched the top over and the girl caught it in both hands.

'Keep going,' said the gunman.

Each time Ged removed an item of clothing and threw it over, there was a shuffle from a different direction as if the ring of steel were growing anxious that they were running out of reasons to kill him. He strung the striptease out as long as he could until he was butt naked and shivering.

'Happy?' he said, his hands out in supplication.

'I'll tell you if I'm happy, but you've got some reassuring to do.'

'Ask away mate but I promise you, I'm much better company with my clothes on.' As he was saying this, another of the lieutenants stepped up and, with his mobile phone torch, checked every inch of Ged's naked flesh. 'Each to their own,' said Ged.

A couple of minutes passed before the excruciating exercise was over and the man with the flashlight and the girl checking the clothes grunted that they'd found nothing.

'Get dressed,' came the command.

Ged complied as quickly as his icy fingers would allow. As he zipped up his jacket, the man jabbed the pistol into his side. 'You ever cross us, fam, we won't be so nice. You get me?'

Ged stepped back and turned. 'Listen pal, if this thing is going to work, we have to show some mutual respect and . . .' He cast his hand around. 'You didn't need to do that.'

'I ain't taking no chances.'

'And what's this shit about being a grass or fed?'

'Fam, I trust you for now. No wire, no piece.'

'So, are we doing this?' said Ged.

'Sure. The brown should be here by the end of the week. You got the "ps"?'

'I don't carry money like that. Not on me, as you've just seen, but I'll get it.'

'£250k by tonight, the rest when we deliver.'

'Sure, like we agreed,' said Ged, his inner terror only now starting to dwindle.

The boss set out the terms and where the drop would happen. Ged nodded and checked some details which, as only he knew, were completely irrelevant.

Fifteen minutes later and having succumbed to the temptation to blow the thug manning the door a kiss, Ged was back on the street pacing to his next meeting.

Having doubled back a few times, stopping suddenly to look in shop windows and jaywalking the bustling high street, Ged disappeared down an alley and in through a nondescript door. Taking the stairs two at a time he burst into a room to be greeted by his cover officer, Nick, holding a Starbucks Americano and a doorstep bacon sandwich while busting a gut to stifle his giggles.

'Just fuck off,' Ged said as he grabbed the coffee and sarnie. 'And stay fucked off.'

'I'm sorry mate, but put yourself in my shoes. Or any shoes come to that.'

'Ha, fucking, ha.'

'*You seeing my todger, such as it is in these temperatures, might scar you for life.* Fucking priceless, mate.'

For the first time Ged cracked a smile. 'You've no idea how cold it was down there. Then the bloody bird piped up. Shit, I wish the ground could have swallowed me up.'

Nick chuckled, then switched into work-mode. 'Well, the good news is, we got it all on tape.' Ged subconsciously twiddled his ear stud. The only thing on him they didn't search, thank God. 'Obviously the bad news is that we still haven't got a nailed-on drop time. You going to be able to work on that?'

'I reckon so. Providing they don't make me go through that palaver again, I think I can start getting a bit impatient.'

'Just be careful of Code C,' said Nick, referring to the Police and Criminal Evidence Act guidance that was the bible for undercover officers.

'You didn't get an egg and straw with that butty, did you?'

'No one's teaching you to suck eggs. I'm just doing my job as your cover officer to ensure the right people end up in prison.'

'Fair dos,' said Ged just as the encrypted app on his undercover phone buzzed. Ged opened the screen and scanned the message, a beam lighting up his face. He turned the phone to Nick. 'We're on,' he said just as his mind started to race about how he'd work this, the final stage of the two-year operation.

2

Three months later

Chief Superintendent Jo Howe, her deputy, Superintendent Gary Hedges, and 'the father of the station', Detective Inspector Bob Heaton, shuffled away from the crematorium, snatching what shelter they could beneath the overhanging trees that lined the 500-yard driveway.

At any other police funeral, the hearse would have been flanked by a white-gloved guard of honour, snapped to attention. As close friends, Jo, Gary and Bob would have been among the lucky ones to have allocated seats inside but, for most, it would be standing room outside with the proceedings relayed through loudspeakers.

This was no ordinary send-off though. Phil Cooke, now being vaporised in Woodvale's furnaces, had suffered a catastrophic fall from grace, and the fact that his only living relative had been whisked back to HMP Pentonville in a prison van seconds after the committal only underlined the reason why so few ex-colleagues wanted to be associated with him. Alive or dead.

The tiny plus point of the sparsity of mourners was that rather than having had to park miles away, Jo's car was within sight of the chapel.

Each were lost in their own thoughts, memories of a man they all had reason to admire and love. A man to whom, whatever he later did and became, they each owed their careers.

Jo zapped the key fob as they approached the police-issue Peugeot 508 Hybrid. The hazard lights winked their hello, accompanied by the reassuring clunk that invited them to step in from the rain. Jo and Gary removed their hats and both unbuttoned their dress-tunics, while Bob, the only one in plain clothes, slid into the back seat.

The two more senior officers went to the boot of the car and carefully laid their jackets inside, resting their caps on top. As Jo closed the lid, Gary broke the silence.

'Christ on a bike, have they no respect?'

'Who?' said Jo, following Gary's gaze to the grass verge.

'Bloody junkies,' he said, as he kicked the three hypodermic needles further from the road. 'Can't they go somewhere more suitable to pump that muck into their arms?'

'In fairness, at least it's not a park or the beach. Probably the safest place.'

'They could just not do it at all,' said Gary as he squeezed between the trees and the car to get in the passenger side.

'Simple as that,' muttered Jo as she climbed into the driver's seat.

'What is?' asked Bob as he looked up from his phone.

'Oh nothing. Attila the Hun here is moaning about some needles on the road and I'm just saying where else do you expect them to go?'

'Not that again. Just leave me out of it,' said Bob as he returned to his screen.

'Well, if you did your job, Bob, and nicked the dealers, we'd have no issues,' said Gary.

'Not now. I haven't got the energy for this,' said Jo as she pulled out of the space and snaked her way towards Lewes Road.

Gary huffed, then changed the subject. 'Nice eulogy, Bob. I'd love to have seen the old boy running naked down Old Shoreham Road that New Year's Eve.'

'Really?' said Bob. 'It's an image I've not been able to shift in twenty years.'

'I bet. Shame there weren't a few more there to hear about the true man. I counted ten, including the prison officers, and I reckon two of the rest were journalists.'

Jo kept quiet and let the men chatter inanely. She was lost in her own thoughts. It seemed only yesterday she'd driven from this very spot having said a premature farewell to her sister, Caroline, after she'd succumbed to her heroin habit with a massive overdose.

The two Gary had spotted were indeed reporters and she predicted the headlines later that day would not be pretty. Instead of carrying on into the city centre, Jo circumnavigated the Gyratory roundabout and headed out of town.

'Hey, where we going?' said Gary.

'Pub,' she said.

'I'd love to,' said Bob, 'but I've got a conference with CPS re Op Vellum at three. I'm taking them through all the undercover evidence.'

'We'll be back by then,' said Jo. She caught his eye in the rear-view mirror. 'I can make it an order if that helps.'

3

In his early days in the police, Sergeant Dale Scott would have been somewhere near the foot of anyone's list to be the friendly face of the war on drugs. A former county-level weight-lifter, he spent most of his PC years in riot vans. He almost never got into a fight, as his mammoth presence was more than enough to subdue the most truculent of crowds.

Since promotion he'd flitted between the response and neighbourhood teams before Phil Cooke, the former divisional commander, created the Street Community Policing Team, put Scotty in charge and vowed to keep him there. He even allowed him to handpick two PCs and a PCSO to work alongside him.

In the five years since Scotty's unit had been running, they had built up an encyclopaedic knowledge of the toings and froings of Brighton and Hove's homeless and begging population. His only flaw was that he rarely committed much of this to paper so, when one of his clientele was murdered – as happened all too frequently – one of his officers would be seconded to the Major Crime Team to share all they knew.

Dodging the traffic as he crossed Grand Junction Road, heading for the arches by the Palace Pier, Scotty felt a gust of wind sting his face. 'There better be the mother of Indian summers coming to make up for this,' he grumbled to PC Saira Bannerjee. She threw him a look, tinged with a half-smile.

'Am I allowed to say that?' he asked.

'Bit late now if not.'

'I can't keep up,' he said, pacing ahead.

They reached the other side and headed to the steps that led towards the lower promenade.

The area beneath the pier had used to be rich pickings for drug users and dealers but since the council blocked it off, they nestled in whichever arches hadn't been taken over by arty gift shops or boutique cafés. Scotty spotted a pile of rags nestled by the door to a vegan 'seafood' restaurant. He prodded it.

'All right chief?' he called out. 'We're police. Stand up for me, will you?'

'Fuck off. You ain't Old Bill and I ain't got nuffin you can rob.'

Both officers reached for their warrant cards while Saira said, 'Surprisingly we are. You're not in any trouble, we just want to see who you are and what you're up to.'

'I'm sleeping.'

With that they held out their credentials and Saira illuminated them with her torch. 'PC Bannerjee and Sergeant Scott from the Street Community Team.'

The man shuffled to his feet and Scotty and Saira took a precautionary step back.

'I've heard of your lot. They say you're the only pigs I can trust.'

'Nice,' said Scotty, almost gagging at the stench of urine and pound-a-pint cider. The man could have been anywhere from late teens to mid-thirties. His matted hair was dragged into a ponytail held in place by a knot of twine. His stubble had long since abandoned any designer pretence. The parka coat that hung off him might once have been green but now was mottled with grime, vomit and unrecognisable foodstuffs.

15

Same with his jeans, although there might have been some other bodily fluids added to the mix there.

His complexion had an all too familiar pallor.

What surprised Scotty most though was that he didn't recognise the man. That meant he was new to town, and newbies brought challenges; never in a good way.

'What's your name fella?'

'They call me Spanners.'

Scotty and Saira looked at each other.

'Why Spanners?'

The man said nothing.

'Righto. Where are you from?'

'Originally from York but I was in Winchester nick up to a couple of weeks ago.'

'You been here since?' said Saira.

'Nah. I went to Eastbourne, then Hastings. Shitholes.'

'Hold up. I'm from Hastings,' lied Scotty.

'No offence.'

'Listen chief. Obviously we're Old Bill but we are here to help. By the look of it, you need a bloody hot shower, a change of clothing and to score. Not necessarily in that order. Am I right?'

Spanners shrugged.

'Now you'll forgive us if we can't help you with the last one – our boss is funny like that – but we can find you somewhere to get cleaned up and some food.'

'Why would you do that?'

''Cos you're killing the tourist trade looking like that. No, honestly, we're the opposite of your average drug dealer. We woo you with hot water, shower gel and clean clobber. Fill your belly with McDonald's—'

'Other fast foods are available . . .' Saira interjected.

'Indeed,' continued Scotty, 'then we have a little chat about all the wonderful things we can do if you go into drug treatment and all the

16

horrible things we'll do to you if you don't.'

Spanners looked at each of them in astonishment. 'Is this some kind of wind-up?'

'Not at all. We call it Operation Eradicate. In a nutshell, you go into treatment while the dealers go into prison. We'll even speak up for you in court if you fall off the rails. You do have to play ball though. There's a limit to our benevolence. What do you say?'

'Do I have a choice?'

'Always, but that involves iron bars or a wooden box.'

4

Jo felt obliged to pay for the light lunch they'd enjoyed at the Devil's Dyke pub, although she did wonder what Gary would describe as a heavy one if the mixed grill, chips, onion rings and garlic bread he chose fell into the slimline category. The corner table gave them the privacy they needed yet stunning views of the South Downs National Park which, as ever, brought Jo a rare inner peace. She and Gary had removed their ties and epaulettes but that did little to disguise who they were.

As wakes went it was tame, but at least they could raise a glass of something soft to Phil and swap stories not suitable for a wider audience. He'd have been proud of them, if a little humbled by the fact they'd all forgiven him for the utter stupidity that had spelt the beginning of his end.

'Coffee anyone?' asked Jo.

Bob checked his watch. 'I really ought to be getting back.'

'It's only half one,' said Gary. 'We'll get you back by three, no worries.'

'He's right, and as I'm having a drink and have the car keys, you're kind of stuck.'

'I'm calling my Federation rep about you two bullies.'

'Bring it on,' said Jo. Using the pub's app, she ordered two Americanos and a hot water. As she pressed confirm, a Twitter notification flashed up. Idly she clicked it and wished she hadn't.

Brightonherald @Brightonherald

'Brushed under the carpet' Police chiefs conceal drug use while leaving jailed cop's funeral. #OpEradicate #Policecoverup #Drugs #Brighton @ ChsuptJoHowe @Sussexpolice Read more https://BH.co/77PTSbbJRik

She scanned the article, which led with a long-range shot of Gary kicking the needles into the crematorium's grass. It went on to explain how the negligent senior officers, one of whom – her – had gone on record calling for the decriminalisation of drugs, had ignored evidence of blatant law-breaking in a place which should be reserved for grief and repose. It asked why they were paying their respects to a convicted criminal during working hours. Was this another example of how little the police, amid the highest drugs death per capita in the UK, cared? it asked rhetorically.

'You need to see this.' She turned her phone round on the table and watched both men as they took in the trashing. Gary's face gave away his escalating rage while Bob's suggested this was one more layer of bullshit that was making the job intolerable.

'Wanker,' said Gary, a little too loudly for a public restaurant.

'Keep it down,' snapped Jo.

'Christ, what the hell gets these scum out of bed in the morning? I'm telling you, there's a special place in hell for reporters.'

'All reporters?' said Jo, with a raised eyebrow.

'Well not your Darren, obviously,' Gary replied. He'd bonded with Jo's husband, who worked for the *Daily Journal*, over her hospital bed the previous year and they'd been friends since. 'Anyway, how did they get that picture?'

'Never mind that. We'll do the usual rebuttals, trot out the arguments and the stats, but we need to get used to this.'

'If I'm honest boss, it does make things tricky in the run-up to the Op Vellum trial,' said Bob as the drinks arrived.

'How so?' said Jo.

'Most of our witnesses, those who aren't cops that is, are addicts and we don't want to be batting off accusations that we've given them special treatment in exchange for their evidence.'

Jo sipped her hot water. 'It's because we got them into treatment that they're alive to give evidence. If only someone had done that for Caroline.' As she said it, her eyes pooled at the thought of her sister, riven with the depression and addiction she'd battled since she was twelve. It was being branded a tart during the trial of the councillor who'd been abusing her for years that tipped her over the edge, especially as he walked free from court. Jo still beat herself up for not doing more to help her.

'I'm just being practical,' Bob replied.

'I know you are, but I'm quite happy to come to court and explain what we are trying to do. Users in treatment, dealers in prison. Reduce the demand while choking off the supply and you stand half a chance of saving lives.'

'We get it,' said Gary. 'The thing is . . . well sometimes you sound a little, what's the word. Preachy.'

'Preachy? If you'd gone through what I have then maybe . . .'

Gary showed her both palms. 'Sorry,' he mouthed.

'This is a long term approach. Everyone wants results overnight but that's not how these things work. Sorry, Bob, if it causes problems at trial, but we still need to get the message out that users entering treatment will be supported. We're trying to save lives here.'

'All right, calm down,' said Bob. The two senior officers stared at him, shocked by this rare flash of insubordination. 'I'm just saying there's more than one big picture here and the one I'm concerned about is locking up the organised crime group we spent two years catching. Now, can we drink up and go?'

Jo and Gary obediently drained their cups, then Jo clicked the app to settle the bill while the two men put on their coats and headed for the door.

'Thanks,' said Jo, as the server held the door.

As she followed Gary and Bob, her phone buzzed. A WhatsApp from Darren.

Hi darling. I hope the funeral went OK. Don't forget you're picking the boys up as I've got to go to London for a meeting with the editor. Leaving in a mo. Love you xxx

'Bugger,' said Jo as she passed an elderly couple coming through the pub door. She quickened her pace to catch Gary and Bob up.

'Get in the car. I'm going to have to drop you off at the front of the nick. Something's come up.'

She spotted the two men looking at each other quizzically, then saw something tucked under her wiper blade. She grabbed it.

National Trust Car Parks Penalty Notice – Failing to Pay

'Just when it couldn't get worse, eh,' said Gary, with that sickening smirk he seemed to save for her.

'Darren's place in hell can go to parking wardens if I get my way.'

She barely waited for Bob to close the door before spraying gravel behind her as she wheel-spun away.

Before working from home became a thing, delayed trains to London had been a daily bind for Darren Howe so, despite his summons to the editor's office being for 5 p.m., he gave himself a full two hours to get there from Brighton.

It was just as well as following various 'operational incidents' and

21

unspecified congestion, when he finally jumped off at St Pancras station he had just twelve minutes, rather than the twenty he needed, to make his way to the glass monolith that served as the *Daily Journal*'s head office.

He'd spent the journey reminding himself of some of his more groundbreaking articles and totting up his recent page one bylines. He was surprised how few of those there were. Was that why his presence in person had been demanded?

Catching his breath after the dash from the station, he trotted up to the security desk and, in vain, scanned the white-shirted guardians for a familiar face. He swung his rucksack off his back and fished inside for his security pass. His heart sank as he thought he'd left it behind, but eventually he found it wedged inside his Kindle cover.

He flashed it to the guard, put his worldly goods on the X-ray machine and ambled through the metal-detector arch. Grabbing his bag, he pressed the card against the reader and, to his utter relief, the glass door in front of him clicked and he was in.

He chose the escalators over the stairs to rise the three floors to Sam Parkin's lair in the hope they might settle his pounding heart and red face.

As he expected, the newsroom outside the editor's office was throbbing with activity: the subeditors shouting demands and profanities at the youngsters hammering away at keyboards. It was one thing not recognising security, but to be unable to name even one of the senior staff made Darren realise how long it was since he'd stepped foot in here.

Darren tapped on Sam's open door, relieved to see he'd made it on time and that Sam was on his own. No one from HR, either.

The editor looked up from his screen and his fresh face beamed. 'Hey! Thanks for coming up here, mate. God, it's been so long.' He shoved back his monstrosity of a gaming chair and strode over, his neatly manicured hand outstretched. Darren shook it and, as ever, was surprised by Sam's incongruously firm grip.

'Yeah, good to see you, boss,' said Darren, not fooled by the effusive welcome.

'Shut the door, then you can call me Sam like the old days. Wouldn't want those snotty kids out there getting ideas above themselves,' he chuckled.

'Thanks. How have you been?'

'Oh, you know. Struggling with my work–work balance to tell you the truth. Have a seat, have a seat.'

Darren grinned and settled himself in one of the easy chairs by the glass table near the door.

'Drink?' said Sam, grabbing two glasses before waiting for an answer. He sloshed a good three fingers of Scotch into each, placed one in front of Darren and took a slug from his before sitting opposite.

'Listen, mate, I'm sorry to drag you all the way up here but some things are better done face to face.'

'No worries,' said Darren, desperate to read the signals. Warm welcome. No HR. Comfy chair. Whisky. Why was he still worried?

Parkin checked the time. 'I'll cut to the chase. Bit of a delicate one but a massive opportunity for you. And it needs your skills. No regurgitating press releases or Freedom of Information requests, this one.'

Darren sat a little straighter, his interest piqued. 'Go on,' he said, sipping his drink.

Sam leant forward, his hands outstretched and eyes on fire. 'The owners wanna get back into investigative features. Deep, meaningful stuff our more intelligent readers lap up. Now you can get all the headline news as it happens on your bleeding phone, we need to offer more. I told them that bit, by the way.' He seemed proud of that. 'So, who else was I going to ask to do just that than my old pal Dazza?'

Darren cringed. He was the only one who still called him that. He'd told everyone – including Sam – he'd always hated it but the editor persisted nonetheless.

'OK, so what did you have in mind?'

'A monthly long read, well researched, getting into sources no one else can, which exposes a huge contemporary issue, home or abroad, but, and here's the cherry, poses an ethical dilemma for our readers to debate in the forums over the weeks before the next one. Looks at the heart of an issue and gets people thinking and debating. We just sit back and watch them joust. Great, innit?'

Sam's feet were jigging under the table and his whole body followed in step. This was clearly his own idea, as Darren had never seen him so excited about anyone else's.

'And you want me to do that?'

Sam nodded.

There seemed to be no downside. It played to every skill Darren had and it meant he could continue to work from home and in his own time, which was great for childcare. The alternative, outside this very room, just didn't bear thinking about.

'I'd love to. Thank you, Sam.' He beamed, chiding himself for the sense of doom he'd felt since he received the invitation.

'Amazing. Amazing. The owners will be delighted. They wanted you to do it,' said the little man opposite as he stood to refill their glasses. 'Cheers. You've got free rein. You find the stories. Run them past me first of course but we'd like to get started on one of our choice. You know, save you the effort of sniffing around. Hit the ground running and all that.'

Darren took another drink. 'OK.' He just hoped it wouldn't involve short-notice travel. Jo wouldn't be happy given how full-on her job was since the scandals of the last two years.

'Yes, and it's a great one. Perfect in fact. Right on your doorstep.'

'OK.' Darren stretched that out for a full two seconds.

'Yes, we want you to do a complete exposé of this drugs thingy in Brighton. What's it called? Operation Irradiate?'

'Eradicate,' mumbled Darren.

'Yeah, that's it. All this legalisation nonsense, paying for druggies to get treatment and not bunging them in jail where they belong. How much public money is being pissed away? The police picking and choosing what they'll enforce. Dig the dirt and get us the inside track. Say, five thousand words cutting through the namby-pamby spin, then leaving it to the readers to natter about what they think.'

Darren breathed heavily, trying to steady his tremors and prevent himself grabbing his old colleague's throat.

'You know I can't do that,' he said.

Sam stared at him for a good ten seconds. 'What do you mean, you can't do it? You said a moment ago that you would.'

'You know who's behind Operation Eradicate, don't you?'

'Of course I do. That's why it's a perfect one to start with. You and the missus must chat about it all the time. I reckon half the big players were round your gaff for barbecues most of the summer. If I were a betting man, I'd say you could write the piece now.'

'But you know it's both ethically and morally impossible. Would you write an article trashing your own wife?'

'Which ex-Mrs Parkin are you talking about? In short, I'd jump at the chance,' he laughed.

'I just can't.'

Sam's face hardened and Darren recognised that infamous rage rising. He chose to sit and take it.

'You fucking can and you will. You'll do as you're told and make like you're enjoying it. It might have seemed like a request, but let me make it clear, if you refuse or fuck it up, the best you can hope for is a box for your things and an escort to the door. On the other hand, if we dig deep enough we might just find you once dabbled in a bit of phone hacking or bunging a copper a few quid for a story. We were all at it, weren't we?'

'No.'

'Really? Well I'm sure we can make it look like you were.'

'Why does this story mean so much to you?'

'It's what the owners want and it's what they'll get. So I'd trot off now and start tapping that keyboard, as I want it ready to publish in two weeks' time.' Sam went back to his desk, while Darren remained where he was. 'You still here? Off you pop.'

Darren didn't remember leaving Sam's office, or the building, as he walked on autopilot to the Lighterman pub behind King's Cross Station. Only on his fourth pint of Peroni did it sink in that Sam was right; he had no choice. He just couldn't imagine how he'd break it to Jo.

5

The following morning, with five minutes to spare, Jo slipped bleary-eyed into the briefing room expecting it to be standing room only. The row with Darren last night had been horrendous. How could he even contemplate writing the article? They'd have round two later but, sleep or no sleep, she had to focus now.

Between the ranks of slouching blue-overalled officers, chatting, slurping drinks and tapping at their phones, there were too many spare chairs for her liking. She checked her watch then sidled up to Bob who was running through a PowerPoint presentation on the ageing laptop.

'It is a 7 a.m. start, isn't it?' she asked.

'That's right, ma'am.'

'Where is everyone?'

'This is it. Two PSUs. One from here and one from East Sussex.'

Jo looked puzzled. She'd been authorised to second a Police Support Unit – eighteen PCs, three sergeants, an inspector and a medic in each – from all three divisions.

'What about West Sussex's unit?'

'They're a no-show I'm afraid. There's some animal rights protest at one of the hunt kennels near Chichester. They've gone to that.'

'Jesus. When were you told?'

'About an hour ago. I just need to tweak a few things.'

'Can you do all seven warrants with just this lot?' She glanced around the room, trying not to show her anger to the officers watching them.

'It's tight. We need to do them all at once, otherwise word will get out and the sewers will be swimming in crack and heroin – but I'll work something out.'

'Righto, I'll leave it with you.' She took a seat in the empty front row and sent a text to her West Sussex counterpart.

Not happy that you've stood me up. Op Eradicate is a force priority yet your PSU had a better offer. We need to speak.

On seeing the laughing emoji she received in return, she was about to call him and ball him out but Bob called the room to order. The chatter stopped instantly and everyone was fixed on the DI standing by the screen.

'Right. Listen in everyone. You'll have spotted we are a little thin on the ground so we've had to make some choices. I think you've all been on an Op Eradicate arrest day before but I'll just remind you of what it's all about. We are going to execute seven warrants issued under the Misuse of Drugs Act, at separate locations around the city. Your sergeants have the individual arrest packs. Each of the people you're arresting has been positively identified as having supplied class A drugs to undercover officers. They won't be told that last point until they are interviewed, so keep that to yourself.

'Each premises will be searched for class A drugs, paraphernalia and evidence of supply. Now, all that's pretty standard. The difference with these operations is that once you've taken the prisoners to custody, Sergeant Scott and his team—' Scotty waved to show who he was, as if there were anyone in Sussex Police who did not know. 'Thank you Scotty. As I say, the Street Community Team will float around the area of each warrant to pick up any users who might be expecting to get their fix from our suspects. The team will engage with them and start the work to get them into one of the dedicated Op Eradicate drug treatment places. Scotty, anything to add?'

'Thanks, guv,' said Scotty from the back of the room. 'PC Bannerjee and I' – he waved his hand to introduce Saira to his right – 'will be joined by a drugs worker who we'll pick up later. If you come across anyone who looks like they might be ripe for a treatment place, then call me and we'll come to meet them. Boss, just one thing. We usually have a back-up unit in case things get spicy. Is that the case today?'

'That might be a stretch. Can you manage without? Call up divisional response if you need any help.'

Scotty sighed. 'I suppose so, but it's not ideal.'

Bob shrugged and looked to Jo. She stood and turned to face the room.

'I'm sorry you've been left short. We only found out this morning and I'll deal with that but hopefully, as we've done this many times before without incident, today will be no different.' As soon as she sat down she wished she'd engaged her brain before opening her mouth.

Bob rattled through the deployments, call signs and the ever-important overtime code, then sent the units off for their specific briefings by their sergeants.

Jo waited by his side while he finished a conversation with DS Luke Spencer, charged with coordinating the interviews once the prisoners had been processed. When Luke had stepped away, Jo said, 'I'll try to get you some more bods but don't hold out too much hope. I'll make damn sure it doesn't happen again though.' Bob gave her a doubtful look which made her even more determined.

* * *

29

As Jo slumped into her office chair, to her surprise, Chief Superintendent Kevin Curtis picked up her call after just two rings. 'Morning, Jo, how's life in your little township?'

'I'm not in the mood Kev. Where the hell were your PSU this morning?'

'And a very good day to you too.'

'Piss off. You were supposed to send a unit over for Op Eradicate. Where were they?'

Just then Gary Hedges walked in, red, sweaty and still in his running gear. 'Morning,' he mouthed. Jo just shook her head.

'We had some hunt protestors at one of the kennels on Lord MacInnes's estate. I had to send them there,' said Curtis.

'Really, a whole PSU? How many protestors are we talking about?'

'I'm not really sure but His Lordship was kicking off to the chief, so I decided to show some strength. These things happen, Jo.'

'That's bollocks. In any case you should have told me. We plan these raids to the last detail and it causes mayhem if we don't have the right numbers.'

Jo signalled to Gary to pass his mobile. Reluctantly he handed it over, then she flapped her fingers for him to unlock it.

'You do these arrest days every other month. The world doesn't stop for your vanity projects.'

'If saving lives is a vanity project, I'll take that,' she said as she zapped a Google search on Gary's phone. What she was looking for came up straight away.

'Four pensioners, Kev.'

'Eh?'

'Three elderly women and an even older man. That's your animal rights protestors who warranted twenty-three highly trained riot cops plus drivers. Really?'

'I'm not sure we knew that when we deployed.'

'That is such crap. You've been had over and it's me that suffered, like always.'

'I'm not having this conversation. If you don't like it, speak to the ACC.' With that the call went dead.

'For fuck's sake,' Jo yelled.

'And there ends the sermon,' said Gary with a grin plastered across his face.

'Read the fucking room, Gary.'

6

Scotty and Saira had spent the morning cruising the target areas, spotting drug users desperate for their next fix. Their unmarked Toyota was in dire need of a valet, the bodywork having been used as target practice by Brighton's ever-present seagulls and the inside carpeted in rancid kebab wrappers and crushed coffee cups. Scotty's rationale for not cleaning it was that its revolting state added to its anonymity. The fact that just about every drug user and homeless person in the city could spot it from a hundred yards did nothing to disabuse the sergeant.

Lizzie, the red-headed, sprightly, Op Eradicate drugs worker teamed up with them today, seemed less than impressed with this mobile hovel. Scotty also sensed her fidgeting in her stab vest, something they all did until they became a second skin. He knew his secret lover would give him hell about this later.

As he pulled off the seafront into Oriental Place, a prime dealing area due to it having more than its fair share of hostels and bedsits, half a dozen bewildered druggies of questionable ages were scurrying in the road.

'You know the saddest sight I've ever seen?'

'No, but I'm guessing we're about to find out, Sarge,' said Saira, as she half turned to raise an eyebrow at Lizzie.

'I was driving down the M4 and up ahead brake lights flashed on and all the cars swerved from the middle lane. I thought something had fallen off a lorry but as I got closer, I saw there were seven or eight tiny ducklings dashing around the carriageway, no sign of the mum. It was too dangerous to stop but I knew it wouldn't be long till the inevitable happened.'

'Right, well that is sad, but why are you telling us that now?'

'This lot reminded me of them, that's all.'

'Is he always like this?' Lizzie asked Saira, as if she didn't know.

'Not at all. Once, around Christmas time, he talked sense.'

'I heard that. Right, let's have a word with them.'

Scotty dropped Saira and Lizzie off by a builders' van, cover enough for the low-key surprise they were used to springing, while he drove past the group and pulled up beyond them. He parked up, slowly got out of the car and ambled towards the group as Saira and Lizzie did the same from the opposite direction.

As he closed in, Scotty recognised all but one and knew they'd have little fight in them. Anticipating them running though, he readied himself. He was proud to see the other two mirror him – both owning the middle of the road, their arms out at forty-five degrees.

It was a pale, scraggy young woman who made the first move. Her efforts to power-walk past Scotty lasted no more than a few seconds as the huge sergeant stretched out his right arm.

'Now that's just rude, Trish. Fancy not even stopping to chat.'

A couple of men met the same end trying to edge past Saira and soon all six were huddled between Lizzie and the two officers.

'Now, what are you all up to?' Scotty asked as he switched on his body-worn video camera, its red light flashing to show that it was active. 'As if I can't guess.'

It was Trish Kenyon who became the spokesperson. 'We ain't doing no harm. Just need to score then we'll be out of your hair.'

'I'm afraid that's a bit of a problem today,' said Saira. 'See, our colleagues have been busy sweeping up the dealers and, well, most of your gear is now in our drug store.'

The panic was palpable – these, like every other addict, had just one goal in life.

'We don't cause no trouble but we'll be clucking in a couple of hours. You lot keep doing this shit and no one gives a toss about us.'

Lizzie stepped forward. 'It doesn't have to be like this, you know.'

'Oh no, not the fucking Op Eradicate chat again,' said Trish as she tried to walk away. Scotty stepped across, blocking her path. Just then a furniture lorry trundled down the road.

'Come on, let's do this on the pavement,' said Saira, shepherding them out of the truck's way.

Lizzie continued. 'Well if you've heard it before, you know the deal. You can come with me now and we'll get you enrolled on one of the funded treatment programmes today. No waiting lists, no eligibility criteria. One form and you're in. Do that and we'll all be here to get you off drugs and crime.' Her hand gesture included Scotty and Saira in that pledge.

'And if we don't?' said the only person Scotty did not recognise.

'Then we hound you, nick you for farting in public and when you tell the magistrates you need to go into treatment, we show them this video,' said Scotty, tapping the camera. 'Some call it assertive outreach. I prefer Hobson's choice.'

Just then a blue panel van crawled up the road. Scotty barely glanced as it eased to a silent stop. It was only when the side door flew open that his antenna was spooked.

Three masked, stocky men jumped out, one of them shouting, 'Get the fuckers.' They closed the two-metre gap in half as many seconds, blades flashing in their clenched fists.

Saira stabbed the red button on her Airwave radio and screamed, 'Code Zero, Oriental Place.' This was the call that trumped all others, sparking every available officer to come running. It also left her microphone open for a few precious seconds. 'Urgent assistance. Plainclothes officers and one civvy being attacked by three with knives.'

Scotty drew his baton and PAVA spray, holding the stick in an aggressive stance while aiming the synthetic pepper solution at his attackers' eyes and simultaneously roaring, 'Get back! Get back!'

Saira shouted the same, rushing to their flank. She swung her own baton at the right-hand man's knees, but missed the target. The distant sirens were a welcome sound but Scotty knew they couldn't hold the knifemen back for long.

The blades swished terrifyingly close and Scotty's spray canister was all but empty. Just then he notched up a hit with the burning liquid as the middle man collapsed to his knees holding his eyes and screaming. This only drove the others on, and Scotty could only focus on the next few seconds.

He bellowed louder and saw Saira draw her own spray and take aim. Suddenly, the two in front of them stopped and dragged their stricken colleague into the van. *Thank God*, thought Scotty as they retreated, but then he felt a fourth person barge past him from behind. He glanced and saw it was the one from the original group he didn't recognise. Scotty tried to grab him but the man slipped from his grip and jumped into the van, milliseconds before it sped away.

Scotty was about to run after it when he heard 'Help me' to his left. He looked round and to his horror saw Lizzie writhing on the ground, eyes pleading and blood jetting across the front wing of the white Vauxhall Corsa she was wedged against.

'Saira, get an ambulance,' he ordered as he sank to his knees and rammed his hand against the open slash where he guessed her jugular vein was. 'Urgent, she's bleeding out,' he yelled before looking back at the sheer terror contorting the drug worker's face, tears streaming down his.

'Keep calm, Lizzie. I've got you. You're going to be OK,' he said with far more conviction than he felt. The blood sprayed between his fingers as the colour evaporated from Lizzie's cheeks.

The first police car squealed to a halt and the passenger was instantly at Scotty's side. He couldn't have been more relieved to see it was PC Wendy Relf, not only one of the calmest and most experienced officers the division had but a trained medic too.

'Keep doing that Sarge, I'll grab my kit.'

Seconds later Wendy was back, her advanced first aid pack already open on the pavement and a huge bandage wad in her hand. 'Sarge, on three, move your hand and I'll clamp this on. One. Two. Three.'

In no time the white pad was sodden-red. 'Get me another,' said Wendy and Scotty obeyed without question. When that too soaked through and Lizzie's eyes closed, Scotty prayed.

Five pads later, the ambulance arrived. The first paramedic was straight at Wendy's side, ready to take over. Wendy shuffled over and the paramedics worked furiously to stem the blood, exchanged a look, then one started CPR. Scotty paced up and down, muttering desperate pleas. Time stood still, then the paramedics' demeanour and urgency waned. 'She's gone,' one said to no one in particular. Wendy sank back on her haunches, as if she'd been waiting for this confirmation.

'NO! Keep going,' yelled Scotty, dropping to his knees, barging the paramedic out of the way. Then, two hands on his shoulders gently pulled him back.

'Sarge, it's too late,' said Saira in barely a whisper. 'You did all you could.'

He looked around at the battlefield, Lizzie's lifeless body the only casualty.

'Where are the rest of them?' he demanded.

'They all scarpered,' said Saira. 'We'll get whoever did this. We will find them, Sarge.'

'Fucking right we will. And where the fuck was our back-up?' he shouted before lung-bursting sobs overtook him and he collapsed into the pools of Lizzie's blood.

7

Jo rubbed her eyes and popped a couple of paracetamol from the stash in her desk drawer. She knew what was coming her way as Op Eradicate Gold Commander. Contrary to the adage, shit travels uphill. Ever since she'd learnt of Lizzie Reed's murder she knew every plan and decision would be subject to the most forensic of investigations, mainly by those whose understanding of operational planning was what they'd picked up from TV.

Having been at the centre of more crises in the last two years than many experienced in a whole career, Jo should have spent the day getting her notes in order before the vulture descended. Instead, she spent it with Lizzie's parents. How you explained why a clever, funny, deeply compassionate young woman could go to work and never come back was beyond Jo. She hated that she could not give them the answers they demanded and deserved.

She glanced at her watch and couldn't believe it was 4 p.m. already. Just an hour until the Gold Group – the high-level, arse-saving meeting which some chief officers used to bury or spread blame in the aftermath of critical incidents. In fairness, Assistant Chief Constable Leon Mills was a breath of fresh air and, despite him calling the meeting, Jo felt she could trust him. He'd phoned her shortly after the murder to check how she was and whether she had all she needed to manage the immediate fallout. It was during that call that he'd suggested they meet an hour before the main meeting so she could brief him privately.

She pulled into Police Headquarters at Lewes, then slammed her hand on the steering wheel. She'd only just remembered she'd promised to be home by 5 p.m. so she and Darren could continue their discussion from last night. She was still livid that he'd not told the snidey editor where to shove his job but hoped that they'd both have cooler heads this time round. She tapped his number on her phone and waited for the hands-free to click in.

'Hi,' said Darren. Frosty, but two can play at that game.

'Hi. Look, you've probably seen what's happening. I've no idea when I'll be home so are you OK feeding the boys? Probably putting them to bed too.'

'Yep. I worked that one out.'

'Oh and Liam has got PE tomorrow, so can you make sure his kit's clean?'

'Already done.'

Jo left a silence, hoping Darren would fill it. As she spotted a parking place she gave in.

'Look, I can't help this. A young woman lost her life today and the buck stops with me. Give me a break.'

'I'm not heartless but I'd love you to understand it from my point of view.'

Fuck's sake, she mouthed. The gears crunched as she lined up to back into the space.

'We'll talk but not now. I've got to see Leon before the Gold Group. I'll be home as soon as I can.'

'Fine. See you later.' The phone went dead.

'Love you, too,' said Jo to the silent handset. She hated that things were so glacial between them. Life, or rather the job she adored, kept chucking boulders in the way of her heartfelt intentions to get back to how things were before work became such a shit storm. God, she missed their date nights, days out with the boys, even running. Was she sleepwalking towards the same fate of most police relationships?

Five minutes later she was knocking on the ACC's door. His velvet public-school voice summoned her in immediately and, as ever, he was out from his desk and shaking her hand when she'd barely cleared the threshold.

'Jo, what a dreadful day for you and your team. I hope everyone is bearing up.'

'Thank you, sir. We're fine compared to Lizzie's family and friends.'

'Of course, of course. Anyway, thank you for popping in early. I just thought it would be helpful to understand and clear a few things up before the main show at five. That sound OK?'

Jo would have loved to say no, just to see what Leon would say. He was such a charmer, and so old-school for his age, that she wondered how he'd ever survived the violence and abuse that came with everyone's early years in the police.

'Sure.'

'Good, good. Listen, I've taken the liberty of inviting Nicola Merrion, the CEO of Lifechoices, to join us. After all, Lizzie was one of theirs. She'll be here in a moment. That OK?'

'Of course, sir, but I thought you'd like me to update you on the operational matters.'

'Nicola can hear that. No secrets in partnerships now, are there? Oh, where are my manners? Can I get you some refreshments?'

Jo waved her Chilly's water bottle at him. 'I'm fine, thanks.' Why did this feel like the world's most civilised ambush?

There was a tap on the door and the ACC's PA poked her head in. 'Ms Merrion's here. Shall I show her in?'

'By all means,' he said, then gave Jo a look which asked whether that was OK. *Bit late.*

A tall, athletic woman, dressed in a green New Balance hoodie and grey jogging leggings, walked in as if she owned the office. Jo had met her a few times and, at best, tolerated her. The ferocity that speared from her laser-blue eyes unsettled Jo. No prizes for guessing whose blood she was after.

'Thanks for inviting me, Leon,' she said, shaking the ACC's hand, then just nodded at Jo.

'Do take a seat. I was just saying to Jo—you do know each other, don't you? Of course you do. Anyway, I said it would be helpful if we understood things before everyone else arrives.'

'I quite agree,' said Nicola. 'To kick off, how did a member of my staff get stabbed to death in front of two police officers on a pre-planned operation? Any idea?' She glared at Jo, who hoped Leon would chip in, but he just stared at her too.

'Can I first say how deeply sorry I am, we all are, for Lizzie's loss.'

Leon spluttered in agreement.

'She was with two of the most experienced officers on the street policing team and was wearing a stab-proof vest with "Drugs Worker" on the front and back. It's early days but from what I understand Sergeant Scott and PC Bannerjee were threatened by some men who turned up in a van and, while they were dealing with that, another man stabbed Lizzie in the neck. My officers did all they could to save her but I'm afraid . . . well, you know the rest.'

'I'm fully aware of that,' said Nicola. 'What I want to know is, where was the back-up? We have a signed service-level agreement that on arrest days our workers accompany your officers to engage with users but there will always be uniformed back-up immediately available. Where was that?'

Jo looked at Leon, hoping he'd read the signs that this was not for the CEO's ears. The ACC just smiled and waited.

She had no option but to plough on. 'We didn't have the number of officers we were expecting. One division had, er, they had another

40

commitment so at the last minute their PSU, that's a team of officers, didn't come.'

Leon cut in. 'That's not altogether unusual. I'm sure Jo has recorded that unforeseen issue and has a clear decision in her policy book which sets out how she adjusted the operation.' Jo's mind flashed back to her very brief conversation with Bob before the briefing:

'*Can you do all seven warrants with just this lot?*'

'*It's tight. We need to do them all at once, otherwise word will get out and the sewers will be swimming in crack and heroin – but I'll work something out.*'

'*Righto, I'll leave it with you.*'

'We did look at it,' she muttered, hoping not to be drawn further on the point.

'There you go. Tragic, but I'm sure we did all we could.'

Why the hell was he always so chipper?

'So, here's where we stand,' said Nicola. 'My staff are refusing to be part of Op Eradicate until this whole matter has been investigated and there are some cast-iron reassurances about their safety. They have a point.'

'That's a bit premature,' said Jo. 'We both know how many lives Eradicate has saved, how much crime it's cut and how much money it's saved the city. Three pounds saved for every pound invested.'

'Spare me the lecture. I have a duty to my staff, not saving your career.'

'That's not fair. I've put my reputation on the line with this operation. Where else have the police challenged the war-on-drugs narrative with something more humane which treats addiction as the illness it is? I thought you of all people would understand.' She nearly mentioned her sister, Caroline, but stopped herself just in time.

'Now, let's not get excited,' said Leon. 'The fact is that Nicola has lost a dear member of staff while she was in our care. We need to find out why and this might be the time to pause Eradicate while we take stock. After all, it's not the most popular of our policing models.' Jo looked at him in horror. How could he even consider that? Momentum was everything.

'Who says policing has to be popular, so long as it works? "Protection of life and property." That's our job. That's exactly what Eradicate does.'

'Jo, we need to calm down a little. The Home Secretary has been on the phone to the chief this afternoon asking some very difficult questions about all this. She did her best to reassure the Right Honourable Lady but, suffice to say, this has brought some unwelcome interest in the force, and you. Anyway, I think we're done here.'

Jo had a thousand more things to say but Leon and Nicola Merrion were both on their feet and making for the door, the CEO scowling at her as she went.

It was just the wrong side of midnight when Jo finally pulled onto her driveway. Any eighteen-hour shift would leave her feeling battered but this one was among the worst she'd experienced. At least after previous marathons, home had been her sanctuary. Now, the glowing lounge light told her that she had one more battle to fight before she could catch a few hours of sleep.

She eased the key in the lock and the door open, careful not to wake Ciaran and Liam. She hoped that Darren had fallen asleep on the settee and she could put the inevitable off for another day.

'Hi,' came his voice from the door on the right.

Shit.

'Hi. Sorry I'm late. You didn't have to wait up.'

Darren stood, walked over to her and took her in his arms. 'Of course I did,' he said before he kissed her auburn hair. 'You've had a hell of a day.' He held her and his stubble on her face triggered a rush of feelings she'd not felt for months.

His natural empathy, one of the things that had attracted her to him when they met in Liberia, was back. Sometimes it was his most infuriating quality though, especially when her feistier side was rising up. At the end of tricky days, just when she wanted to rant, he'd have the right words, the warm hugs and the level head to put things into perspective. But what was between them now felt different.

She eased herself out of his embrace. 'Let me get a glass of wine, then we have to talk.'

'I'll get it. You sit down.'

Jesus. Stop being so bloody reasonable.

Darren returned carrying two large glasses of what Jo hoped was Pinot Grigio. 'I don't want to row,' he said as he handed one to her.

'Me neither,' she replied as she shuffled over to make room for him. 'But we have to sort this out and better now than with the boys earwigging.'

'It's just a job, Jo. It's one article which, if I write well and the readers like it, will lead to many more and that's stability for us. Not to mention flexibility so I can cover when you pull shifts like this one.' He paused. 'And fulfilment for me.'

'Are you saying you're not happy?'

He paused again.

'Darren?'

'It's just . . . Don't get me wrong, I love you and the boys but since you took on this job' – he nodded towards her chief superintendent epaulettes – 'I've become . . . Oh God, this is going to sound Neanderthal. I've become a house-husband in all but name.'

Jo pulled back and glared at him. 'What, like I was – in all but name – for three years? Is this a woman's place then? Barefoot, pregnant and up to my elbows in dishwater? I thought you were different.' She gulped her wine and turned away.

'No, no, please listen. Of course I don't begrudge you success. God knows you've earned it. And the way you've come through the last couple of years has been awe-inspiring, but I've been filling the gaps and I'm bored.'

'Bored?'

'Not with you or home. With work. This is a fabulous opportunity to get back into traditional investigative journalism and flex my brain cells again. To show that idiot Sam, and whoever is pulling his strings, that there is still a place in the industry for people like me.'

Jo stood and paced the room. She needed to choose her words carefully.

'Darren, I understand that. I promise I do. I've been where you are and I know how it demolishes your self-esteem. All I'm saying is that you cannot write a flagship piece crucifying me. We are bloody married, for Christ's sake.'

'Who says it will crucify you? It could go the other way and be the golden opportunity to tell your side of the story.'

She sat back down, in the armchair opposite. 'Oh come on. You know Sam will never accept that. He's completely in the pocket of the owners, who have their own hateful agenda. You might as well send in your resignation than a piece supporting this lefty, soft-on-crime disgrace to the uniform. Tell him where to stick his job.'

'It's more complicated than that,' Darren muttered.

'How? We can survive for a while on my salary. No amount of money is worth sacrificing a marriage.'

'Is that a threat?'

'Of course it's not, but just imagine the pressure we'll be under if you're forced to write a fascist piece about how drug laws should be tightened, addicts cold-turkeyed in prison and the police should get back to locking up anyone not like them. Just leave the newspaper.'

Darren jumped up, knocking his wine glass over in the process. 'You have no fucking idea,' he yelled as he stormed out.

8

As with any undercover briefing, Bob arrived ten minutes late so the UC and cover officer could talk through things they'd rather he didn't hear. As the covert operations manager for the deployment, he was entitled to know everything, but sometimes a deaf ear served a bigger purpose than blind compliance.

The flat they were using as a safe house was ideal. The block had numerous entries and exits and the residents' transiency meant that strangers rarely stood out.

Bob came by bus, another tactic to preserve anonymity, and took the bin-store entrance before climbing the concrete steps to the second floor. He rapped twice on the door, saw the spyhole darken then heard the rattle of chains and the clunk of the lock. No greetings were offered as he stepped in, so he headed straight for the lounge at the end of the short corridor.

Bob took in the tabletop rammed with used coffee mugs and pasta-encrusted bowls. 'You want me to get a cleaner in here?' he said, once Nick had closed the door.

'That silver spoon in your mouth must play havoc with your drinking, guv,' said Nick.

'Crockery is reusable. You do know that, don't you?'

'Every day's a school day,' said Ged, the UC, slouched in the easy chair.

'Cup of tea, boss?' said Nick.

'Are you serious? Right, there's two things we need to discuss.'

'Two?' said Nick. 'I thought we were talking about the trial. What else?'

'You heard about the drugs worker who was murdered yesterday?'

'Who hasn't?'

'Well, the pressure is on to find out who's responsible. We've got some body cam footage we'd like you to look at Ged, but we want you to go back on the ground and see what you can find out. It's pretty urgent, as you can imagine.'

Bob caught Ged's frantic look to Nick.

'Problem?' asked Bob.

'Only that my missus is due to drop our first sprog in a couple of weeks. I've kind of booked paternity leave,' said Ged, as he anxiously rubbed his beard.

'Well, congratulations,' said Bob. 'It might only be for a few days. Pick up the buzz, that sort of thing.'

Nick chipped in. 'I get it's important, guv, but so is family to him. You've got kids, so you know you don't get these moments back.'

'Look, I promise, two weeks max. If you've got nothing by then, we'll pull it. You've got my word.' Bob wasn't sure how he'd explain that to the powers that be, but he was not going to deny this brave cop the birth of his first child. 'I'll go through the briefing in a bit but are you happy to do it?'

'Yep,' Ged and Nick replied simultaneously.

'Two weeks though,' said Ged.

'You've got my word,' said Bob. 'Right, on to the trial . . .'

* * *

Scotty's eyes were aflame from the last two days scouring the body cam footage in his vain attempt to identify Lizzie's killer. Even the facial recognition software they used to compare images against prisoner photos was coming up blank. The Major Crime Team had swept up the other users who'd seen the attack, but all had been released under investigation when it became clear that they either genuinely did not know the man or were uncharacteristically consistent in their lies.

'Saira, grab the car keys, we're going for a drive,' he said as he stood up from his desk.

'Really, Sarge? I've got a ton of paperwork and I'm on leave for a few days next week.'

'I'll have a word with your sergeant about the reports. I've heard he's a pushover.'

Five minutes later they were crawling the streets of East Brighton in the team's Toyota, Scotty at the wheel. He snaked around the labyrinthine streets of Whitehawk drifting aimlessly into Kemptown.

'Sarge, I'm not being funny but what are we actually doing?'

Scotty did not reply, just crawled along examining each passing car and glaring at every pedestrian.

Three streets and as many minutes later, his copper's nose twitched into life. 'Over there,' he said, louder than necessary.

'What, where?' said Saira.

'There.' He pointed at a scruffy man who'd just emerged from some basement steps on the left. 'Grab him.' He stopped and Saira jumped out and sprinted after the man. Scotty caught up in the car.

'Sarge, this is the bloke we stopped by the pier the other day,' she said as she hung onto the bewildered man's arm.

'Yeah I know,' said Scotty, still in the car. 'Spanners.'

'Well he's not the guy we're looking for.'

Spanners flicked his eyes between the two, making no attempt to interrupt or escape.

'I know. Put him in the car.'

'What for?' said Saira and her reluctant guest in unison.

'I want a word.'

'Can you even do that?' said Spanners, his eyes pleading with Scotty, then with Saira.

Scotty opened the door and pulled himself up to his full six foot four.

'Why, got something else to do?' he said as he opened the back door. 'We need a chat.'

Spanners looked pleadingly at Saira but she just shrugged.

Once they were all belted up, Scotty pulled away and headed for the coast road.

'Where are we going?' said Spanners.

'For a little drive, then we're having a chat.'

They skirted the Palace Pier roundabout and headed west towards Hove. As they passed Oriental Place, Scotty slowed down. 'A very dear friend of mine died there the other day. All she did was help people like you.'

'Yeah. Sad.'

'Her name was Lizzie,' said Scotty. 'She was a human being. A lovely one at that. Remember her name and remember how we're all feeling. Now think about everything you've heard about what happened, because you're not getting out of this car until you've told us the lot. You get me?'

'But I know nothing.'

'It'll take us about twenty minutes to get where we're going. That's how long you've got to rack that stewed brain of yours to come up with something.'

Scotty felt Saira's hard stare but he kept his eyes fixed on the road, his thoughts filled with Lizzie's gentle touch.

Scotty pulled into Shoreham's Widewater car park exactly twenty minutes later. During the summer and school holidays, it was packed with day trippers eager to bask on Shoreham beach, walkers who would traipse the shingle to Worthing or twitchers keen to spot a rare breed on the lagoon.

Today, it was all but empty and there was plenty of space to park out

48

of earshot, if not eyesight, so he pulled up, facing the bank that shielded them from the beach.

'What are we doing here?' said Spanners, his voice betraying his trepidation.

Scotty ignored Saira's glare which silently asked the same question.

'I want to know more about you,' said Scotty as he turned in his seat. 'You rock up in town, no one – and by that I mean us – knows anything about you, then a few days later my friend gets stabbed to death.'

'Man, you can't think that's got anything to do with me?'

'Go on then, chief, what's your story?'

'I told you. I'm from York. I got a habit which landed me in the nick and they released me from Winchester after serving six months. I moved around then thought I'd see what Brighton was all about for a while.'

'What's your real name? I'm assuming you weren't christened Spanners?'

Saira scribbled the details down as he rattled them off.

'So, tell us about you,' said Scotty.

'There's not much to tell. I was in the army for five years, fought in Iraq and Afghan. Saw some bad shit out there. Lost two of my closest friends to an IED. Killed a couple of insurgents, at least that's what we were told they were. They were just kids, man.' He paused and Scotty saw he was back in the desert.

'And?' he prompted.

'I got sick. PTSD, although they said it wasn't treatable. I had counselling and shit but the nightmares and sweats never went away. Still haven't. I got a medical discharge and tried to get a job as a mechanic, like in the army.'

'Hence Spanners?'

'Yep. So I tried a few garages, the type you find under railway arches and in lock-ups. I thought that would help get me back on my feet, but it was the worst thing I could have done.'

'How so?' asked Saira.

'You ever served, either of you?'

'No,' they both said.

'It's hard to explain but you have this rage. It burns deep inside and it only takes someone to give it oxygen and up it flares. Proper explodes.'

Both officers remained silent.

'Well, this customer came in. Flash geezer but seemed OK. I'd serviced his car and was handing it back when he said I'd nicked a £20 note from the door pocket. He got proper angry and the boss tried to reason with him but he was ranting about me being a thief and that.'

'And had you?' asked Scotty.

'No man, I wouldn't. Anyway, he got right up close to me. Right in my space. Next thing I know he's on the floor, blood gushing from his nose, crying like a baby. I don't remember butting him, but that's what the boss said I did and I could feel it on my head. I don't blame the gaffer for letting me go there and then but that's when I thought, what's the point?'

'What did you do?'

'Well I lost my bedsit, had no job, no friends. Living on the street, I did what so many ex-squaddies do. Drink, drugs eventually, then crime to buy the next fix. I'd gone from someone with a real pride to this.'

Scotty and Saira had heard the same story countless times before but it never failed to sadden them.

'What happened next?' asked Saira, breaking the silence.

'I don't like to talk about that.'

'OK, another time. So, back to the other day. Look at this bloke.' Scotty pulled up an image taken from his body cam. 'Know him?'

Spanners took the phone and zoomed in on the face. Scotty and Saira shared a look while he examined it.

'No, sorry man. I recognise the others behind him though.'

'So do we. You've never seen this bloke around at all?'

'No, as I said I'm new to Brighton.'

'It's just it's a bit of a coincidence. Saira and I, we know just about everyone living on the streets or who has a habit. Yet all of a sudden you turn up and so does this bloke. Take another look.' He thrust the phone back at him.

'I don't need to. I'm good with faces and I don't know him, but I can tell you something.'

Scotty's heart pounded an extra beat. 'Go on.'

'I'm not the only new bloke in town.'

'What are you saying?'

'Well, I wasn't exactly telling you the truth when I said I wanted to see what Brighton was like. Nor about them other places I went.'

'Right,' said Saira.

'Well, the discharge grant ain't enough to last one day. Even when they put it up to £76, it's nothing. There's these geezers in all the nicks south of Birmingham. Just when you're coming up for release they offer you a monkey to go to Brighton, keep your head down, proper down, until you get a nod to do something. I'm telling you man, most of us have never seen £500 so, like me, they take it. If you get nicked or come to notice in some other way, they give you a kicking and you pay the money back.'

'Prison officers?'

'Not directly but they must know it's going on.'

'What do you have to do for the money?'

'Just lie low and wait. Then when they have something, they'll find you and you do what you're told.'

'So you reckon . . .'

'Yep, I reckon your man is here for the same reason I am. And I'll tell you something else. He'll be long gone by now. You'll never find him.'

9

Following every other Op Eradicate arrest day, Bob and DS Luke Spencer had relished briefing the Crown Prosecution Service on the quality and quantity of evidence they'd amassed on each suspect. The undercover officers' evidence, shored up with volumes of technical and physical surveillance, rendered top-end charges inevitable. As before, some were charged on the day, others relied on drug analysis, but it was a foregone conclusion that all would have their day in court, then prison.

Bob's team had become so expert at these operations that all those they caught pleaded guilty. In some ways he was staggered that the tactic of embedding covert cops into a criminal network then watching as they were gleefully sold drugs still worked. But work it did, not least due to the ingenuity and courage of the UCs, but partly down to the stupidity and greed of their targets.

Today had been different though. Whilst it didn't affect the strength of the cases, Lizzie's death brought a sombre mood to the meeting. Due to the guilty pleas, she had never appeared as a prosecution witness in any Op Eradicate trial. But she had given character evidence on many occasions, describing to the judge how well the defendant was progressing through treatment and asking them to consider non-custodial sentences to allow them to continue their path to recovery. Sometimes it worked, sometimes it didn't. But, given the overall Op Eradicate objective was to get people off drugs, the police were more than happy for those who had strayed into low-level dealing to be handled leniently and get back into treatment.

So far as the cases themselves were concerned, the CPS lawyer was as happy as ever. The undercover officer who went by the name of Ged was particularly strong in tying together the higher echelons of the organised crime group. True to type, the prosecutor was keen they eke out more regarding the controlling mind – but Bob had explained that not only had the original covert objectives been met, but Ged was going off on paternity leave so would be heading back to wherever he came from for a good few weeks. He overlooked the fact that he'd agreed to have one last go and was already embedded and making promising progress around Lizzie's murder.

As they handed in their visitor's passes at the front desk and bade the receptionist goodbye, Bob held the heavy glazed door for Luke and followed him out. 'We should do something, you know,' he said, partly to the DS and partly to himself.

'Eh? About what?'

'Lizzie. We should have a memorial or something. Not sure what though. She never struck me as religious.'

'Ask Scotty.'

Bob paused to allow a car to reverse out of a space in the tiny car park. 'What would he know?'

'You're kidding me,' said Luke. 'You know they were an item, don't you?'

'He never said.'

'Of course he didn't. He's not told anyone, especially not his wife. They were seeing each other for months.'

'How did you know?' asked Bob as they walked down Dyke Road towards where they were parked.

'Blimey, guv. Call yourself a detective? Have you never heard them called Charles and Camilla?'

'What are you on about?'

'It's like them two. Everyone knew they were having an affair but no one mentioned it. And the size of Scotty, there's no wonder.'

'I definitely need to get out more,' muttered Bob as Luke chuckled to himself.

'We'd have been better off walking from the nick,' said Luke as they turned yet another corner.

'Sorry about that. I remember when you could reserve a spot at their office but apparently that might impinge on their independence, so now we battle with the great unwashed for a space. The walk will do us good though.'

Once they were close to where Bob thought the car was, he zapped the key so he could spot where they'd parked. The car crawling behind him was no doubt cruising for a rare place and Bob could imagine his optimism when it became clear from the flash of lights on the opposite side of the road that he'd strike lucky soon. He didn't look round but subconsciously quickened his pace so as not to keep the other driver waiting.

'Do you need to grab a sandwich on the way back?' Luke asked.

'Not for me,' said Bob. 'I'm on a fasting day today. I don't mind stopping off if you need to though.'

'Cheers, boss.'

Bob still sensed the car. He'd give them a nod when he was opening the door. When he was about ten yards away, he spotted a gap between a parked van and car he could squeeze through to cross over. He stepped off the pavement, Luke following a pace behind. The trailing car was a good fifteen yards away and, given this was a narrow one-way street, Bob didn't glance up. There would be no other cars coming.

The next five seconds seemed to take thirty.

First the scream of the engine. Then the screech of tyres clawing for grip. Finally, the eyes above the driver's mask. Naked rage. He didn't feel the car smash into him at all, just heard the thud, then the sensation of tumbling up, over and down. That and Luke screaming for someone to stop.

He had no idea how long he'd been knocked out but was woken by his right arm being squeezed. He thrashed against it until he heard someone say, 'Mr Heaton, you need to keep still while we take your blood pressure.' He opened his eyes to blinding fluorescence.

'He's coming round,' said the same soft Mancunian accent. 'Mr Heaton, you've had an accident. You're in the ambulance. Can you tell me where it hurts?'

'Where's Luke?'

'Is that the other officer you were with?'

'Yes, is he OK?'

'He's with your colleagues outside.'

'How is he?' Bob twisted but his ribs had other ideas. 'Shit.'

'You're better off staying still until we get you checked out. Your colleague is fine, if a little sweary!'

'What about the other car? Did it stop?'

'No. I think your lot are looking for it now.'

'They better bloody find it,' muttered Bob, before the lights went out again.

10

Ged was no football fan, certainly not where Brighton and Hove Albion were concerned. But he was more than happy after schmoozing his way back into the organised crime group to scrub up and be their guest at the Liverpool game. As a kid, his dad used to take him to Anfield to stand in The Kop and cheer Gérard Houllier's reds on. He often wondered if his dad would have enjoyed the game so much in their leaner years.

As he ambled towards the West Stand Reception, from where he would be shown to the box, his heart fluttered as his thoughts wandered to the impending birth and how he'd spend his Saturdays with his new son.

As this was just a getting-to-know-you deployment, he and Nick agreed they could brief over the phone. The cover officer would monitor the audio feed from Ged's covert microphone but neither were expecting anything earth-shattering to emerge. In any case, the stadium was full of cops so if he needed extracting, he was in the best place.

'Oi, Ged,' came a familiar voice behind him, followed by a smack on the back which nearly caused him to bite his tongue. 'Found it then.'

Ged laughed. 'All right, Nathan? Bit hard to miss, with American Express Stadium plastered across its fucking walls. Any case, I got a cab. Just in case I was struck blind.'

'You should have said. I'd have picked you up.'

'You driving? I've got every intention of spanking the free bar.'

'Me too,' said Nathan with a wink. As they entered the reception, Ged flashed his e-ticket to the reader and was grateful when Nathan said, 'Follow me.'

They climbed the stairs, showing their tickets to the yellow-vested stewards who guarded the various stairways and lounges against ticketless interlopers. Nathan didn't even look at them as he passed, but Ged's legend was that he was a polite, if hard-nosed, businessman so he said hello to each.

He'd worked undercover in a lot of settings but this was new to him. It was hard to reconcile the affable host, Sir Ben Parsons, as an associate of Nathan's who, once you scratched the surface, was just a ruthless gangster. Brighton had an underworld of the suspiciously wealthy: those who operated a don't ask, don't tell policy around how they afforded their champagne lifestyle.

Sir Ben was a Brighton boy through and through. Leaving school at fourteen, he worked his way up through the market trade to somehow acquire a chain of pharmacies which he expanded to become a staple on every UK high street. His charitable work earned him a knighthood in 2013. The following year he became chair of Respite Pharmaceuticals, a multinational drug research and manufacturing company based along the coast in Worthing. He'd recently shot into the headlines when Respite won a licence to trial a new heroin substitute, Synthopate, which promised to revolutionise addiction therapies. That and his scalpel-sharp intelligence, innate business acumen and unforgiving ways kept wary rivals at bay.

Nathan, on the other hand, had a more traditional career path through the ranks of organised crime: children's homes, borstals, vicious turf wars and prison. He had as much nous as Sir Ben but was less subtle in how he kept order. His name had been linked to half a dozen contract killings across the south-east of England, yet no one could pin anything on him.

It never ceased to surprise Ged how villains with so much pedigree failed so miserably in the due diligence department when meeting new contacts. The faces bustling around the food table and free bar were more suited to a criminal intelligence briefing than a VIP box at a Premier League stadium.

'Sir Ben, can I introduce Ged, the buyer I was telling you about?'

Sir Ben locked eyes with Ged then, after an uncomfortable pause, smiled warmly. 'Nice to finally meet you, Ged.' His working-class roots rang through his earthy Brighton accent. 'Nathan's been telling me all about you.'

Bet he hasn't, thought Ged.

They shook hands. 'Thanks for inviting me, Sir Ben. I'm really looking forward to the game.'

'Please, call me Ben. The game's just the sideshow. This is all about getting to know one another and enjoying the hospitality.' He indicated the huge buffet spread out at the back of the room. 'No pies or pints here. Unless that's what you fancy, of course.'

'This'll do,' said Ged, suddenly aware he might just be talking to the main man. He knew Nathan deferred to someone high up, but a knight of the realm?

'Remind me what line you're in,' said Sir Ben as he handed Ged a glass of chilled champagne.

'Thank you. I'm in acquisitions and sales. Imports and exports.'

'I see,' said Sir Ben, clearly understanding the code. 'Similar sector to me I gather.'

'I believe so but maybe less high profile.'

'Indeed. It's a troubling time for both of us though,' said Sir Ben. 'There are some that would prefer to see our customer base reduced to nothing, and that can't be good for anyone.'

'Indeed,' said Ged. 'We're feeling the pinch too.'

'Well don't worry, we have plans. It'll soon blow over.'

Ged knew not to probe, just to open the door. 'Really?'

'Absolutely. We can't have naive personal agendas taking down multimillion-pound businesses. Think of the taxes the government would lose.' Sir Ben shook his head.

Ged couldn't have been more relieved when the players' walk-on music, 'Sussex by the Sea', bellowed out through the stadium's speakers.

'Time to take our places gentlemen,' said Sir Ben as he held the door to the premium seats with bird's-eye views of the pitch.

Ged had struggled to keep a lid on his instincts when Liverpool converted a penalty in the second minute of first-half stoppage time. 'Never disrupt your environment' was a mantra the instructors on the Level 1 Undercover Course drummed into every prospective UC. To cheer an away goal at the Amex would not so much disrupt as explode his.

On the referee's whistle, Sir Ben and his guests filed from their seats for their half-time refreshments. Ged joined them, texting a coded message to Nick to check the comms were still working.

You at the gym tomorrow?

The reply came back straight away. *Sorry mate, I've pulled my calf.*

Shit, thought Ged. That was Nick saying he couldn't hear a thing. These earring mikes were great when they worked but they were packing up all the time recently. That was why he always carried a spare in the stitching of his belt. He could do with a piss anyway, so he'd have to swap the stud over then and hope no one was looking. With dozens of drink-fuelled, middle-aged men filling the lounges, the toilets at half-time were unlikely to be deserted but needs must. If Sir Ben was planning on becoming looser-lipped, Ged needed Nick to both hear it and have it recorded for evidence later.

He slipped out of the box and glanced round the lobby, spotting several men from other boxes disappearing through a blue door. Clocking it as the toilet, he followed, hoping for a cubicle. He was out of luck. Each of the three were firmly closed and the noises coming from behind the doors told him they'd be in use for a while. He couldn't afford to wait as he didn't want to be missed by his new contacts, so he took his turn at the urinal. Trusting the unwritten rule that men never looked down or at each other while peeing, he took the chance to unpick the loose stitches in his belt and palmed the spare earring microphone.

Next was the tricky bit. How to remove one ear stud and replace it with an identical one without drawing attention to himself. He worked out that if he did it in stages, the chances of anyone seeing the whole manoeuvre were slim to the point of being negligible.

As he stepped away from the basin, he pretended he was scratching his ear and managed to take the faulty stud out, slipping it into his pocket.

'Thank you,' he said to the man who held the door for him. He stepped into the lobby and, as he ambled back to Sir Ben's box, he repeated the scratching ear technique and the fresh device was in. It was only when he opened the box door to rejoin the others that he noticed a bald man with a birthmark on his head behind him.

Not paying much attention to him, Ged helped himself to a plate of food and walked over to Nathan. 'Oh cheers,' he said as the gang leader handed him a glass. In his peripheral vision, he saw the man who'd followed him pull Sir Ben to one side and talk rapidly but inaudibly to him. The host flicked Ged a glance and his genial expression hardened into something quite terrifying.

He tapped a text to Nick.

How about a beer then?

Sounds good, came the confirmation that the cover officer could hear him loud and clear. Ged was about to fire off a text about Sir Ben but, at that moment, someone near the door shouted, 'Second half.' He decided it would be safer leaving it for the debrief.

The crowd around him downed their drinks and wandered out to retake their seats. As he followed on, he heard Sir Ben call out, 'Nathan, you got a minute?'

No one quite knew where the referee got the six minutes of stoppage time from, as the equaliser Brighton scored with ten minutes to spare would have made ninety per cent of the crowd happy enough. However, when the Liverpool centre half clipped a Brighton player's legs following a ninety-fifth-minute corner, the crowd erupted.

With seconds to go, the Brighton striker slotted home the penalty in what was the last kick of the game, and three rare points against the champions-elect were in the bag.

The party mood in the box after the game was more like Mardi Gras than a networking meeting at a football match, and Ged joined in despite being gutted for his late father.

After about half an hour, he was ready to go. Sir Ben had given him a wide berth and he wasn't making much progress with anyone else. Nathan was downing the free bubbly like it had a 'use by' date and the wisdom of sharing a car with him on the way home was evaporating. He made the snap decision to give the gang leader the slip. He couldn't wait to sign the deployment log, hand in his comms and head up north to become a dad. It was all he could do to stop himself telling his wife he was on his way.

Out of politeness he wandered over to Sir Ben. 'Sir Ben, I'm off. Thanks so much for this afternoon. I wouldn't have missed it for the world.'

'I'm sure not,' came the frosty reply. 'Take him with you too,' he said, nodding at Nathan. 'He tends to become embarrassing the later it goes on.'

'Sure,' said Ged, his heart sinking. Maybe he could persuade Nathan to share a cab.

Ten minutes later, Nathan was fumbling with his keys in the car park just outside the South Stand. 'Mate, let's get a cab. There's so many Old Bill around here you're bound to get nicked.'

'Fuck that. I drive better with a few sherbets inside me.'

'Well, I'm getting a taxi.' Ged looked around but, other than a couple of coaches, there was nothing that looked like public transport anywhere near.

'Get in the fucking car, you wuss. I'll drop you off in Rottingdean.'

Ged calculated that was ten minutes max. If he pushed the point it would cause a scene, and the last thing he needed was to draw attention to himself.

'Just drive carefully then.'

To his surprise, Nathan seemed remarkably in control as he eased out of the parking space, navigated the one-way system then filtered onto Village Way. Thankfully, as most supporters had not enjoyed post-match hospitality, the roads were clear. Nathan waited at the red light then completed a flawless right turn onto the Drove as soon as the green light shone.

Ged took in the patchwork of fields either side of the narrow country road, wondering who allowed the stadium to be built in such stunning countryside. The road swept gently to the right, then to the left, and the shimmering English Channel on the horizon finished off the landscape perfectly. Ged vowed to himself that this was the image he'd take home of Brighton, not standing stark naked in a beer cellar with a gun to his head.

As they pressed on, two cyclists appeared in the near distance riding abreast.

'Fucking bikes,' muttered Nathan.

'Chill mate. We'll get past them soon,' said Ged, hoping to dissuade the drunk-driver from some ill-judged overtake.

Nathan just muttered and settled in behind them, the oncoming traffic and bends preventing anything more ambitious.

If Ged didn't know better, he'd have thought they were deliberately blocking the way, but he kept quiet. The cyclists seemed oblivious and Ged could sense Nathan getting more and more agitated. It wasn't unusual for bikes to create tailbacks but Ged's sixth sense screamed that there was more to them than their lack of road sense. Just as Nathan dropped down a gear, the bikes split like a Red Arrows display team at the precise moment that a glint came from a copse at the roadside ahead.

The last thing Ged ever did was to grab the steering wheel, but it was too late to save either of them.

11

For someone with such an ingrained fear of hospitals, Jo seemed to have spent an inordinate amount of time in them over the last couple of years. Her phobia stemmed from when her dad was dying from prostate cancer and spent weeks withering away in Brighton's main one.

She'd visited the sick, the dying and even had a spell as a patient following a car crash, but this incessant exposure had only heightened her aversion. The Pavlovian sweats came on the second she walked through the door and she knew if she didn't keep going, she'd bottle it.

She followed the signs to Keymer Ward, and slowed as she walked past the desk. As the only nurse there was on the phone, Jo didn't trouble her but walked straight through to Bob's bay. When he'd been admitted the day before she had posted an officer by his bedside just in case someone came back for a second go, but Bob had sent them away, using his rank to reinforce his order. As a compromise the ward agreed to move him to a private room and to monitor people coming in and out. She'd just discovered how empty that promise had been.

Jo tapped on the door. 'Are you decent?'

'Luckily for you I am,' came the reply.

She pushed the door and stepped in. Bob's fractured arm was immobilised in a brace and the bruises gave him the look of a street brawler, but other than that he looked like he'd had a lucky escape.

'I brought you some biscuits,' said Jo.

'Ah, Bahlsen's. Your favourite.'

'Well, you can't eat them all, what with you being stuck on your arse for the next few weeks. Think of your waistline. Steve would kick you out.'

'You've just missed him. A ball of sympathy he was too, saying how he could get used to having our bed to himself.'

'He's too good for you anyway.' She opened the biscuits, took one then offered the pack to him.

He shook his head. 'Can't stand them, as you well know. Anyway, haven't you got better things to do on a Saturday evening?'

'Not really. Let's say Darren and I are getting on better when we're apart at the mo.'

'Oh, I'm sorry to hear that.'

'It'll blow over. Just work stuff. His, for a change. Anyway, have you remembered any more about the driver?'

'No, but he was definitely masked up. That says to me it wasn't some joyrider with shit driving skills.'

'You still think you were targeted?'

'That's the only explanation. Why else follow us along the road then hit the gas as I'm crossing?'

'But why?'

Bob looked at her as if she were simple. 'I've not exactly been running shoplifting enquiries over the last few years. There's probably a queue of people waiting to bump me off.'

'Don't flatter yourself,' said Jo as she took another biscuit. 'Most of those are dead or in prison. Oh, sorry.' She kicked herself for such crass insensitivity, remembering Bob's brief period of incarceration.

'It's OK. No, I think it's more what I'm doing now than anything from the past.'

'What, Eradicate?'

'Sure. It follows. Lizzie gets killed the day we lock up the city's recent batch of drug dealers, then someone tries to wipe me out just after my meeting with CPS.'

'Why not take Luke out too?'

Bob shrugged, then winced. 'Maybe that was the intention but they could only get one of us.'

'It's a bit two and two equals five, isn't it? We don't know why Lizzie was killed but it could be a hundred reasons, including her affair with Scotty.'

'You knew about that?'

'Of course, it's common knowledge,' said Jo.

'Just me then. But why kill her on an arrest day in front of two cops?'

'You've got a point but, as you say, you are universally hated so it doesn't have to be connected.'

'And you came here to cheer me up, did you?'

'Yep. How am I doing?'

Just then Jo's phone rang. *Unknown Number*. That usually meant it was the force control room or someone from the intelligence world. 'Jo Howe.'

'It's the Ops room inspector, ma'am. Are you free to speak?'

'Yes, sure.'

'Are you on your own?'

Jo frowned. They never usually asked that. 'Give me a minute.' She shrugged at Bob and stepped out of the room to find a quiet corner. It took a minute but she pushed a door and stepped into a linen cupboard. 'I am now. Go ahead.'

'Ma'am, there's been a double shooting on the Drove near the Amex stadium.' A chill washed through her.

'Fatalities?'

'Yes, two dead in a car. It's early days but it seems the gunman shot through the windscreen while it was moving. Killed the driver and passenger outright.'

'That's no mean feat. Sounds like a hit.'

'That's what the duty DI says.'

'Suspects?'

'Not yet but the driver was Nathan Challenor. He's a National Crime Agency target, I'm told.'

Jo paced the room. She'd put Challenor away a couple of times when he was a small-time dealer and had featured in the Op Eradicate intelligence. 'Sad for his family but no great loss. Any ID on the passenger?'

'That's why I'm calling you. His name is . . . was, Pete McElroy.'

'Not ringing any bells.'

'No it wouldn't. He's a Cheshire detective. But he's also an undercover officer down here working on Operation Eradicate. His pseudonym was Ged.'

Jo's world slammed to a halt. She could barely hold her trembling phone. 'Are you sure?'

'Yes, ma'am. His cover officer has identified him. ACC Mills is making his way to HQ and asks if you can join him.'

'Yes, yes, of course. I'll be there in half an hour.'

Thoughts crashed through Jo's mind as she thought first of the officer's family, and then what this all meant. The shakes kicked in almost straight away and she took some deep breaths to settle herself down. She stepped out of the cupboard to quizzical looks from a healthcare assistant, headed out of the ward then turned, remembering Bob.

When she walked in, Bob was staring at the door, phone in his hand. He did not react to her arrival but looked totally stunned. 'You've heard then?' she said.

He gave the faintest of nods. 'How could it happen? Where was his protection? Christ, what have I done?'

Jo went over to the bed and put her arm round him. 'We'll find all that out but don't blame yourself. I promise we will get to the bottom of this.'

'But he was due to go off on paternity leave when I asked him to have one last go.'

'Paternity leave? Oh my God. It's still not your fault. But I'll tell you something.'

'What?'

'I was wrong earlier. Two and two definitely equals four.'

Living with Jo was becoming impossible. From the moment he met her in the Liberian hospital camp when she was helping rebuild an amoral police service and he was reporting on the West's complicity in supporting the corrupt government, he'd been head over heels in love with her.

After the week and the rows they'd had, she'd promised him a family day, taking their boys, Ciaran aged six and Liam aged five, swimming and then piling all the calories back on at their favourite Greek restaurant, Archipelagos, in the city centre. Then came yesterday's call about Bob being mown down in Hove. Jo owed Bob more than her career. Darren got that, but the way she broke the news this morning that she'd have to work today, before they'd even got out of bed, was brutal.

Even when she was head of Major Crime, she'd at least tell the boys herself if she had to renege on a promise, even if then they were too young to understand. This morning she'd been out of the door before they had so much as stirred. So, once again, it was down to Darren to burst their balloon.

They took the news with a shrug of inevitability, Ciaran spinning it into a positive with an arm around his bereft brother, building him up for a lads' day out. This perked the sportier sibling up, so Darren added a kick-around into the mix and found a live stream to watch the Albion game on. They didn't even baulk when he traded the restaurant visit for the promise of a pizza courtesy of Deliveroo.

'I'll get it, I'll get it,' screamed Liam, as he jostled with his older brother when the doorbell rang. They used to save such elation for when

Jo came home but, as that was becoming a rarity before bedtime, the fast-food delivery boy received both barrels.

'Calm down,' said Darren, understanding that the promise of a Meat Feast and garlic bread on top of Brighton's last-minute win against Liverpool could never induce serenity. Liam opened the door and he and Ciaran just stared at the glum-faced pizza-bearer.

'Thanks, mate,' said Darren, as he edged past the boys. He slipped the man a fiver and took the boxes through to the kitchen.

'Are we saving some for Mummy?' said Ciaran.

Darren thought for a second. 'I think Mummy might be late, so maybe I can cook her something else when she gets in.'

'Will she be sad?' said Liam, his face a picture of worry.

Miserable yes, but sad? Probably not. 'She'll be fine, darling. Come on, let's get these in the lounge and watch the late kick-off.' They settled down, three abreast on the settee, pizza boxes set out on the table in front, Cokes by their side.

The Wolves v Chelsea game was twenty minutes in and no score. Darren enjoyed watching as a neutral but, if pushed, he'd prefer to see the home team edge a 6–0 victory. He was halfway through his second slice when his phone rang from the kitchen. Hoping it was Jo to say she was on her way home, he sprung up. 'Won't be a second, boys. Make sure Chelsea don't score while I'm gone.'

Ciaran and Liam chuckled in a way that melted Darren's heart. Whatever he and Jo were going through, he couldn't sacrifice this beautiful family.

Spotting the phone on the island unit, he swore under his breath. *Sam Parkin*, the display announced.

'Hi Sam,' said Darren, with more glee than anyone could believe was genuine.

'Dazza, glad I got hold of you. Are you in Brighton?'

'Well, Hove actually.'

'Great. Listen, I need you to get across to near the football stadium. There's been a double shooting and I want it covered. The trains are all to fuck this weekend so I can't send anyone else down. You don't mind, do you?'

'Well, to be honest, Sam, it's not great timing.'

'I don't reckon it is for the two geezers lying on slabs in the morgue either, but some things you just can't plan for. Be a good mate and pop over there, see what it's all about.'

'But I've got the boys.'

'Not my problem, Dazza.'

Darren wandered into the lounge and saw the boys snuggling up, glued to the football.

'Look, are you sure there's no one else? I thought I was on features these days.'

'Like I said, it's you or you. Anyway, talking of your feature, this is your opening paragraph on a plate.'

'Eh? Is it gang related?'

'In a manner of speaking. One of the stiffs is some big-noise villain called Nathan Challenor. Ever heard of him?' Darren had, but said nothing. 'Nah, me neither. The other though, and this is where it gets sexy.'

'Go on?' Despite himself, Darren's interest was piqued.

'Now this ain't confirmed and certainly not for publication yet, but the other one, we are told, is a copper.'

'A police officer? What, a corrupt one?'

'No, the opposite. We've had this from more than one source that he's an undercover detective from up north somewhere.'

Suddenly Darren was all ears. If this was what it seemed, he could be on the verge of the most explosive scoop of his career. His mind raced. There was no way he was missing this. He reassured himself that the boys would love a sleepover at Nanny's.

Darren sighed. 'Send me the details. I'll sort the boys out and be over there within the hour.'

'I knew you wouldn't let me down. Oh, just to let you know, there's a press conference at police HQ at 7.30 p.m. Make sure you're there after you've snapped some pics at the scene. I better tell you also, it's being led by your missus.'

He was about to protest but Sam interrupted with a question he must ask Jo, come what may. Suddenly everything fell into place.

12

Having checked the huge iron gates had firmly closed behind him, Sir Ben Parsons drew up outside his porticoed ten-bedroom mansion within which he now rattled. Taking half a dozen deep breaths, he steeled himself for the transformation necessary every time he stepped over its threshold. Would it have been easier had his wife not left him a decade ago, or if they had managed to produce the family they so craved? At least there would have been someone to share the burdens with.

God, he could do with that now. The afternoon's events had hurtled out of control. He was furious that Nathan had brought an undercover detective into the fold, more so that he had the temerity to introduce them. The order he'd given at half-time was ruthless but necessary. He didn't enjoy playing God, but what choice did he have?

He pulled himself out of the car, blipped it locked and walked like a condemned man to the front door, which opened with a glance at the iris-reader. As he did each time he got home, he paused in the hallway to sense what kind of crisis he was walking into. Now, the house was silent except for the chatter from a television upstairs.

'Mum, it's me,' he called, as he climbed the sweeping staircase. The stench of faeces and urine hit him the second he reached the top. That bloody care agency.

The scene that greeted him as he stepped into his mum's room brought tears to his eyes and bile to his throat. The room had once been the main guest bedroom and, before he'd moved Audrey in, a work of art. Brighton's finest designers had given it the feel of a suite at the Dorchester. The furniture alone would buy you an average city starter home.

Now, it resembled a crime scene; his mother entangled in a mesh of sheets, her grey wispy hair matted with unidentifiable foodstuffs. Even from the door the multicoloured stains of human waste splattered across her nightie and the linen were as plain to see as they were to smell.

On the table by her arm was an upended mug and a plate with encrusted, untouched, salmon en croute.

But it was the fear in her eyes that hit him the hardest.

'Don't hurt me. Take the money and go, but please don't hit me,' she sobbed.

'Mum, it's me. Ben.'

'I don't know a Ben. Please go now before my husband gets home.'

He edged closer, careful not to scare her. The dementia had been getting worse and while Ben was determined to keep her at home as long as possible, he was actively scouring for remedies which would give her dignity in her twilight years. So far, only the USA seemed to have the right treatment programmes but most were unproven despite the six-figure sums they were asking.

'Mum, Dad died ten years ago. It's just you and me, Ben, now. What's happened?'

'Ben who? I don't know you.'

'We've been through all this. Look, let's get you cleaned up and we can sit and chat. Maybe look at some photos.' She flinched as he went to touch her, cowering on the other side of the bed. 'I'll tell you what, I'll put some music on.'

73

He pressed some buttons on his phone and *My Fair Lady*'s 'Ascot Gavotte' purred from the Bose Wave sound system. It was as if he'd flicked a switch in her.

'Hello, darling. Enjoy the football?'

'Yes, it was good thanks. Just like the old days,' he lied. 'Look, let's get you cleaned up and we can have a good natter.' He walked her to the en suite and eased her into the wicker chair just inside the door while he ran the bath. 'Did the carers come in today?'

'Who dear?'

'The carers. Have they been?'

'I don't think so. I'm not sure they do at the weekend, do they?'

'Never mind, I'll give them a call.'

Half an hour later, his mum now clean in a fresh nightie and with the bedding replaced, Sir Ben was on the phone to the care agency. It turned out they had been that day, twice, but the first time his mum had just told them to 'get the fuck out of my caravan', and the second she'd threatened to call the police. They apologised for not being able to reach him on his mobile, which he accepted. He stayed quiet about the notoriously poor signal at the Amex stadium on match days.

He checked his watch. 7.00 p.m. The others would be round soon, so he popped up to his mother's room again to check whether she needed anything. 'I've got all I need with Ant and Dec,' she said, pointing to the TV. 'See, you could have made something of yourself if you'd have followed in their footsteps.'

She had a point. He bet those cheeky chappies never had to order executions while nibbling a buffet.

His phone chirped and he saw on the Ring doorbell app that both Nicola Merrion, the CEO of Lifechoices, the city's drug treatment provider, and Arjun Sharma, the Prison Service regional executive director, were standing side by side. He strolled downstairs and opened the door.

'Nicola, Arjun, do come through,' he said with the warmth of a long-lost buddy.

They took their seats in the drawing room, the baby monitor in the corner humming away with sounds of tacky TV and his mother's mumbling.

'I'll get straight to the point. We've got a huge problem.' He didn't insult either's intelligence by recounting what had happened at and after the match. If they didn't know by now, then he'd seriously underestimated them as business partners. 'Christ only knows what damage this undercover officer's done. Him and Challenor are, of course, no longer a problem, but we need to embark on some serious damage limitation and up our game.'

'How do we know there aren't any more?' said Nicola. 'What the hell do we do if there are moles elsewhere?'

Sir Ben glared at her. It unnerved him when she returned the stare with equal menace, but he continued nonetheless. 'You better hope for your sake there aren't. If I have any chance of breaking even, let alone profiting from the Synthopate trial, we need a flourishing heroin market, which means lots of users. Now's the perfect time for you to pull out of Eradicate.'

'I'm trying to, but it's not easy without losing the commission and the funding that goes with it. Lizzie's murder has terrified the staff though, so I'm fuelling that. If we're seen to pull out, the powers that be will just find someone else to take over from us.' Nicola knew her stuff – that much was obvious from her previous role as Director of Public Health.

'Leave that side of things to me. We all know Chief Superintendent Howe's evangelical quest is born out of the guilt of not being able to save her sister. However, if she succeeds here then others will follow suit, and I don't need to explain what that will do for not only our pockets but our shareholders' too.'

'She's like a dog with a bone,' said Sharma, piping up for the first time. 'I've even heard her quoted at Prison Service HQ meetings. "Cut the demand, choke the supply." "Users in treatment, dealers in prison,"' he mimicked. 'And if I've heard those supposed crime reduction stats once, I've heard them a thousand times.'

Sir Ben glared at the prison director. 'Then do something about it. The bloke I'm going to replace Nathan with will need you to keep the steady flow.' He noticed how they both looked at each other when he talked of a replacement before Nathan's body was even cold. 'Get your prison governors to send more ex-cons to Brighton. And not just from Lewes nick. Drip them from prisons right across your domain so no one joins the dots. You've got an endless source of bribable labour, we just need more of it.'

Both guests nodded.

'This isn't more of the same. This is a turbocharged effort to make sure that bloody woman's leftie ideology is buried under an avalanche of heroin, users and, if necessary, overdoses.' Nicola flinched. 'Anything to keep the business going and crash Op Eradicate.' He stood. 'Happy? Good, I won't keep you any longer.'

Other than mumbled goodbyes, no one said another word on the way out. Sir Ben closed the door behind them, a ripple of optimism trickling through him for the first time since the football.

13

There was never a good time to be sat around the chief constable's conference table.

Jo's presence here was rarely for a pat on the back or to present one of her crime-cutting ideas. Either, in the chief officers' eyes, she had royally fucked up or, as was the case today, something devastating had happened and it required the collective brains to stop it getting any worse.

She was surprised that it wasn't the actual chief constable chairing the meeting. Most of her senior colleagues accepted his invisibility when it came to operational matters but if the execution of an undercover officer working on a Sussex operation didn't make him step up, what would?

'Right. I think we're all here,' said the chair. 'Shall we introduce ourselves? I'm ACC Leon Mills and I'm the duty chief officer this weekend.' He turned to his left.

'Chief Superintendent Jo Howe. Divisional Commander for Brighton and Hove and Gold Commander for Op Eradicate.'

'DS Nick Dillon. I am, er was, Pete McElroy's cover officer.'

'DCI Claire Jackson. Senior investigating officer.'

'Superintendent Gary Hedges. Strategic firearms commander.'

'And on the screen?' said Mills.

'DI Bob Heaton, I'm the covert operations manager for this deployment. I'm sorry if I cut in and out. The hospital Wi-Fi's not great.'

'No problem, Bob. I hope you're on the mend.'

'Thanks, sir.'

'And I'm DCC Nigel Hughes, Cheshire Constabulary. Ged, or Pete as we know him, was one of ours.'

'Thank you Nigel. I'm sure I speak for us all when I say how sorry we are for your loss.'

The deputy chief constable gave the faintest of nods.

'Claire, if you can tell us where you are with the investigation and what, if anything more, the force can provide.'

Claire took the meeting through the various lines of enquiry, what her priorities were and how she had drawn in staff from across the region.

Gary talked through the armed policing plan which, until Claire came up with any viable suspects, amounted to armed response officers cruising the city poised to respond while trying to reassure the community they had their backs.

'Nick, can you tell us about today's events and what Ged, er Pete, was doing?'

'Sure, thank you. As you probably now know, Pete had infiltrated an organised crime group led by Nathan Challenor. It was all to do with getting into the higher echelons of those subject to Op Eradicate.' Jo felt all eyes fall on her. She shuffled uncomfortably. 'Yesterday, he received an invitation from Challenor to go to the Brighton v Liverpool match at the Amex. He told Pete he'd introduce him to some useful contacts. Usually I'd have run it past DI Heaton but, as we know, he was rushed to hospital so I couldn't get hold of him.'

Jo looked up at Bob.

Nick continued, 'I agreed that, providing it was literally a networking meeting in a crowded public place, the risks were low and he should go.'

'I'd like to come in on that. Was that a formal risk assessment?' said the Cheshire DCC.

'Nigel, would you mind awfully if we leave that side of things to the IOPC?' said Mills.

Jo winced at the mention of the Independent Office for Police Conduct, as did Bob. A couple of years ago they'd been responsible for the closest to a miscarriage of justice Jo had ever been involved in, resulting in Bob serving time on remand.

The DCC was about to reply, but Mills ploughed on.

'What happened at the game then?'

Nick recounted how Pete had travelled by taxi, but his covert microphone had stopped working so Nick had no idea what happened or who he met before they realised this and he had switched earrings at half-time. He said that Pete had instructions not to travel in any vehicles but Nick could tell, once the comms had been restored, that he had no other option. He took a sip of water. 'I heard all the conversation while they were in the car. It seems Challenor was drunk, or at least over the limit. I tried to text Pete to tell him to get himself out of there but the message wasn't delivered. Next thing I hear is two thuds then a crash. Presumably that was Challenor's car hitting the truck after they'd been shot.'

There was reverential silence as they all bowed their heads.

'Jo, anything to add from a divisional or Eradicate perspective?'

'Not a lot. We know Nathan Challenor of old. He's the highest level in the Organised Crime Group who we've identified. He kept his network on a tight leash, and we were starting to look at him for any connections with Lizzie Reed's murder and the attempted murder of Bob.'

'Really?' said the ACC.

'Really,' she said as if talking to one of her sons. 'I'm convinced they are all drugs related and that he was the controlling mind. Or one of them.'

'And did Pete uncover anything to corroborate that?'

Bob chipped in. 'If I may, sir, no, not yet but we were optimistic he would one way or another. Can I add that whilst Nick wasn't able to get hold of me, if he had I would have authorised the football visit.'

Nick looked at the screen and nodded a thank you to Bob.

'OK. What I need to establish is whether there is any current threat, how we play this in the media and what we tell our staff. Here and in Cheshire,' Mills added in what seemed like an afterthought.

'In terms of the current threat,' said Jo, determined they'd hear it from her, 'I'm sure Claire will consider which of Challenor's rivals had the capability to do this.' She waited for Claire's nod. 'It's highly possible that he was the target and Pete just happened to be in the wrong place at the wrong time. There's nothing to suggest that he was compromised so, whilst we can't rule it out, we have to be looking for another gang and to prevent reprisals.'

The group chatted around this point for a good ten minutes and agreed that was the likely scenario.

ACC Mills paused. 'Here's what we are going to do. Jo, you're not going to like this, but we must show strength. I'd like you to tone down the outreach aspect of Op Eradicate for the time being and concentrate your resources on coming down hard on anyone, and I mean anyone, involved in drugs. Users, street dealers, gang members. We need to send a strong message that we will not tolerate such violence.'

'But, sir . . .'

Mills held up his hand. 'No, Jo. I agree these three events could well be linked so we must show them who's boss. I'm not having a bloodbath on my watch. Please brief the council chief executive before you front the press conference, but if we can have a word in private first. Thank you everyone else. You may go.'

Jo shuffled uncomfortably as the ACC stood up and made sure the video conferencing monitor was switched off once, other than the two of them, the room was empty.

'Cup of tea?' he said.

'I don't drink tea but I'm fine. I'd rather just get on if it's OK with you.'

Leon Mills sat back down opposite Jo, the huge mirror-polished table a welcome barrier.

'Are you OK with the press?' he asked.

She allowed her eyebrows to shoot up at his patronising tone. 'Yes, I'm fine. I'm assuming we are just throwing them some titbits so they don't create the story for themselves.'

'Yes, indeed. It's unlikely we'll get drawn on one of the dead being an undercover police officer. There's nothing to suggest that's out there. Fob any questions around identification off with the old "next of kin are being informed" line.'

'But they've already been told I understand.'

'Yes, but the press don't need to know that. Anyway, just the basics. What I really wanted to talk to you about was the viability of the whole operation. Make no mistake, the IOPC will be all over this and that includes whether the undercover deployment was proportionate.'

'But . . .'

Mills lifted a finger. 'Don't get me wrong. I absolutely support the experiment of reducing crime by collapsing the drugs market, but a lot of people are getting twitchy.'

'Who exactly?' said Jo, more abruptly than she'd intended.

Mills broke her gaze, pretending to flip through his notebook. 'Well, the Police and Crime Commissioner, the Home Secretary – as I told you after Lizzie's murder – and several of the Sussex MPs, one of whom I don't need to remind you is the current Policing Minister. We have to play these people very carefully if we are to keep our funding level.'

'But, sir, don't you see, a little investment cuts crime which cuts demand which cuts costs. It's a win–win.'

'But not at any price. We've had three murders and one attempted murder in a few days, all with one thing in common. Op Eradicate.'

'What are you suggesting? Wave the white flag?' Jo could barely get her words out. Of all the chief officers she'd worked with, Leon Mills was the most affable, but he still lacked backbone. She wondered whether they had them surgically removed on day one of the Strategic Command Course.

'I'm just saying, we are going to be under a lot of scrutiny for the next few months and maybe we should pause and try more traditional methods to reduce crime. Frankly, those who sign the cheques don't share our patience for long term strategies. They need results yesterday. Or sooner if you can manage.'

Jo had had enough of this. She didn't need a lecture on politics, or on the merits or otherwise of her flagship project. She was the one beaten up at each monthly performance meeting when burglaries went through the roof or robberies soared. Who did they think was committing the crimes, her own officers? She had done the research, scrutinised policing models across the globe and always came back to the same conclusion. Operation Eradicate worked and would continue to work. She knew she wasn't going to get the top-cover she needed, so had to leave before Mills converted his mealy-mouthed suggestion to end the operation into a direct order.

14

Once he'd dropped the boys off at his mother-in-law's house, Darren drove towards the scene of the shootings but couldn't get anywhere near, so he headed to Sussex Police HQ.

He had no idea how to play this but was convinced Sam Parkin was setting him up. It was one thing to be asked to cover a run-of-the-mill press conference where the police would say nothing yet promise the world, but the question he'd been told to ask was suicide. Not only would it show their hand to every other news outlet but it would almost certainly detonate his marriage.

He parked in the Tesco car park, five minutes' walk from HQ, to give himself thinking time and to get his act together. His mind drifted back to the hold Parkin had over him.

He was sure he hadn't been involved in the dark practices others had gone to prison for, but could he be certain his fingerprints weren't somewhere in the evidence trail? In those mad days of angry editors and impossible deadlines, he'd helped whoever asked. They all had. Could he have inadvertently handled some nugget obtained by nefarious means? He couldn't take the chance and, when the dust settled, Jo would understand. Surely.

As he reached the top of the hill he could see that he'd left it late for a front row seat. Arc lights and cameras were already set up and the press pack was five deep and ten abreast. Maybe he could use the sheer numbers as an excuse not to get his question out. Would Sam accept that? Who was he kidding?

He recognised fewer than a handful of the waiting journalists. Hardly surprising given most of them looked about twelve and he rarely covered news events like this. He was grateful for the comparative anonymity that would bring, and the fact he could avoid inane small talk while they were waiting.

He pretended to message on his phone while prima-donna camera operators around him whinged about the failing light and whether they could get the spokesperson to stand against a neutral background.

Suddenly, the pack shuffled and surged, shutters clicked and voices called out questions they knew would never be answered.

Over the shoulder of a biker-jacketed woman in front of him, he glimpsed Jo as she strode out, clipboard in hand and rock-like expression across her face. He recognised the red-haired woman by her side as press officer Clarissa Heard. Jo liked her and she enjoyed a good reputation with the local media.

Darren wondered whether now was the time to slip away and take the consequences. He glanced round. Even if he wanted to, the latecomers had now boxed him in.

'Thank you, thank you,' Jo boomed in a voice Darren was more used to hearing calling the boys in for tea. 'I have a short statement to give, after which I will take one or two questions. Please remember though, this is an active and fast-moving investigation and I won't have that much to add beyond what I'm about to say.' As ever, she was doing this from memory. They shared a pet hate of senior officers reading their carefully worded statements, giving the impression they wanted to distance themselves from the party line.

'Today, shortly after five-thirty, two men were shot while travelling in a car on the Drove in Brighton. Police and paramedics arrived within five minutes but sadly both men were declared dead at the scene. Next of kin are being informed. Our initial hypothesis is that this was a targeted attack and there is no reason for people to be alarmed. That said, we would ask the public to remain vigilant and report anything suspicious to the police. We'd ask anyone who was in the area of the Drove between five-fifteen and five-forty-five today to contact us whether or not you think you've seen anything, particularly if you might have dashcam footage. Thank you.'

A cacophony of questions erupted, but Clarissa chose who'd get the floor. 'Mike Parker.'

'Thank you. Chief Superintendent, do you believe this is gang related?'

'It's too early to say,' she replied, as they all knew she would.

'Karen Pollard,' Clarissa called out.

'Mrs Howe, this is another horrific event on your watch. Is Brighton becoming a no-go area?'

'Of course not, but I'm not going to speculate on what's behind this.'

She parried a handful of similar questions with the same disdain and Darren thought he'd got away with it. He could just say he hadn't been invited to speak. Then his mind flashed to images of Ciaran and Liam watching him being led away in handcuffs. Just as Jo was turning to walk away, he took a breath and called out.

'Is there any truth in the rumours that one of the dead men was an undercover police officer working on a drugs operation?'

Jo spun back and, even from this distance, he could feel her rage. Clarissa called out, 'Sorry, can you say who you are and where you are from?'

Jo hissed, 'I know who he is and I'm not dignifying that with a reply,' and then she stormed off.

Suddenly, Darren was surrounded by journalists demanding to know more. He forced his way through them, ignoring their pleas while trying to work out where the hell he would sleep tonight.

Having been too enraged to pick up his first three calls, Jo knew Gary Hedges wasn't going to give up until he'd hunted her down. She needed time to process what had just happened, to work out a future and to cry. Ideally she would have sprinted out of Headquarters and up the hills that climbed above it. But that would have literally played into the easy stereotype of female leaders that some insisted on.

Instead, she headed for her favourite bolthole at HQ: the Operations Department. During the day there was enough buzz to make it feel like a proper police station, and by night it was blissfully deserted.

The phone buzzed again.

'Yes.'

'Are you where I think you are?' said Gary.

'Probably.'

'Just stay there.'

She thought about slipping out of the fire door but that would be childish. A far door squeaked then closed just as the motion-sensor lights floodlit the corridor. A few seconds later, Gary appeared in the open doorway. 'I bet your boys wipe the floor with you at hide and seek,' he said.

'I'm not in the mood, Gary,' she mumbled.

He raised his hands in surrender. 'I heard what happened,' he said, as he took a seat on the other side of the desk.

'I mean, what the fuck?'

Gary shrugged, then said, 'People are wondering if you told Darren about the UC.'

'How fucking dare you. Who the fuck do you think you are?'

Gary stood his ground. 'Hey, hey. I'm not saying I think that, but you need to know the gossip. I thought it was better you hear it from me than from snide comments in the corridors.'

Three deep breaths later, Jo said, 'Of course I didn't. Why would I? We don't talk about stuff like that. He knows about the operation but I never go into details.'

'Before you throw that laptop at me, I'm being devil's advocate here. If you didn't tell him, how did he know?'

'Don't you think I've been asking the same question ever since I heard his weaselly voice pipe up?'

'Have you asked him?'

They exchanged a look then stayed quiet as the door to the corridor opened and closed again. Footsteps came closer, then the faint hiss of inaudible radio chatter took over.

A firearms officer walked past the door, then back and poked her head in. 'Evening, ma'am, sir. Everything OK?'

'Fine thanks, Nahida,' said Gary.

She nodded and walked on. Waiting for the far door to open and close, they stayed silent. Once Jo was happy there were no potential eavesdroppers, she replied, 'Of course I haven't. I can't imagine a time when I'll ever have a civil conversation with him again.'

Gary leant forward. 'I know you're angry – Christ, I would be, but take a moment. I don't know Darren as well as you . . .'

'I'd hope not.'

'But he's not the sort of person to drop a bomb on you like that for no good reason.'

'Any decent husband wouldn't do it at all.'

Her phone buzzed on the desk. She picked it up and showed Gary the display: *Darren Mobile*.

'Answer it.'

'Why are you whispering? He can't hear you until I press "accept",' she said, cracking a smile for the first time since she'd stormed away from the press conference.

'That's better,' said Gary as the call rang out. 'You've got to speak to him. I'll leave you to it. Oh, and whatever you do, don't look at any news apps.' He stood and walked to the door. 'Good luck and let me know how it goes.'

The beauty was completely lost on Darren as he stared across the Downs from Ditchling Beacon. How would he explain this to Jo? Would she even pick up his calls? With his career on a thread and his marriage sunk, were it not for the boys he'd seriously contemplate taking the ultimate alternative. He weighed up which would be the quickest and least painful way to end it all. Just thinking about that made him realise he still had a grain of fight left in him.

His ringing phone snapped him back to the present. *Jo.*

'I'm so sorry,' he said, as he picked up.

'Where are you?'

'In the car, trying to work things out.'

'Where are the boys?' It felt like she was grilling him as a suspect.

'At your mum's. Look, I can explain. I had no choice.'

Silence, then, 'There are always choices, Darren, and you took the wrong one. Have you seen the news? Bollock all about the shooting, just the fact that the reporter who asked about an undercover officer happens to be my fucking husband. And the picture of me storming off; that's the cherry on the icing on the fucking cake.'

'You shouldn't read those things.'

'Says the journalist. What the hell were you playing at?'

'Can we do this face to face?'

'No, let's do it now.'

His mind whirred for the right words. 'Look, I'm being blackmailed, of sorts.'

'That's like being a bit pregnant. You either are or you aren't.'

Darren tried to gather the right words. 'I'm not sure but I may have been involved in something years ago and, if it comes out, I could end up in prison.'

'Prison? What the hell have you done?'

'That's why I need to explain in person. I'm not sure what they have on me.'

'Who?'

'The newspaper for starters, but maybe others.'

Darren listened expectantly for some hint of understanding. The silence was killing him.

Finally, 'I can't deal with this shit now. We'll talk later but it better be fucking good if you have any desire for our marriage coming out of this intact.' The silence as she ended the call crushed Darren and he choked on his sobs.

15

From the moment last night's Teams call ended, Bob had been churning over what he should have done differently. How he could have prevented a woman he'd never met from becoming a widow and an unborn child fatherless.

He'd been in charge of the operation. Ged, or Pete to give him his real name, had just been applying his exceptional skills to Bob's bidding. He was responsible for keeping him and the operation safe and now, with what happened and the leak that he was a UC plastered over every news site, he'd failed at every turn.

Two days on from his own brush with death, his pain screamed louder than ever. The morphine pump did its best, but he was in for a long and frustrating recovery. At least he was alive though, which meant he had a chance to make amends.

A gentle tap on the door and then, before he could object, his favourite nurse, a small woman with a permanent smile but tired eyes, came in.

'Good morning, Mr Heaton. How are we today?'

'As well as anyone who's acrobatted across a Peugeot four-door could be.'

'See, it's always best to look on the bright side,' she replied with a wink. 'It's time for your obs I'm afraid.'

While she crushed his arm with the blood pressure sleeve, poked the thermometer in his ear and shone a torch in his eyes, he wondered what the chances of the readings having changed in the last two hours were.

'How long until I can go home?' he asked.

The nurse chuckled. 'The doctor should be round soon but you've had a nasty trauma. Don't be in such a hurry to leave us,' she said as she made to leave the side-room. 'Your husband has made that a special request too.'

Bob feigned a laugh then turned back to his phone, horrified at the shitshow that was playing out on social media. What the hell was Darren Howe playing at? It took him just a couple of minutes more before a plan started to form. He flicked to the phone app and tapped a recent caller.

'Boss. You OK?' came the reply with more than a little surprise.

'Not bad, thanks. Listen, Scotty, I know it's a Sunday but are you working?'

'Hold on.' Bob could hear footsteps, then a door closing. 'Sorry. No, I'm training this morning. Why, what's up?'

'Shit. OK, not to worry.'

'No go on, what is it?'

'I wanted you to come and pick me up from the hospital but I'll get someone else.'

'Blimey, have they discharged you already? They can't wait to free up beds in that bloody place. Did I ever tell you about my nan? Eighty-five years old and . . .'

'No, they haven't,' Bob interrupted. 'I'm checking myself out. I need to do stuff that can't be done from in here.'

'But boss . . .'

'Mate, if you can't, you can't, but spare me the lecture.'

For a second Bob thought Scotty had put the phone down. He was about to do likewise when the sergeant said, 'Give me half an hour. Text me the ward name and . . . boss?'

'Yes?'

'Have all the rows before I get there. I'm not happy with this and if I get roped in I might just side with the doctors.'

'You're a diamond. I love you Scotty.'

'No you don't, you owe me.'

True to his word, Bob had driven the hospital staff to the point of surrender by the time Scotty arrived. As he helped the DI out, he shrugged an apology to a nurse who, despite her smile, looked genuinely concerned.

As they turned out of Brighton and started up the A23, Bob piped up. 'Where are we going? I don't live this way.'

'I know you don't,' said Scotty. 'We're going to meet some people. Springing you from hospital is way above my pay grade.'

'That's over-egging it a bit. I did all the springing and I could have got a cab.'

'Why would you get a cab when you've got me for free.'

'Fair point. Who are we meeting?'

'You'll see.'

Scotty pushed on past the Hassocks turn-off then took the slip road marked *Henfield.* He loved how close to the urban hustle of Brighton these seas of golden cornfields were. He didn't look at Bob as he waited for a tractor and trailer to clear the mini roundabout, then turned right, leaving his indicator on and slowed to turn into a car park.

'Rushfields?' said Bob. 'You've brought me to a bloody garden centre?'

'I think you'll find it's a "Plant Centre, Farm Shop and Café",' said Scotty as he spotted a parking space to the right.

'Well I hope we're here for the latter, as I'm not in the mood for bedding-plant shopping.'

'Bit late in the year for that boss.'

'Whatever.'

Scotty straightened the car and turned the engine off. When he was out, he walked to Bob's side and opened the door. As he went to take his arm, Bob shook him off. 'Don't you bloody dare. We might be in God's waiting room but you're not treating me like your granddad.'

'Suit yourself,' said Scotty as he walked through the gates to check whether their guests had arrived. He was in luck. They'd nabbed an outside table far enough away from most not to be overheard.

'Ma'am. Sir,' Scotty said.

'Don't make him struggle,' said Jo, deadpan. She stood and made towards Bob, shambling a dozen yards away.

'Good luck with that,' mumbled Scotty, then said to Gary Hedges, 'Bit my head off for helping him a moment ago. Thanks to you both for coming. I needed someone to talk sense into him.'

'You might have picked the wrong pair in that case. Actually, it was handy you called, as Jo's in a right state and needs a focus. And I've never been known to turn down a full English.'

'Is she paying?' said Scotty.

'Either her or Bob. I forgot my wallet, as did you I gather.' He winked.

'Bugger,' said Scotty with a grin as he tapped his pockets.

Bob and Jo approached. 'I can't believe he made you hobble,' said Jo, glaring at Scotty.

'Me neither,' replied Bob.

Bob lowered himself onto the bench opposite Scotty and Jo reclaimed her place across from Gary.

'First things first, what the hell are you doing out of hospital?' she asked.

They all listened as Bob explained his reasons, then talked about aspects of the covert operation that to Scotty were breaking news. Despite the tragedies that had brought them all here, he felt a warm glow. Now, he might finally be able to avenge Lizzie's death, lawfully or otherwise.

Once the breakfasts had been ordered and served, Jo's phone rang.

Darren. Despite her conflicting feelings, she let it ring out.

All of a sudden she'd lost her appetite. Shuffling the sausage and bacon around the plate, she was relieved when Gary piped up.

'You not eating that?'

She shook her head and pushed the plate to the middle, whereupon the three men descended on it liked starved piranhas.

'Listen,' she said. 'I need some ideas. We've come too far to ditch Eradicate and I'm sensing the eye-catching benefits are just around the corner.' The others' conspiratorial looks seemed to question her. Bob spoke first.

'Don't you think we ought to listen to the ACC and just ease off for a little while? After all, we're all going to be busy enough tracking down Pete and Lizzie's killers so maybe we should take some time to regroup.'

'He's right,' said Gary. 'Let's focus on that and meanwhile work out what's gone wrong.'

'Who says anything has gone wrong?'

Gary put his hand on her arm which she instantly snatched away. 'I'm not saying you've done anything wrong but two murders . . .'

'Three.'

'Three murders and an attempted murder,' Gary continued – they all looked at Bob – 'isn't exactly the hallmark of success. Something has changed and we need to find out what and how we stop it.'

'If it's any consolation, we hadn't tracked down anyone higher than Nathan Challenor, so maybe whoever shot him has done us a favour,' said Bob.

Jo came straight back. 'In what world is a murdered police officer a favour?' Her phone rang again and this time she rejected it straight away.

'He didn't mean that,' said Gary, giving Jo a look which said *Everything OK?* She broke his stare.

'Can I come in?' said Scotty, whom Jo had realised was not used to these heated exchanges between her and her closest colleagues.

'Of course,' she replied.

'Thanks. I might know what's changed.'

They all looked at him with fixed curiosity.

'Saira and I met this guy the other day. Goes by the name of Spanners.'

'Spanners?' said Gary.

'Something to do with him being a mechanic.'

'Imaginative.'

'Anyway, he says that inmates being discharged from most of the prisons from Birmingham southwards are being offered £500 to come to Brighton and lie low until they are given a task.'

'By who?'

'Other inmates he says, but he reckons the screws know it's going on.'

'What sort of task are they given?'

'Attacks, dealing. That sort of thing I gather.'

The three others were stunned into silence.

'And I take it you've fed this nugget into the intelligence system,' said Jo.

'Er, not yet. I was going to but . . .'

Bob slammed the table with his good hand. 'How many times, Scotty? There is no point in giving you free rein amongst the druggies and homeless if you keep everything to yourself. You have to submit the intel.'

Gary's glare beat Jo to it in reminding Bob where they were.

'I'm sure Scotty will do that the second we've finished here. In the meantime, tell us what your guy is saying,' said Jo.

Scotty took them through everything Spanners had told him, including how he felt he was different from the others who drifted through the city.

'Let's be clear. He took the money too, yes?' said Jo.

'So he says.'

'In that case, how do we know he hasn't been used already?'

'You need to be bloody careful,' said Bob. Jo raised her hand to him, then killed another call.

'In truth, we don't. But why would he tell me about it if he might already be wanted? No, to my mind, he's looking for a way out and hoping we can break up whatever's happening before he's forced into something which lands him back in prison.'

'Do you think you can keep him onside?' asked Jo.

'I reckon so. He seems a smart guy and he's been through some shit. I think I can package it as a lifeline for him. Depending on what you want him to do, of course.'

'Er, can I just butt in?' said Bob. 'If we are talking about running an informant, we have a dedicated unit for that. And Scotty isn't on it.'

Jo turned to Gary. 'I don't think we're talking about that, are we Gary?'

'I'm sure we're not,' he replied.

'No. There you go Bob. Just a public-spirited citizen willing to help us protect lives and cut crime. Not an informant, never.'

Bob shook his head in surrender.

'Good, we're agreed.' She turned to Scotty. 'If you can keep in touch with this new friend of yours and if he happens to tell you what's going on from day to day, who's running the show, what he knows about the attacks and, most importantly, who if anyone is taking over from Challenor, that would be fabulous.'

'And write it all down,' grumbled Bob.

'Yes please,' said Jo. 'Anyway, as I recall it, ACC Mills asked me, rather than told me, whether we should pause the operation. There was definitely a question in there so, whilst I didn't say no, I wouldn't want him to think we are flying in the face of that suggestion. Therefore, everything we do needs to be under the radar and reported to me.'

Gary pointedly looked at the *Missed Call: Darren* messages totting up on Jo's phone, then said, 'With respect, don't you think you've enough on your plate just now?'

'We are doing this,' she said, a little too loudly for a public place.

Gary spoke in barely above a whisper. 'I know *we* are, but *you* can trust others to run things for once. We are all behind you, but you do have some pressing domestic problems to deal with.' She didn't like the way he emphasised the syllable 'press'. 'Secondly, Mills suggested *you* ease off, not us. And thirdly, operations are my domain, despite you insisting on being Gold Commander for this one.'

'What are you saying?'

'Let us get on with it.'

'But . . .'

'No buts.' Gary raised his hand before she could argue. 'Trust us, Jo. You might just like what happens when you do.'

16

The noisier and more aggressive the newcomers became, the more certain Spanners was that it was time to move on. The sweetener for coming to Brighton had seemed a gift from heaven when the alternative was a revolving door back to C Wing, but with a £100 per day habit you didn't need to be a mathematician to work out how long that windfall lasted.

Moving on was great in theory but, in practice, it could be a death sentence. He had been told to sit tight until he was called, so what choice did he have?

But this squat was a shithole. The landlords had kicked the community bookshop out when, surprise surprise, they couldn't meet the 100% rent increase. However, they failed to appreciate how quickly the city's burgeoning homeless would swarm and, with current squatting laws and zero interest from the police, there was nothing they could do about the takeover.

So, Beach Books had become the Dubai Airport of Brighton's underclass; most rough sleepers transited through there at some stage. Spanners was here for the second time in a month and he'd already noticed the difference in clientele. It wasn't that he was scared – he'd moved through enough prisons in recent months to know what arseholes some people could be – it's just there seemed to be an entitlement in the lot that had arrived over the last few days, almost as if they were starting a coup.

Most of the time he sat in a corner near a long-obstructed fire exit and just watched. Rarely emerging from his prized possession – a blue and grey survival sleeping bag – he feigned sleep or stupor and took it all in.

The windows were all boarded up, but they'd made such a poor job of it that slivers of daylight still leaked through. Enough for him to be hypnotised by dancing wafts of crack-pipe smoke and the euphoria of those who seemed to be permanently puffing away.

Spanners swigged from his Tennent's Extra beer can and wondered whether attracting the attention of that bull of a policeman and his gentler sidekick would be the end of him or his salvation. He'd never been a grass, not even before his night terrors and flashbacks turned him to drugs and crime, but he'd been foolish to get himself locked in the talons of those forking out the £500. He'd heard what had happened to those who'd even whispered that they might run.

Suddenly among the snoring and the rumble of chatter came a yell.

'Fooking wake up mate. Stop pissing about,' a voice he didn't recognise shouted, with more panic than he'd heard from someone not demanding a fix. 'Somebody help me over here. He's not fooking breathing.'

Spanners' army training kicked in and he sprung up, barged his way through the mêlée of brain-dead spectators and dropped to his knees beside the flaccid body.

The strings of vomit ran as much from his nose as his mouth. His Wedgwood-blue eyes were so glazed they'd put a master potter to shame and his Adidas sweatshirt, which might have once been grey, was caked in so many substances Spanners couldn't work out what was fresh and what was there to stay.

'How long's he been like this?' he demanded. No one answered. He became conscious of feet shuffling away. He grabbed the weasel who'd raised the alarm by the leg as he tried to follow suit. 'Stay here and help me,' he said and gave him a look which countenanced no debate. 'Help me get him on his back.'

'I ain't doing no mouth to mouth.'

'No one's fucking asking you to. I just need to see if there's any hope left.'

Spanners grappled for a pulse on both wrists and the man's neck, bent his head by his mouth to hopefully capture a whisper of breath and then, in the absence of proper light or anything else that might help with more humane checks, he took out his pocket knife and dug the blade into the man's cuticles.

Nothing.

Spanners went through the checks again. Still nothing. Christ, he looked familiar. He turned and looked at the weasel, whose face had also taken on the colour of death.

'He's gone mate. Who was he?'

'Fooked if I know. I don't know any fooker here.'

Spanners took a closer look but couldn't place where he'd seen him before.

'How did he get like this?'

'I don't know, one minute he scored off me, the next minute he's like fooking gasping for breath.'

'Where did you get it?' said Spanners.

The weasel eyed him up with steel. 'What's with all the fooking questions, man?'

Spanners leapt to his feet and grabbed the man up by his throat, shoving him back to the wall, nearly stumbling over a prostrate couple who'd been too out of it to notice the panic ensuing beside their heads.

'Because you've fucking killed him.'

'You fooking Old Bill or summat?'

'You'll fucking wish I was if you don't tell me.'

Just then Spanners' legs gave way and his neck jarred like a 240 volt current had been fired through it. He collapsed on a teenage girl in the process of sticking a needle into her crotch. 'Get off me you fucking perv,' she shouted. 'Look what you've done to my gear.'

Thankfully he didn't pass out but, as soon as he'd reorientated himself, he was hauled to his feet and dragged backwards through a door to what must have been an old stockroom. He was thrown back to the floor and when he could focus, two steroidal men in surprisingly clean black sweatshirts and cargo trousers were glaring at him, one ratcheting out a polycarbonate baton.

'Get that fucker out of here,' one shouted back towards where the body lay.

'Meanwhile, we need to have a little chat about who the fuck you are,' said the other.

The two stepped forward, and Spanners curled up like a foetus in the vain hope of protecting his vital organs from the onslaught that followed.

Sir Ben had lost count of how many of his peers had badgered him to get a full-time driver. It wasn't that he couldn't afford it, it was just that his working-class roots made him regard such luxuries as bourgeois peacocking. In any case, despite the fact he could work in the car if someone else were behind the wheel, he enjoyed the headspace driving himself gave him. And some of his calls were not for a chauffeur's ears.

However, he drew the line at battling the capital's traffic so opted for the lesser evil of the Brighton to London train, despite punctuality being an optional extra. As it pulled into Victoria Station, just thirteen minutes late, he gathered up his coat and shoulder bag. He squeezed past the student who'd spent the journey bunking in first class from Three Bridges, invading his personal space and tapping the table vaguely in time with the tinny beat leaking from his AirPods.

If only there had been a ticket inspection.

Once through the barriers, Sir Ben opted to walk the short distance to the Busby Club in Pall Mall. Trains were one thing, but the Tube? Never.

Striding down Buckingham Palace Road, he wondered how peaceful these streets must have been in the 1800s when the Palace became the monarch's official residence. No swarms of buses, impatient white van drivers or darting Deliveroo riders, just genteel horses pulling gentry-filled carts. But, then again, the manure must have brought its own challenges.

In less than fifteen minutes he was climbing the steps to the Busby and didn't have to break stride as the door was invisibly pulled open.

'Afternoon, Angus.'

'Afternoon, Sir Ben, I trust you're well.' The doorman's clipped Highland brogue was both respectful and authoritative. There were rumours that he'd led an SAS advance party onto the Falkland Islands following the 1982 Argentinian invasion. Sir Ben had never asked him, and if it was true, he knew Angus would never tell. 'Mr Baker is already here. Your usual booth.'

'Thank you.' Sir Ben slipped him a £10 note, for which he received the shallowest nod of thanks. He swept through the hallway, watched by the distinguished past members' portraits adorning the imposing walls. The maître d' mumbled 'good day' as Sir Ben walked through the door at the end, turning sharply left, smiling at the Brighton MP and policing minister fidgeting at the secluded table.

'So sorry to keep you waiting, Edward,' said Sir Ben with no trace of contrition.

'Not at all, although I do have to be back in the House for a vote at 2.30 p.m.'

Sir Ben glanced at his watch. 'Plenty of time.' If he'd had his way, he would have much preferred to meet the Home Secretary herself; she would certainly have made time for him, had done ever since he'd dropped her backstory into a conversation. Unsurprisingly, she'd been desperate to keep that out of the headlines. But meeting the grown-ups was tricky in terms of both what he needed to discuss and distancing himself when they fell off their perch, which they always did.

Baker, with his constituency role, ministerial appointment and the fact he was the mentor of Sussex's Police and Crime Commissioner, was an acceptable substitute.

Both men picked up the menu, Edward Baker reading it closer than his host.

'I'm having the lobster bisque and the beef. What about you?' said Sir Ben.

'Oh, I'll have the same and a sparkling water.'

'Nonsense. We'll share a bottle of claret.' He glanced at a white-tied waiter, who scurried over. Rattling off their order, once the flunky had stepped away, he cut to the chase.

'Now, Edward, we have a few problems in the city as you well know, and we'd really appreciate some support from the centre.'

'Yes, the chief constable briefed me on the shooting. Is it true it was an undercover officer? The Home Secretary has been asking but even she seems to have been stonewalled.'

'I have no idea I'm afraid. Anyway, as I was saying, you'll be well aware of the irritating voices in Brighton naively spouting that reducing the demand for certain substances might improve the fabric of the city. Unfortunately these ideas seem to be developing some traction and, were it to happen, I don't need to tell you how many very influential people might feel the pinch.'

'I see.' Baker might have been slightly moist behind the ears but Sir Ben could tell from his reaction that his point had hit home.

'Now, we are doing what we can on the ground but some additional persuasion at, shall we say, a more strategic level would be appreciated.'

'What did you have in mind?'

Sir Ben waited while the wine was poured and tasted, and the glasses filled.

'I know you have to balance your local and national roles – but how right is it, for example, for the police to have such ready access to goods and services others might struggle to procure?'

'Such as?'

'Nothing that will completely cripple them, but I was thinking fuel, utilities, the web. Maybe private contracts for, say, custody, forensics, maintenance, estates. Perhaps if they felt a squeeze on their infrastructure they might be more inclined to focus in on their core responsibilities rather than these vanity projects which, in the long run, would create significant difficulties and embarrassment all round.'

Baker hadn't touched his wine. 'I'm not sure how we'd even go about that. It's really not that simple.'

Sir Ben took a sip of claret and leant in. 'Of course it's not, but wouldn't a father do anything to protect his children?'

Baker's expression had taken on an air of shock and puzzlement. 'What do you mean?'

'How's young James getting on at Cambridge? First year, isn't he?'

'Er, yes?'

'Well he's certainly fitted into the Tory-boy stereotype quicker than most.'

'Listen. We are both busy men so, unless you've got something to say, let's finish our lunch and go about our days.'

Sir Ben reached into his inside pocket, opened his phone and navigated to his photos. 'Some nice snaps for the family album.' He handed the phone to Baker and watched his expression change as he swiped through the images. Each showed young James Baker dressed in a Nazi uniform, clearly wasted on drink or drugs. A couple more photos confirmed it was the latter, as in them he was crouched over a black girl held down by four unseen people, snorting a powder through a £50 note off her naked breasts. Just enough of her face was in shot to suggest she was far from a willing participant. The final crystal-clear picture of him with three others giving a 'Heil Hitler' salute removed any doubt as to his identity.

'You must be so proud,' said Sir Ben.

'Where did you get these?'

Ben tapped the side of his nose.

Baker's eyes flared and he scoured the vicinity in case any other diners had glimpsed the screen. 'I don't know what to say. I'll speak to him, I promise, but please don't do anything.'

'No. You will not speak to him. He seems to be having fun, so why spoil it? In any case I might need some more like these and if my source is compromised or he moderates his behaviour, where would that leave me?' He leant in. 'If I get a whisper you've told him, these will be on every news site, in every paper. Am I making myself clear?'

The minister blanched. 'Of course, of course. I'll see what I can do, but you appreciate I'll have to speak to other departments. What you're asking is not all in the Home Office's gift.'

'I'm sure you're right and if you're concerned about ministerial approval, don't be. All your lot and the majority of those elsewhere, especially the Department of Health, have already been persuaded in a similar way to be helpful, if I ever need them to be. Like now.' He held the silence and his glare for a good five seconds. It was Baker who broke it.

'Yes, of course. But please keep James out of it.'

'That's up to you, Mr Baker.'

The minister stood up, nearly toppling a glass in the process. 'I understand. I've just remembered an urgent meeting back at Marsham Street. I'm sorry, I'm going to have to leave.' He grabbed his briefcase and dashed for the door.

17

Microsoft Teams took an age to load as usual and Darren Howe wondered, not for the first time, whether he could use that as an excuse to cancel his meeting with Sam. The last time he'd pulled that stunt though, the bastard had made him rent a room at a business centre and log on from there. At his own expense.

Eventually his image appeared on the screen, so he checked his background was blurred, took a breath and clicked 'Join Meeting'.

'DAZZA!' Sam shouted as soon as they'd connected. 'What a blinder you played on Saturday. I'll be honest with you, I thought you'd bottle it. Then we'd be having a very different conversation.'

'Yeah, thanks.'

'Cheer up mate. You're the man of the moment. No other bugger had that snippet and no one would have had the gumption to ask the police – or should I say your missus – there and then. We've made bloody thousands on your copy and the reaction you got from your old lady. That pic is going to pay for my next cruise.'

'I couldn't be happier for you, but you do know it's effectively wrecked my marriage.'

'Bloody hell, mate, if you'd been through wives like I have you'd know that's just collateral damage. Anyway, she'll get over it.'

Darren edged the cursor over the 'Leave Meeting' button but thought better of it. He needed to see this through if he was to keep his liberty. Or was he catastrophising, just like he always pulled Jo up for?

'I can't see that. I'm staying at my brother's for the time being, it's that bad.'

Sam guffawed. 'Been there, got the divorce writs, mate. Listen, we need to keep up the heat. How are you getting on with that article? You must have shedloads by now what with the three murders and that copper getting bowled over.'

'Bob's a friend of mine,' said Darren.

'You need to separate work from leisure, mate. I make it my business never to have actual friends, just useful people to butter up. Listen, crack on with the piece and don't forget the deadline.'

Darren's phone buzzed on the desk beside him. *Jo*. He prayed this meeting was coming to an end. The last thing he wanted was for the call to ring out and Jo to think he was ghosting her.

'Look, gotta go. Got the chairman on the other line. Ciao ciao.'

Before the screen blanked, Darren hit 'accept'. 'Hiya. Everything OK?'

'Not really. We need to meet.'

The last time Jo had been at Devil's Dyke was after Phil's funeral. So much had happened in those short weeks and, at the time, she'd thought her world was coming to an end. Little did she know what was round the corner.

Sitting outside the pub, on a picnic bench, she mulled over how many times her life had been ripped apart. The first time was when her twelve-year-old sister, Caroline, was abused and that monster walked free.. She'd gone off the rails then, and now Jo beat herself up over what more she could have done to support her, to stop her spiralling into addiction, homelessness, the ravages of PTSD – ending in a lonely, squalid death.

What were big sisters – who happened to be senior police officers – for if not protecting their nearest and dearest?

The one thing she had left that was sacred was the very thing she was certain she was about to lose – and that would kill her.

Eventually, Darren's car appeared round the bend and he parked next to hers. As he got out he fiddled with his phone, looking up at the parking instructions as he did so.

'You have to pay,' said Jo as he approached.

'That's what I'm doing. Listen, before we start, can I just say I'm so, so sorry about the other night. I really had no choice.'

Jo looked up at him. Those eyes. 'Get me an orange juice, then we'll talk.'

He sloped off to the bar, returning a few minutes later with their drinks.

'Start by telling me why you thought our marriage was worthless enough to burn.'

'We're not going to talk about this as adults then? I might as well go.' He went to stand.

'No, please wait. I'm sorry but I'm so angry. Do you realise how much trouble you've caused? It's not just the shock of having your husband throw in a hand grenade like that. It's the whispers, the gossip. I was specifically told not to reveal what you asked, then ten minutes later, out you come with it.'

'You know I love you. I'd never have done that by choice.' He reached his hand across the table but she drew hers away. 'I swear I was forced. I wish I'd never picked the phone up but Sam's got something on me, I'm certain of it.'

'So you said.'

'Look, you've heard of Operation Elvedon, right?'

'Of course. The Met even arrested one of my sergeants for leaking stories to the press. Ended up doing six months. But you weren't involved in that were you?'

'Not knowingly, but Sam certainly was. We all suspected he was one of those who got away. Whether he bought his way out of it or was just too clever for them to catch, he built his reputation on how quickly he could get the inside track on anything they wanted. Police cock-ups, political scandals, exclusive stings on celebrities, the whole nine yards. I was working closely with him and all the others. I don't know what I might have dirtied my hands on. He's now using that to get at me.'

'But surely he'll reveal his own involvement if he digs anything up on you.'

'He'll have thought of that.'

Jo took a sip of her drink and watched a hang-glider take off from the hill opposite.

'What sort of things did you do?'

'Let's get some lunch, then I'll tell you. I can't do this on an empty stomach.'

Jo's 4G was patchy so she browsed the lunch options on a paper menu instead of the app. She wasn't that hungry but if she wanted to get to the bottom of why Darren would so readily betray her in front of the world's media, she'd have to humour him by picking at a sandwich.

She plumped for the jackfruit wrap while Darren chose the brisket ciabatta. She went into the pub to place the order. One of the staff, slightly older than her but immaculately presented in her white blouse and black pencil skirt, seemed to be staring. With her media profile over the last couple of years, Jo had this from time to time – but she couldn't help feeling this recognition was due to Saturday's debacle, or the ubiquitous photos that followed on just about every news app.

Jo slipped her credit card from her purse but the woman told her she could pay later, 'in case you want a dessert or coffee'. *No chance of that*, thought Jo, but she nodded anyway.

When she rejoined Darren, she was pleased to see the adjacent table was still vacant.

Thankfully the food didn't take long. The server, possibly a student given his pimply face and patchy stubble, took a long look at both Jo and

Darren and she was certain she detected a smirk as he placed their plates down. Once he was safely back indoors, Jo said, 'Go on then.'

Darren took a huge bite of his sandwich, then wiped stray juices from his chin with a napkin. 'Do you remember when that newsreader Edward Stark was arrested for abusing his daughter and granddaughter?'

'How could I forget?' said Jo. It had been a national scandal with echoes of Jimmy Savile. Stark had been an icon, the fearless voice in the face of filibustering politicians and businessmen. Rolled out for any emerging crisis, he took the people's side and had a knack of asking the unanswerable questions in laypersons' language which left the interviewee with nowhere to go. When it emerged that he had fathered his own grandchild during decades of horrendous sexual abuse of his daughter, and his wife knew all about it but had been beaten into silence, the tables were turned. For Jo, it brought back bitter memories of her sister's abuse.

'Well, and I promise this is true, the first I knew was the rolling live news of the police crashing his door down and him being dragged out in his pyjamas.'

It was hardly that dramatic, thought Jo. As she remembered it, they tapped on the door and were let in. He came out twenty minutes later, unhandcuffed, with a detective on either side. But, being a journalist, it was in Darren's DNA to sensationalise the truth.

She nodded.

'Well, if you remember, there was an uproar from his wider family and those who thought he was innocent about why there were TV cameras there to capture his downfall. For a few weeks, until he was charged, there were headlines about a phase two of Op Elvedon and how the rot of police and press corruption was alive and kicking.'

'I remember, but what's that got to do with you? You've never worked in TV.'

'I know and, if you remember, the executive producers of Days News were hauled up in front of the Parliamentary Digital, Culture, Media and Sport Committee to answer where they got their information from.'

'Along with the Met Police Commissioner, as I recall. Weren't some of the investigators suspended for a while?'

'That's right, and two producers and the head of news were quietly let go.'

Jo bit into her wrap. She could easily become a vegan, she thought. 'I'm still not with you.'

Darren took a breath. 'Well, the night before, I was working in the newsroom. Sam was the duty subeditor but, as usual, he'd disappeared. Probably to the pub or to see some woman. Anyway, whenever he vanished he'd always leave strict instructions that if anyone called for him we were to take a message on paper, put it in an envelope and leave it on his desk.'

'Why didn't people call him on his mobile?'

'He was paranoid. Ever since the phone-hacking scandal he thought everyone, the police, MI5, News International were bugging his every word.'

'He was never that important.'

'Exactly. Anyway, I was just finishing this piece on . . . I can't even remember what it was, but I was up against a deadline. His desk phone rang and as I was nearest, I picked it up. Well, after the usual preambles of asking for Sam there, the caller got a bit tetchy.'

'Was that unusual?'

Darren sipped his beer. 'Not really. We all have our sources who give us tittle-tattle, and some think their world will implode if they're caught talking to the press.'

'They might be right.'

Darren ignored the jibe and continued. 'This bloke asked me how quickly Sam would get any message. I told him he'd have to be back for when the paper went to bed so he told me to write down exactly what he said. I grabbed a pen and he dictated something about it being on for five-thirty tomorrow morning at the Queen Anne's Road address. I had to add that it was exclusive so he could only tell the ones they agreed. I wrote it down word for word. He made me read it back then he put the phone down. I popped it in an envelope as usual and left it for Sam.'

'Queen Anne's Road? Ed Stark's address?'

'So it turned out, but I didn't know that at the time.'

'Did these sorts of calls come in often?' Jo was wondering what kind of Pandora's box Darren was opening on himself. Part of her wanted to tell him to say no more but she needed honesty, if only to save their marriage.

'Not like that. Most were bollocks but this one stood out as something different. Anyway, half an hour later Sam wanders in, all flushed and sniffing, and asks if there had been any calls. I just said, "Yep, there's a message on your desk." He went over and to be honest, I was so wrapped up in what I was writing I didn't even see him open it – but the next thing he's bolting out of the door saying something like "Won't be long". He came back about ten minutes later and he was like a kiddie on their first trip to Disney but wouldn't say why.'

'Didn't you suspect something was up?'

'Not really, although being made to read the message back was a first. Some in the office called him Sam Turing as he was always creating enigmas about himself, so I didn't give it another thought. I just assumed it was Sam being Sam.'

Jo was aware she was on the verge of treating this like a police interview rather than a marital share-all. 'And then?'

'As I say, the penny dropped when I switched on the TV the following morning and saw Stark being arrested. It was when they mentioned the road name that I put two and two together.'

'How do you know the coverage was down to Sam? Whoever it was, and let's assume it was a cop, could have told anyone.'

'I don't know if you remember but it was in early December.'

'Not especially.'

'Well you will remember that hamper that we found on the doorstep when we came back from IKEA.'

Jo nodded. A 'Royal Standard' luxury hamper, full of stuff she'd never even heard of, let alone tried. Who really eats ragu of wild boar and black winter truffles? And who would spend £840 on such stuff? No one she knew.

'Anyway,' Darren continued. 'Even though we ended up chucking most of it, the wines and champagne were something else. I was desperate to find out who'd sent it but the shop wouldn't tell me. I just put it down to some grateful benefactor. Frankly, I didn't care.'

'You told me it was from the newspaper owner,' she said.

'That was a lie.'

Jo bit her tongue.

'I never mentioned it at work but when we were at the pub on Christmas Eve, Sam sidled up to me, wiggled his glass of wine and said, "It's OK but not quite the Châteauneuf-du-Pape La Chasse you'll be quaffing is it?" That was one of the bottles in the hamper.'

'Oh, come on,' said Jo. 'That's hardly conclusive.'

'Maybe not but I know him. He'd want me to know it was a thank you from him.'

'Did he buy the hamper?'

'Not personally. He's too tight-fisted, but I'm certain that's what Sam's got over me.'

'And if you don't write the article the way they want it, he'll go to the police about that?'

'I'm certain of it.'

Jo pushed the wrap away, wondering whether she could have a Pinot Grigio instead of her orange juice. 'The police aren't stupid – they'll find the link with Sam, even if you don't mention it.'

'They're in his pocket. Even if he hasn't covered his tracks, which he will have, they won't go anywhere near him. It's more than the Met's worth. He'll rain decades of shit and scandal on them and none of the top team will escape.'

Jo's mind raced. This was either her career or his liberty if he was right. He certainly thought that's what would happen but, really?

'How about you give him an article. Not the article he wants but one that sets out the truth. One that shows that what we are doing here is saving sons, daughters, brothers and sisters. Real people. He won't like it but what can he do?'

'Deliver me to His Majesty's Prison Belmarsh? Anyway, won't that play to people who think you leak stuff to me?'

'You're overthinking. I'll just tell you where to find all the material you need and trust me, no one is getting nicked. You might just need a new job.'

They spent the next fifteen minutes throwing around ideas for an article both knew the *Daily Journal* would never publish but that would set out, in one place, how society and not just the addicts, benefitted from progressive drugs policing.

Then the conversation moved to holiday plans and promises to make more time for each other. Jo could only hope they'd stick to them for once.

'We better be off,' said Jo. 'I'll just nip in and pay. Are you going to wait or are you off?'

'I just need the loo.'

They both walked into the pub and Jo went to the bar while Darren headed for the gents.

'We were table twelve outside,' she said to the woman who'd taken her order, offering her credit card. The woman took it and Jo nonchalantly gazed out of the window to the rolling hills beyond. With all the pledges they'd just made to each other, Jo promised herself that she, Darren and the boys would come up here at least once a month and ramble their way across the stunning countryside they were always too busy to enjoy.

'I'm sorry, it's been declined,' the woman said in barely above a whisper.

Jo snapped round. 'Oh, are you sure?'

'I'll try it again.' Jo watched this time. 'No, I'm sorry. Have you got another card?'

Jo fumbled through her purse for her debit card and presented that, now feeling the spike of irritation.

'I'm sorry, it's not taking that either. Sometimes it's these machines.' Jo couldn't decide whether the sympathetic look was feigned or not. 'I could try another, unless you've got cash.'

Jo was about to argue when Darren emerged from the toilets. 'Problem?'

'Their machine is playing up. Have you got any cash on you?'

'She's always doing this,' said Darren, winking at the server. 'How much is it?'

'£27.45,' she replied, stony-faced.

Darren handed over three £10 notes and told the woman to keep the change, while Jo made straight for the door.

18

Scotty knew, the second Saira let slip that she thought it had been 'quiet' for a weekday, that the beasts of hell would be unleashed. Police officers never used that word. The closest they'd come was 'Q'. There was a time when anyone daring to use the full word would be banished to the bakery to buy their weight in doughnuts as punishment.

Those days were gone but it didn't stop him berating the young PC like a *Newsnight* interviewer.

Thankfully, so far she'd been right, and having enjoyed a rare coffee overlooking the opulent yachts in Brighton Marina, she was now driving them down Bear Road for a meeting with University of Sussex security about drug dealers on the campus.

'Charlie Oscar to any unit for Hollingdean Waste Transfer Centre,' came the distinctive tones of Linda Simons, who'd been a radio controller since before Scotty was a fresh-faced probationer.

'Shall we offer up?' asked Saira.

'She's not said what it is,' said Scotty. 'Could be a load of shite. Let's see if uniform respond.'

'Really, Sarge? We're literally down the road.'

Scotty sighed. 'Is it your mission to piss me off today?' He picked up his radio from the centre console. 'Charlie Sierra Nine One, PC Bannerjee and I are close by. What have you got?' He turned to Saira. 'I'm not getting my bloody pen out, this is all yours.'

'No change there then,' she said with a smirk.

'Charlie Sierra Nine One, thanks for that. We've had a call from the site manager. A landfill truck has just dumped its load and there appears to be a body amongst the rubbish. Can you attend?'

They looked at each other and Scotty shook his head.

'Roger that, ETA two minutes.'

Scotty shuffled in his seat as Saira upped the pace. She circled the Gyratory and headed up to the dump. Having parked up in a visitors' bay, they'd spent a good ten minutes trying to find someone in charge when they saw a man ambling away from a line of dustcarts.

'Can I help you?' the man, dressed in what could charitably be called smart casual, said.

Instinctively, Scotty and Saira reached for their warrant cards, unfolded them and waved them in the man's general direction. 'Police, you called us?' said Scotty.

'Oh, I was expecting the proper police. I'm Sean Baxter, the site manager.'

'Sorry to disappoint,' said Scotty, looking at his jeans. 'You've found a body?'

'Yeah, he's a bit mashed I'm afraid. One of the trucks dumped him. Bound to be another bin sleeper. Wanna have a look?'

'That's what we're here for,' said Scotty, following the man towards a stadium-sized warehouse.

Since Brighton and Hove City Council had replaced individual waste collections with huge communal wheelie bins, they had become the shelter of last resort for the homeless and late-night revellers alike. Thankfully, most woke to the sounds of the bin lorry machinery hooking on just as they were about to be lifted. Some weren't so lucky and they were tipped into the crusher, only emerging when the lorry was emptied. Half the problem for the police was identifying the mangled corpses.

It seemed that Baxter and his team were well used to the protocols when a body was found; all operations had paused, which didn't seem to bother the workers as they vaped away outside the guarded area.

'Just over here.'

The stench almost felled Scotty as he stepped into the gloomy cavernous dump. Saira seemed to be bearing up better but the cocktail of rotting food, excrement and a thousand other stomach-churning odours made keeping his breakfast where it belonged his sole priority. If he so much as hinted he was about to puke, word would be round the police station faster than a dose of dysentery.

As he approached, the vague shape of the body emerged from the surrounding waste like a magic eye picture. It was almost impossible to distinguish where the body's tattered rags stopped and the garbage started.

'Well, he's definitely dead,' said Saira.

'Thank you, Dr Bannerjee,' was all Scotty could risk saying in case solid matter chased the words from his mouth.

He sneaked a hand to his nose as he neared the mass. By some fortune it lay face up and the jaws of the truck, whilst making mincemeat of his lower limbs, had spared his head.

Despite his initial reaction, Saira had made a great call in choosing to respond to this, as they had the best chance of identifying the corpse if it was a rough sleeper.

The site manager watched on as Scotty girt himself to move in for a closer look. Saira hovered behind him.

The light wasn't great and, while the man's head was intact, the remnants of what looked like a kebab and dirty nappy made his task tricky. He shone his torch in vain.

'You got a stick, or a pole or something? I need to get a look at his face,' he called to Baxter.

'Sarge, should we take some photos first?' asked Saira.

'Yes, I was about to,' he lied.

He took out his work phone and snapped half a dozen pictures of the man's head as they had found him. When he'd finished, Baxter handed him a litter-picker. Scotty gingerly clipped the nappy and moved it to one side, then did the same with a lump of pitta bread. Nudging a few stray teabags and chips aside, Scotty held his nose and went in for a second look.

In an instant his nausea deserted him and something between rage and excitement took over. He flashed three more photos, then stood up.

'Right, I want everyone out of here,' Scotty barked to Baxter, despite the fact the site manager was the only one in the warehouse.

'What, has he been murdered?' came the reply as he did as he was told.

'I've no idea but, if it's who I think it is, he'll be glad he died before I met him,' muttered Scotty as he dialled Bob Heaton's mobile.

Despite having his arm locked into a cast for the foreseeable future, and the indescribable agony he endured with every step, Bob was in his office. The murder of DC Pete McElroy had plunged every officer and civilian, past and present, into deep mourning. As usual when any member of the police family died, colleagues from across the country replaced their Facebook profile picture with a blue horizontal line on a black background as a mark of respect.

Bob would never shake the feeling that he was responsible. But there was no time for self-pity and reflection. He and DS Luke Spencer had a trial to prepare for, and they needed to work out if that was still viable with their star witness dead.

Bob rested his injured arm on the desk, shooing away a pile of files that he dared not open. He brought up the latest CPS memos and updates from Luke on his computer, just as the sergeant walked into the room.

Unlike Bob's default look of having dressed drunk and in the dark, Luke was incapable of appearing anything but ready for an audience with the king. In his spare time he played semi-professional football in the

National League South and bore the look of a sportswear model.

He sat down without Bob having to invite him.

'Boss, you sure you should be here?'

Bob grinned. 'Did you know you are the first person to say that? Oh, no, hang on, you're the hundred and first. What else would I be doing? Trusting you to run the show?'

Luke shook his head and smiled. 'Fair enough,' he said as he tapped at the laptop on his knees. 'How are you feeling about Ged? I mean Pete.'

'Gutted, guilty, worried all his hard work was for nothing. That's just for starters.'

'Me too,' said Luke. 'I never met him but you still feel it, don't you?'

'A hundred per cent. Have you told CPS?'

'Yes, and they don't see it as so much of a problem to the trial as we do.'

'Really?' Bob shifted in his chair, then his back screamed for him to make no sudden movements.

'Yep. I'll ping you this. It's their latest advice, which confirms what they told me on the phone just now.'

Bob waited for his emails to refresh, opened the most recent one from Luke and scanned the attachment.

He nodded. 'Blimey, I wasn't expecting that. So, providing we can produce the original recordings and Nick, the cover officer, is available to give live evidence, we've got an arguable case to have Pete's evidence admitted.'

'That's the gist of it, guv. On the phone they were at pains to point out that it's not a foregone conclusion and we're no doubt going to get battered by the defence, but at least they're not throwing the towel in.'

'Did they say whether the jury would be told Pete had been murdered?'

'Yeah, I asked that. They thought we might lose that argument. They would just be told he'd died, but I'll take that if we can get all the conversations in.'

'Me too,' said Bob. 'Have you given your statement yet about this?' He raised his plastered arm a fraction.

'Yes, on Friday. I don't think I was much help, mind you. For a detective, my powers of observation were on a par with Mr Magoo's.'

'I'll use that in your next appraisal.'

Luke was about to reply when Bob's phone rang. He raised a finger to ask the sergeant to hold on, then accepted the call.

'Hi mate, what can I do for you?'

Bob felt his face drop as he took in what Scotty was telling him. He wedged the phone between his shoulder and ear then typed, bringing up the incident log on the computer-aided dispatch.

'Give me the CAD number,' he said, and typed again, then beckoned Luke to come round to his side and pointed to the screen.

As he listened he interjected with the occasional 'Right' and 'I see'.

When Scotty had finished, it was Bob's turn.

'Send me a photo of the body and don't let anyone near it until Luke and I get there. Let Major Crime know. If this is the bloke who killed Lizzie, they'll be all over it. Great work Scotty.'

Bob stood up. 'Grab some keys, Luke and, this time, try to get me back here in one piece.'

Half an hour later, Bob, Luke, Scotty and Saira had been joined by the duty senior investigating officer, DCI Claire Jackson. All had pored over the body-worn video footage of Lizzie's killer and the corpse in front of them.

'Shame we couldn't get any offender's DNA from Lizzie,' said Claire. 'Still, despite him being mangled by a dustcart, I'm certain it's the same person.' They all nodded and mumbled their agreement. 'I'm not treating it as suspicious yet but as an unexpected death under investigation. I want to know who he is, why he killed Lizzie and how he got here. Thanks everyone, leave it to us now.'

All but Claire stepped away from the body and Bob wandered out of the warehouse. He glanced back and saw Scotty's head drop. He was about to walk over, then had second thoughts. The big man needed a few moments alone.

Instead, he found the number of someone who should know and tapped it. It was answered on the second ring.

'Bob, don't tell me you're at work,' said Jo.

'Where else would I be, ma'am? You got a minute?'

'One sec,' she said and Bob heard a door close then footsteps. 'Go ahead.'

'Take this how you want, but a couple of pieces of good news.'

'God, I could do with that,' she said.

'It looks like the trial is still on. It's not going to be easy but CPS think we're in with a chance providing we, or rather they, can persuade the judge.'

'Excellent, and the other bit?'

Bob described what had happened at the refuse centre and how Scotty, having his wits about him, might just have closed the Lizzie murder enquiry. Jo's response was more guarded than he'd expected.

'Assuming Scotty is right, it's a bit of a stretch to accept he happened to turn up dead, don't you think?'

'It does happen,' argued Bob.

'On the telly maybe, but given what Scotty's unauthorised source said . . .'

'Spanners?'

'Yes, bloody stupid name by the way. Given what Spanners said, we can't assume this bloke, whoever he is, acted alone. Nor can we assume he wasn't taken out himself.'

'As in murdered?'

'Why not? He's served his purpose, but in front of witnesses. If there is this big conspiracy going on, the sooner he's out of the way, that's one less vulnerability. Let me speak to Claire Jackson. She needs to put some effort behind this. See you later.' She ended the call, leaving Bob to stare at the mute handset, wondering why he'd stoked her fire in the first place.

19

Sir Ben paced up and down the lounge, seething. He paid the carers to arrive at 8 a.m. sharp when he needed them here all day and, time and again, they treated that as a 'from' rather than a 'by' time.

He'd let it get to 8.15 a.m., then he'd give the agency a rocket and their final warning. As his watch ticked to 8.11 a.m., the gate buzzer sounded and, seeing the Totalcare-liveried Peugeot waiting, he buzzed it through. On its tail was a white and turquoise Toyota Avensis with *Brighthelm Taxis* emblazoned on the side.

Sir Ben cursed as he dashed for the front door, determined that the driver of the first car didn't meet the second. He gave the taxi driver the international signal for 'I'll be five minutes', and ushered the carer in. The mid-fifties woman, who looked like she'd lived twice her years and skipped more than the odd meal on the way, couldn't stop apologising, blaming traffic, her grandchildren and a host of other excuses Ben couldn't give two shits about. 'I'll be back about five. Call me if you need anything,' he said as he strode out of the door, shouting, 'Bye Mum,' almost as an afterthought.

He slammed the door and was in the back of the cab in seconds. 'Jesus,

Tony. There was a time when people actually turned up on time.'

'You said 8.15 a.m. so that makes me four minutes early by my watch,' the driver replied with disdain.

'Not you mate, that bloody care agency. I can't remember the last time they were actually punctual.'

'Give them a break, Ben. Not everyone's as reliable as we are.' Sir Ben caught Tony's eyes twinkling in the rear-view mirror. Tony Evans was one of those characters who defined Brighton's blue-collar elite. As well as owning the city's biggest taxi company, Brighthelm, outright, he also had controlling stakes in most of his rivals' firms, and ran a multimillion-pound commercial cleaning and environmental services company plus three late-night restaurants. His control over the door supervisors at the major Brighton clubs was hazier, certainly nothing Companies House could confirm, but it was an open secret that he pulled all their strings. To the ill-informed he easily passed as a humble workaholic, grafting to make ends meet, rather than the ruthless truth.

'Are you sure we're safe to talk in here? That CCTV camera is making me nervous.'

Tony pulled out onto the busy road, weaved through the lanes then turned right towards the A27 bypass. 'Don't let appearances deceive you, nothing in here is what it seems. Great cover, eh?'

'What, swanning about in an eye-smarting cab with your company's name and number plastered on the side? Hardly under the radar.'

'You're kidding aren't you? How many Brighthelm taxis do you see on an average day?' Tony darted out on the roundabout and off at the second exit, which would take them to Worthing.

'I've no idea.'

'Well have a look.'

It was then that he realised almost every other car seemed to be identical in shape and colour to the one he was in, and they all had either *Brighthelm Taxi* or one of Tony's rivals' names on the side. 'Oh, I see.'

'Yep, no one notices us. Unless we cut you up, that is. Perfect, eh?'

Sir Ben grunted in grudging agreement. 'Where are we headed?'

'I thought we'd look like we were going to your office, but I'll find some traffic jams to give us some time.'

'Fine. Listen, I haven't thanked you properly for sorting out our problem so promptly on Saturday.'

Tony met Sir Ben's eyes in the mirror. They both knew this was the only place they could speak of what had happened after the football.

'I'd like to say it was no problem, Ben, but I'd never lie to you.'

'What, getting the gun?'

'No, that wasn't the problem. You try getting hold of a sniper who can embed himself in a hedge then shoot straight with an hour's notice. Not to mention two cyclists happy to ride in the firing line.'

'That's what I pay you for.'

'Talking of which . . .' said Tony, as he glared in the mirror.

'It's on its way. Listen, obviously the weekend's events have highlighted some chinks in our armour.'

'I thought something must be up when you suddenly wanted your main man and an undercover cop slotted.'

'I'm not worried about Challenor, but I was sloppy trusting him in the first place.'

Tony didn't answer, but trundled along the inside lane as they entered Southwick Tunnel.

'Did you hear me?'

''Course I did, I just don't know what you want me to say. I could have told you years ago that he was a liability. A gob on a stick, that one.'

'Why didn't you?'

'You never asked,' said Tony as he eased his speed in reply to the sea of red lights illuminating the near distance.

'Fair point. Look, I need someone with more business acumen to run that side of things. Someone who understands strategy, is discreet but has the wherewithal to do what's needed, no questions asked.'

Tony stared ahead. 'Are you kidding? Listen, I don't want to offend you but I'm not exactly scrabbling round for work at the moment. Anyway, I'm not even sure what it is you're doing. I mean I know what you do, but why?'

'Well I haven't got a business plan I can share if that's what you mean, but it's really simple. Like it or not, we all profit from the city being the drugs capital of the UK.'

'Former.'

'Exactly, and don't tell me you've not felt the pinch of us losing that crown – and I don't mean just by you creaming off the street dealers. It's the goods and services a drug problem relies on. Substitute drugs, hostels, treatment services, cleaning and of course the tourism pound of being a party city.'

'Is this about this Synthopate you're trialling?'

'Yes, but it's not just Respite Pharmaceuticals who'll benefit if we get the licence to produce, it's the whole city. Wider, even. The UK.'

'But I thought it was supposed to get people off drugs. Isn't that just going to accelerate the pinch you're on about?'

The traffic ground to a halt as they emerged into daylight, only to be met with yet another stretch of carriageway improvement works.

'That's the beauty of it. It's a massive sticking plaster. A fucking expensive one to develop but a sticking plaster nonetheless. It's never going to cure anyone, they'll just get addicted to that instead, so in effect we get to print our own money. The more heroin there is on the street, the more addicts who'll need treatment and the more people on a lifetime prescription of Synthopate. But the police seem to think it's in everyone's interests to cure addiction, dry up the demand and stop the flow of drugs in, just to save a few pitiful lives. That can't happen.'

'How do I come into this? I don't like getting my hands dirty you know.'

The traffic lights at Shoreham Airport turned green, although you wouldn't know it as the logjam remained stubbornly stuck.

'I wouldn't expect you to. I've got people in place who can provide muscle, those who can access the users, I've even got someone at Whitehall pulling strings – but I need someone to oversee it all and, as I say, have the capability to come down hard on whoever gets in our way.'

'While you sit back and watch.'

'I'm the main investor. I've put millions into the trial and if it doesn't succeed I'll lose everything.'

'What's in it for me?'

Sir Ben named a fee which was twice what he'd paid Challenor, but he knew to attract someone with Tony's contacts and influence, he needed to talk big numbers.

The traffic thinned and Tony didn't answer for a good minute, which seemed like ten.

'Here are the conditions.'

Sir Ben punched his thigh in glee. 'I'm all ears.'

'I get full control. You can say what you need to achieve but you leave it entirely up to me how I go about that. No arguments and no questions. Oh, and no red lines. If someone needs taking out, I'm free to make that happen. I don't mess about, Ben, but in return you'll be isolated from all the mucky business. You can honestly claim innocence. But there must be total trust. You breach that and, well, you've seen what I can make happen and I'm not entirely sure how your dear old mum will cope on her own, are you?'

20

Jo wondered, not for the first time, which business school taught that interspersing tinnitus-inducing hold music with 'your call is important to us' increased market share. She'd spent two hours last night listening to the same marching band tunes while she helped Darren research his article. There was no way she was staying with this excuse for a bank once she'd got her blocked cards sorted.

Thankfully Gary Hedges wasn't in the office, so at least she was able to put it on speaker and crack on with some work. She was about to open the third directed surveillance application of the morning when Fiona, her PA, tapped on the open door. Jo looked up and smiled. Great personal assistants were hard to come by, so she'd landed on her feet when she inherited this one from Phil Cooke, her predecessor. She was a rare breed in that she always had Jo's back, batting off more tripe than there were hours in the day to deal with, and rarely bringing bad news to her door, just solutions.

'Jo, don't you think you ought to be heading off?' she said in her rich, soft Glaswegian accent.

'Off? Where?' Jo flipped her screen to her diary page. 'Oh shit, I'd forgotten all about that. Yep, on my way. You're a bloody saviour.'

'No problem, see you later.'

Jo hung up on 'The Bank That Cares', grabbed her shoulder bag, slipped on a civvy jacket and headed for the door, just as Gary breezed in.

'Had enough for the day?' he said.

'I forgot I'm meeting Nicola Merrion at the Lifechoices offices in ten minutes.'

Gary looked at his watch. 'Good luck making that. Oh, try to avoid Amanda if you can.'

'Why so?' Amanda Short was the business manager, the most senior non-police officer on Jo's Command Team. She'd been in that role for longer than anyone could remember and without her the division would be broken and the whole place would grind to a halt.

'You not heard about the petrol deliveries?'

'Still nothing?' The station fuel tanks had been dry for three days and it was causing chaos. During the height of the cuts, some bright spark at HQ had removed all the fuel cards to save a few pence per litre by making officers fill up using their own cheaper supply rather than at public petrol stations. That was fine until theirs ran out.

'Nope and she wants you to kick the chief officers' arses.'

'All at once?'

'Don't say I didn't warn you.'

'Consider me warned,' she said as she deliberately took the long way down to the car park. As she passed the Street Community Team, Scotty looked up from his desk.

'Ah, Sergeant Scott, are you busy?'

'Always, ma'am.'

'Good, how about a trip out to see Nicola Merrion with me? I could do with someone who knows what's actually going on.'

Scotty looked around the office. 'How about PC Bannerjee? I get all I know from her.'

Saira's look was one of someone whose plans for the day were about to explode in her face.

Jo picked up a photo from her desk which showed Saira being awarded her judo black belt. 'She's a trained killer. We don't want to waste her talents at some boring meeting, do we now? No, get your jacket, it looks like you could do with some fresh air.'

Scotty shoved his chair back from his desk, grabbed his warrant card and coat, then sauntered to the door while both Jo and Saira stifled giggles.

'We'll take my car,' said Jo.

As they made their way onto the Kings Road in front of the Palace Pier, Jo revealed the real reason she'd taken the opportunity to bring Scotty along. 'How are you?'

'How am I? I'm fine. Why do you ask, ma'am?'

'Call me Jo. You know why I'm asking. You and Lizzie were the world's worst-kept secret. I think only Bob Heaton didn't know.' She left a silence for him to fill. He didn't disappoint.

'And my wife.'

'I wouldn't bank on it,' said Jo. 'You must be devastated. Is there anyone you can talk to?' She glanced across and caught Scotty wiping a tear away. 'Want me to pull over?'

'No, no, I'm fine, honestly. It's just so hard. I have to put on a brave face at home and at work. My missus knew Lizzie – really liked her – and she was fine that we worked closely but I have to pretend she was just a colleague. Shit, it's such a mess.'

They passed Oriental Place where bouquets of wilting supermarket flowers still bunched along the railings.

Scotty stared at them and then wiped his eyes again. 'I'm sorry.'

'Don't be daft. Look, I can sort some time off for you if that helps. You need to find someone to unload on. Someone who'll listen, hug you if you want, but won't judge.'

'No, please don't. I need to be here. It gives me a purpose. I need to find Lizzie's killer.'

'You've already done that.'

'We both know he was just a patsy. I'm talking about the people behind her murder. And that undercover officer's. I want to rain hell down on whoever's pulling the strings and I won't fucking stop until I do.' He shouted the last sentence, then softly said, 'Pardon my language.'

'Swear all you fucking like,' said Jo with a glint. 'But talk to someone, promise me that.'

'Promise.'

Darren couldn't be sure that he'd pulled his marriage back from the brink, but the signs were more positive than they'd been twenty-four hours ago. He and Jo had talked long into the night and she'd done her best to reassure him that the chances of him being even interviewed, let alone arrested and charged, for his apparent involvement in the Ed Stark affair hovered millimetres above zero. Outwardly he accepted that, but his editor's connections and raging psychopathy niggled away; he'd put nothing past that bastard.

Yesterday, while Jo's phone had hummed the on-hold music on speaker, she'd talked him through how he could show how many lives Operation Eradicate had saved. She'd shown him online testimonials from erstwhile addicts who had found work, housing and love as a direct result of the operation. He was a journalist so didn't need Jo to tell him how to contact them. He'd been on to that first thing and wondered why so many were desperate to tell their story.

Then it was just a case of researching the data, triangulating everything and juxtaposing the macro with the micro. Readers loved human stories, but equally they'd be all too quick to dismiss them as convenient anecdotes if the bigger picture didn't prove otherwise.

What the hell was he worried about that for? No one would ever read this.

As he sat on the breakfast bar stool re-reading the draft, doubt surged through him. He'd worked for the *Daily Journal* for around fifteen years and he was under no illusion that the moment he pressed send, his tenure, and probably his journalistic career, would be snuffed out like a candle at the Easter Vigil. This was the polar opposite of what he'd been told to write. He was not only handing Parkin the gun, he was loading it, cocking the hammer and shoving it in his own mouth.

What then? Just resign and hope the threat was as empty as Jo said? That would be the coward's way out. Write the article Parkin wanted and lie to Jo that it had been sabotaged by the subeditors? She'd rumble him straight away.

He re-read the piece. So far as investigative journalism went, it wasn't his most impactive effort, but it was OK. True? For sure. Balanced? Tick. Yes, this was the article he wanted to write. This was the one that, whatever the consequences, would allow him to sleep at night, save his marriage and keep him true to his journalistic values.

He scanned it one more time, opened an email, typed Parkin's address, attached it and pressed send.

21

By the time Jo pulled into the visitors' bay at Lifechoices HQ, which served as its outreach, treatment and dispensing centre, you'd never have known Scotty had broken down just a few minutes earlier. Game face on, he strutted ahead of Jo as if he owned the place.

The way he was received, he might as well have. Jo knew he was a familiar face amongst the drug-using community but the balance of those who held him in awe and those who feared him was split fifty–fifty.

The greetings reflected on which side of the fence each patient – as that's what he told her to call them – sat. Some mumbled a reluctant 'All right Scotty,' others practically hugged him. None though dared snort like a pig or mutter insults under their breath.

As they were about to enter the squat prefabricated building, Scotty stopped short. A scruffy twenty- or thirty-something man in a filthy parka with raggedy stubble and hair yanked back into a ponytail had caught his attention. 'Spanners, over here.'

The man looked edgy as Scotty took his arm and walked him towards what looked like a storage shed. Jo followed, the name registering immediately.

'Man, I can't be seen talking to you here. Them lot'll shank me.'

'Relax. I have little chats with everyone here. Don't think you're so special. So long as no one hears what we're saying, they won't give it a second thought. Ma'am, this is Spanners. I mentioned him the other day. Spanners, this is my big boss so no swearing, got me?' Spanners eyed Jo suspiciously, then flicked his attention back to Scotty. 'Say good morning to Mrs Howe, then. Where are your manners?'

'Honestly, call me Jo.' Spanners just nodded, still wary.

'Do you know anything about a bloke who ended up in a bin? Needle marks all over him. Dumped by the dustcart.'

'How would I know anything about that?' His head flicked left and right, clearly terrified he'd be labelled a grass.

Scotty took hold of Spanners' elbow and from his squirm, Jo knew he'd found the pressure point.

'Think harder.'

Jo touched Scotty's shoulders to suggest he relaxed his grip a little.

Spanners rubbed his arm. 'There was this geezer in the squat where I was dossing. He took too much or maybe a bad batch. I tried to save him man, honest to God.'

'Woah, back up. You saying you were there when he died?'

'Yeah, but it weren't nothing to do with me. I was just there. I tried CPR and shit but it was too late.'

'So what happened?'

Spanners shrugged and Scotty finally let go. 'They took him, man.'

'Who? Where to?'

'I don't know. They took me away and did this.' He pulled up his T-shirt and showed a rack of black and yellowing bruises.

'Jesus,' said Jo. 'You need to get that seen to.'

'I'm sweet, Jo,' he said, then gave Scotty a sardonic smile. 'They took the geezer away, and last I heard he was dumped. I don't know where, I swear.'

'You and I need to talk more about this,' said Scotty.

'Sure.'

Jo and Scotty walked back towards the door, leaving Spanners to scurry in the opposite direction.

'I wasn't expecting that,' said Jo.

'I was. They'd all know something about it. There are no secrets among this lot, whatever they'll have you think.'

'You were expecting him to have tried to save the bloke's life?'

'Er, no. That was a bonus, I'll give you that. I'll squeeze some more out of him tomorrow.'

'Just be gentle on him. You've done enough squeezing.'

They walked up to the reception desk, where a stunningly pretty young woman with the most piercing eyes and neat cornrows leapt up from her desk and came and gave Scotty the tightest of hugs.

'I'm so sorry about Lizzie,' she said with genuine feeling.

Scotty shrugged awkwardly. 'Er, yes me too, Ayo. My boss and I are here to see Nicola.' Jo read the code which said, *Don't say too much in front of her.*

Ayo understood, unlocked the embrace, smiled at Jo and disappeared out the back. A moment later, Nicola Merrion appeared. Unlike last time she'd seen her in ACC Mills's office just after Lizzie's murder, she was sporting a smart business suit, incongruous with her surroundings. 'Come through, come through,' she said with a painted-on smile.

Jo had only met Nicola twice here before and she'd forgotten how spartan her office was. 'Scotty, grab another chair from the corridor will you?' said Nicola. Jo was surprised at how he obeyed like a lapdog.

'Nicola, thanks for making time,' said Jo as Scotty dragged a plastic moulded chair in and flounced down.

'Well we do seem to be in a bit of a crisis. Such a shame given all we've achieved.' The words said one thing but Nicola's expression seemed to disagree.

'Well, I don't think we need to get ahead of ourselves. To my mind, and Sergeant Scott here agrees with me' – she glanced at Scotty, who returned a *Do I?* look – 'we should be redoubling our efforts given what happened.

We don't know whether Lizzie's murder and that of the two after the football are connected, but if they are, we need to get even tougher on the dealers and reduce their customer base by getting more through to recovery.'

'Haven't you been told to leave it well alone? For now at least.'

How would you know that? she thought. That was a private conversation between her and the ACC. She let it go for now.

'Not in so many words. This is the perfect opportunity. After all, we've got the trial coming up which should send shockwaves through the gangs. It's a perfect time to get our joint teams back on the streets while upping our covert efforts. We're ready to go whenever you are.'

Nicola twisted her daith piercing, an irritating habit Jo put down to her buying time. 'I'm not so sure. Most of the outreach workers are terrified they'll be next. You have to remember they've lost a very dear friend. If Lizzie could be murdered with two police officers by her side' – she looked accusingly at Scotty, then back at Jo – 'then what guarantees can we give them?'

'That's a little unfair,' said Jo as she felt Scotty rise from his seat. Still looking at Nicola, she put her right hand out to stop him. 'We obviously need to review how we look after your staff, but surely they'll understand that it was a one-off and we need to get back to what we were doing.'

'As I say, we'll think about it. We've got this Synthopate roll-out to grapple with too. It's a difficult time. You said you were resuming the covert operations?'

'Yes, as soon as we can get some more UCs we'll be back in business. Be prepared to get busy.'

They spent the next ten minutes talking through the hotspots and the drug trends. Scotty's grasp of both was phenomenal and Jo started to feel by the end of it that Nicola was coming back on board. Her worries were valid but they couldn't give up at the first hint of trouble, devastating as it was.

'Thanks Nicola, we won't take up any more of your time. It's been very productive.' Jo stood and Scotty followed suit. 'We'll see ourselves out.' They headed for the door and had turned the corner back to reception when Jo stopped and retraced her few steps. As she walked back in, Nicola looked up from her phone with a jolt like she'd been caught watching porn. 'Sorry, just taking the chair back for you,' Jo smiled, but she couldn't shift the thought she'd interrupted her somehow.

When she was back in reception, Scotty was talking to Ayo, his face riven with concern. 'Leave it with me. I'll look into it.'

Jo smiled at them both. 'We done?'

'Yes, ma'am.'

They walked in silence to the car. Once both doors were closed, Scotty spoke. 'Did you know two of their patients were found dead from drugs overdoses this morning?'

'Er, no.'

'Ayo had just been told by the medical director. A bloke and a girl. Both found in their bedsits.'

'Separate then?'

'Seems so. I'll look up the CAD.'

'If the medical director knew, Nicola would have, surely?' she said. 'Yet she didn't mention it. Suspicious or forgetful.'

'Not the sort of thing you'd forget, is it, ma'am?'

'My thoughts exactly.' She started the car as her mind raced.

Jo still wasn't convinced that Scotty was OK to work or would talk to anyone about his grief.

As they drove back to the station, they swapped theories about the drugs deaths and why Nicola hadn't mentioned them. Neither came up with any concrete connection but both voiced how uncomfortable they felt.

Scotty tapped away at his mobile data terminal, or 'phone' as he called it.

'That's interesting,' he said, more to himself than Jo. She let the silence settle. 'Both of these were doing really well with their treatment.'

'What, the drugs deaths?'

'Yeah. They've both been in a holistic treatment programme for around six months. A few relapses but they'd got back on it and were looking really good.'

'Still using though?'

Scotty shrugged. 'I suppose they must have been. There doesn't seem to be any third-party involvement . . .'

'Except the dealer.'

'Except that. Something must have triggered them both to relapse on the same day.'

'But would a normal dose kill them, perhaps after a period of abstinence?'

Scotty shrugged again. 'That's why these ODs can be the almost perfect murder. Unless there is sign of a fight or some of the gear left behind to analyse, we never really know how much they've taken and why it's killed them and not the next person.'

'Is that what you reckon?'

'My job is to stop them getting to that stage. Cleverer people than me decide what's happened when they do.'

Jo thought about that. These could be nothing more than an unhappy coincidence. After all, they'd slashed drugs deaths over the last ten months from one a week to fewer than one a month. But now there had been three in a few days. She'd been around long enough to know that blips like this weren't a forecast of things to come but were worth watching.

She pulled into the car park at Brighton Police Station and was intrigued to see a police community support officer standing sentry at the back door.

She and Scotty got out of the car and ambled over to where the bored young woman was standing.

'Everything OK?'

'Power cut, ma'am. None of our passes are working.' She pointed to the card reader next to the lock.

'Oh. Been out for long?'

'An hour or so.'

'I'm sorry. It might not feel like it but you're doing a great job.'

Jo walked past and called Gary. 'You in the nick?' she said as he picked up.

'Yes, I'm with Amanda trying to work out how to get the leccy back on.'

'Jesus. Is everything down?'

'Yep, and it seems it's just us. I tried UK Power Networks and they've confirmed it's an isolated mains cable fault. As it is though, we have no lights, the comms are all dead and there's no IT. If it goes on much longer we'll have to trigger the contingency plan.'

She nodded a goodbye to Scotty and fast-walked towards the stairs.

'You sure it's just us? Have you checked American Express across the road?'

'Jo, I'm not an idiot. Just trust me.'

22

As soon as Sir Ben had rung him to relay Nicola's message, Tony Evans made some calls of his own. His cab made the perfect office, complemented by his secure phone which he ran through a virtual private network. He kept on the move and always used WhatsApp to call. So long as he didn't lose the handset, he reckoned he was below most radars. It didn't bear thinking about if he was wrong.

He and Ben had discussed how they needed to not only flood the streets with drugs and kill off enough of those in treatment to make it appear high risk, but also sap the morale and capabilities of the police to act.

He'd made it appear as though Saturday's shooting was not the hardest thing to set up, but in fact it nearly hadn't happened. Knowing that Nathan Challenor was one of the targets, however, had given him extra impetus to find the right sniper. He'd predicted it would create a vacancy for him to fill.

The previous night's drugs deaths were child's play. Just accessing some high-strength heroin and getting his men to make it look self-administered was all it took.

If he was to meet the conditions of his seven-figure contract, he'd need every ounce of his ingenuity and willing brains and brawn to make the more challenging sabotages pay off. He knew that cutting the police station's power would only have a temporary effect but by chipping away like that, he'd distract them enough to give him time to rock their foundations. Or at least Chief Superintendent Jo Howe's foundations. And to get to her, he needed to get to those she loved, or those who did her bidding.

Now was the hiatus that came with a hands-off approach, but which he found the most frustrating of all. He'd given his orders. All he could do was wait.

He pulled away from the Brighton Marina car park and joined the conga of traffic heading up the slope and back into the city, hiding in plain sight as usual. He guessed that one of the reasons Ben had asked him to replace Challenor was his reputation. There were plenty of people out there able to make life a tad uncomfortable for the odd business or who could unearth a scandal or two on a public official, but Tony was the go-to person if you wanted creativity combined with utter brutality.

He wondered how long it would be until he got the call that the job was done. He didn't doubt that it would be, it was just the waiting that was unbearable.

As the Brighton Aquarium roundabout came into view, the three police cars overtaking him, sirens blaring and lights flashing, together with the helicopter swooping in from the north told him things were happening.

PC Wendy Relf was first on the scene and wished she'd not been. Missing children reports were always chaotic and getting any reliable information was nigh on impossible.

The George IV swimming centre was smack in the middle of town, which meant that access, even on blue lights and sirens, would test the patience of the Dalai Lama. Unlike many police drivers though, Wendy had become hardwired to bully her way through congestion and was

141

not averse to flicking the odd finger at any dickhead who didn't shift themselves.

She ran into the foyer to be greeted by a hysterical woman, wrapped in a peach and yellow beach towel, and half a dozen skinny teenagers whose blue T-shirts proclaimed them as lifeguards even though they were behaving like frightened puppies. One slightly older but no more in control woman in yellow had the word *Manager* emblazoned on her back.

Wendy headed straight for the frantic woman, who was the boy's mother, Mrs Spencer.

She took the woman by the shoulders and turned her so she could lock onto her. 'Listen to me. I know you're frightened but we're all looking for him . . .'

'Leo. His name's Leo.'

'Leo.' Wendy ventured a smile, to reassure rather than to minimise the gravity of the situation. 'We need to know what happened and what Leo looks like. Shall we go in here?' She turned towards an office and guided Mrs Spencer in, gesturing to a soft, high-back chair behind the desk, in which the mother reluctantly sat.

'Can you get the lady a robe or something? And can you get your lot to do a thorough search of the building?' Wendy asked the manager, who nodded and left. Turning back, Wendy said, 'Now, tell me what's happened.'

Between sniffs, Mrs Spencer managed to explain that she'd brought Leo swimming as she did most Thursday mornings. They'd been there for half an hour, playing in the water and her teaching him to swim a few strokes to the side, when she needed the toilet. She stood Leo outside the cubicle but when she came out he was nowhere to be seen.

'What happened then?'

'I-I-I looked for him all over. He never runs away. Oh please find him, don't let anything happen to him.'

'Every available officer is looking for him as we speak. The helicopter's up and we're doing everything we can to find him.' No promises. That was lesson one in police college.

'Please, please.' The woman collapsed forward and her shoulders shook uncontrollably. The wail that came jolted Wendy. She needed to get more information, but there was no consoling this mum. Thankfully the call handler had managed to eke out the basics, enough for a search. How many three-year-old blond boys in Spider-Man swimsuits would be wandering the North Laine, after all? Suddenly, the mother heaved a deep breath. 'My husband. Is my husband coming?'

'Er, I don't think so. I'll check but I'm not sure we have his details. We can get him if you tell us his number.'

Mrs Spencer glared at her. 'Luke Spencer. DS Luke Spencer. You work with him don't you?'

'One minute.' Wendy dashed out of the door. She tapped her inspector's number on her Airwave radio and, thankfully, she answered immediately.

'Yes, Wendy, have you got an update?'

'Not as such, ma'am, but did we know this is Luke Spencer's boy who's missing?'

'Christ, no we didn't. Leave it with me. I'll restrict the log. Do you want him over there?'

'Yes please. Unsurprisingly, his wife's a wreck.'

'Roger that,' said the inspector and they both ended the call.

Wendy walked along the corridor and the sirens coming from outside hit her like a wall, in stark contrast to the huddle of lifeguards to her right chatting and gazing at their phones. 'I thought you were looking for Leo?'

The group looked as surly as her thirteen-year-old brother. The manager ambled round the corner. 'We've got half the police force out looking for this boy. The least you could do is get your shower of shit motivated to do a proper search,' said Wendy.

'There's no need—'

Wendy cut her off with a scowl and fully loaded finger. 'Just do it.'

Wendy took a breath and stepped back into the office. Mrs Spencer was on the phone.

'Sorry, Mum, I've got to go. No, no, I'll be OK.' She put the handset down on the table.

'Luke's on his way, Mrs, er, sorry what's your first name?'

'Judy.'

'Judy, Luke's on his way. Sorry no one made the connection. Now can I get some details from you?'

Wendy tapped away on her mobile data terminal as Judy answered her questions between sobs. Updates chirped through Wendy's earpiece, but none so far were the good news she was desperate to hear. Judy might not know, but Luke certainly would: the longer a child is missing, the less likelihood of a happy ending.

Suddenly the door burst open, and for a moment Wendy thought she was hallucinating. DS Luke Spencer filled the threshold with a small boy in his arms, enveloped in an oversize suit jacket.

'Oh my God,' said Judy as she leapt to her feet, flicking the chair over as she did. In a second, she grabbed Leo from Luke's arms and squeezed him so tight, Wendy feared for the little boy's ribs.

'Where have you been, darling?' she said, nuzzled in his neck.

'He was walking up Barrack Yard outside,' said Luke. 'Why the hell didn't anyone see him?' He wrapped his arms round both mother and child.

Wendy gave the update everyone was waiting for into her radio, then stood back while the touching reunion played out in front of her. As the hug released, Leo said, 'The lady looked after me.'

Luke and Judy exchanged a look. 'What lady, darling?'

'The lady. She's your friend, Daddy.'

Judy threw Luke an accusatory glance.

'Leo, darling,' Judy cut in. 'How do you know she's Daddy's friend?'

'She told me to give him the picture.'

Wendy was about to take over but Luke's outstretched arm barred her way through.

'What picture darling?'

Leo fiddled in the pocket of his swimsuit and pulled out a folded photo, handing it over to his dad.

Luke opened it and his face took on the colour of ash.

'What?' said Judy, taking hold of Leo again, but Luke handed it over to Wendy.

'You don't need to see it,' he told his wife.

Wendy opened the picture and saw an image clearly focused but almost certainly taken with a zoom lens. Luke was walking out of the police station front door, talking on the phone. Superimposed, smack in the centre of his forehead, was a single bullet hole. Underneath was the text, *You have been warned.*

23

From the moment Leo Spencer was found with a blunt threat to his dad's life in his tiny hand, Jo's day became turmoil. There was a time, when she first took senior command, that the oh-so-important meetings that cluttered her diary took precedence over real police work. Over the last two years, however, she had recalibrated her priorities to the degree where some accused her of actively looking for operational distractions. Gary Hedges had turned it into an art form long before she'd arrived on the division and she was happy to learn from the master.

The kidnap of any three-year-old boy in broad daylight from a crowded swimming pool always trumped strategising round a table, whether or not he was a police officer's son. Jo had taken direct control of the hunt for the woman whom Leo had said gave him the picture, alongside managing the pandemonium the press were creating and the very real threat to DS Luke Spencer's life. Gary had offered to take charge but she felt she owed it to Luke and his family, given the abduction and the warning were surely linked to Op Eradicate. It was after midnight before she'd got home and now, seven hours later, she was back behind her desk.

Glancing down the 240 unread emails hoping to spot one that might be vaguely important, she was aware of a figure lurking in her doorway. She looked up and saw Bob, shifting from foot to foot, rubbing his injured arm.

'Well, come in if you're going to.'

'Thanks.' He walked over and stood, vaguely to attention, in front of her desk.

'Well we're not doing the headteacher–pupil thing. Sit over there.' She gestured to the small round conference table which filled the space between her and Gary's desks, and walked to join him, closing the door on the way. 'What's up? Luke OK?'

'Oh, yes. Well sort of. He's taking a few days off to recover.'

Jo nodded. 'Good. So how can I help?'

'Well, we've got a bit of a problem with Eradicate.'

'Understatement of the year,' she muttered.

'No seriously, I can't find anyone to work on it.'

'What? Well pay some overtime or something. I get that we're busy but this is part of what we do now.'

Bob shook his head. 'It's not staffing levels. We can manage those, for once. No, people are refusing to work on it.'

'What do you mean, "refusing"? When did we stop becoming a disciplined service?'

Bob avoided her gaze, then met it. 'It's not that straightforward. Firstly, we can't get any replacement undercover officers. That's not just a case of ordering someone to do it. The National Crime Agency are saying there's no one available, but I know that's code for they don't feel safe.'

'Well I'll get the ACC to escalate it.'

'It's not just them. The whole CID are saying they don't feel protected enough to work on it.'

'Protected? This is the bloody police service. We're the ones who do the protecting.'

Fiona, her PA, appeared at the door, her raised eyebrow asking if she could come in. A terse shake of the head was all it took to send her away.

'With respect, ma'am, you need to see it from their point of view. They've seen Lizzie murdered in front of two cops, me get knocked over, an undercover officer and his target shot dead and now the case officer's little boy snatched and returned with a death threat. Why should they feel safe?'

Jo heaved a breath out and rubbed her eyes. 'I do understand, but we can't give in to intimidation. We all know where that would end, don't we? At least you're still onside, eh?'

Bob paused just a beat too long.

'Bob?'

'I'm getting too old for this shit. Look what I've been through over the last couple of years. I should be winding down for retirement. Steve and I have plans and I've every intention of living the good life with him, not watching over my shoulder.'

'For God's sake Bob. You're supposed to be a leader. I know how people are feeling, but you need to show some steel. Get out there and reassure, inspire, bribe if you have to, but we can't have people picking and choosing what they'll investigate.'

Bob stood, the look of an exhausted warrior across his face, shook his head, turned and began to walk out. As he got to the door, he turned and said, 'You're not going to be able to dictate your way out of this. You must do something or your pet project goes down the drain.'

Jo stood, about to shout for him to come back when her mobile phone rang.

'Jo Howe.'

'Ah, good morning, ma'am, it's the custody sergeant at Worthing.'

She took a breath. 'How can I help you?'

'Yes, it's a bit sensitive but we have a Darren Howe here who says he's your husband.'

'What do you mean?'

'Is he your husband, ma'am?'

'Well yes, of course he is, but what do you mean, "here"? In what capacity?'

Jo's heart thumped.

'Mr Howe has been arrested by the Met Police on suspicion of corruption, aiding and abetting misconduct in a public office and conspiracy. He's asked that you be informed.'

Jo grabbed the desk to steady herself. 'Is this some kind of joke?' She regretted that outburst the second it left her lips.

'With respect, ma'am, you know the answer to that.'

'What's it in connection with?'

The sergeant's voice dropped to a whisper. 'From what I can gather it's an historic allegation. Something about paying the police for information about an arrest.'

Jo could barely get her 'thank you' out before the blood drained from her.

Years ago, Jo had returned home after a burglary, but somehow this invasion of her privacy seemed far more intrusive.

Unlike last time, this carnage was the work of a so-called specialist search team. Whether the Metropolitan Police had deliberately left the house looking like a war zone in some spit back at her being in the job or whether this was their normal modus operandi she had no idea, and frankly she didn't care. All she was worried about was how to get the place back into some semblance of normality before her mum dropped the boys back.

Standing in the lounge, she didn't know where to begin. Drawers were strewn all over the floor, their contents left scattered as if by an explosion. Cables hung redundantly where laptops, the Xbox and even printers had once sat. Nothing that could feasibly hold data was left. No phones, tablets, memory sticks, not even that know-all Alexa which in better times she'd have paid someone to take away. This was spiteful, plain and simple.

She set about numbly stuffing the debris where it might have once belonged, but her mind was fixed on what would become of Darren, her and the job now.

It took a good four hours, close to 10 p.m., before the house looked halfway respectable. She Whatsapp'd the all-clear to her mum and within fifteen minutes her car drew up outside.

Jo coughed subconsciously and straightened her back as the bell rang and the excited chatter of the lights of her life rippled through the door. She'd barely opened it when the boys burst through and latched onto a leg each. Her mum threw her a *It'll be fine* look, with a wink and a smile, before she eased past Jo.

'Mummy, we've had the best time. Nanny took us bowling and we had pizza and ice cream afterwards,' said Ciaran as he ran into the lounge.

'Tell her who won,' shouted Liam as he chased after his brother.

'Only 'cos you had the ramp and gutter-guards, didn't he, Nanny?'

Jo looked at her mum, who grinned and nodded, as they followed in the boys' wake.

'Hey, where's the Xbox?' said Ciaran as he stood at the nest of wires on the TV unit.

'And my iPad. It was here,' said Liam, running to the empty coffee table.

It broke Jo's heart to see the tears burst from both boys' blue eyes.

'Come here, come here,' she said, her arms stretched out to receive each of her distraught darlings.

'Drink?' mouthed her mum. Jo nodded and waited for her to leave.

'Listen, it's fine. Some people have had to borrow them for a little while but they'll bring them back soon.'

'But why didn't they ask?' said Ciaran. 'If you want to borrow something you have to ask.'

'That's stealing,' said Liam, summing up where his brother was going with this.

150

'Not really. They needed to borrow them and Mummy and Daddy said they could, but we'll get them back.' Jo hated the hole she was digging with these lies. How would she ever explain that Darren had been arrested for corruption and that God knows how many pairs of size ten boots had stomped through their house ripping everything apart, looking for evidence of some trumped-up allegation.

'I hate you,' said Ciaran with a venom she'd never seen in either of the boys before. 'I hate you, hate you, hate you. I want Daddy.' Jo grabbed his shoulders and twisted him to face her. 'Ow, you're hurting me. DADDY. DADDY!'

Jo instantly let go of him, letting him flop back on the settee. Liam stared at her in terror.

What was happening to her? This was a nightmare but to take it out on the kids?

Her mum came running back in. Jo felt like a little girl again as she spun her head round and, with a look, implored her mum to help.

As only a mother can, she instantly got it. 'Boys, how would you like a sleepover at Nanny's tonight? I'll even make pancakes for breakfast.'

Jo mouthed 'thanks', as the boys scurried to their grandmother as if Jo were the stranger the school insisted on warning them about. 'I'm sorry boys. Mummy's very tired and just waiting for Daddy to come home. I'll pick you up tomorrow and we'll do something fun.' Even that promise didn't seem to cut it and both boys nestled tighter into their nanny, looking terrified of Jo.

Thirty seconds later, they were gone and Jo was inconsolable on the same settee she'd practically dropped Ciaran on moments before. Why couldn't she stop these things happening? She felt her whole world crumbling and there was nothing she could do to stop it. All she could do for now was numb the pain, and she was relieved to find a bottle of wine chilling in the fridge.

* * *

Jo woke with a jolt when the key scraped in the lock. She was still on the sofa, her head pounded and her mouth was arid. 'Hello. Who's that?' she said as she rubbed her eyes, conscious that she was in no state to receive visitors. She checked her watch as she heard the distinct growl of a diesel taxi engine fade outside. 3.30 a.m.? She stuffed the empty wine bottle behind a cushion and put the picture of her sister Caroline she'd found by her side back on the mantelpiece.

'It's me,' said Darren, flatly.

As he stood in the doorway, she realised that compared to him she looked banquet-ready. His hair was spiked in all directions, the jacket and shirt he'd pressed that morning looked like it had been slept in and his usually proud posture wilted.

'You OK?'

'Jesus Christ. What the fuck have they done to the place?'

Jo struggled to her feet and moved to embrace him. 'Thanks, this is after I've tidied up.' She wrapped her arms around him but his hung limply by his side. Releasing him, she stepped back. 'What?'

'I'm on bail but I'm pretty certain I'm going to prison.'

Jo reached out and took his hands, this time determined not to be rebuffed. 'Come and sit down, it'll be fine. Tell me what happened but let me get you a beer first.'

Over the next two hours he took her through everything. The arrest, the handcuffs, the body search at custody, the solicitor – if that's what he really was – then the interview. That was the worst bit. They made it sound like he was some kind of traitor ready to bring down the monarchy, the government and a whole way of life.

At intervals, Jo tried to reassure him that these were just the games some officers played, while mentally noting how to make their worthless lives a living hell when all this was over.

Darren topped it off with the bombshell she knew she was expecting.

'They said they're coming after you, Jo.'

'Me? *I've* done nothing wrong.'

'Oh, but I have, have I?'

'No, no, I didn't mean that. Someone's fitted you up, I get that, but how does that extend to me?'

Darren just looked at her. Then the penny dropped.

'The undercover officer thing? Oh, please, how can they think I was behind that?'

'In fairness, that's what you'd think isn't it?'

He was right, of course he was. It was not so much a leap, more a skip to think: if he's taken a bung from a corrupt officer before, then why not marry one?

'Anyway, I'm out on bail and there are conditions.'

'There always are. What are they?'

'Report to the police three times a week, surrender my passport, and here's the killer.' He paused.

'Go on.'

'Other than signing on or reporting a crime, I'm to have no contact with any serving police officer.'

'Except . . . ?'

'No exceptions. I can't even be here now, but I had to tell you in person and collect some stuff. I'm allowed no contact with you, so can't even live in my own house.'

'YOU WHAT?' Jo instinctively grabbed her phone and stabbed in the passcode.

Darren took her hand and eased the phone from her. 'Leave it. I've got to live at my mum's. We'll get a proper lawyer, but for now I'll just grab a bag and go before I get found out. The best you can do is act normal, look after the boys and keep yourself safe.'

Jo grappled with what to say, her emotions were seesawing so much. It was an obvious bail condition when she thought of it but, for the first time, she was feeling the turmoil she'd inflicted on so many over the years. She'd never given it a moment's thought until now.

'It should be me saying all that stuff to you, you know.'

Darren smiled for the first time. 'Yep, but I got fed up waiting. Look, I need to go. Can you book me an Uber while I get my gear?' They both stood, looked at each other, then hugged as if it were their last day on earth.

Ten minutes later, Darren was gone and Jo had no idea how she'd carry on.

24

Word must have spread like wildfire as, not long after 7.30 a.m., the banging on her door made Jo think the Met were coming back for another go.

After a cursory glance in the hallway mirror, she filled her lungs and opened the door. A wave of relief washed through her as she was greeted by the only two people she'd trust to be on her side.

'Are the boys here?' said Gary, as he stepped over the threshold.

'Er, do come in,' said Jo, moving to one side, allowing Bob through too. 'No, my mum's got them.'

'Great, we're going for breakfast.'

Jo looked at Bob, hoping he'd offer more explanation than her bullish deputy. He just shrugged and remained silent.

'Don't you two do anything without food in front of you?' said Jo. 'I do have some shit going on you know.'

'No one's forcing you to eat, although I'd recommend it. Let's go.'

'Why not here?' said Jo.

Bob looked around. 'I see you've had the Met Police's finest through

155

here, although their housekeeping skills could do with some work.'

'None taken,' said Jo, wondering why the blokes in her life couldn't spot that she'd tidied up.

'As I was saying, not the best place to talk.' He touched his lips. Jo instantly twigged. As well as taking every electronic device they could find, who was to know whether they'd planted one or two? Suddenly, she remembered Darren breaking his bail conditions just a few hours ago. Christ, how could either of them have been so stupid? If this place was bugged as Bob was suggesting, she'd be in as much trouble as her husband.

Fifteen minutes later, they'd grabbed a table outside Carat's Café behind Shoreham Harbour. They'd chosen wisely. The soulless, pencil-straight and barely used road that served the harbour's warehouses, the beach and the café was perfect for ensuring they weren't being followed. However, Jo did think it was slightly unnecessary to turn off her location settings before they left, but she was beyond arguing.

'What you having?' said Gary, making the three words sound like one.

'The works for me,' said Bob.

'Bacon sandwich and a coffee please,' said Jo.

Gary and Bob looked at each other in shock. 'Coffee?' said Bob. 'Not hot water?'

'I need a booster. Strong coffee and stick an egg in that sandwich.'

'You're the boss,' said Gary as he went inside to order.

'You OK?' said Bob.

'Not really. I should have expected this.'

'Eh?'

'Darren was being blackmailed by his editor. He had to write an article throwing me under the bus or he'd rake up stuff from the past.'

'Are you sure?' She glared at him. 'OK, what sort of stuff?'

'Crap about him buying information from the Met, but it was all down to the fucking editor himself.'

Bob fiddled with a stray plastic stirrer. 'Why would he do that? It's a bit close to home.'

'That's what I've been thinking. He's thick as shit so I'm convinced he's been forced into this by someone higher up.'

'Who?'

'If I knew that, don't you think I'd have gone after them? Whoever it is though, they're not going to stop, are they?' She massaged her temples. 'I know you warned me yesterday but when it hits you personally, it feels kind of different.'

'Darren's innocent, we know that, but we've seen them do far worse than this to those who've got in their way.'

'But why go for him? This is on me.'

'Exactly, and what better way to attack someone than take the ones they love.'

Gary shouldered the door open, balancing three mugs on a tray. 'Food's coming.' He placed it on the table, sloshing the overfilled contents as he did so. 'Bollocks,' he said.

Jo helped herself to a wad of napkins from the dispenser on the next table and mopped up the mess. 'You need more practice.' She took the nearest cup and sipped. 'Jeez, that's disgusting. How do you drink this tar?'

'Working with you, I need all the chemical armour I can get.'

Jo couldn't help but grin, but it did little to soothe the angst that was eating her up.

Once Gary had taken a seat, he cut to the chase. 'Right, Darren's in the shit.'

'Thanks for that.'

'No, listen. As I say, he's in the shit and with everything we know it's not of his making, but whoever is behind this knows what they're doing and it's not the endgame either.'

'Really? What is then?'

'Not sure, but given we know they are prepared to kill police officers, drugs workers and addicts to further their cause, it's going to be more than trumping up a charge against the top dog's husband . . .'

'Charming.'

'This is only a means to an end. Bob?'

'Thanks boss. I'm doing some digging. Trying to work out who's not only got the most to gain by attacking those who threaten the drugs market, but also who's got the capability. And that means money. Big money.'

'Don't keep me in suspense. What have you found out?' said Jo.

'Nothing just yet.'

'Great.'

'Hear me out. This is not some local tier-three dealer protecting their patch. It's far bigger than that, and I wouldn't mind betting it's someone who has direct access to massive wealth but high-level influence too.'

'Who then?'

Bob was about to continue when a cheery forty-something man in a blue and white striped apron appeared with two huge breakfasts and Jo's bacon and egg butty.

'Get you anything else? Sauces?'

Before either of the men could reply, Jo said, 'No, we're fine, thanks.'

Once he was out of earshot, Jo repeated her question.

'No idea just yet but we need to look at all the big-money people who have anything to lose by Op Eradicate and, between us, target them.'

'Target them? How are we going to do that with bugger all intelligence?' said Jo, the irony not lost on her that she'd once thrown Bob into mortal danger on far less.

'Well, I'm not going back undercover,' said Bob, clearly thinking the same. 'We need to provoke them. Make them do something . . .'

'I know what provoke means, you don't need to mansplain.'

'Make them do something to show out, then we hit them.'

'Really?'

'Really,' said Gary. 'Bob's right, and unless we do this soon, more people will die and they might be closer to home than we could imagine.'

Jo instantly lost her appetite and any residual taste for coffee. She dialled her mum, barely able to speak when she eventually picked up.

25

'Bail? Fucking bail? How the hell did that happen you worthless amoeba?'

When Sir Ben had received Sam Parkin's text saying he had an update, with a Zoom link attached, he'd assumed the newspaper editor had wanted to see the delight in his eyes when he told him it went swimmingly. He wasn't expecting this.

'I agree, boss. It's not great but what can I do?'

'Don't give me that,' said Sir Ben. 'And get rid of that bloody beach background, will you?'

Sam glanced down at the keyboard, then back at the screen. 'Sorry boss. Look, this is just a glitch. I had a right old row with my Met contact but he said the Sussex custody officer was being an arsehole.'

Wishing he could reach through the screen to rip Sam's throat out, Sir Ben took a breath. He couldn't get in a shouting match if he wanted this idiot to focus.

'I'm not paying you the amount I am for you to fob me off with "it's just a glitch". I pay you to get things done and I thought I was clear enough that if Darren Howe didn't play ball, I wanted him out of the picture.'

'And he will be, boss.'

'Stop calling me boss. It's Sir Ben to you.'

'Right you are. As I say, the Old Bill don't like to keep their mates' husbands banged up but we'll sort it. I've already got a plan to keep Sussex out of it.'

'Christ. Why were they involved in the first place?' The signal juddered for a second which gave a rather desperate freeze frame of Sam, as if he was thinking of an excuse. He probably was.

'Breakdown in communication. What more can I say?'

Sir Ben rubbed his eyes, wondering how to get rid of this supercilious clown. He jotted *Spk Tony E re SP* on a Post-it note by the side of his keyboard. Sam had the gravitas of a failed *Love Island* contestant and, when the time was right, Tony would have to do the necessary.

'What have you got on him so far?'

Sam paused. 'Let me just open my messages, so I get it right.' He was really trying Sir Ben's patience, but what could he do? 'Here we go. They say he gave a no comment interview on solicitor's advice. They are going through all the gadgets they took from his house but that'll take some time. They've got a statement from one of those who was nicked for this leak before and they've put him right in the frame. Oh, and they've kept me out of it.' Sam looked up. 'Early days, then, but things are coming together.'

'And if they don't find anything? All they've got is the word of some disgraced journo.'

'Don't worry about that. Those digital forensic geeks have all sorts of tricks up their sleeves. It's not just getting stuff off computers they're good at . . .'

Sir Ben knew not to ask for the details, although with Sam he felt sorely tempted. 'Well just make sure next time he's in custody he leaves in a prison van, or else you'll be travelling in something much more permanent.' Without the closing etiquette of most video calls, Sir Ben clicked the red 'Leave Meeting' button, spun the chair round and stormed off to see his mum.

* * *

160

Jo had rammed her day with meetings and appointments so she didn't have to think about the inevitable conversation that loomed. On the way home she'd stopped off to get a quarter of a tank of petrol she didn't need, just to delay the moment. Thankfully her new card worked.

Given Darren's bail conditions, her mum had collected Ciaran and Liam from school. They'd argued earlier whether she should be there when Jo told the boys why Daddy wasn't coming home but, for once, Jo won, stressing that it was better for grandmothers to remain a force of good than become complicit in breaking the boys' hearts.

Jo pulled up outside the house, locked the car, took a breath and walked to the front door. Slipping the key in the lock, she silently counted to three then, on cue, the bedlam commenced.

'Mummy, Mummy. Nanny brought us an Xbox game.'

Jo bent down and hugged them both. '*Bought.* Nanny *bought* you a game but to be honest, maybe Nanny could have asked Mummy first.' Her mum appeared from the kitchen wearing a guilty smile. Jo chose not to mention that they didn't have anything to play it on at the moment.

'I'm sorry, dear, did you say my name?'

Jo shook her head in defeat. 'Never mind. Thanks, Mum. Have they eaten?'

'I managed to find enough to make a bolognese. Would you like me to get some shopping in for you? Your cupboards are rather bare you know.'

Jo's eyes filled as she stepped over to her mum and hugged her. 'It's fine, I'll get a delivery. It's been so . . .' She felt her voice tremble so cut off the sentence before it cracked completely. Her mum gave her an extra squeeze which only served to wring more tears out. She broke the embrace and gave the slightest nod.

'Boys, I'm going to leave you with Mummy now. Be good and don't fight over that game.'

'Ohhhhh. Can't you stay and play?' said Ciaran.

'Yes, stay, stay, stay,' Liam said, backing up his older brother.

Jo's mum sniggered. 'I need to share you with Mummy. I can't keep you all to myself.'

Both boys feigned a sulk but their nanny gave them a hug and a kiss, then the same to Jo, and left.

'Mummy, when Daddy comes in, can we show him our new game?' said Ciaran.

She took them each by the hand and led them to the lounge which, true to form, her mum had tidied up from the mess it had been this morning. 'We need to wait until we get the Xbox back, then you can play it with Mummy?'

'Can you get it back now?'

'Soon, darling.'

'Do ladies play computer games?' said Liam, in all innocence.

'I think we need that gender stereotype chat soon,' mumbled Jo as she sat them on the settee. 'Now listen, boys, I've got something to tell you.' She tried to read each of their eyes but both flicked between curiosity and fear. This felt like giving a death message.

'Look, Daddy isn't going to be living with us for a little while. He's going to stay at Nanny Howe's.'

She left the silence to hang while the boys were each processing the bombshell in their own way. Ciaran spoke first.

'Are you getting a divorce?'

Straight for the jugular then.

'No, no darling. We're not. It's just. Well it's complicated and, he can't come home just yet.'

'Poppy in my class, her mummy chucked her daddy out,' said Liam. 'Poppy saw him and another lady wrestling in the bedroom, so when her mummy came home and they were having tea, she asked her daddy why. She hasn't seen her daddy since. Was Daddy wrestling with a lady?'

Despite herself, Jo found herself grinning. She'd love to know more about Poppy's dad but now wasn't the time. 'No, Mummy and Daddy

162

love each other. It's just something has happened that means Daddy's not allowed to live here for now.'

It was Ciaran's turn. 'Toby's mum got an injection against his dad. Now he lives in a bedroom with a kitchen in it.'

'I think you mean an *injunction*. And that's not what's happened. I promise we both still really want to live together, with you, here, but we can't – so you're going to stay with me and Nanny will help look after you when I'm out. Just until this is sorted.'

Again, she could tell they were mulling this over. This time she moved first to stop their imaginations running away with them. 'It's a work thing.'

'It's always a work thing with you,' said Ciaran, loaded with a ton of blame.

'No, this is Daddy's work.' Then a cowardly idea came to her. 'Why don't we pretend Daddy's had to go to America for a story, like he's done before?'

'Or China,' shouted Ciaran, suddenly excited.

'Or Africa,' chipped in Liam.

'Australia,' said Ciaran.

'No, Timbuktu!' Liam's final contribution had them giggling incessantly, rolling around on the settee.

'Yes, any of those places and before you know it, he'll be home.'

Then a switch flicked and the mood changed.

'But that's only pretend, isn't it, Mummy? Daddy's not really gone on a plane and he's not coming back, is he?'

Jo was about to answer when Liam screamed, 'He is. He is, is, is. Mummy wouldn't lie to us 'cos she's a policeman. Mummy, tell him Daddy's coming back.'

Jo bit her tongue to stop herself correcting Liam's second gender error. 'He will come back. We just don't know when, and you can still see him.' Why hadn't she led with that? Reassured them from the start. They'd agreed not to reveal the real reason Darren was absent, not yet in any case, but she could have been kinder in the order she broke the news.

'Can we see him today?' asked Ciaran.

'Not today, it's a bit late. Maybe tomorrow. We'll see.'

'We'll be good Mummy, won't we, Liam?' His little brother nodded, looking as brave as any five-year-old who'd lost his hero could. 'And, until Daddy comes home, I'll be the man of the house and look after you, Mummy. And you, Liam. I'll be as strong as Daddy.'

Jo could take no more; she pulled both boys into her and wept like no one was watching.

26

Despite being more prepared than he'd ever been for a trial, Bob had been at his desk since 7 a.m. The events of the last few weeks had shaken not just him but the whole force. The Crown Prosecution Service remained sure that, in light of Ged's murder, they had an arguable case to persuade the judge to admit the undercover evidence anyway.

As he cross-checked the contents of the exhibit box with the schedule, he was interrupted by a gentle tap on the door.

DS Luke Spencer's usual pristine appearance had given way to a grey two-piece suit which was passable at best, a pastel green shirt in dire need of an iron and a black tie which seemed as if it had been knotted by someone in boxing gloves.

'Mate, you might want to have a shave before we head off. And maybe swill some Optrex round those eyes.'

Luke didn't react, just stood in the doorway, his Adam's apple throbbing above his unbuttoned collar. Bob sprung up and dashed round the desk. 'Sit down, sit down,' he said as he shut the door and closed the window blinds against prying eyes. 'What's the matter? Is it Leo?'

Luke sniffed and nodded.

'I know it's easy for me to say but he's safe. Yeah, that was a fright, but you can't let them win.'

'I know, I know, but what if they take him for good next time? Judy won't let him out of her sight and she blames me.'

'I suppose that's natural but once we bang these bastards up, you'll have nothing to worry about.'

Luke gave Bob a look which said *We both know that's not true.*

'Should I speak to Judy?' This time Luke threw Bob a different look. 'Yeah, you're probably right. Maybe not. Look, help me with this lot, take your mind off it a bit. I just want to check we've served all the unused material we should have. Can't lose this on a technicality.'

Five miles past the Hickstead showjumping ground, en route to Croydon Crown Court, the A23 traffic came to a sudden and total stop.

'Good job we left early,' he said to Luke, who seemed distracted tapping messages on his phone. A quick glance at the screen told Bob he was trying to appease his wife, so he pretended he hadn't noticed.

After fifteen minutes, they'd still not moved an inch and Bob was starting to get concerned. 'Luke, can you get on to comms and find out what's going on?' Bob rubbed his arm, then tapped impatiently on the steering wheel. He tried to fill in the gaps when he heard Luke say, 'Oh I see . . . Anyone injured? . . . Christ, poor bastard . . . How long?'

As Luke finished the call, Bob said, 'Well?'

'There's an artic jack-knifed and overturned a couple of miles up here. The driver's in a bad way. Looks like we'll be stuck here for hours.'

Bob looked in the mirror and saw the traffic stacked up behind. 'Better give the court a ring,' he said, more to himself than Luke.

Scrolling through his contacts, he found the number for the court's CPS office. It rang and rang. He checked his watch: 9.05 a.m., so there should be someone there. After it automatically cut off, he tried again and again but still no one picked up.

'You haven't got a mobile number for the caseworker have you, Luke?'

'I don't think so. Let me see if it's on the footer of any of his emails.'

While Luke checked, Bob looked around. People were out of their cars, stretching their legs and chatting to one another as if long-lost friends. Bob would have liked to join them but he needed to get a message to the court that he'd be late. Just then everyone looked up as the thump thump thump of a helicopter ricocheted the air around them.

'Sorry guv, nothing.'

'No worries. I'll get someone to see if they can get a message to him.' Bob was about to call the CID office when *Unknown Caller* flashed up on his phone. He looked at Luke, shrugged and tapped 'accept'.

'DI Heaton.'

'Where are you Mr Heaton? We're waiting for you at court.'

'Sorry, who is this?'

'Lance Redmond, CPS.'

'Well good morning to you, Mr Redmond. I've being trying to contact you. Currently, DS Spencer and I are stuck in traffic on the A23 with all the exhibits in the boot of our car. The way things are looking, I think we might be here for some time.'

'Well the judge is already getting very anxious. Defence counsel are talking about making applications to dismiss the case given your absence and that of the other police witnesses.'

'What other police witnesses? One's dead so I'm sure he can be excused, but the others should be there.'

'I'm afraid not. They've all called in sick.'

'What? All of them?'

'Every one. Even that cover officer on whom we were so relying.'

'How didn't I know that?'

'I have no idea, but I've come in to a string of messages to say each of them has gone off with this, that or the other. The judge wants to hear from us on what we propose in fifteen minutes and he's determined to start the trial today.'

'Hold on. You've got to give me more time. I'll find out what's going on. I'll see if I can get out of this jam somehow. I'm sure there's a way round this.' He ended the call and turned to Luke.

'He's changed his tune. Look, everyone's thrown a sickie. Find out what's going on. I need them all spoken to and at court ASAP. I'll try to get the chief crown prosecutor in to bat for us.'

Bob ignored the gridlock surrounding him as he tried to pull every string he could think of, including Jo Howe and ACC Leon Mills, but no one seemed to be getting anywhere and the minutes were ticking away. He sensed that Luke was having no more luck as he was locked into a rhythm of dial, wait, redial, wait, try new number, repeat.

After forty-five minutes of dead ends, Bob knew he was coming to the end of the line. On seeing the other carriageway empty of traffic, in a last throw of the dice he called a traffic sergeant friend to see if they could be picked up and driven down that side of the road. He punched the dashboard when he was told that was where the air ambulance had landed so nothing was passing any time soon.

Then his phone rang. *Unknown Caller*. He checked his watch.

'DI Heaton.'

'Yes, it's Lance Redmond. I'm afraid you've had your chance. The judge has dismissed the case.'

'You what?'

'There's no need to shout. The judge has dismissed the charges against all the defendants and they are being released as we speak. I did warn you.' It was Redmond who hung up this time, which was just as well given the invective that came from Bob's mouth. He looked at Luke whose face, despite the region's top drug dealers now being out on the street, showed a flicker of relief.

In all his years working with the street homeless and drug addicts, Scotty had learnt that appointment times were a movable feast, sometimes by days. He was surprised therefore when, bang on midday, Spanners shuffled across the road from the Brighton Centre towards where he stood beside Shelter Hall. He flicked his head, indicating that his guest was to take the east steps down onto the beach, while Scotty himself took the west ones.

Scotty then turned and headed for the subway that led from the beach under Kings Road – far from inquisitive eyes.

Scotty checked for any rough sleepers. Happy they were alone, he beckoned Spanners into the shadows.

'Bit of a bombshell you landed on me in front of the boss the other day.'

'Well, you did push it. What did you want me to do, lie?'

'You wouldn't be the first. Anyway, tell me what you know about that bastard we found at the tip.'

Spanners took him through everything that had happened in the squat and how he'd tried to save the man's life. He choked a little when he recalled how no one had seemed that bothered that the man had died.

'You do know who it was, don't you?' said Scotty.

Spanners shrugged. Scotty was about to go on when a figure came towards them, boots shuffling among the discarded food wrappers. 'You got any gear, mate?' slurred the interloper.

'Is this who you're serving up to?' Scotty shouted at Spanners, dragging him forward.

'Oh, fuck, Sergeant Scott,' said the would-be drug buyer as he spun round and ran at a pace that belied his wasted appearance.

For a second both Scotty and Spanners chuckled. 'Not sure we'll be seeing him back here for a while.'

'Does everyone know you?'

'I hope so. Anyway, as I was saying, did you recognise the bloke who died?'

'No. Well he looked familiar but he was fucked so, well, I don't know.'

'I showed you a picture of him when I took you out to Shoreham. Remember? That was the bastard who killed my . . . the drug worker.'

'Oh shit. Of course. In my defence, it was bloody dark in there. I'm

169

certain I've never seen the other geezer before though.'

'What about those other two who OD'd the other day? They were regulars. Do you know what happened to them?'

'Shouldn't I be asking you that?'

'We know how they died but what we don't know is why. They were doing well and it seems a bit of a coincidence they died so soon after that bloke.'

'Maybe there was a connection, maybe it's a coincidence. Want me to find out?'

That took Scotty aback. He'd asked many a drug user for information but none had ever volunteered quite so readily. 'Why would you do that?'

'The way I see it, you lot have got no hope of finding out what's going on. If you had someone on the inside who could find out, maybe it might just save a life or two. Makes sense?'

Scotty's heart leapt at the thought that he might just be able to find out who was behind Lizzie's murder and, with a fair wind, he might get to them before his detective mates. He pushed Bob Heaton's warnings about running unofficial informants to the back of his mind.

'You sure?'

'If you want.'

'What's in it for you?'

'I get to live,' said Spanners.

Scotty nodded then took Spanners by the hand and pulled him in for an embrace, whispering, 'Thank you mate. I owe you,' as he released his grip.

For the remainder of the two hours it took for the traffic to clear, Bob was raging at whoever would take his calls. He insisted Luke give him personal contact details for all the police witnesses, even those in covert roles, as it was impossible to believe so many officers were genuinely sick on the first day of a major trial.

He didn't want to be accused of bullying the genuinely ill, but he wanted answers and was determined to see the rat he could smell.

For wily, streetwise cops, their efforts were pitiful. The range of ailments, from diarrhoea to bad backs and migraines, lacked more imagination than a 1970s soap opera storyline. Equally superficial were their excuses as to why they'd not told him directly. It was not only in the regulations, but also common decency to let your boss know you were off sick, especially on a day like this.

The crash had been just bad luck, but Bob still felt that the morning's events leading to the judge pulling the plug on the case had more behind them than he could put his finger on. Judges never worked that quickly.

Luke had taken over the driving, leaving Bob to make some calls. The last one, before he sulked on the journey back to Brighton Police Station, was to Jo's PA. He'd already texted her the bad news but wanted to speak to her face to face.

Jo spun her chair round when Bob appeared.

'Come in, and shut the door.'

He did as she asked, then pulled up Gary's chair. After all these years, he'd only recently stopped waiting to be invited to take a seat.

'I can't believe it, ma'am.'

Jo coughed and pointed to the closed door.

'Sorry. I can't believe it, Jo.'

'Better.' She tried to lighten the mood but with her personal and professional lives crumbling around her, that was a struggle. 'Tell me what's happened.'

Bob took her through the morning's events, giving particular emphasis to the formulaic excuses each of the officers gave for being sick.

'Something's up,' he said.

'I agree,' she said. 'I'll buy one, or even two, forgetting to call you. Especially the ones who were puking, but all of them? That's never happened.'

'I reckon they're scared. You should have seen Luke this morning.

171

What happened to his boy has destroyed him. They don't want the same to happen to them.'

'They're all grown-ups and they all know we can look after them if they feel under threat. Withdrawing labour is not what we do.'

Bob's expression said it all. If the last two years had taught them anything it was that nothing and no one could protect even the burliest of cops against an ingenious and determined force.

'What about the crash?' asked Bob. 'Coincidence?'

'It's early days yet. The headlines are the driver died at the scene. That does happen, and hundreds, if not thousands, of motorists will have had their plans disrupted. However, if whoever is behind recent events is as connected as they must be . . .'

'And ruthless.'

'Yes. If they are as connected and ruthless as they seem to be, we can't rule out that the crash was staged to trap you before you got to court.'

'They must have had great intelligence. Sure, there's only one sensible route to drive to Croydon Crown Court, but they'd have had to know when we left, et cetera. Who's to say we wouldn't have already passed where they chose to stage the crash?'

Jo gave him a *do catch up* look.

'What?'

'These are clever people. I take it you left your phone behind, Luke too? I take it you scanned the car before you set off? And, how about your counter-surveillance tactics? All up to scratch?'

'You reckon?'

'I don't know. All I'm saying is that if we assume that they're this determined to pull the plug on anything connected to Eradicate, there must be a serious reason for it and that must be money. Big money. So, if what we are doing is affecting their coffers so much, they're going to protect their investment.'

'Right.'

'And that means they're not going to stop. I don't want to bring this back to me but if they can engineer Darren's arrest, then what else can they do?'

'What do you suggest?'

'Let's do what we are good at. Get out and pay them all visits.'

'Is that it?'

'Let me finish. Get everything you can on all the officers' phones, pay them the welfare visits they're entitled to and get all the CCTV around their homes checked. I want to know who they've been speaking to, when, where and how, and then we might just pick up some patterns.'

'You going to authorise all that?'

'No. I'm not nearly independent enough to satisfy the legislation. We need to find someone who's removed enough to be objective.'

Just then, Gary Hedges barged the door open, bellowing down his phone which was wedged between his shoulder and ear, his other hand clutching his laptop case. As he caught sight of Jo and Bob, he mouthed, 'Sorry.'

'Speak of the devil,' said Jo, stifling her laugh when she saw Gary's face drop in dread.

27

Sir Ben had spent the last few hours providing his mother with what the care agency euphemistically termed 'personal care', but which was, when you stripped it all back, mopping up piss and shit. That only put him in a worse mood than ever but once the carers had finally arrived, he did as Tony Evans had suggested: donned what he thought might fit the description of 'dog walking gear' and headed for Ditchling Beacon in his ropiest car, a grey Peugeot 308. The drive itself was uneventful except for a trundling tractor, which drew a tail of traffic like the Pied Piper with children. Eventually the machine swung off into a nearside field and the traffic thinned out as everyone made up for lost time.

Just before the road fell away towards the Beacon's eponymous village, Sir Ben turned left into the circular car park and squeezed into the last remaining space, behind the ever-present ice cream van. He switched off the engine, picked up his phone, then thought better of it and left it on the centre console. He stepped out of the car, zapping it locked.

As instructed, he clambered up the bank, turned left and, having held the gate for a couple of speeding mountain cyclists coming the other way, walked through and headed for the trig point two dozen yards away.

A sense of relief washed through him as he saw Tony Evans waiting with two Labradors straining at their leads.

Evans, dressed in green combats and a black sweatshirt, nodded. 'All right, Ben?'

'Been better, so I hope you've got some good news for me.'

'In good time. Got your phone?'

Sir Ben frowned. 'No, I thought I'd better leave it in the car. You know, in case I'm being tracked.'

Tony leant against the stone pillar which marked the highest point on that particular hill, and sighed. 'How did you get to be so successful? You've got to think.'

Sir Ben pondered for a second. 'I thought that's what I was doing.'

'Far from it, mate. Listen, if anyone's tracking you, which I very much doubt by the way, they'll have you making your way up here then, what?'

The penny dropped. 'Sitting in my car for an hour?'

'Exactly, and while you're there, not using your phone in any way, shape or form. How often does that happen?'

'Well, never. Unless I'm doing something else, I'm always messaging, calling or emailing.'

'And do you ever leave your phone behind?'

Sir Ben shook his head.

'Right, well go and get it and let's create a nice innocent trail of you driving up to a beauty spot to meet an old mate for a dog walk.'

Sir Ben grunted in acceptance and scurried back to his car, grabbed the phone – checking for messages and firing back replies to the two most urgent ones – then walked back up to Tony.

'Right, let's walk and talk,' said Tony, having checked for eavesdroppers. He thrust one of the dog leads into Sir Ben's hand and they strode off west along the ridge, giving the air of two middle-aged friends having a long-overdue catch-up in the fresh air of the national park.

'Well this morning couldn't have gone better. We got to all the police witnesses, one way or another, and persuaded them all they deserved a day off. Then the crash worked like a dream. I've heard they're still trying to identify the driver and Twitter's gone mental with people ranting about how long it took to clear the traffic.'

'And the judge did as he was told, I see.'

'Wouldn't you if you were in his shoes?'

Sir Ben chuckled. 'Too right. Anyway, out of curiosity, how did you stage the crash at just the right time and place?' Tony looked at him, his face making any words redundant. 'Seriously, I'm fascinated.'

'What did we say about deniability, Ben?'

'Humour me,' said Sir Ben with an edge designed to remind Tony who was in charge here.

'Well, it was simpler than you'd imagine. The hardest bit was nicking and storing the lorry beforehand. Once we'd crossed that bridge and plated it up so it looked legit, the rest was simple. We were lucky that Elmley Prison just released a lorry driver who'd done three years for importing millions of dodgy fags. So all we needed to do was doctor the front tyres with some remote-controlled charges and give the driver a story about needing to get to Harwich on the hurry-up.'

Sir Ben was impressed. 'That it then?'

'No, of course not. We had a few disgruntled ex-cops follow Bob Heaton after he left the police station.'

'And?'

'We judged their journey and, as the driver was told he had to go hell for leather for Harwich, just at the point when the coppers couldn't pull off, we detonated the charges and hey presto, the lorry jack-knifes and overturns. Gridlock.'

'And a dead driver?'

'Well, yes that was unfortunate, but no one said this was without risks.'

As they approached the next field, Sir Ben saw there were around twenty or so Hereford cows crowded round the gate. Stopping, he said, 'These dogs OK with cattle?'

''Course they are. They'll move. Not scared are you?'

'I was more concerned about the dogs,' lied Sir Ben.

Tony chuckled. 'You're like my daughter. Loves all other animals but can't be in the same postcode as a cow. God knows why.' He paced ahead, opened the gate and as predicted the cows ambled away.

Satisfied the immediate danger had passed, Sir Ben continued.

'You sure the trail won't come back to us?'

'It's fine. They'll identify the driver soon enough but to all intents and purposes he nicked a lorry and got unlucky driving it. The phone we gave him happened to be from where the rig was nicked from and at the right time. The charges and detonator disintegrate on ignition so it'll just look like another ex-con heading back into crime, driving too fast and unable to keep control of a blowout.'

'And . . .'

Tony stopped, turned and glared at Sir Ben. 'No. No more "and"s. You've got to trust me. I shouldn't have told you all that. Let me get on with what you pay me for, and you sort out whatever you do as a result.'

He was right, of course he was, but Sir Ben needed one more question answered.

'What about the court charges? Any chance they'll be resurrected?'

'Nope. Not a hope.'

It had been a few years since Bob had carried out an in-person welfare check on an officer's first day sick. And that had been following a particularly nasty assault.

The first two calls had gone as well as such things ever can. The two officers had come to the door, after he strong-armed their partners a little. Both looked pasty enough and certainly there was no smell of alcohol. It was interesting that, when asked whom they had told that they couldn't make the trial, they both mentioned the same witness care officer.

The third call meant a trip north to Burgess Hill, a commuter town between Brighton and Gatwick Airport. It took a few reverses out of dead ends before he found the right house on the new-build estate.

Squeezing his car into a space, he checked the number and walked up to the tiny terraced house wedged between two larger homes. The trim postage-stamp front garden was enclosed by low picket fencing. The pink scoot-along 'Little Tikes' car suggested why.

Bob pressed the doorbell and waited. Nothing. He rang it again. This time a woman's voice yelled out of an upstairs window.

'Yes?'

'Oh, hello. It's DI Heaton from the police. I've come to see DC Josh Mitchell.'

'He's in bed.'

Bob sighed. 'That's good, but I need to see him.'

'You'll have to come back. He's ill.'

Bob was about to reply when the woman slammed the window. A minute later, the door opened. He thought it would be Josh's partner, ready to give him both barrels, but he was shocked to see the DC himself.

He was even more surprised to see him in suit trousers and a crisp white open necked shirt. His red eyes contrasted with his otherwise immaculate look.

'Come in, boss,' he said, stepping aside.

Bob walked in and found himself in a small lounge/diner with more furniture than clear floor space.

The blonde woman who'd a moment ago told him to leave stood by a door Bob assumed led to the kitchen. The rage written across her face was unnerving. She glared at him, both arms shielding a toddler in front of her.

'Boss, this is Lyndsey and our little girl, Faye.'

Still the woman said nothing but scowled.

'Look, I'm sorry to intrude, it's just I need to check you're OK. You know, that there's nothing we can do for you while you're ill.'

'On day one?' said Josh. 'Bit unusual isn't it?'

'Bloody harassment if you ask me,' said Lyndsey.

Bob thought he could front this out and pretend it was just a run-of-the-mill visit, but he knew that would just anger them even more so he came clean.

'Look, can I sit down?' He didn't wait for permission but perched on the edge of a blue velour armchair. Josh did likewise but Lyndsey and Faye remained rooted to the spot. 'I'm here because you, and every other police witness in the Eradicate trial, have gone sick and, well, it's a bit odd don't you think?'

Josh looked as if he wanted to say something, but he'd thought better of it.

'Is there something you need to tell me? The trial has been pulled because of this, so it's serious.' He paused. 'You don't look sick, just terrified.'

'Are you a fucking doctor?' said Lyndsey. Bob saw Faye look up at her mother in astonishment.

'Lynds, leave it,' said Josh. He turned back to Bob. 'Honestly, I just felt rough. I'm sure I'll be back tomorrow. I'm sorry about the trial but I couldn't go and throw up in the witness box.'

Bob wasn't taken in for a second. 'Josh, you need to tell me.'

'Fuck this,' said Lyndsey, striding forward. 'If you're not going to tell him, I will. See her?' She pushed Faye almost into Bob's lap. 'You got kids?'

Bob nodded.

'Natural?'

'I'm not sure that's . . .'

'Did you have them the natural way?'

'Well, yes but . . .'

'Lucky you,' she said. 'Four miscarriages and three failed IVF attempts it took us before we fell with this little miracle.'

Josh stood and touched Lyndsey's shoulder, which she shrugged off. 'I'm not saying you love your kids less than we love Faye but after all that, when someone threatens them across your own garden fence, you do whatever it takes to protect them. And if that means Josh here has to throw a sickie and ask no questions, well that's what'll happen.' Her face was scarlet now but there was no stopping her. 'It's only 'cos I happened to look out of the window that I saw the bastard. I thought he was going to snatch her.'

'What happened?'

'He told me next time I wouldn't be quick enough. Then he told me what Josh had to do, and he fucked off. You tell me, Detective Inspector, what would you do?'

Bob had no answer for that. 'I'll leave you now. But Josh, come and see me first thing tomorrow.'

He saw himself out, walked to the car in a daze and called Jo Howe, who listened in dumbstruck silence.

28

Darren's life was on hold. When he'd left home for university, he had no reason to think he'd ever live back here. As the years passed, the very thought of it brought him out in hives. Now though, it was his only sanctuary. Whilst he couldn't see, even speak to, his wife, Ciaran and Liam were allowed to visit and his mum made it as homely as possible for him. But still, on days like this which stretched out ahead interminably with nothing but daytime television and the odd bit of cleaning the already immaculate bungalow to occupy him, he wondered whether life was worth living.

Just before midday, he'd flipped the channel to catch *BBC News* in the sure knowledge that nothing much would have changed since the 11.30 a.m. update, when there was a ring followed by a rapid knock on the front door. 'I'll get it, Mum,' he called as he heaved himself up from his chair and ambled to greet what was no doubt yet another impatient delivery driver.

Unhooking the chain and turning the deadlock key, he looked for the already dumped parcel but saw instead a familiar, smartly dressed woman and bull of a man stood shoulder to shoulder in front of him.

'Good morning, Mr Howe,' said the woman. She and her partner needlessly showed him their Metropolitan Police warrant cards; he'd already met DS Julia Shiel and DS Ian Jones across the interview table at Worthing Custody Centre.

Icy goosebumps erupted on his skin. 'Yes?'

'Darren, I'm arresting you on suspicion of corruption.' She rattled off the caution but Darren was too dumbfounded to take it all in.

Darren stretched his arm across the open doorway. 'Hold on a second, I've got a bail date. You can't just come and rearrest me before then. Surely I have *some* rights.'

'Do you really want to do this on the doorstep?' said DS Jones, nodding to the barrier that Darren had created.

He dropped his arm, then stood to one side while the two detectives squeezed past and found their own way to the lounge. 'Mind turning that off?' said Jones, helping himself to the remote control. Darren snatched it out of his hand and pressed the off button.

'Gentlemen, please put your willies away,' said Shiel. She turned to Darren. 'I know this is a shock but if we have new evidence, we are perfectly entitled to rearrest you.'

'What new evidence?' Darren's head swam. He'd expected them to realise it was all a terrible mistake by now, yet here they were saying they had even more on him.

'All in good time,' said Shiel softly but firmly. 'Now we've got a long drive ahead so we're going to have to handcuff you. For everyone's safety.'

Darren stepped back and found DS Jones's bulk blocking his way. 'Surely that's not necessary. Worthing's not that far and I promise I'm not going to fight or try to escape.'

'Like to see you try,' muttered Jones.

'Enough, Ian,' Shiel said to her partner. 'Health and safety,' she continued, to Darren. 'We're not going to Worthing, we're taking you to London.'

Darren wasn't sure whether to cry or run. 'Why? Can't we do this in Sussex?'

'Nope,' said Jones.

'Can I speak to my solicitor then?' said Darren.

'When we get to the custody centre. In the meantime, if you can put your hands out like this.' DS Shiel stacked her arms in front, about six inches apart. Obediently Darren copied. Jones produced a pair of rigid cuffs and fixed them to Darren's wrists.

'It could be worse mate,' said Jones. 'Often we cuff to the rear and you'd bounce around the back of a van like a frog in a box.'

Just then Darren's seventy-six-year-old mum appeared in the doorway. 'What's going on?' she said to Darren but looking directly at the two detectives.

DS Shiel stepped towards her. 'I'm sorry to disturb your day but we've arrested Mr Howe and we're taking him to custody now.'

'I don't understand. He's done nothing wrong.'

'Said every mother, every time,' muttered DS Jones.

'You can't take him. Don't you know who his wife is?' she said, becoming hysterical.

'Mum, it's fine,' said Darren. 'I won't be long.'

'I wouldn't bet on that,' said Jones. With that, DS Shiel ushered Darren by the shoulder to the door and whispered to Jones, 'Can't you shut the fuck up?'

As Darren was helped up into the waiting van, he was sure he could hear his mother's howls from behind the front door.

When he was appointed to the force, ACC Leon Mills had been a breath of the freshest air. A born and bred gentlemen, he treated his chief superintendents with the utmost respect and, unlike some of his predecessors, valued their dignity, even in troubled times.

Those who didn't know him well mistook these traits as weaknesses. That was forgivable, given their experiences with previous chief officers. Jo knew different. A raised eyebrow, a disappointed look or a quiet razor-edged question from him stung sharper than the hairdryer treatment.

However, she had never been summoned to his office – 'in person and immediately' – before, and something told her she might be about to see another side to him. On the journey up she'd called the renowned gossip-sponge, Gary Hedges. If there was anything afoot, he'd know. Unfortunately he didn't pick up but flicked a text to say, *In meeting. Call you later unless urgent.*

She left it.

Having snaked around the HQ complex for the miracle of a parking space, she thanked the Lord she wasn't sure she believed in when a blue Lexus pulled out of one on the far side of the campus. With a wave, she thanked the driver and dodged in.

Five minutes later, she was outside Leon's office, still none the wiser. Although the door was open, she tapped lightly and expected an effusive welcome. Instead the ACC looked up from his desk, and with no hint of a smile said, 'Come in. Close the door.'

Jo was grateful for small mercies when he deigned to move round to the easy chairs. She followed suit and sat opposite him, facing the window which elegantly framed the South Downs beyond. Before she could break the ice with small talk though, Leon launched into her.

'Have you heard?'

Jo's mind raced, frantically flipping through its filing systems to wonder what on earth he was talking about. There was plenty they didn't see eye to eye on, but what had triggered this now?

'I'm sorry, sir, I'm not sure . . .'

'Your husband? Darren?'

'We've spoken about that nonsense with Darren, which by the way has the potential to breach our human rights to a family life, but . . .'

Leon turned a colour she'd never seen before. One so like the previous chief constable's that it struck terror through her. 'How dare you start quoting human rights to me. You've no idea the efforts I've gone to so that you can still sit there in that uniform. Your human rights should be the least of your concerns after this morning.' She looked at him blankly and saw a minute softening in his eyes. 'You don't know, do you?'

Jo's mind raced with possibilities, each one coming back to Darren and the conspiracy he had been sucked into. 'Know what?'

Leon shuffled in his seat, eons outside his comfort zone. 'You don't know that Darren was rearrested this morning?'

'What, Darren? There must be some mistake.'

'No mistake I'm afraid.' The ACC recounted the new evidence, or the version that a Metropolitan Police deputy assistant commissioner had given to him. He was careful in couching the story in caveats such as 'so it seems' and 'allegedly', which to Jo indicated that he might be harbouring some doubts as to its authenticity. When he finished he waited in silence.

'Boss, you've obviously got your doubts. Thank you for that.'

'Maybe, but all this is becoming rather a distraction. We still need to discover how it was your husband who broke the news about DC McElroy being an undercover officer. A fact only a few of us knew.'

'Sir, I have nothing to hide.'

'Of course, but due process must follow. However, the work you're doing in Brighton is crucial – but sometimes we have to compromise, and you're becoming the story.'

Jo was terrified that as well as losing her family, she was about to once again lose the job she loved more than any other.

'If you've got a direct instruction for me, please spell it out?'

Jo could see Mills was struggling. For the first time she was convinced he was someone else's mouthpiece here. She'd had first-hand experience of being temporarily relieved of her command when she didn't toe the chief officers' line, and they all knew how that had ended. She hoped they'd not be stupid enough to do so again.

'We're giving you four weeks to wrap up Op Eradicate.'

'Four weeks? This is a long term—'

Leon raised his hand. 'I'm going out on a limb here. Others would have shut it down straight away. Four weeks, then it's over. Unless something dramatically changes in that time, you then move on to other things.'

Something in the way he looked at her confirmed her earlier thoughts. Whoever was pulling the strings wanted her blood on the carpet, but Leon must have grabbed the initiative and insisted he speak to her. Only he would have the decency to give her a chance and a way out. 'Consider the message passed.'

'Are we done, sir?'

'You know, I think we are.'

It was only on the way back to Brighton that it dawned on her what a crucial ally Leon Mills could be – or what a lethal enemy, if she crossed him.

29

Darren had spoken to enough miscarriage of justice victims in his time to have some understanding of how disorientating and scary police cells could be. His relatively short stay in Worthing custody had been positively ambient compared to this. Upon his previous arrest he'd sensed that him being married to a senior, and by all accounts popular, officer played in his favour. However brusque and by the book the Metropolitan Police detectives had been, the Sussex detention officers were not shy in going the extra mile for him.

Now, he could be the worst kind of paedophile the way he was being ignored and treated. Sat in the blanched ten-by-eight-foot cell furnished with just a three-inch-thick, blue, plastic-coated mattress atop a moulded bench, a stainless-steel toilet with no seat and a sink with cold running water set into the wall, he could see why whoever designed these hellholes went to great pains to remove any possible ligature points.

He had nothing but his own thoughts and the din of the invisible drunk, drugged and desperate incarcerated along the same corridor for company. He'd sat through three interviews so far and, for no other reason than the duty solicitor had told him to, answered no questions. When he heard that advice, he did question it. Surely incessantly trotting out 'no comment' again would merely confirm the police's suspicions. The solicitor said that until the police had disclosed all their evidence, it was best to let them work for their money and not sleepwalk into the bear traps they were undoubtedly laying. So, he'd kept his counsel and drawn some ironic satisfaction from the detectives' rising anger as the grilling continued.

He was pretty sure now that they had no more questions, so why the wait?

He happened to be looking at the spyhole in the door when it darkened, and then the security hatch clanked down.

'Want anything to eat?' came the voice which, from this angle, belonged to just a nose and a beard.

'What are the choices?' said Darren.

'Now let me see. You can choose between . . .' The detention officer paused. 'Yes or no.'

'Oh, I see. Yes please, then. Can I have a cup of tea too?'

The hatch was wrenched up as violently as it had been dropped.

'I'll take that as a "yes" then,' said Darren to himself.

In the brief moment the hatch had been open, the putrid stench of urine, vomit and feet had wafted in to accompany the shouts, screams and slam of metal doors and grilles. He had no idea how long he would have to wait for his meal or any kind of update, let alone release. Given the complete absence of natural light but the constant flood of the artificial alternative, he'd lost all sense of time.

After a while, the hatch opened again and the same humourless oaf called through. 'Food.'

Darren stretched himself off the bench, took the three paces to the door on the opposite side of the cell and took the airline-style blown-plastic plate and cup. As he did so the spork fell on the floor. He didn't waste his breath asking to be brought another. The hatch only just missed him as 'Beard' racked it shut.

Darren looked at the congealed mess masquerading as a lasagne and realised that the fingers holding his tea were not burning as they should. He put both down on the floor by the toilet, his appetite gone.

Desperate to kill time, he went back to the bench and thought he'd try to sleep. The noise, the smell and his own fear would make success unlikely but without anything to read, no one to talk to and none of his personal possessions to occupy him, he had to try to speed this nightmare up.

He was certain it had only been about ten minutes – twenty tops – when the door clanked and was thrown open. For the first time he saw there was more to 'Beard' than facial hair and nose, and he realised why he'd chosen a career where looks and charisma weren't essential criteria.

'Out you come. The officers need you.'

'Is my solicitor here?' It had been drummed into him not to talk to the detectives without legal representation.

Beard just shrugged and stepped to one side so Darren could pass in front of him. 'Didn't fancy dinner then,' he said as he looked at the untouched meal and tea.

As he walked down the corridor, the banging and cat-calling were deafening. He wasn't sure if it was him the others were sizing up but he hoped he'd never find out.

As 'Beard' unlocked the gates and grilles, the custody centre grew more spacious and he soon recognised the futuristic booking-in area. Much cleaner, much lighter and without the gagging smell.

He immediately saw Detective Sergeants Shiel and Jones standing stony-faced in front of a desk, behind which sat an equally impassive custody sergeant. Despite his dread he smiled, hoping to evoke one back. He didn't.

With no preamble, Shiel locked eyes with him and said, 'Mr Howe, we have presented the evidence regarding you to the Crown Prosecution Service and they have authorised you be charged with conspiracy to commit misconduct in a public office, so listen to what I have to say . . .'

189

Darren's head swam and he stumbled back. He was aware of Shiel spouting some legalese but he couldn't take it in. This had to be a mistake. He'd done absolutely nothing wrong. Where was his solicitor? Jones held onto him while Shiel finished. All he took in was 'Do you understand?'

'Well no. This can't be right.'

With no attempt to reply, the custody officer took over. Her sharp Irish accent made it hard for Darren to understand her but he got the gist of it. He was being held in custody to appear at court in the morning where the CPS would object to bail. Something about interfering with witnesses, absconding and committing other offences.

'But . . . but . . . Can I speak to my solicitor? My wife? There must be some mistake.'

'Later,' said the custody sergeant who then nodded at 'Beard'. 'Back to his cell please.'

He walked in a trance to the same racket he'd received on the way out. Only when his cell door slammed and he found himself slumped on the bench did he allow his world to collapse.

30

If there was one thing being the former head of the Major Crime Unit brought Jo, it was kudos. It had been a while since she had investigated a murder herself but she'd always made it her business to be across any that happened on her patch.

Her reputation and knowledge ensured she always received a warm welcome at murder briefings. DCI Claire Jackson had jumped at Jo's offer to be there today and, while Jo gave her customary assurances that she was there to listen, not to contribute, both knew that promise was unlikely to be kept. They did agree to a pre-meet though.

Squashed between the tiny circular table and the far wall, Jo waited for Claire to finish her phone call, using the time to scan the wallpaper of association charts, maps and photographs which plastered the office.

'Sorry, Jo,' said Claire as she put her phone down and took the chair opposite. Jo raised a hand which said *No need.*

'It's been frenetic on the phone work overnight. Lots to wade through but we're seeing some overlaps with a couple of the burner phones and the ANPR hits on one of our vehicles of interest.'

ANPR, or Automatic Number Plate Recognition to give it its full title, was a system of fixed and mobile cameras which recorded every registration number they captured. Through it the police could pick up on vehicles of interest, such as stolen cars or those believed to be used to carry guns. More crucially though, providing a driver triggered enough of the ANPR network, you could track their movements, discover who they might have been in convoy with and, like today, link cars to phones.

'Can you spill the beans?' asked Jo.

Claire gave her a wan smile. 'All in good time.'

'I trained you too well,' said Jo. 'So was it the right move to link all the jobs?'

'Yes, it seems that way. And don't you dare give me that "I told you so" look.'

'As if.' It had taken some battling with Claire's detective superintendent, but eventually they'd prevailed. Lizzie's and DC Pete McElroy's murders together with Luke's son being snatched and Bob being run over all had the irresistible denominator of Op Eradicate. Despite the accusations that she was blinkered, they couldn't ignore the common factors.

'Before we go into the briefing, there's something you need to know,' said Claire.

'OK.'

'It might just be a reaction, but there are rumbles from a lot of the officers that they'd rather work on another enquiry.' Jo was about to interrupt but Claire continued. 'Don't get me wrong. They're as keen to catch the bastards behind this as we all are but, well, they're scared.'

'I understand that. We're all feeling at risk.' Claire gave Jo a nod of understanding. 'But they're murder detectives and if they aren't going to get to the bottom of this, who is?'

'I know, I'm just saying. Ready to go?'

Jo stood and followed Claire into the briefing room, which had far more empty seats than she'd been expecting. As Claire took to the lectern, Jo peeled off and took a chair on the back row.

'Good afternoon everyone,' said Claire. 'Phones away and let's have your attention. We've a lot to get through and not much time.' She turned to one of the detective sergeants. 'Is everyone here?'

'Er, yes, this is it, ma'am. We've had quite a few gone sick.' Jo was about to erupt but caught Claire's cautionary glare, which was a hallmark of her legendary talents in managing upwards. This was her show, Jo reminded herself, so let her crack the whip.

'Let's chat afterwards,' she told the sergeant. 'I want to review the sickness.'

Jo could tell that was as much for everyone else's benefit as it was the DS's. Nevertheless, this further example of detectives voting with their feet did not bode well.

'Let's get started then. Any update from the firearms expert?'

'Yes, ma'am,' said the same DS. 'Their provisional findings are that the rounds came from a .308 rifle which the National Ballistic Intelligence Service have no record of coming to light before.'

'Do NABIS link with other countries?'

'That's their next step, ma'am. They believe the gun was fired from that small copse on the west side of Falmer Road. The car was travelling around fifty miles per hour when it was hit and was only on the straight stretch for about four seconds.'

'I've no idea how they work all that out, but it says to me that whoever pulled the trigger has done this sort of thing before,' said Claire. 'Well, update me when we have more. I take it there's no trace of the shooter in the copse.'

'None at all. No spent cartridges, no broken branches, nothing.'

Jo pondered that. She knew this was no amateur execution but did this mean they were looking at ex-Special Forces? That worried her more than she'd ever admit.

'Babu, can you update the meeting on what you told me earlier about the phones and ANPR?'

'Yes, ma'am,' said the senior intelligence analyst. 'From the phone work we did in and around the George IV swimming pool when Luke's boy was snatched, we've identified ten unregistered phones there or thereabouts. One of those was in the Seven Dials area – sorry I can't be more specific than that – when Mr Heaton was run over . . .'

'Not much of a burner phone then,' came a call from the front.

Babu continued. 'And the other was close to Bedford Square when Lizzie was killed.'

'That's two streets away from where it happened, isn't it?'

'Correct. And the interesting thing is that one moved quickly away shortly after the murder, as did a car that happened to be near Warninglid just before the lorry crash. Well, that's what ANPR says.'

They all knew that ANPR was excellent for picking up on registration numbers but couldn't differentiate a real car from a 'ringer' if someone was using false plates.

'Why were you researching Warninglid?' said that DS. He then turned to Claire. 'Is there something sus about the lorry crash?'

Babu chipped in. 'I wasn't especially but I ran everything through the software and that's what came up.'

Jo was itching to ask something, but held it back.

The rest of the briefing was as mundane as they all become, with those few present updating on their plans for the day and offering no more snippets. Jo was about to leave when the DS turned round.

'Mrs Howe, as you're here, is there anything you can say to reassure us about all these attacks on officers?'

Jo walked to the front of the room. 'I'm not going to insult your intelligence by saying there's nothing to worry about. We all need to be vigilant . . .'

'It's not just us though, is it? We can look after ourselves most of the time. It's our families. They didn't sign up for this, and whilst I love this job, if I have to choose, my husband and my kids come first.'

'I understand that. I've got young children too and I worry about them every second.'

'Especially with a villain for a husband,' a mumbled voice uttered.

'Who said that?' shouted Claire.

Jo put her hand on her shoulder. 'It's OK. Look, the sooner we catch who's behind this, the safer we'll all be. We can't give up and I thank you all for your courage in being here. We will stop this, but only with your efforts.'

The DS spoke up again. 'You've spotted that half of us aren't here and I'm sure those who say they're sick really are. All I'm saying is I'll do what it takes to protect my family.'

'You need to think very hard before making comments like that. You took an oath to do a job and that's what you're expected to do. I'll not have people picking and choosing.' As soon as the words had come out of her mouth, Jo regretted every syllable. She'd stood here to reassure, but now she was threatening them. 'That'll be all.'

She walked towards the door, nodding an apology to Claire. The last thing she heard before she was in the corridor was the same mumbling voice from before say, 'Corrupt bitch.'

Once sleep had overcome the boys, Jo began her telephone quest for Darren. Firstly, more in hope than expectation, she tried his mobile. When that went straight to voicemail, she rang around the Metropolitan custody centres. Each answered with the robotic 'We can neither confirm nor deny that. No one of that name has given us permission to reveal whether or not they are here.' It was like a bloody script.

Infuriating as these responses were, they were only doing their job if Darren had said he didn't want her told where he was. But why wouldn't he though?

Once she'd exhausted everywhere he was likely to be held, she toyed with trying surrounding forces or even going back through her Met list again once there had been a shift change.

She must have dozed off, as when she checked the clock above the fireplace it read 5 a.m. At least two hours before new staff would be on duty. She heaved herself off the settee and padded towards the kitchen when suddenly her phone burst into life. She ran back and hit 'accept', briefly registering the display. *Unknown Caller.*

'Jo Howe.'

'Mrs Howe, it's Croydon Custody Centre here,' came a Birmingham accent she'd heard a few hours ago.

'Didn't I speak to you earlier?'

'I don't know. I have your husband here. He'd like to speak to you but please be aware we are monitoring the call, so do not discuss the charges or arrange to bring him any illicit items into custody.'

'Charges? Are you fucking joking?' she replied. The caller didn't reply but the next voice was very familiar.

'Hello, darling.' *Was that a sob?*

'Babe, what's going on?'

'I tried to get them to tell you . . .'

'Fuckers. Sorry, it's just I've spent all night trying to find out what's happening.'

'They've charged me with Misbehaviour in a Public Office.'

'Misconduct. Misconduct in a Public Office and it must be conspiracy as you're not in a public office.'

'Yes, whatever. Anyway, I'm going to court this morning.'

'Court? Not bail?'

'No. They said I was a flight risk and I might interfere with witnesses or something.'

She heard the same Birmingham voice in the background say, 'Careful.'

'Tell him to fuck off,' said Jo. 'In fact, don't. Listen, what did your solicitor say when they charged you? Didn't he argue to get you bail?'

'He wasn't here. I did ask.'

'Jesus. Give me his name and which court you're appearing at.'

Darren spelt out the solicitor's name, then she heard him call out, 'Which court am I going to?'

She heard the reply yet Darren repeated it. 'Croydon Magistrates.'

'Listen, I'll be there,' she said before she had a chance to think it through.

'Are you allowed?' Darren said. She could hear the hope in his voice.

'Courts are open to the public. That means me. Look, stay strong and tell your solicitor I want to talk to him before the hearing. OK?'

'Sure. Jo, is this thing serious?'

Jo hesitated. 'Don't worry. Love you.'

'Love you,' Darren muttered just before she put the phone down.

What the hell should she do? How could this even have happened? She needed some thinking time, then to speak to the one person she could trust who'd experienced the side of the system Darren was now being plunged into.

Despite her intentions to first talk to Bob, Jo reflected and dialled Gary's number. No time was too early for her deputy but she gave it until 7 a.m.

She held nothing back and was grateful that he patiently took it all in before offering any suggestions. They'd come a long way since she pipped him for the divisional commander's job when Phil Cooke was removed. For the first few weeks Gary had been frosty, some might say obstinate. But now they were a formidable partnership, each flexing their different strengths as required so you couldn't get a slither of baking paper between them.

Once she'd finished, even though she'd already decided, she said, 'What should I do, Gary?'

He let the question hang, then came up trumps. 'Well, if it was me, I'd be at court the second it opened, find the solicitor and make sure he makes the mother of all bail applications.'

'That's what I hoped you'd say.'

'Oh and I'd take back-up. What's Bob up to today?'

'I've already checked. Nothing his chief superintendent can't cancel.'

'Jo, why have you even called me? You've already planned this haven't you?'

'Always worth checking my thinking.'

'I'll remember that. Listen, to save you the humiliation in asking, yes of course I'll take your commitments today and ask Fiona to move those I can't?'

'Oh, would you?'

'And book you a rest day in lieu so there can be no conflicts?'

'Thanks so much. I owe you big time.'

'Stick it on my tab.'

Jo surprised herself when a snigger escaped. 'You're such a star.'

'Good luck, Jo, and give him my best. I mean that.'

'Sure, bye.' She hung up, choked at his loyalty.

31

It had been the worst night Sir Ben could remember since his mum's dementia diagnosis. The episode two years ago when his neighbours had been so concerned about the screaming that they'd called the police was bad enough. Thankfully, one of the officers' fathers had been going through the same terrors so he understood. With everything that was happening, the last people he needed banging on the door and asking all sorts of awkward questions now was the Old Bill.

Previously he'd been able to calm her down. Not last night though. She'd grown more and more terrified, so much so that he couldn't get near her until six that morning. Given how short-tempered he was at the best of times, even he realised that it was not the greatest idea to call the doctor right now, but he couldn't carry on like this.

Dr Blaketon answered in two rings.

'Trevor, I need you round here pronto,' said Sir Ben, as soon as the call connected.

He heard a sigh, then, 'Ben, I've got a full clinic this morning. If it's urgent, dial 999.'

'Not good enough. I'm sure your NHS patients will understand. You've no idea the night she's had and I need you to prescribe her something.' As he paced the landing, he caught sight of the wreck he looked in the mirror.

'I've told you before, there really is nothing I can do. She has dementia and all we can do is manage the symptoms.'

'Then come and manage them or I might have to review the sponsorship we provide to your private practice.'

'Are you threatening me?'

'Not at all. I just want to make sure my investments realise a reasonable return.'

Just then an almighty scream jolted Sir Ben from his rant. 'Coming, Mum,' he called, then back to the doctor, 'Here in thirty minutes Trevor, or else.'

After about fifteen minutes of him settling her, she fell asleep. Sir Ben dashed off for a quick shower and change of clothes before Trevor arrived.

He'd only just pulled on his blue polo shirt when the gate buzzer sounded. Sir Ben checked the app on his phone and, without a greeting, pressed 'open' and watched the doctor drive in. He reached the door before Trevor and grunted a gruff 'Morning.' Trevor was equally curt but both knew where the balance of power lay.

'She's asleep now, so let's talk,' said Sir Ben, leading the way to the drawing room.

'I really am in a hurry. I wasn't joking when I said I had patients waiting.'

Sir Ben pretended he hadn't heard that and, with a flourish of the hand, invited Trevor to take a seat on the two-seater settee. He remained standing.

'Now listen. I don't want any of this "we can only manage the symptoms" nonsense. We've spoken before about the US treatment. All I need is for you to certify her physically able to travel, then we're off.'

Trevor paused, as if trying to find the words. 'There is no robust evidence that this so-called treatment is beneficial to anyone, let alone someone with such advanced dementia as your mum. It would be professional negligence of me to green-light her to fly. One, I don't think she'd survive the flight and two, the invasive procedure the treatment involves would be useless at best, but I'd suggest pointlessly cruel.'

Sir Ben walked behind Trevor's position on the settee, with the sole intention of putting him on edge. 'If you'd spent a night like I did last night you'd know how arrogant that comment is.' He paced back round so he was two feet in front of Trevor, forcing the doctor to crick his neck to make eye contact. 'I'm going to take her. All I need you to do is sign whatever it is you need to sign, and I'll sort the rest.'

He saw Trevor's eyes flit round the room. 'Can't you buy your way round that? I don't mean to sound impertinent, but surely with your wealth, you can. Yes, it's likely to be six figures by the time you've factored in return flights on a fully staffed critical care air ambulance, pre and post op care, the procedure itself and convalescence but, come on. You can afford a few extra quid to waive the need for my signature.'

It took every sinew Sir Ben had to stop himself from exploding.

'Now listen here, you little worm. My financial situation is nothing to do with you, so sign this off as being clinically necessary and leave the rest to me.'

'But . . .'

'No buts. The doctors across the pond are ready and waiting, so grow a pair and do your bit or start looking for another investor.'

By 8.00 a.m., Jo and Bob were on what was paradoxically labelled a semi-fast train to London, with Gatwick Airport being the only stop between Brighton and East Croydon. She'd hate to experience the slow option.

Once she'd spoken to Bob, he'd immediately jumped at the suggestion but with one alteration to her plan. After his last attempt to get to Croydon, they were not driving. She let him have that one concession, even though it did mean they were severely restrained in how much planning they could do among the crowded commuters. At least they got seats across the aisle from one another.

As the Sussex, then Surrey countryside passed the window, they kept the conversation light, keeping off any subject that would give away their jobs, let alone their mission. Once the Gatwick passengers had boarded, the carriage was so packed that every patch of floor space was taken. They could no longer see each other despite being about eighteen inches apart. Finally, the conductor announced the next stop was East Croydon, so they struggled to their feet and 'excuse me'd their way to the nearest door.

As soon as the train stopped they were off, battling through the opposing press of passengers who seemed to think the world would end if they didn't embark that very second. Bob had Googled the best route to the court and it seemed walking would be quickest and had the bonus of giving them some plotting time.

On the way, Bob reminded Jo that she'd be unlikely to meet Darren and that they should focus on getting the solicitor to deliver the most impassioned and reassuring speech of his life, so that the magistrates had no choice but to grant bail. There was no chance of getting the charges quashed at this point, but getting her husband out would be the first battle.

When they reached the white concrete utilitarian slab of a building with *Croydon Law Courts* carved in the stonework, a small crowd was milling around by the steps. Jo walked past them and pushed the door.

It was supposed to open at 9 a.m., but twenty minutes later it was still locked with just a security guard reading a paper on the other side of the smoked glass. Jo had had enough. It could have been the worry about Darren. It could have been lack of sleep. It could just be her utter hatred for jobsworths.

She curled her fist and banged on the glass so hard it jolted the man from his *Daily Mail*. 'Get your warrant card out,' she muttered to Bob as she thrust hers against the window. The guard folded his newspaper, put on his hat, slid his chair back and ambled to the door.

Instead of opening it, he pointed at a sign, taped drunkenly to the glass. Jo looked at it. *Court Closed Until 9.30 a.m. Smoke Alarm Testing.* Jo shook her head. She mouthed 'Open the fucking door.'

To her surprise, the guard complied. 'We're not open for another ten minutes.'

'I can see that.' She held her card out again and Bob did likewise. 'Chief Superintendent Howe and DI Heaton. We have an appointment.'

'Who with?'

Jo reached in her bag and pulled out her phone. 'Never mind, I'll call the district judge myself. While we're at it, what's your name?' She squinted at his name badge for effect.

'Er, look, it's OK. I'll let you in. I'm sorry but . . .'

'I know . . . Samuel. You had your orders. Thank you.' She and Bob rushed past him before he had second thoughts. As they walked across the atrium Jo checked behind and saw Samuel was back at his desk taking in the *Mail*'s latest outrage. She spotted a court listing, glanced down and saw Darren's name straight away. 'Court one, Bob. Let's go.'

Once they found the courtroom they were surprised to find it not only open but someone already in there, a pile of files stacked in front of them. As the frazzled young lady dressed in a charcoal-grey business suit was sitting furthest from the dock, she was likely to be the prosecutor. And by the look of her, she was in no mood to chat. Jo risked one question. 'Excuse me, do you know if the defence for Mr Howe is here yet?'

The woman huffed then looked up. 'Sorry, who are you?'

Bob stepped in. 'DI Heaton. We just need a word.'

'Oh, I'm sorry I've no idea who that might be. I'm agency counsel and, as ever, I've been dumped these remand hearings this morning. Do forgive me, I must get on.'

'Sure. His name's Mr Springer in case you need to know.'

The barrister looked up again. 'Thanks, I'll bear that in mind.' She immersed herself straight back into her files.

Jo and Bob took a seat in the public area at the back of the court and waited. It was a bit late to realise they had no idea what Darren's solicitor looked like and despite both frantically searching the web, they were still none the wiser when the three magistrates paraded in and court started.

It reminded Jo of her days as a detective constable when the court clerk – or legal advisor as they were now called – seemed to pick the running order from a tombola and, more often than not, her cases were last.

With each defendant called, a different defence solicitor rushed in, bowed to the bench, apologised and made a half-hearted attempt to get them bail. The overworked prosecution counsel gave no sign that she'd only picked these cases up an hour ago, such was her grasp of the facts and the quality of her advocacy.

As each decision went the prosecution's way, Jo felt a deeper and deeper dread. Granted, most of those who preceded Darren were drug-addicted recidivists for whom prison was probably just an occupational hazard, but at the moment it was CPS 9, Defence 0. What troubled her even further was that none of the defeated solicitors had introduced themselves as Mr Springer. Surely he wouldn't be a no-show?

Finally, the legal advisor called, 'Darren Howe,' before phoning down to the cells to repeat his name.

Five minutes later, the door at the back of the dock opened and in walked Darren, flanked by two heavily tattooed custody officers. He looked like she felt. Red-eyed, anxiety and terror plastered across his face and in clothes which gave the impression he'd worn them for a week. He glanced around the court and she gave him what she hoped he'd receive as a reassuring smile. He just nodded and looked forward.

Suddenly the back door to the court crashed open and in ran a wiry, middle-aged man in a crumpled green linen suit with a Bobby Charlton comb-over, a battered brown leather shoulder bag swinging behind him. He nodded his head in the most perfunctory of bows and said, 'I'm so sorry, Your Worships. I was delayed in another court. I'm Mr Springer for Mr Howes. If you'll give me a moment.'

The chair of the bench, a robust-looking woman with tightly pulled-back blonde hair, said, 'The court does not appreciate you being late and disorganised. Ms Morgan can open while you sort yourself out, then, if

204

you must, you can make any application you see fit.' She turned to the prosecutor. 'Ms Morgan.'

By contrast, the prosecutor was eloquent, respectful and to the point. She reminded the magistrates that this was a matter that could only be heard in the Crown Court, so she invited them to send the case there, then trotted through the facts.

Were Jo not so coached in courtroom etiquette, she would have called several points of order. Ms Morgan couldn't even name the officer who was supposed to have sold Darren the information regarding the raid, couldn't quantify how much he'd been paid, and as for the hamper? Really? If this was it, then any half-decent defence counsel would shred it on the first hearing.

Then Springer stood up and she was snapped back to reality.

'If it pleases Your Worships, I would like to make a bail application on behalf of Mr Howes.'

'I think your client is called Mr Howe,' said the bench chair.

'Yes, quite. Mr Howe. As I was saying, my client has no previous convictions and, until recently, had a steady job. He's a family man with a permanent address where he lives with his police officer wife who, I might add, is a chief inspector in Sussex Police.'

'Chief superintendent,' whispered Ms Morgan to his right.

'Yes, that's correct. In any case, my client is prepared to surrender his passport, observe a curfew, wear a tag and report to the local police station. You do not need to remand him in custody as there is no risk of reoffending or interfering with witnesses.'

Jo waited for him to continue, but he sat down. *Was that it?*

Ms Morgan stood up. 'Your Worships, contrary to what Mr Springer says, Mr Howe presents a substantial risk of committing further offences and interfering with witnesses. His wife is, as the court have heard, a chief *superintendent* of police, who is suspected of leaking information to him and has ingratiated herself into court today.' She glanced round.

How the hell did she work that out? Bob put his hand on her arm, presumably sensing she was about to do or say something that would Exocet her career.

'Insofar as interfering with witnesses, for now only Mr Howe knows who those witnesses are so it's impossible for the police to ensure he would be complying with any condition you may impose. I agree, in normal circumstances he would be unlikely to abscond, but given the seriousness of the charge and its likely sentence should he be found guilty, a man of his means could be driven to desperate measures.'

'Could isn't good enough, Ms Morgan.'

'Of course, Your Worships. That said, the Crown object to bail given the substantial risk of Mr Howe reoffending and interfering with witnesses.'

She sat down, glancing again at Jo, giving a combative wink.

The magistrates did not even retire, they just whispered between themselves.

'Stand up, Mr Howe. We are refusing bail in this matter for the reasons given by the Crown. We will send this case to the Central Criminal Court and you will be remanded in custody. Take him down.'

As he sombrely turned back to the door, Jo couldn't help herself. 'We'll get you out. This is a stitch-up,' she shouted. Before the chair of the magistrates could rebuke her, Bob bundled her out into the corridor and away.

The words 'remanded in custody' tripped over and over in Darren's mind as he sat head in hands on the tiny bench in the court holding cell. He wondered whether he'd ever get used to the yelling and banging that rang out down here. Would it be quieter in prison?

How could they be sending him there though? Other than some debatable naivety in accepting a Christmas hamper, he'd done nothing wrong. At best this was a massive mistake, at most – and more likely – it was a monumental stitch-up.

When that useless solicitor Springer popped down to see him after the damage was done, the only good piece of advice he had was to stay silent about who he was married to. In the eyes of most prisoners, being married to a cop was only one step removed from actually being one.

The rattle of keys in the lock nearly caused his bowels to empty.

'We're off,' came the command that courted no debate. Darren walked to the cell door and instinctively offered his hands out for cuffing. Once the guard checked them for comfort, he locked a linked set to his own wrist. 'This way,' he said, like Darren had any choice.

The breeze on his face during the few steps between the back door and the white van was possibly the last Darren would feel for the foreseeable future, so he sucked it in. After two breaths he was climbing into what he had been told was 'the sweat box'.

The narrow corridor between the line of cellular pods was barely wide enough to walk down, especially with the security officer by his side. In a second, he was ushered into a tiny cubicle. The cuffs were removed and he sat on the moulded seat, a minute window to his right being the only feature. As the door was closed and locked, Darren lapped up the silence.

Seconds later that was broken by shouts. 'I'll rip your fucking throat out you filthy screw.'

'Bring your mates,' replied the guard, which just fuelled the idiot's imagination as to what other atrocities he'd perform when he got out of there.

After a few less agitated travel-mates were locked up, the van drove off with the angry man still bellowing tirades to not only the staff but his unseen fellow prisoners too.

Darren had no idea how long the journey would take. In one way he'd like it to be long enough to bawl his eyes out and recover so no one spotted his weakness when it was time to de-bus. On the other hand, that near-accident he'd had when the guard had opened his cell door was not just down to fear. He was desperate for a poo.

Somewhere between an hour and a half and two hours later, the van seemed to have arrived. Through his needle-eye window, Darren couldn't work out where they were but the stopping and starting suggested they were waiting for endless gates and doors to open, presumably following reruns of the same security checks at each. The gobshite in the back hadn't let up throughout the whole journey but Darren had all but switched off from him.

When the van finally drew to a stop, Darren readied himself to be taken off. If he'd been frightened before, he was terrified now. He'd watched *The Shawshank Redemption* and that Sean Bean drama and hoped to God they were outlandish exaggerations of prison life. He'd always walked away from trouble, but he knew well enough that to show weakness here would be a death sentence.

It seemed to take another hour before he was finally unlocked.

'This way,' said the same guard who'd locked him in. He escorted Darren out and to a door marked *Reception*. Reception? He bet he'd be offered no complimentary cocktails and cold towels here. The door heaved open and Darren found himself stood in front of a gentle-looking, fiftyish, grey-haired woman sporting a white shirt, black epaulettes and matching trousers. The radio and flashing body camera clipped to the shirt-hoops reminded him of the police officer who'd investigated his burglary a couple of years ago.

'In here, sir,' she said, ushering him into yet another holding cell.

'Can I use the toilet?'

'In a bit. Let's get you booked in first.'

'But . . .'

'It won't take long,' she repeated, with a hint of a genuine smile.

It dawned on Darren that this was just a small taste of how every decision, every dignity, would be for others to bestow from now on.

Thankfully, he was only in the stifling cell for about fifteen minutes when he was called forward. In that time he'd resolved that compliance and keeping his head down was the key to survival. So, when the prison officer who'd replaced the kindly lady insisted on strip-searching him, making him crouch so he could peer at his anus, then sit on something called a BOSS in case he had the latest iPhone shoved up him, he just went with it.

The questions kept coming and coming. Was he depressed? *What do you think?* Did he use drugs? *Not yet.* Had he ever self-harmed? *See above.* Those were what he wanted to reply but instead he played a straight bat in the hope he'd be deemed a model prisoner and looked after.

Before long he had hooked his ID badge on and was carrying his bed pack and meagre provisions, following yet another prison officer.

Desperate for conversation, he asked, 'Where are we going?'

'First-night centre is full so you're going straight on the wing, I'm afraid.' Darren had no idea what a first-night centre was but the wing did not sound like a good thing. He presumed he was being hurled straight into the fire.

As they marched around countless corridors and up and down steel staircases, the eerie sound of invisible men shouting, crying and screaming from behind cell doors made Darren want to throw himself off the landing. As they walked along what he worked out was the fourth floor, he sensed the eyes at the spyholes and made out the kissing noises. 'Will I get a cell to myself?' The officer just laughed.

If he'd been hungry he might have asked for food, but he guessed the answer to that would be the same.

Finally, they stopped outside one of the graffitied green doors. The officer looked in, turned the key and opened up. 'In you go.'

Darren stepped inside and almost tripped over the shirtless man pumping out press-ups. 'Sorry,' he said as he stepped round him. The man didn't miss a beat as the door slammed shut.

He sat on the bottom bunk and the man, without looking, said, 'Top.' Darren looked up and saw the bread-slice-thin mattress on the steel frame and chided himself for being so stupid. He put his pack on the bed when suddenly the man stopped and sprung up, offering a fist pump. 'Ivan. No English.' Darren wasn't going to leave him hanging and as soon as the pleasantries were over, Ivan was on his bunk snoring.

He noticed the toilet surrounded by an opaque shower curtain in the corner, then looked round at Ivan. All of a sudden his bowels clamped shut. Call it stage fright, or just fright, he didn't know, but he could never imagine shitting with an audience.

He climbed on his bunk and wrapped himself in the cheese-grating grey blanket. He guessed from the light straining through the A4-size barred window that it was about 8 p.m., but who knew? Did it matter? He would not be able to sleep. He looked at the paint peeling off the ceiling which was only a handful of inches away from his nose. The pale cream walls were pitted with what looked like blobs of toothpaste.

The noise from other cells was unremitting and he wondered how Ivan could sleep so soundly. Maybe he would one day.

He closed his eyes. His mind goaded him with images of Jo lying in their huge empty bed, sobbing at the void his stupidity had created and the future he'd cremated.

Then the boys came into view. He'd drummed into them for as long as he could remember that only bad people went to prison. How would he disavow them of that ridiculous distinction? What would happen to bedtimes? Their nightly story ritual? Baths and teeth-brushing? God, he needed to feel their sloth-like arms hanging round his neck as they battered him with kisses.

Oh to be called Daddy, darling, Darren, sweetheart. Oh to rewind the clock. Once the tears started there was no stopping them and he'd lost any will to try. He didn't care if Ivan heard him. His world was over, so nothing mattered.

Suddenly a shout, echoing from the landing, froze him. 'Fed fucker, we're coming for you.'

32

As Spanners grabbed the begging pitch outside Tesco Express on Queens Road, he wondered whether Scotty would protect him if what he was doing went tits up. When he was in prison he'd heard talk of registered informants, handlers, controllers, text letters and a whole language which suggested there was more to being a grass than a nod from a police sergeant by the pier.

One thing he did know was that if he was outed as a police informer, his life on the streets, or anywhere else for that matter, would be over. He took his plastic beaker and the scrap of cardboard on which he'd scrawled *Hungry and Homeless* from under his coat. He placed them in front of him and adopted the doleful look so many others used to inject enough guilt in the occasional passer-by for them to throw some loose change. Nowadays, people were so worried that beggars just spent their money on drugs that they gave meal-deals instead. He often felt like shouting that he had dietary requirements but never quite found the courage.

As he settled, he became invisible. The commuters and day trippers power walking from the station seemed to accelerate as they approached so his destitution wouldn't rub off. Some lied that they were 'sorry' or 'had 'no change' but most just pretended he wasn't there.

This was one of the prime sites though, given the footfall and it being right by a cash machine. It was rare that a newcomer like him would be allowed anywhere near this square foot of pavement. In all communities there are hierarchies and he knew he'd soon be booted off by one of the bigger guns. But that was why he was here; to provoke.

It didn't take long.

'Eh bruv, what the fuck you doing here?' came the voice from somewhere behind the beard. Spanners looked up and squinted into the sun. He'd certainly seen this walking scarecrow before but couldn't place him.

'What's it look like? I'm grafting innit.' Spanners looked back down at his feet, feigning disinterest.

'Not fucking here you're not,' said the scarecrow. 'Get your stuff and piss off somewhere else.' Now he was crouching down, his compost breath suffocating Spanners, who sprung to his feet.

'Really? I didn't see your beach towel.'

At that the scarecrow's right hand punched out and grabbed Spanners' throat, thrusting him back to the cashpoint, scattering the queue. All but the woman who was mid-transaction scurried away. She followed a moment later once she'd snatched her cash.

By now the two homeless men were grappling, Spanners clawing at the man's choking hand while trying to aim knees at his most delicate parts. He made contact.

'What the fuck's that all about, you wanker,' shouted Spanners as the scarecrow writhed on the ground.

He groaned, then staggered to his feet. 'You got to show some respect, bruv.' People were now walking past even faster, trying not to stare.

'Respect? I ain't respecting no one who kicks off like that, man.' Spanners turned away.

'Not me, bruv, "Manc Mick". You can't just jump in his grave like that. That's low man, real low.'

'You talking about? Who the fuck is "Manc Mick"?'

For a second, Spanners thought the scarecrow was going to attack him again so he tensed, but then tears bubbled in the man's eyes. 'Hey man, you OK?'

'Mick? He was a legend. This was his pitch. You can't just take it before he's even cold.'

The scarecrow's transition from raging bull to weeping lamb was bewildering. Whoever this Mick was, he was special to this rag of a man. Spanners chanced it and put his arm round him. 'Tell me about him.'

'He looked after me, bruv. Like proper had my back. In jail and out. Shit, I'm going to miss him.'

Spanners looked around. They were attracting stares and whatever this man was going through, it was not a spectator sport. 'Come with me.'

They walked in silence down the hill, just twenty yards or so to the junction with North Road, and waited for the pedestrian lights to turn green. Ahead of them was a neon sign slapped against the wall of Community Base, an office building for charities and small businesses. The sign flicked from why you absolutely could not live without the new BMW in your life to warnings not to give money to beggars.

They crossed, took the path to the right of the yellow-brick Brighthelm Community Centre and found a vacant bench in the public garden behind it.

'Tell me about Mick,' said Spanners as soon as they'd sat down.

'Top bloke. Top bloke,' said the scarecrow between his tears.

'What happened?'

'Killed in a lorry crash.'

'A lorry crash?' Spanners was sure he'd have heard if one of the homeless community had been killed by a lorry.

'Yeah, he flipped it and that was him, bruv.'

Spanners tried to process this. 'Why was he driving a lorry?'

'The gaffers. They told him to. I was with him when they came up. Just where you were man. They told me to fuck off, but I was slow to go and heard them say something about a driving job and that he had to go now.

213

He used to be a lorry driver, see. Got nicked for importing cigs.'

'And?'

The scarecrow shrugged. 'All I heard was that he was driving to London or Essex or some other shit place and he turned it over. I can't see how. He was legendary behind the wheel.'

This was making no sense. 'Where did it happen?'

The scarecrow delved into his jacket pocket and pulled out a square of newspaper. Spanners half expected it to be piss- or cider-stained but it looked almost pristine. He carefully unfolded the front page of the *Argus* from a few days ago. It showed an aerial shot of an articulated lorry tipped over on its left side, with firefighters clambering over the cab. In either direction there were queues as far as the eye could see.

'ONE DEAD IN HORROR CRASH' read the headline. Spanners scanned the article for more details. 'They don't name anyone here. This could be anyone.'

'It's Mick, I'm telling you. It's what happens. We take the bung at the gate, wait to get the tug, then.' He drew his finger across his throat.

All Spanners could think to do was to let Scotty know before the next 'Manc Mick' was sacrificed.

'Will you put your bloody phone down,' said Sir Ben as Nicola Merrion looked at the caller ID for the umpteenth time.

They'd chosen to meet at a health club between Brighton and Crawley, one where Nicola was a member and where they could be assured relative privacy without arousing suspicion.

'It's easy for you to say but I've got my staff, the police and even the NHS commissioners on my back, not to mention the patients laying siege to my treatment centre.'

Tony leant across the table and snatched the phone from her. He switched it off then handed it back. 'Problem solved.'

Nicola flounced back in her chair. 'I'm going to have to tell them something.'

Sir Ben took a sip of coffee and waited for a couple of women who seemed lost in their own conversation to pass by. He leant in.

'It's not just you. I've stopped Synthopate deliveries to every other pharmacy in the city too. It's a massive risk for me and the trial but if we can keep calm and ride it out, the long term benefits will be astronomical.'

'But pharmacies sell other stuff. If we can't get Synthopate or are allowed to go back to methadone, our whole business model implodes. If we can't meet people's needs the powers that be will find someone who can.' Nicola looked to Tony as if for back-up but he just stared back.

'First of all, going back to methadone will invalidate the trial,' said Sir Ben. 'Secondly, let me give you a quick masterclass in economics. Respite Pharmaceuticals develop, manufacture and provide medicines to a population who, often through their lifestyles, have become dependent on them.'

'That's a bit harsh,' said Nicola.

Sir Ben raised a hand. 'People need our products, ideally for life. What becomes problematic is when the medicines cure rather than just maintain. Then the investment goes down the pan and with it, our profits.'

'But isn't that the business we're in? Curing people.'

'No. New diseases and conditions come along for sure, but the cost of developing drugs is astronomical. So, here we are since the 1960s in a perpetual heroin pandemic where police tactics had been all about quashing supply yet not touching demand. Drug dealers come and go, always to be replaced by someone else who sees the colossal amounts of money to be made in pushing what the state has deemed illegal.'

'Yeah, but . . .'

Sir Ben continued. 'Then along comes little Mrs Howe and starts sucking the demand out of the market. With you as an ally, I might add. And it's working. Your own figures tell the story. A seventy per cent recovery rate in two years with a marked reduction in users lapsing in the first six months compared to two years ago. In essence, she – and you – are curing people too quickly. That's affecting demand for Synthopate, which, in case I need to remind you, is still unproven and costing me a fortune.'

'But we've still got two hundred clients going through treatment.'

'Yes but this time next year it will be one hundred and fifty, then the year after, it'll be double figures. There just aren't the users coming through to make us profitable.'

'So why have you stopped supply? Surely that's affecting your bottom line.'

'Temporarily, yes, but not only have we stopped anyone getting their scripts, we're flooding the streets with a new strain of smack.' Nicola's face blanched. 'Close your mouth,' said Sir Ben. 'All those users banging on your door need something to get them through the day. Well, now they'll get it.'

'What?'

'And, because it's a new strain, there may be some casualties, isn't that right, Tony?'

'Guaranteed, I'm afraid. Still, all in a good cause.'

'Quite. Before long, heroin addict numbers will be back up to the numbers we were seeing a few years ago, because no one can get the healthier alternative. Tony will be able to ask whatever he wants for a fix and then you come in, our very own knight in shining armour doling out my new drug.'

'How?'

'Suddenly the supply chain opens again and people can start cashing in their Synthopate scripts. Those who want to get back on track, can. Meanwhile, we've built some longevity into the market and everybody's happy.'

'When?'

Tony cut in. 'We're putting enough gear out there to keep people going for about ten days then, to all intents and purposes, the supply disappears. My guys put the prices up, the quality plummets and, with your people back out there coaxing people back into treatment, the smackheads see an alternative.'

'But some of these people have made such good progress.'

'Yes, too good,' said Sir Ben. 'So we need them back to square one. You and that copper have just been too successful. You're treating yourself – and me – out of business, so all we're doing is a factory reset and soon the good times will return.'

'You sure?'

'Look, if you want out then that's fine. Obviously that nice little supplement you get each month will stop. Oh, and maybe that Howe woman might hear you're playing for both sides, if she's not worked it out already.'

Nicola was about to argue back when it was Tony's turn to lean in. 'Is all that clear?'

'Are you threatening me?'

'Not threatening. Promising.'

33

Spanners had always known it was only a matter of time before his sleeper role was rescinded.

He'd often thought of fleeing the city before he felt the tap on the shoulder, but he'd heard that for those who'd tried, retribution was drawn out and savage. Spanners had no choice but to wait until the police could act, but he wasn't confident they would.

Having left the scarecrow to the Tesco's begging spot, he walked to a new pitch on the London Road. Mid-afternoon, a Brighthelm Taxis car pulled up alongside him, making him jump. He quickened his pace but once the driver did likewise, he knew escape was futile. As soon as the rear passenger door was flung open, he got in the cab to hear the inevitable.

The man sitting behind the driver seemed affable enough but, even in the half-light, Spanners saw granite in his eyes. He spelt out the mission with startling brevity and it seemed surprisingly simple at first glance, but Spanners knew to look deeper. After all, it was unfathomable that all he had to do was deliver fast food.

A few hours later, sporting a motorcycle jacket and with a thermal top box liveried with *Brightnosh Deliveries*, he waited on his moped outside

McDonald's among half a dozen identically dressed riders, ostensibly waiting for his next job to come through. The truth was, he already knew each of the six pickups and where to deliver. The man in the cab had made it abundantly clear what would happen if he forgot the tiniest of details.

He browsed the phone he'd been given – the one he'd been told not to make any calls or send any messages on – and waited for the first appointed time. Bang on 7.30 p.m. he fired the moped into life, riding as fast as he could to Leaning Tower Spaghetti House on Lewes Road. It dawned on him how many fast-food delivery bikes there were buzzing around the city. What an inspired way to distribute whatever you liked.

He found the tatty takeaway quicker than he'd anticipated, hoicked his bike onto its stand and, keeping his crash helmet on, ambled into the deserted shop. The spotty youth behind the counter was clearly expecting him as, with a quick exchange of the coded confirmation question and answer, he handed Spanners the bag, which was much heavier than it looked, then disappeared out the back with no further words.

Spanners walked as quickly as he could out of the shop and slotted the package in his top box, fastened the clip, mounted the bike and headed off to Stephens Road, not five minutes away. He tried not to think too much about what might happen once he'd made his last delivery. He had thought of telling Scotty what he was up to but was sure he'd stop him. However good it looked in the movies, police protection only delayed the unavoidable.

Scanning the numbers on each of the red-brick blocks, he found the address he was after, grateful it was a ground-floor flat. He unlocked his top box, removed the sleeve and walked up the path to the communal entrance. He was about to heave it open with his shoulder when he spotted the intercom on the wall.

Shit.

He'd hoped to be in and out as quickly and as anonymously as possible, but this was an added hurdle. Still, what could he do? Balancing the weighty bag on his knee, he prodded the button, hoping for no reply. Although the chances of that happening on all six deliveries were microscopic.

A flash of light caught his right eye. He turned and saw a curtain falling back into place. Then the speaker on the wall box crackled.

'Yeah?'

'Brightnosh. I've got your delivery.' The only reply he received was the door clicking and buzzing. 'I'll come in then,' he mumbled.

He'd already worked out from the twitching curtain which was his customer's flat, so it was no surprise when that door opened. Spanners didn't know who to expect but was still shocked to see a bespectacled grey-haired man in his fifties, sporting brown flannel trousers, a cream open-necked shirt and a puce thick-knit cardigan, waiting.

He instantly recognised him.

Spanners took the package out of the thermal bag, the aroma of Italian cuisine noticeably absent. Despite the charade, wouldn't any self-respecting cop pick up on that, were they to carry out even the most rudimentary of searches?

He handed the package over and, despite himself, couldn't resist quipping, 'Bet you've missed these where you've been.'

The man just glared at him and slammed the door. Spanners sniggered, then turned and headed back to his bike. He rode away, meandering through Hollingdean, then pulled over. He took out the phone and despite his instructions, Googled 'Brighton Drugs Trial Defendants'. Instantly a page of hits rolled out, most of them leading on how absent police witnesses were cited as the reason for the administrative acquittal of six charged with conspiracy to import and supply controlled drugs. He selected the 'Images' tab and there his last customer was, in a three-by-two gallery of the now technically innocent kingpins. It said his name was Nicklas West, aged 59. He would bet any money that he'd be bumping into the other five before the evening was out.

True to his prediction, the other deliveries were in a similar vein. Each collection from a mute, but very prepared, underling at a different fast-food shop, and the customers were equally reluctant to chat. Only two of the other lucky drug dealers answered the door – the others were taken in by women or, in one case, a boy who couldn't have been older than ten.

As he mounted his moped to leave the last address, his phone rang. It was no surprise that it was a withheld number but, despite his usual habit of ignoring them, Spanners answered. 'Hello?'

'Finished?'

'Unless you're going to tell me otherwise, yes.'

'Right, take the bike down to Shoreham Harbour. There's a deep wharf at the back of the pub. Get rid of it and the phone in there.'

'Is that it then?'

'For now. We'll be in touch.'

The phone went dead and Spanners stared at it for a moment. He revved up the tinny machine and headed for where he'd been told. Now he'd completed the task he promised himself that if this was his last twenty-four hours on earth, he'd make it count.

He found the quay the caller had directed him to, then dialled a number he'd found easy to remember. In two rings it was answered.

'Scotty, it's me. I've got something to tell you. Quite a lot actually.'

He outlined to the sergeant what he'd been up to, then listened very carefully what he was to do next. When Scotty hung up, Spanners secreted the bike and the phone behind a row of bins, then waited in the shadows. It wasn't long before headlights washed the deserted dock road. Spanners instinctively stepped back further into the dark, watching as the car eased to a stop five yards away.

Only when he was sure did he run up and throw himself on the back seat, the car squealing off before he'd had time to close the door.

34

If there was one thing that made otherwise passive drug users rage, it was when they didn't know where their next fix was coming from. And if there was one thing Scotty could sense the second he ventured out, it was when there was a shortage. From what Spanners had told him last night, he was expecting the opposite, even though, as Bob Heaton told him in no uncertain terms, six dubious fast-food deliveries were not grounds for any magistrate to issue search warrants. His gut feeling told him the city was about to be flooded with heroin, so why was everyone clucking?

He grabbed Saira and they drove up to Lifechoices HQ to see if there was anything they knew that might explain the phenomenon. As they turned the corner, Saira slammed on the brakes. 'Christ, Sarge. Where's this lot come from?' The entrance looked like Wembley Stadium on Cup Final day, minus the revelry. Crowds of men and women of all ages, each wearing their pain across their face, jostled to get to the front of what was far from an orderly queue.

'Park up here. We'll kill someone if we try to drive through.' They both alighted from the car and Saira locked the doors.

'Excuse me,' said Scotty as he forced his gym-toned frame through.

'Come on, out the way.' Saira followed up close behind, offering the apologies Scotty forgot.

As he neared the door, Scotty accidentally on purpose stood on a few feet to encourage them to give way.

'What the hell's happening?' he asked Trish Kenyon, one of those they'd been speaking to when Lizzie was murdered.

'They ain't got no Synthopate and they ain't doing methadone no more. There's none here nor at the chemist. I'm clucking man but can't get my script.'

'Is that the same for everyone?' said Saira.

Trish looked around. 'Reckon.'

'Come on,' said Scotty, 'let's find out what's occurring.'

They muscled their way the final few yards to the door and nodded at the two security guys blocking it. Scotty made a beeline for Ayo, on reception. She wore her fear bravely but the tear-streaks gave her away. Saira dodged past Scotty and gave the woman a hug.

'It's OK,' she whispered. 'Just tell us what's happening.'

They waited while she composed herself, then between sniffs said, 'It's been getting bad all week. Something to do with the supply chain, but we can't get any Synthopate. The pharmacies are the same. There's none in the city.' She pointed out to the crowd. 'This lot. They're all doing well, or were. If we don't get supplies soon they're going to look for alternatives and all our work will be for nothing.'

'Where's Nicola Merrion?' said Scotty.

'I dunno. I tried to call her but she's not picking up.'

Scotty took out his phone and found the number he was after. As expected, the Lifechoices CEO didn't take her call either. 'Jesus. Ayo, would you like us to get some bodies up here to clear this lot? They're not going to get what they want just by hanging around.'

'I know,' she said, 'but at least we know where they are. I'd rather them here hoping to get their meds than trawling the streets looking for whatever muck is out there today.'

'You and me both, but I'll not have you intimidated. Is there any indication when you might get some more stock?'

'No. I've been on to Respite Pharmaceuticals and they were about as much use as a waterproof sponge.'

'It must be in their interests to speed things along,' said Saira. 'It can't be good for business or the trial.'

Scotty turned to his colleague. 'All the while this trial is going on, they've got the monopoly on heroin substitutes here. If they can't supply for a few days, where's the alternative?'

Just then a commotion rumbled outside. Scotty ran the short distance to the door and saw pockets of users gathered around each other's phones, their angst swept away by excitement.

'What's going on?' he asked one of the security guards.

'I dunno.'

Scotty pushed his way out and found Trish. 'What's happening?'

'Wouldn't you like to know?'

'Yes, if it's police business.'

'I ain't no grass so fuck you, Scotty.'

He was about to grab her and give her a piece of his mind when a shout from the back went up. 'Let's go.'

The crowd turned and rushed back through the very gates they had been choking up moments before.

Trish was about to run when Scotty grasped her T-shirt. 'Tell me what the fuck's going on,' he said as she writhed in his grip.

'That's assault. I'll fucking have you.' By now Saira was by his side. She forced her way between the two, breaking Scotty's hold but replacing it with a judo collar-grip.

'Trish, just tell us where everyone's going and we'll let you go.'

Now Trish was looking desperate as the crowd had all but dispersed. 'Get off. I've gotta score before it's all gone.'

Scotty and Saira glanced at each other, then he looked back at Trish. 'Don't do this. You're making progress, don't mess it up.'

'What choice have I got? It's like the Lord's given at the same time he's taken away. I need myself a slice of whatever this new batch is.'

With that, Saira released her and Trish was sprinting to catch the others heading for the city centre.

For the third shift running, PC Wendy Relf had begged her sergeant for a couple of hours to write up the more urgent investigations he'd piled on her over the last couple of weeks. There were only six other officers on duty for this three to midnight shift and they were already deployed, but her sergeant had been true to his word. She'd never say the Q word, but things were looking promising as she sat down, opened her work tracker on the computer and browsed those with red flags to see which of the hopelessly overdue ones might be job-threatening if she left them any longer.

She clicked on a stalking case involving a particularly vulnerable victim. Her heart sank when she scanned down all the tasks she'd yet to complete. 'God, we are so good at being shit,' she muttered to herself. She was about to call the victim when her radio interrupted her.

'Charlie Romeo Zero Two.'

She paused in case she'd misheard. She was, after all, marked on the dispatch system as unavailable.

'Charlie Romeo Zero Two,' the controller repeated.

Reluctantly she reached to her left shoulder and pressed transmit.

'Go ahead, over.'

'Charlie Romeo Zero Two, are you available for a suspected drugs death in New Steine Mews?'

'Charlie Romeo Zero Two to Oscar. I am shown "on reports". Can someone else go?'

'Negative Charlie Romeo Zero Two, I'm afraid. Everyone else is tied up. I'll try to keep you free once you've finished but, in the meantime, the details are on the CAD.'

Wendy looked up from her screen over towards the sergeants' desks for some support, but they were empty.

'For God's sake,' she mumbled, then pressed transmit again. 'Roger, Charlie Romeo Zero Two, assign me. Making from John Street.'

The only positive from this deployment was that New Steine Mews was just a couple of minutes away so, with a fair wind, Wendy could get there and deal with it within an hour or so. But in all the time she'd been in the job, the winds had almost always been inclement.

Five minutes later, she was reversing into a 'Loading Only' bay half a dozen houses from the squat she'd been assigned to.

Without the luxury of a partner, she'd not only have to secure and preserve any evidence of drugs supply but render first aid, deal with grieving and irate friends, and give at least a nod to tracing any witnesses all on her own.

As she approached, she pressed record on her body-worn video, then pushed open the already splintered door. As expected, the stench of weed, sweat and stale cider hit her. She'd been to enough drugs deaths in her time to know that when she eventually found the room where the body was, it would be rancid – but no son or daughter deserved to end their days in such a wretched way. She remembered Chief Superintendent Jo Howe confiding in her how her own sister had died in a drugs den and the guilt she felt that even she couldn't save her.

Once she'd waded through the river of flyers where a doormat should be, Wendy spotted a callow man, hunched up on the stairs, his hands clamping his head to his knees. 'Oi, mate. I've been called to an OD. Do you know where it is?' At once he sprung up, turned and ran up the stairs out of sight. Her instinct was to chase after him, but she needed to focus so she could get back to her stalking victim.

Having checked the downstairs rooms of this once-elegant Regency townhouse, she risked the stairs that the scaredy-cat had taken two at a time. As she reached the first landing, she sensed movement in the room to her right. 'Hello, it's the police,' she called out. 'You called us?'

She inched the door open and saw two young women, both dressed in stained T-shirts and leggings, crouched over a vaguely familiar third on a threadbare mattress by the window. She'd struggle to age any of them but as drug users generally looked much older than they were, she'd bet next month's rent on none of these being much over twenty.

She rushed forward and knelt, shouldering one of the others aside while she snapped on her nitrile gloves. The trail of vomit running from the side of the victim's mouth, across her bra strap and to the floorboard did not bode well. Nor did the alabaster skin – although that might be normal – or her icy touch. She wiped the muck from her face with a grimy towel which looked like it was culturing something radioactive. While frantically searching for a pulse, Wendy said, 'How long has she been like this?'

'Dunno,' the two girls said in unison.

'Well who found her?'

'Dunno.'

Unable to detect any sign of life, Wendy spotted a mirror nestled among a pile of used needles and scorched foil on a small unit by the single bed. 'Get me that.'

'What and put my prints all over it . . .'

'Fuck your prints, just pass it to me.' The girl nearest tried to pinch it by the edges but kept dropping it. 'Get out of the way,' said Wendy and grabbed it herself. She held the mirror in front of the woman's nose and mouth, praying against the odds that it would steam up, even just a little.

It didn't.

She could try CPR but years of experience told her that all that would achieve would be to break bones and knacker her. The woman was dead, there was no getting away from the fact. She reached for her radio. 'Charlie Romeo Zero Two.'

'Charlie Romeo Zero Two, go ahead.'

'To confirm, re the job I'm at, this is a G5. Can we have CID, coroners' officers and undertakers to the scene, please?' Using the code G5 for a sudden death avoided blurting out the obvious to loved ones, or in this case, those who had the misfortune to end up at the same rock bottom.

'Roger.' After a couple of minutes, the controller was back. 'Sorry Zero Two, I've just checked, there are no coroners' officers available. They are deployed at the others.'

'Others?'

'Yes, unfortunately this is the fourth drugs death today.'

'What about CID?'

'Same problem I'm afraid, although it seems DI Heaton is attending them all on his own. He's asking you to gather the evidence and take photos. Package it all up and return it to him. For the same reason, we've got a three-hour wait for undertakers. Apologies for that.'

Wendy rested back on her haunches and sighed. She knew that three hours would become four and any hope of updating her stalking victim evaporated. As she looked up, she realised she was on her own.

'Oi. Come back,' she shouted, more in hope than expectation. The two women must have slipped out when she was updating comms. Any hope of finding out how the girl had died had left the room with them. If only she was double crewed, then her partner could stay with the body while she chased them down. But single crewing was the price of austerity.

Wendy looked at the woman, then she remembered.

'Charlie Romeo Zero Two,' she said.

'Zero Two, go ahead.'

'For the log, I've dealt with this G5 victim before. Her name's Trish Kenyon.'

It was when the fourth overdose came in that Bob realised an unstoppable flow was hitting the city. He'd called Scotty and told him to meet him in Gary Hedges' office in ten minutes, wishing that Jo could be there too. She had other priorities though, trying to reconfigure her family's lives in the wake of Darren now cowering on remand.

'Thanks for seeing us so soon boss,' said Bob, shutting the door then taking Jo's chair.

'No worries. It's me who should be thanking you for picking up on this so quickly. Where's Scotty?'

'He'll be here in a mo. I just need to update you on something before he arrives. Last night he called me saying that this unofficial snout of his . . .'

'Spanners?'

'Yep. Spanners was forced into running some fast-food deliveries and he was convinced he was delivering drugs.'

'Scotty or Spanners?'

'Well, Spanners but he called Scotty and he agreed with him.'

'Hold on. Just rewind. How does dropping off fish and chips suddenly become drugs supply?'

Bob explained.

'Do you reckon this was the task Spanners had been allocated in exchange for his bonus when he left prison?' said Gary.

Bob shrugged. 'I can't be sure but it seems to fit. Sounds like the lorry driver who crashed on the A23 when I was heading to court was one of them too.'

Gary raised his hand. 'Hang on. Are you thinking the lorry crash was staged to force the judge to dismiss the trial?'

'Why not? It seems he didn't need much persuading. Someone at the court told me that he was practically gagging for a reason.'

'Had he been bought then?'

'It's hard to buy judges. Much easier to find something in their past they'd rather not get out. We need to dig more, but it is beginning to look as if there is some conspiracy going on . . .'

'Don't let our leader hear you say "if".'

'Fair dos. As there is a conspiracy going on, then whoever is behind it has some serious pull at very high levels.'

Just then there was a tap at the door. Gary looked up and beckoned Scotty in.

'Sorry I'm late, boss.'

'Don't apologise. Bob was just bringing me up to speed. Now you're here I might as well hear it from the horse's mouth. Tell me what happened once you'd spoken to Spanners about his deliveries.'

Scotty looked at Bob and the DI saw the conflict in his eyes.

'That's OK,' said Bob. 'I'll explain. Scotty rang me and said we should get warrants to search where Spanners had dropped off to.'

'Sounds reasonable.'

'Possibly, but we had six addresses with at least six unknown people behind each door, including a child. Spanners says he thought he recognised them as the defendants in the drug trial.'

'Some of them,' Scotty said.

'Yes, some of them. In any case, if we were going to get warrants we'd need an idea what was in the packages and more on the addresses themselves. That's before we tried to find the dozens of staff we'd need for simultaneous raids.'

Gary had a chilling look in his eye. 'What did you do instead then?'

Bob had been on this hot seat many times before, but that didn't make it any more comfortable. 'I told Scotty to write it all down and I'd allocate it to a development officer in the morning.'

'And did you?'

'Yes, we're working on it as we speak but it's a massive task. In my defence, if we'd jumped too soon we'd have spooked the whole network.'

'Instead the streets are awash with what's probably a lethal batch of heroin and we've had three months' worth of drugs deaths in one afternoon.'

Bob wasn't sure whether Gary was genuinely angry or just rehearsing for the inevitable press and public kangaroo court when all this got out. He was about to come back when Scotty interrupted.

'Boss, one thing I hadn't got round to telling Mr Heaton was what Saira Bannerjee and I found at Lifechoices treatment centre this morning.' Bob and Gary listened intently while he spelt out the crush at the gates, the Synthopate drought and the desperation in the eyes of all the addicts who, up until then, had been making all the right progress on their road to recovery.

'Bit of a coincidence, isn't it?' said Bob. 'The day we get this fatal batch is the day our users can't get their scripts.'

'There's more,' said Scotty. 'I've checked and all our pharmacies are suffering the same shortages. But out of county, those not on the trial who also get their medicines from Respite Pharmaceuticals are seeing no problems.'

'So it's Synthopate that's in short supply?' said Gary.

Scotty nodded.

'Maybe it's a production issue. Can't they just switch back to methadone?'

'Apparently not. I'm not sure whether that's for clinical or contractual reasons though.'

The pieces of the jigsaw swam around in Bob's head. He was all too aware of confirmation bias but this was looking intuitively obvious. All he needed to do was prove it.

35

Jo had no idea how she'd managed to arrive at Brighton Police Station in one piece. The drive was a blur and she knew working was a stupid thing to do, but if she spent another day in the silence of home imagining what purgatory Darren was going through, she'd go mad. He'd had two nights in that hellhole already. How would he survive a third?

As she expected, her trudge up the stairs to her office brought awkward stares and murmurings of 'Morning, ma'am' to which she just grunted replies. She'd brave one of her station walkabouts later but for now she needed to reacquaint herself with the normality of her office and hopefully empathy from Gary.

She'd almost reached her door when Fiona looked up from her phone call. The PA's warm smile and wink reassured Jo that no one and nothing would be allowed to intrude on her return until her gatekeeper deemed the time was right. She smiled back and pushed the handle down. It was only then that she looked up and saw Gary deep in conversation with Bob and Scotty.

All but Gary stood up.

'Oh do sit down,' she mumbled.

'Morning, Jo. Listen chaps, can we continue this later?' said Gary. Scotty was the first one to gather up his iPad and head out. As he left, Bob was about to follow but as he walked past Jo she touched his shoulder.

'Stay.' She shut the door.

Before she could open her mouth, Gary said, 'What are you doing back? Shouldn't you be taking, you know, some time?'

'What, with my family? Not sure I'm that welcome in Belmarsh.'

'No, I mean . . . The boys.'

Jo sat down in the vacant chair, leaving Bob to retake her usual one.

'I'm going mad at home. What were you lot plotting?'

'You really want to know?'

'What do you think?'

'You tell her,' said Gary. Jo detected a frostiness towards the DI.

She looked at Bob as he hesitated. 'Well?'

Bob sighed then brought her up to speed, warts and all. He looked more contrite than she'd ever seen him and she now knew why Gary was so pissed off.

'To sum up then, we had intelligence that drugs had been distributed and we did nothing. We heard of a city-wide lack of Synthopate and we did nothing. Then people started dying when the heroin hit the streets and still we did nothing. Is that about it?'

Gary chipped in. 'I think that's a little harsh. Bob had his reasons for not getting search warrants, but yes, we could have done a little more.'

It would have been so easy for Gary to throw Bob under a bus, but she was impressed he wasn't shirking his part in this. She was sure he'd made his feelings very clear to the DI in private but now he was the buck-stop point.

Jo was starting to feel more like her old self already. 'Let's get back to basics. This Spanners fella. How do we know he's not playing us? He wouldn't be the first to ingratiate himself to us, would he? What do we actually know about him?'

Bob started to give his background and the information he'd been feeding to Scotty, but she raised her hand. 'I know all that but what's driving him? He rocks up from nowhere and all of a sudden he's spilling his guts to a sergeant he's never met. He says he's scared but, really?'

'He did phone Scotty as soon as he finished the drops,' said Gary, taking the underdog's side now.

'When he'd finished. Not when he started. Why would he do that? If you're right then he's deliberately distributed drugs to a gang of people who have just swerved double-digit jail time, and now we've got addicts dropping like conkers.'

'Maybe he had no chance earlier . . .'

She cut Gary off. 'He had a choice. He could have called us and we'd have looked after him. Sure, we wouldn't have known where the drugs were going but at least we'd have had them and they wouldn't be poisoning God knows how many people as we speak.'

'In fairness,' said Bob, 'he didn't know they were drugs and we still don't. And even if they were, how do we know it was that batch that's killing people?'

She hated doing this, but two of her closest allies had let her down and they needed to know. 'How do we ever know there are drugs anywhere we look? We don't. We gather intelligence and we make a judgement. He should have told us before he went all Santa Claus. He's got blood on his hands.'

There was a silence that Jo was determined not to fill.

'What are we going to do?' Gary finally said.

So many colleagues, Gary included, had told her she was becoming a control freak, but here he was ducking responsibility. 'Gary. I'm not being funny but surely you can work that out. What do we usually do with drug dealers?'

She could almost bite the atmosphere as it changed. Gary looked confused. Bob got it straight away.

'Tell him, Bob.'

'Arrest him?'

'There you go. Wasn't that hard, was it? When you strip it all down, this Spanners fella has done the square root of bugger all for us.'

'Now that's hardly fair,' said Gary.

'Isn't it? He's given us the nod on a few uncorroborated pieces of gossip but that doesn't trump wholesale drug distribution. He needs nicking and we need to do a proper job on him.' She could see the panic rising in both men. No doubt they were totting up Scotty's breaches of a barn-full of laws and regulations, not to mention turning a blind eye to countless petty crimes. The defence would have a field day and no doubt Spanners would walk, probably to his death. 'Let me help you out. He knows more than he can tell us in this uncontrolled, borderline illegal way we are dealing with him at the moment. If we nick him, he's ours. We can debrief him about the other night but also tap him up for other information too. No one's to know.'

'And then?' said Gary.

Jo shrugged. 'Maybe we charge him, maybe we don't. But if we do, he'll be safer on remand than out there.'

'Safe on remand?' blurted Gary until Bob glared at him. 'I, er, I didn't mean that. I'm sorry Jo, that was careless of me.'

Jo stood up, her hands trembling. 'You don't need to spell it out for me. I see it every waking hour, and that's every fucking hour. He's going through hell in there, just like Bob did.' She turned briefly to the DI. 'I wouldn't wish that on anyone, but life goes on and if Spanners is seen to be treated as the common criminal he is, that helps him and helps us. Believe it or not he would be safer inside, which is where he should be already, so stop faffing about and get him nicked.' She turned back to Bob. 'Get a team together and start building a case. These dead kids were loved by someone and they deserve justice.' She opened the door. 'Off you go. And don't tell Scotty.'

36

Sir Ben was old school. While the woke generation espoused the benefits of working from home, he made it clear that anyone employed by Respite had to work *at* Respite.

So, when he texted his PA telling her to put all today's meetings online, he could almost hear the whispering as people's Outlook appointments changed. It was an open secret that the plummeting number of drug users in Brighton and Hove was decimating revenues, and they might be thinking he was absent to avoid those worried about their jobs.

Little did they know what the issue really was. Yet another sleepless night during which, several times, he'd stared at the pillow by his mother's side sorely tempted to put her out of her misery. But he loved her too much for that and the New York treatment programme was his beacon.

He'd been calling Dr Trevor Blaketon on and off for the last three hours. Why couldn't he just prescribe something for her pain and sign her off as fit to fly? In between time, he'd been emailing the clinic hoping to strike a deal on their fee. He'd never been one to beg. He presented to the world as a multimillionaire who could buy whatever he wanted at the click of his finger. Nothing could be further from the truth though. He was asset rich but cash poor and freeing up the money he needed was no mean feat.

Even if he could persuade the doctor to offer a ninety per cent discount – which would never happen – that was still out of his immediate reach, but at least he could raise some legitimate funds to make a dent in it. Looking over at his wheezing mum, he was damn sure he'd make her remaining days bearable.

So video meetings it was today. Firstly so he could look after her in this, her most distressed state, and secondly so he could meet the people who were starting to arrive in person.

Tony Evans was first, as Sir Ben knew he would be. Then came Arjun Sharma, the regional prison director, who was two minutes early. He told them to help themselves to coffee while his temper frothed as they waited for Nicola Merrion. A full ten minutes late the CEO of Lifechoices jabbed the intercom on the gate and Sir Ben despaired. She looked like she'd jogged there.

'I'm so sorry I'm late,' said Nicola, wiping the sweat off her brow.

'Just go through. You really are trying my patience.'

Nicola did as she was told, and Sir Ben couldn't help but notice the smug looks on Tony's and Arjun's faces as they nodded to the latecomer.

'Right, sit down,' said Sir Ben, taking the chair at the head of the table. The three others obeyed with only Tony appearing relaxed.

'Bring me up to speed. Nicola?'

She dabbed her brow again, flashed a smile and locked onto Sir Ben's gaze. 'Well, we've no Synthopate, and with no access to methadone and Subutex our patients are dropping like flies. The reason I was late was the offices were besieged with dealers openly serving up right outside. People are coming to us for help but, as we can't provide it, others are.'

'And you ran rather than drove,' muttered Tony.

'Sounds like at least someone's doing their job properly,' said Sir Ben, to Tony. 'How many days' gear have you got left?'

Tony kept a poker face then hunched forward. 'Well, thanks to them being acquitted, we've got six of the best dealers operating different sectors of the city. The brown needs to be pretty pure, around sixty-five per cent, so they are keeping it just at that but cutting it in with fentanyl to make it go further and take out the weak quicker. I reckon we've got a couple of weeks based on current demand and I've told them not to just serve it up to the same old faces.' Sir Ben nodded approvingly. 'We need to attract a whole new client base, including those who Nicola's got clean.'

'Great stuff. A fortnight sounds perfect. It's a shame we are going to lose some potential Synthopate customers in the meantime but once I open up the supply lines again, demand will be raging. Think you can cope, Nicola?'

For once she looked unsure. 'I don't know. These are good people who are dying. They are on a long programme. A bit like snakes and ladders. It takes ages to make progress, but one slip and they're back to the beginning. I'm not sure we have the capacity to start so many people from scratch again.'

'You'll cope,' said Sir Ben. 'Just be ready. I've explained the delays to my staff as contractual issues but once I turn the tap on, you need to handle everything we throw at you. By then I should have distracted the local police well enough so they won't be the problem they were.'

'But Jo Howe's like a dog with a bone. She's already left half a dozen messages for me demanding I do something.'

'Talking of which. Arjun, how's her hubby getting on in Belmarsh?'

'He's had better days. Unfortunately, someone's already leaked that he's married to a police officer so that didn't go down well.'

'Good,' said Sir Ben. 'Make sure the governor keeps him in general population for now. I wouldn't want him hiding away in the vulnerable prisoners' wing. Keep turning the screw.'

'I've already ordered that.'

'And how are we fixed for getting more dealers out on the street? Is our package still attractive?'

Arjun's grin fell away. 'Some are so desperate that they'll take a few quid whatever the risk, but others are getting a little nervy.'

'Nervy?'

'Even though we are spreading the offer thinly across the southern region prisons, so as not to spook anyone, word's getting out that it's one job and you're gone.'

'Eh?'

'Let's just say it's not escaped the bush telegraph that some who've taken the money have ended up dead. As I say, most will grab whatever you throw at them but maybe we can ease off on the disposals?'

Sir Ben thought about it. This endless supply of labour was only any good if it remained endless. Maybe Arjun was right and a few should be allowed to become ambassadors of the scheme. Who better to allay fears than those who'd been through it?

He nodded. 'Yes, we'll do it. For now just focus on those we can trust to deal drugs. That's the priority, but soon I'm going to ask you to find some proper muscle.' Arjun looked worried. Sir Ben continued. 'We all need a payday and anyone who stands in our way needs to learn not to. Understood?'

All three nodded.

'Right, I need to stir the hornets' nest,' he said, rising to his feet to signify the meeting was over.

Sam Parkin was very careful not to allow his frustration to creep into his voice whenever Sir Ben tasked him. He'd been living on a precipice ever since he'd given the police the concocted story about Darren Howe buying titbits from detectives. When the time came for him to give evidence at the Old Bailey, he would happily perjure himself despite the inevitable battering he'd get from Howe's defence counsel. His only worry was if they pulled something out of the bag that would shine the light on him. A couple of days in the witness box was one thing. Prison was another.

On the face of it, the article Sir Ben had demanded was straightforward but the tone would be tricky. The boss was after substance, but Sam had become accustomed to clickbait counting more than truth. He read it over one last time.

The City of Death
Special Report by Sam Parkin, Editor

If your kids are heading to the once charming and idyllic city of Brighton and Hove, whether to study, work or play, take my advice and send them to Bournemouth instead.

Today the Journal *can exclusively lift the lid on the disastrous policing of this 'London by the Sea', and reveal why, over a few short days, it has once again regained its long-held moniker of being the drugs death capital of the UK.*

What was hailed as being the panacea to drug crime and deaths, Operation Eradicate, is nothing but a vanity project conceived and jealously guarded by the city's controversial police commander, Chief Superintendent Joanne Howe. Fuelled by her own shameful guilt following the death of her sister Caroline in a stinking city squat, Mrs Howe – wife of disgraced journalist Darren who is currently in Belmarsh Prison on remand charged with corrupting police officers – has turned her own failings on the public of Brighton and Hove by refusing to clamp down on druggies and, contrary to the law, diverting them to namby-pamby treatment programmes.

Mrs Howe, who seems to thrive at the centre of corruption scandals, has propagated Brighton's dubious image of a permissive party town by openly advocating the legalisation of drugs.

Well, her obstinance and naivety has come back to bite her. It's no surprise that her whole approach was built on sand and, rather than curing addicts, she's left nearly a dozen dead over the last few days.

Her house of cards was destined to collapse, and it took just one ace being removed – in this case a short-term cut in the supply of a heroin substitute trial drug from Respite Pharmaceuticals – and crashing down it came. Within a few hours of these druggies being unable to get the props that hold them together, a new batch of heroin was on the streets and they started dropping like flies.

Sources on the ground have told the Journal *that the few police who are left – Brighton is experiencing unprecedented sickness levels, but that's another story – are haring around from body to body while the mortuary is overflowing.*

Howe has previously banged on about her aim to reduce the demand and thus suck the oxygen from the drugs market. Well, all she seems to have achieved is to have sucked the life out of vulnerable and troubled young people. Only time will tell how many more must die before this preening officer is removed or she sees sense and returns to the job we pay her to do.

Sussex Police declined to comment.

Sam pressed submit and sat back, waiting for the plaudits to pour in.

Sir Ben couldn't believe his eyes when he saw the piece, the moment it appeared. He scan-read it first, then seethed over it slowly, hoping he had misread it. Why the hell did he mention Respite and the Synthopate trial?

He knew it would trigger a storm, but now feared it wouldn't be the one he intended. Sure enough, ten minutes later, Respite's chief financial officer was on the phone.

Sir Ben didn't give him a chance to state the obvious. 'Yes I've seen it and yes he'll pay for it. What's it doing to the share price?'

'It's free-falling. Thirty per cent down already and there's no sign of a parachute this side of London closing. Why the hell did he mention us by name? He might as well have put out a bankruptcy warning.'

'Jesus,' muttered Ben, taking the phone into his mother's room partly to check she was still breathing, and partly to remind himself what this was all about. He'd come too far to let Parkin blow it out of the water.

Creaming money off Respite relied on there being money to skim from in the first place.

'Leave Parkin to me. I'll get the article taken down too. In the meantime, get some proactive reassurance out there and make it look like it's business as usual. I want the stock to bounce back today or you'll be looking for another job by the morning.' He ended the call and walked over to the bed.

'Don't worry, Mum. I will sort this and we'll get you the treatment you need. I promise, it'll be fine.' He leant forward and kissed her on the cheek.

It was Clarissa Heard, Jo's press officer, who drew her attention to the article. Usually Clarissa would just email or WhatsApp the link but today she came to her office.

'How dare he bring up Caroline and Darren? Surely there are laws against talking about ongoing cases.'

Clarissa tilted her head to one side. 'He's been careful. My advice is to say nothing and let it die.'

'But he's attacking me and my family personally. And he's lying about Eradicate. How can we not fight back?'

'You know why. You'll just bring all the trolls and that will be ten times worse. Honestly, you've had this before and you know, silence is golden.'

Jo huffed as she read the screen again. 'You know why he's doing this, don't you? He used to be Darren's boss but sacked him for this bollocksy allegation of corruption. He's using his venomous mouthpiece to rub the salt in.' She read over it again. She stopped three paragraphs from the end and read it out loud.

'"Her house of cards was destined to collapse, and it took just one ace being removed – in this case a short-term cut in the supply of a heroin substitute trial drug from Respite Pharmaceuticals – and crashing down it came. Within a few hours of these druggies being unable to get the props that hold them together, a new batch of heroin was on the streets and they started dropping like flies."'

'Did you spot that Clarissa?'

'Spot what?' said the usually whip-smart press officer.

'That bit where he's linking the lack of Synthopate with a new batch of heroin. How does he know they might be linked?'

'He could be guessing,' said Clarissa. 'We know he only has a casual relationship with the truth.'

Jo pondered on that, then read it over again. 'No, he's not guessed this. He knows it and, unless I'm mistaken, we've not released this to anyone. That means, unless Nicola Merrion has, which I doubt as she and her staff would rather eat their own poo than talk to the press, he's got some inside information and I reckon Respite are the key.' She thumped out a WhatsApp to Gary and Bob.

For the first time in weeks, the fire in Jo's belly ignited.

37

If Scotty wasn't to learn of Spanners' arrest, then hardly anyone else could.

Given the soaring supposed sickness – the average team's attendance rate was hovering around the forty per cent mark – Bob was hardly awash with choices. The public had yet to spot the shortfalls, such was their low expectation of the police since the cuts, but the force was in a critical state.

If he timed the arrest right, he'd get away with two, maybe three, officers surprising Spanners on a quiet street. If not, it would mean a whole police support unit battering some squat's door down. He'd struggle to find three officers, let alone the twenty-plus he'd need. So he chose a wilier approach and hoped the ex-squaddie didn't kick off.

When he arrived at work on the following day, the station seemed even emptier than usual. Time was getting on and the longer he waited, the more chance word would get out. He'd gleaned from Scotty that Spanners was an early riser and liked to stroll along the lower promenade before the crowds hit the beach. It wasn't perfect but it was the best Bob could think of. All he needed was to find an arrest team.

He was rechecking the duty state when Gary strolled into his office. 'All fit then?' the superintendent asked rhetorically.

Replying in whispered tones, Bob said, 'Not really. Have you ever seen the place so empty? Talk about tumbleweed.'

Gary looked at the empty desks outside Bob's office. 'We can't go on like this. The chief needs to be making an example of one or two of these bloody skivers. That would get them back to work.'

'They're scared. For themselves and their families.'

'It's a tough job, Bob. They can always leave and make room for some less feeble recruits.'

Bob shook his head. 'Anyway, looks like we'll have to leave it to another day.'

'Will we bollocks,' said Gary. 'I know who can do it.'

Fifteen minutes later, Bob and Gary were squeezed into a dark blue Toyota Yaris, on the patch of promenade which separated Marmalade's nightclub and the shingle beach. At this time of the morning they were less conspicuous than they would be later, given the army of cleaners scouring their way through the various clubs, bars and restaurants that occupied Brighton's Victorian beachfront arches.

'You sure you'll recognise him?' said Gary, fiddling with the in-car stereo.

'I hope so but remember this was your idea.' Bob switched off the ignition to stop his boss finding Talksport. 'And it's helpful if we keep a little quiet while we wait . . . sir.'

'This is why I never became a detective,' said Gary.

'They'd never have had you.'

Bob expected some quip back but instead, Gary said, 'Is that him?', pointing to a middle-aged man dressed in ripped camouflage trousers, a blue crew neck jumper and flip-flops.

'That's another reason why you stayed in uniform.'

The man walked past them, not even noticing the car was occupied.

'Rude,' said Gary.

Over the next half hour, twenty or thirty unlikely suspects wandered past and Bob started to wonder whether he'd relied too much on Scotty's casual reflection on Spanners' habits. More to make a point to Gary than in any sense of optimism, Bob was determined not to give up too soon but the cramped car, Gary's attempts at humour and a mounting inbox all chipped away at his resolve.

He was about to give in when a huge dustcart filled the road ahead, lights flashing and machinery gobbling up last night's detritus. It must have come down an unseen ramp but was slowly making its way towards them. Bob realised he'd come off second in any duel. He glanced in the mirror to reverse out of the way.

'Gary, behind us.'

'What?'

'Slowly turn round and have a look at that bloke walking this way.'

Gary snapped his head round as if reacting to a gunshot. Bob tutted.

'Could be,' said Gary.

'Almost certainly is. Let's chance it and if we're wrong, call it a day. On my count, open your door and get straight out. Whoever's side he comes round grabs him.'

'Got that.'

Bob kept watching, hoping he could time it to perfection. 'Looks like your side,' he said as the man ambled between the car and the club. 'Ready. One. Two. Three. GO!'

The doors were flung open and both men leapt out. Bob ran round the front in case the suspect made a dash for it but by the time he got to Gary's side, Spanners – he was sure of that now – was wedged by his throat against a garish orange sign.

'Get the fuck off me,' Spanners croaked, Gary's face catching more than its fair share of spittle.

'You dirty fucker,' shouted Gary as he squeezed tighter.

'Boss, leave him,' called Bob as he pulled at Gary's shoulder to stop him killing their target. Thankfully Gary acquiesced and Bob shoved him out of the way. 'You Spanners?' said Bob.

'Who wants to know?' Bob flipped open his warrant card wallet and almost instantly he saw the fight evaporate from Spanners' eyes. 'What the fuck do you want?'

'I'm arresting you for supplying class A drugs.'

Bob had barely finished the caution before Spanners said, 'You've got the wrong bloke. You do know I've been helping you. Ask Sergeant Scott.'

'Listen, sweetheart,' said Gary. 'Two bits of advice. Firstly, keep your mouth shut until you've got a solicitor. And secondly, if you can't do that, be very careful who you tell that you've been helping the police out. There are some serious health and safety issues associated with outing yourself as a grass.'

Bob took his handcuffs from his covert harness, pulled Spanners' arms to the rear then clipped the cuffs. 'Are they OK?'

'Not really.'

'It's not too far to custody, so providing you behave yourself they'll come off as soon as we get there.'

Spanners nodded a grudging understanding and allowed Bob to help him into the back seat, behind where Gary had been sitting. 'Boss, can you get in the back next to him? Behind me?'

'You're kidding, right? Chuck me the keys. Sorry, privilege of rank.' Bob gracelessly did as he was ordered and slid in the back seat, his knees crunched into his belly.

As Gary pulled away, Spanners stared ahead. 'I think I know what this is about.'

'Save it,' said Gary.

Bob said, 'Oh, do you?'

'Those deliveries. I told Scotty about them as soon as they happened.' Bob left a silence. 'You know I'm dead now anyway, don't you?'

'How so?' said Bob.

'It's the way it is. One job then you're a goner. I think you might have done me a favour.'

'I wouldn't be so sure,' said Bob.

'Well, you've got to protect me now.'

Bob knew that but he thought he'd push it one more time. 'Only if you tell us more. And by more, I mean everything and not to Scotty. To properly trained source handlers all going through the right channels. You do that and we'll look after you. What do you say?'

'Not sure I've got any choice, but you need to tell Scotty. I can't imagine he'll take it too well.'

'Sergeant Scott will do as he's told,' said Gary.

'We got a deal then?' said Bob.

'Of course we have,' said Spanners, as he turned to stare out of the window, with just the glimmer of a smile.

The video that his Cambridge source had WhatsApp'd him last night couldn't have been better timed but with his mother in such a precarious state, there was no way Sir Ben was travelling up to London. So the policing minister would just have to make an unscheduled constituency visit and come to him.

He knew the Right Honourable Edward Baker MP would cry three-line whips if he demanded he travel to Brighton in the afternoon, so he demanded he arrive by 9.00 a.m., for his son's sake.

On the dot, his doorbell app pinged and there, on the screen, was the minister, resembling a boy caught smoking awaiting his fate outside the headmaster's office. He pressed the button and Baker scurried up to the driveway, throwing glances behind him as he went.

For no other reason than spite, Sir Ben kept him waiting on the doorstep a couple of minutes, smirking as he watched him squirm in plain sight.

Eventually he opened the door and Baker squeezed past. 'This really is not convenient, Sir Ben. I can't just hotfoot it down to Brighton at your beck and call. I'm a busy man.'

'Yet here you are. Come with me.' Sir Ben led the way into the lounge. On the coffee table sat a MacBook Pro, screen up and the first frame of a video waiting to play. 'I've something to show you. Do sit down.'

Baker did as he was told and Sir Ben sat next to him. 'This came through last night. I wanted you to see it before anyone else.' He pressed play.

The image flickered on the screen, then stabilised. It was from a mobile phone and it was apparent that whoever was holding it had consumed as much alcohol as those in its frame. The scene was a narrow cobbled street with a high wall on one side and a Sainsbury's Local, a Mountain Warehouse and other ubiquitous chain stores on the other. 'It's Cambridge city centre, in case you were wondering.'

'I know,' said Baker. 'I spent three years there.' He jabbed a finger at the wall, which Sir Ben knew belonged to Sidney Sussex College.

'Keep watching.' The camera operator was following three young men, all dancing in the centre of the road, singing 'The Wild Rover'; one had a traffic cone on his head. All were about the same age, nineteen or twenty, and all were very drunk. After a second, the middle one, wearing 'white tie' but without the tie, turned to the camera. 'Put that fucking phone away you peasant and join in.' Baker looked horrified as there could be no doubt the face belonged to his son, James.

The video continued for a few more seconds when James's attention was suddenly drawn to a charity shop doorway. 'Oh my fucking Christ, what have we here?' he shouted as he turned to face whatever he'd seen. 'A fucking Fraggle on God's fair streets.' The image zoomed in to show a man huddled in blankets with straggly grey hair and full beard. 'Stand up my man,' James shouted. When the man didn't move, he took a step in and swung his leg back, then drop-kicked the man square in the stomach. There was a sickening scream, then one of the others tried to haul him off but James pushed him away. 'I know what the problem is. He's too fucking cold to move. Let's warm him up.' With that, James reached in his waistcoat pocket and pulled out a silver lighter.

'A gift from Daddy?' said Sir Ben.

'Do we have to watch this?' said Baker. Sir Ben remained silent but turned back to the screen.

In the second they'd been looking away, James was bending down and a flame had erupted from the lighter, which he was waving at the homeless man's coat hem. Suddenly the coat caught fire. Panic ensued and two of James's companions pulled him away then jumped in and stamped on the man's burning clothes until they'd gone out. Amid the shouts, James's hysterical laughter cut through. The loudest cries though were from the man in the charred rags trying to get up.

'You fucking idiot,' yelled the man who'd done most of the stamping, clearly to James. The phone swung round to capture him again. He was still giggling like a child, then his expression changed. 'Hold on, he's still on fire,' said James. 'Leave it to me.' He leapt forward, kicked the man back down, then having fiddled with his trousers, an arc of urine drenched the man's head.

'A proper little charmer, isn't he?' said Sir Ben. 'You and he will be finished when I send this out, so this is your last chance. What the hell have you been up to since we last spoke?'

'He's just a kid, please don't ruin his life.'

'Oh, he's perfect Number 10 material if previous incumbents are anything to go by. However, not if this goes viral.'

'OK. OK. We did delay some deliveries and temporarily interrupted the police station power. And we got Mrs Howe's credit cards frozen for a while, but it's difficult to do more than that.'

'Really? For a man of your talents? You have a reputation for waltzing through the impossible, so this should be child's play. Pardon the pun.'

'Leave it with me. I'll try harder but give me your word you won't leak this.' He pointed to the screen.

'I gather the poor man doesn't want to press charges. However, I'm sure that might change – for the right sum.'

'Please.'

'Then do what I asked. You are an important cog in a set of very complex wheels. Well, not you specifically, but what I've asked you to do is. If this whole machine delivers, then we'll all be very rich and young

James can continue in his father's murky footsteps.'

Sir Ben fiddled with the keyboard and a blank message appeared, with the email addresses of twenty or so of the UK's foremost news outlets filled out in the 'To' field. The video was already attached.

'Shall I press "send"?'

'No.'

'OK, so do we have an understanding or should your constituency be preparing for a by-election?'

'What choice do I have?'

'That's more like it.' Baker jumped up and strode for the door. 'Enjoy your day, Minister,' Sir Ben called out, as the door slammed shut.

Jo had ignored half a dozen calls from an unknown number while she waited on hold to Belmarsh Prison. She'd been on the line for the best part of an hour when Scotty rapped on the open door. She looked up and tried to hide the fact he was the last person she wanted to see.

Forcing her best smile, she said, 'Scotty, how can I help you?'

'Can I come in, ma'am?'

'Yes of course.' He stepped into the office and closed the door. 'How are you? You know, after Lizzie.'

'What? Oh yes, I'm getting there. Look, is Mr Hedges around?'

'Er, no I think he's up at custody. Can I help at all?'

Scotty fidgeted. He'd obviously geared himself up for a battle with someone senior, but not this senior. The sergeant took a breath. 'Is it true that the superintendent has arrested my informant?'

'Well, if I know Mr Hedges as I think I do, I'd imagine he asked DI Heaton to actually say the magic words – but, yes, Spanners is in custody.'

Scotty flushed. 'Well didn't anyone think to tell me? He is my contact for fuck's sake.'

Jo wanted to treat him gently but she couldn't let that go. 'Right. Sit down, shut up and listen.' He did exactly as he was told. 'First of all, you never speak to anyone like that, be it me, the chief constable or the newest cleaner, do you understand?'

'Yes, ma'am. Sorry, it's just . . .'

'I know you're annoyed and I would be too, but *I* decided he would be arrested and that you wouldn't be told.'

Scotty's brow furrowed. 'I don't understand. Don't you trust me?'

'Don't be ridiculous. If I didn't trust you, do you think I would have involved you in everything that's been going on? Of course I trust you, but sometimes it's not good to know everything. For your own protection. But, since you asked, Spanners distributed drugs around the city and since then people have been dying. We can't just ignore that.'

'But why does it take a superintendent and DI to arrest him?' Jo was relieved he seemed to be veering away from his original 'don't keep secrets' stance.

'Usually it wouldn't but we're a bit short-handed at the moment. They were simply all we had left.'

'But what about the others?'

'What others?'

'The people he delivered to. Are they getting nicked too?'

She didn't know how to answer that without lighting even more blue touchpaper. All she could manage was, 'In time.'

Scotty unfolded himself to his full six foot four. 'Well, let me make a start,' he roared then stormed out of the door, his mission lasered in his eyes.

'Scotty, Scotty,' she called out but he was gone.

38

The cell became smaller by the hour. When the boys wouldn't give Darren a moment's peace or Jo made demands, he'd idly wonder what it would be like to be locked away from any distractions. Well, three days in, he knew how stupid those thoughts were. With just the monosyllabic Ivan for company and the incessant threats hurled by would-be assailants, he'd kill to have his family back.

At least his cellmate mostly ignored him, pumping out press-ups while Darren spent hours counting paint bubbles in the ceiling above his bunk. That was more than could be said for the few prisoners loitering on the landings when he was finally escorted to the shower and to collect his food. Most growled at him and one spat in his breakfast. Thank God for the trio of prison officers guarding him, even though they were only one peg up on the friendly scale.

On reflection, he thought it was odd that he didn't get his meal shoved through the hatch as others did, but he was still finding his feet so shrugged it off.

He was about to drift off to sleep when he heard the cover to the spyhole scrape, then a shout, 'Get back from the door.' Darren swung his legs off the bed, almost kicking Ivan in the head as he sprung up. The cell door crashed open and three prison officers, two men and a woman who wore a stripe on her shoulder, burst in.

'Cell spin,' said the woman. 'Routine plus. Stand over here while these officers search you.'

Darren had no idea what was going on, nor what a 'cell spin' or 'routine plus' were, but he soon gathered that not only would his pad be ripped apart but he'd be strip-searched too. His instinct was to argue but as the younger of the two warders padded him down like he was kneading bread, he thought compliance was the smart way to get this over and done with. After all, he had nothing to hide.

They say that the punishment was being in prison itself and nothing that happened inside should be for retribution or revenge but, even though he was unconvicted, these three took great delight in robbing inmates of their last shred of dignity.

He put his clothes back on and watched as the two male officers systematically searched every conceivable crack and crevice and upended the few so-called personal items they had.

He watched with mild interest at the two officers' vigour, safe in the knowledge that anything they found would be Ivan's.

'Find.' He looked up at his bunk and, to his horror, the young officer was holding up a black object no more than eight centimetres long by two wide and a small plastic packet containing white powder.

'You've got some explaining to do Mr Howe,' said the senior officer with a smirk.

Jo Howe rubbed her eyes in a futile attempt to erase the pounding headache that had been building all day. Since Spanners' arrest that morning, she'd had to cope with Scotty's outburst, fend off various custody officers demanding she arbitrate in their row with Bob Heaton over why only intelligence officers had interviewed the drug dealer, and her own nightmares about Darren.

She checked her watch: ten past eight. God, she was getting too old for this. She made a quick call to Darren's mum to check on the boys, then yet another to Belmarsh Prison which, quelle surprise, rang until it cut off.

She walked the floors to see who might be around. The few detectives who had bothered to turn up for work were now long gone. She wandered back to her office and turned on her Airwave radio. The clipped chatter reassured her that there were still brave souls out there and not everyone had been scared to their sickbeds.

The radio provided the forlorn commentary to the ever-growing list of uncovered jobs. Fights, domestics, robberies. None would be answered even though the few PCs out there would have been split up to provide more cover. She could take a call herself but that would just tie her up for the whole night, and she needed to focus on whatever Spanners had come up with.

Suddenly, a desperate and familiar voice blasted from the radio, 'Charlie Sierra Nine One, Code Zero urgent urgent, I'm being attacked . . . Arghh fuck off, Code Zero, Code Zero, I need urgent . . . Argh get off . . . Stephens Road urgent . . . urgent. Oh God.'

Jo leapt up. Scotty? What the hell was he doing in Hollingdean? As she flung on her stab vest and utility belt her mind raced. Stephens Road? Where had that come up recently? Then she remembered. 'Oh shit, Scotty, what have you done?' She clipped on her radio and shouted into the mouthpiece, 'Chief Superintendent Howe, I'm making from the nick, any other unit to back up?'

She didn't wait for a reply. Others would be there if they could. Some would abandon equally deserving victims to help one of their own.

She took the stairs three at a time, almost turning her ankle on the first landing. Footsteps pounded above her. She hoped they were also racing to the car park.

As she flashed past her, PC Wendy Relf said, 'Jump in with me, boss.'

A surge of fear coursed through her, but she couldn't lose face in front of Wendy. Nor could she abandon Scotty. She knew what to expect from Wendy's in-your-face driving. If they didn't get there in time – or at all – it wouldn't be for lack of trying. She jumped into the front passenger seat of the marked patrol car, as Wendy flipped on the lights and sirens, slammed the door and squealed away, all in one movement.

Scotty's screams were still blasting from his open mike straight into her earpiece.

'Charlie Romeo Zero Two, tell him the chief super and I are on our way,' said Wendy into her radio. 'Any update?'

'Control to Charlie Romeo Zero Two, nothing yet, we can only hear what you can. He's not answering.'

'Roger that. Any other units making?'

'Just you at the moment. We are trying to get more units to you.'

Wendy powered down Carlton Hill, barely pausing at the T-junction as she turned right onto Grand Parade. The engine screamed for relief as she raced north, through the incessant red lights and onto Lewes Road. She took the traffic island at the bottom of Elm Grove on the wrong side then continued with that ferocity until she reached the Gyratory roundabout which, Jo knew, Wendy would navigate like a fairground ride.

She took over the radio duties.

'Charlie Romeo Zero Two, our ETA is two minutes. Any update or description of offenders?'

'Still nothing. Please update as soon as you arrive. We have units making from Lewes.'

'Jesus,' said Jo, 'he'll be dead by the time they get here.'

Wendy wrenched the wheel left into Hollingdean Road and Jo grabbed the *fuck me* handle to keep herself upright. Wendy struggled to keep control but the wheels managed to grab the wet road, just avoiding a collision with a parked car. She floored the accelerator and the tyres screamed as she took the right turn that fed them into the Hollingdean estate, then swung the car into a series of rights and lefts as it revved towards its destination.

As Stephens Road straightened up, Wendy stood on the brakes. A black sack blocked their path and she stopped the car only two yards from it. It took Jo just a second to realise what it was.

She leapt from the car, as did Wendy who stopped only to grab her medic kit. The engine and blue lights were still going, but they ran to where Scotty lay.

His face and head were unrecognisable. Jo was no doctor but with Scotty's eye socket, nose and cheekbone looking like a Picasso painting and blood oozing from his ear she knew he was in a bad way.

As Wendy fished in the green bag, Jo touched his face. 'Scotty. It's Jo, Jo Howe. Can you hear me?'

Nothing, just the rasp of laboured breath.

'Scotty?'

Nothing.

Wendy checked his airway and breathing then hit her radio transmit button. 'Charlie Romeo Zero Two, urgent. Charlie Romeo Zero Two, urgent,' she repeated.

Then, from the control room inspector, 'All units except Charlie Romeo Zero Two stand by. Charlie Romeo Zero Two, go ahead.'

'Charlie Romeo Zero Two, thank you. I need an ambulance here urgently. Sergeant Scott has severe, repeat, severe head injuries. He's unconscious but breathing, just. Not known if he has other injuries. I want as many units as you can in the area.'

'Roger that Charlie Romeo Zero Two, we have three units making towards you.'

Jo held his head still with one hand while Wendy tried to stem the bleeding.

'How's it looking?' Jo asked.

'Not good. Can you grab a blanket from the car?

'Sure,' said Jo.

She was back in seconds and tenderly laid it over Scotty, hoping that the desperate reassurances she was whispering into his ear were true.

Within seven minutes, the area was bathed in blue strobes. Two police cars, angled across the road, blocked any attempts to breach the cordon. Tape was flung between lamp posts and officers started to push the mobile-phone-wielding crowds back.

A single 'whoop' signalled the arrival of the paramedics. The PC by The Crossway dropped the blue and white 'POLICE' tape to let them through. As the ambulance glided to where Scotty lay, Jo prayed that they were here in time.

While they were still tending to him, Wendy told the medics the little she knew, while Jo watched as they took over.

'How is he?' she asked.

The older paramedic looked up. 'It's touch and go. I think he's had a massive bleed to the brain. We tried to get a doctor here with us but no luck. We are going to stabilise him the best we can then scoop him, er . . . get him to hospital ASAP.'

Dread washed through Jo as she muttered a thanks. She stepped over to Wendy and choked when she saw her sobbing like she'd lost one of her own.

Jo knew Scotty was well liked but, until that moment, not how much.

39

Whilst the oiling of wheels was the police minister's responsibility, the grittier aspects of Sir Ben's plan were down to Tony Evans, who always came up trumps.

Today, Sir Ben had decided to spend the day out with his enforcer to see for himself what was happening at the sharp end.

He'd been impressed that Arjun Sharma had managed to get the phone and drugs secreted in Darren's cell so quickly, but that was the power he wielded across half the prison estate. Planting the calls to Jo Howe was also inspired. He was confident that they'd be able to bury the holier-than-thou Mr Howe sooner than he'd imagined.

The carers had arrived bright and early for a change and once he'd handed over to them, he stood by the front window like a child on Christmas Eve. Five minutes later a plain white van pulled up. Rather than waiting for Evans to press the intercom, Sir Ben stepped out and waved. He made his way across the drive, out of the gate and, in a second, he was in the passenger seat.

'Really?' said Tony as he eyed Sir Ben up and down.

'What?'

'I said dress casual. Stone slacks and a button-down pinstriped shirt is Sunday best where I come from.'

Ben huffed. 'Well, it'll have to do. Why aren't you using a taxi, anyway?'

'Mixing it up, mate.' Tony pulled away and joined the gridlock heading for the city centre. 'Where do you want to go first?'

Sir Ben checked his Rolex. 'Take me to where the drugs are being sold.'

'OK, but only from afar. You never know who's watching so we'll just do some drive pasts.'

'Fine. I heard what happened last night.'

Tony glanced across. 'Yes, silly man. He'll not be bothering us for a little while.'

'A little while? You mean he's not dead?'

'It's not as easy as you think to top someone, especially someone like him. Two of my lads are nursing some nasty injuries after the way he fought back.'

Sir Ben let that go, but it worried him. Too many people were getting lucky and that smacked of sloppiness. Now was not the time to confront Tony about that though.

'How did he get so close? If a lowly sergeant seemed to know where all the main men were, how do we know the higher-ups don't?'

'Don't underestimate Sergeant Scott. Everything the Old Bill know about the drugs scene comes from him.'

Ben huffed.

As Tony crawled down Montpelier Road, the cause of at least some of the congestion was clear. A car had T-boned a bus at the Western Road junction. It appeared to have happened a while ago, and the one PC trying to both direct traffic and marshal the drivers and bus passengers out of the road looked like he'd rather be cleaning out the city sewers.

'They need to get that shifted,' Ben said idly.

'Ain't going to happen,' said Tony as he navigated round the wreckage.

'Eh?'

'A friend of a friend has the police contract for vehicle removal. Or should I say, had the contract.'

'What are you on about?'

'Some of us don't need to be told. I know you're trying to paralyse the police so I've been a bit proactive. He's cancelled the contract so any cars, lorries or whatever the police want moving are staying put for now.'

Ben sniggered. 'You diamond.'

'Cheers. It's not just breakdown trucks though. I've done the same with undertakers, cleaning contractors and vehicle hire. No fast-food place that wants to stay in business is serving the Old Bill for the foreseeable either. Oh, even the fire service and hospital are on a go-slow with anything police related.'

'Blimey you've been busy. I just wish others would follow your lead.'

They joined the line of traffic on the coast road, turning left then taking the next left into Oriental Place.

'Isn't this where that drugs worker was done in?'

'Yep, but that doesn't seem to have put anyone off. Look.'

Ben peered up the road. At first he thought it was a protest. Blocking the road were forty, maybe fifty drawn and bedraggled men and women, desperately bustling around as if in a war zone awaiting an airdrop.

Tony checked his watch. 'Watch this.' Right on cue, two only slightly better-fed and marginally smarter men wandered up. The way the crowd reacted, they could have been film stars. 'See, bloody desperate the lot of them. They can't get enough of this gear. It's like this all day. Come on, we better go.'

Ben nodded. 'Just here?'

'No, all over. I only brought you here as it was close by.'

'I can see you've been busy. Just keep at it.'

'For as long as you want, boss.'

For want of a distraction, Ben took out his phone. He glanced down and saw the BBC News app flashing its 'Breaking News' banner.

Secure 8 cancels Sussex Police Custody Contract with immediate effect.
He read it twice, before tapping it to open the article.

The BBC understands that security conglomerate Secure 8 has withdrawn from its multimillion-pound contract with Sussex Police with immediate effect, citing payment irregularities. Details are still unclear but, if confirmed, the implications are catastrophic. Secure 8 currently provide Sussex Police with all their custody centres and civilian jailers, as well as transport for prisoners to and from courts. This could mean the complete collapse of the force's ability to handle and process prisoners, leaving the county at huge risk of an even greater crime wave than we've seen in recent years. Sussex Police have declined to comment. More follows.

A rush of adrenaline gushed through Sir Ben as he took in the news. 'Seems you're not the only one who's been busy,' he said as he thought of the policing minister. 'Take me home. I've work to do.'

'Can I give you some feedback?' said Evans as he headed back to Sir Ben's house.

'If you must.'

'You need to cut off the snake's head.'

'Eh?'

'Well, we've all been busy getting at everyone and everything around her, but Mrs Howe is showing no sign of stopping.'

'We've put her husband in prison. Surely that will have an effect if nothing else has.'

'True, we've certainly given her a message but there is one thing we've not done. One part of her life that even she couldn't make second fiddle to her job. It's risky but I'm sure you don't mind that.'

'Go on.'

Tony spelt out his idea, step by step.

'And you've got the person in place already?'

'Yep. For a couple of weeks now.'

'How did you know we might need him?'

'Ben, you pay me a lot of money to think ahead. There's lots I've put in place that you don't need to know about. Deniability, remember? All you need to know is that once you give me the green light it can happen.'

'What, today?'

'Yep, it's all set up.'

This time it was Ben who left the silence. He didn't scare easily but this was a terrifying prospect. If it went wrong, none of them would see daylight again.

He nodded. 'Make it happen.'

40

Thank God for grandparents, thought Jo as she walked back from the Royal Sussex County Hospital, still in full uniform. Four days in, there was no news from Darren but of equal concern was how she was neglecting Ciaran and Liam, who needed her more than ever.

The night at Scotty's bedside had been as long as it was traumatic. More than once an alarm had wailed and an army of doctors and nurses had sprinted to his convulsing body, twisted some dials, shone torches then left him wheezing and puffing again. Once the consultant's round started, she decided to amble back to the police station and consume what passed for fresh air in central Brighton.

Fifteen minutes later she opened her office door to see Bob and Gary deep in conversation. They stopped the second they saw her and she knew she'd interrupted something.

'Sorry, don't mind me,' she said as she waved Bob out of her chair and rested her weary legs.

'Well? How is he?' said Gary.

'"Time will tell" was the best I could get out of anyone,' she said.

Gary looked her up and down. 'Tell me you didn't go out in public like that?'

She followed his gaze and for the first time noticed the smear of blood on her sleeves and the grit and gravel marks on her knees. She shrugged. 'He's in a terrible state. Christ, I'm surprised he's still with us.' She paused and stared into the middle distance.

'Want me to take you home?' said Bob, now sitting on one of the guests' chairs.

'No,' she said. 'I need to be here. There's going to be a lot of upset people when they find out and they need me.' Bob and Gary exchanged a look. 'What?'

Gary seemed to be clutching for the right words. 'Jo, best you hear it from me. I've spoken to the nights and the early shift, such as they are, and well, you're not flavour of the month with them.'

In her weariness, Jo thought she'd misheard him. 'Come again?'

'They were quite direct to be frank. They blame all this on you.' Jo went to interrupt but Gary put up his hand. 'Let me finish. They're joining the dots and see everything that's happened as coming from your' – he air-quoted – '"obsession with smackheads".'

'How bloody dare they,' said Jo. 'Smackheads?'

'Jo, it's not what they call drug users that's the issue here; they think you're doing more harm than good and putting them in danger. You're losing their faith and that's not a great place to be.'

'They're also questioning why you're not suspended, what with Darren being on remand,' said Bob.

Jo was struggling to take it all in. She loved this job and had always enjoyed the respect of her troops. Like last night, she was there in the line of fire if needed. How could they think this about her? She just wanted to do what was right. Too many divisional commanders had papered over the cracks insofar as the drugs problem was concerned, but her idea was both radical and long term. Couldn't they see that?

'I need to talk to them.' Weary as she was, she stood up and headed for the door.

'No, Jo,' said Gary. 'Not now. If you stand any hope of winning them back, you need to look and feel the part. Go home, have a shower, get some kip and come back refreshed.'

She sat back down. How could she sleep in this state? But Gary was right. 'OK, but first bring me up to speed on Spanners.'

Bob picked up his notebook. 'Well, he's been very talkative.'

'Great. Give me the headlines.'

'Well, he's confirmed everything he told Scotty about the ex-inmates being paid to come to the city and wait to be called, but there's more. They're from all over so we'd never have spotted it otherwise. He's heard the lorry crash which stopped me getting to court was all part of the same set-up. They didn't mean the driver to die – just to halt the trial, so that part worked.'

'That it?' said Jo, still bruised by Gary's feedback.

'No. He's given a lot more on the night he made the deliveries, especially about the bloke who told him what to do and the car he spoke to him in. First the car. It was a cab. Brighthelm. Could have been one of thousands but Spanners remembered both the registration and the hackney licence numbers.'

'Are they genuine?' said Jo.

'We're working on that. The driver said nothing but the guy who was in charge was a squat, bald bloke with what Spanners described as a "Gorbachev birthmark" over his left ear. The handlers were too young to know what that was but, as we are of a certain age, it's something to go with.'

'And the people he delivered to?'

'As he told Scotty, he said they were all the acquitted defendants from the trial. My guess is that dealing in the drugs was their pay-off for walking from court.'

'Excellent, so plenty to go on then,' said Jo, rubbing her eyes.

'It's still very circumstantial. We've had to bail him by the way,' said Bob. Jo nodded. She understood.

'Will he be safe?'

'Should be. No one knows we spoke to him. Anyway, the good news is we're certain who the bloke in the car was,' Bob continued. He tapped his phone into life and flicked through some apps. 'Here you go.'

It was a press photograph of a charity event the previous year, which all of Brighton's great and not so good had attended. Something about white-collar boxing and an auction brought out all the city's dubiously wealthy and, while they usually preferred to stay under the radar, in this case they seemed more than happy to parade in front of the camera to show off how philanthropic they were. And Tony Evans was no exception.

'This is him,' said Bob. 'Anthony Evans. No previous but a stake in just about every cash-based business in the city. He has the taxis, the door staff and the fast-food deliveries all sewn up.'

'But what's he got to gain from killing, maiming or terrifying half the police force? Things must be going well for him so why upset the status quo?'

'That's what we need to work out, but it's not necessarily him behind everything. The fact is he has access to a never-ending stream of muscle, so maybe he's working for someone even more powerful than him.'

Jo's addled brain couldn't work out how that fitted, but it seemed to. Gary was right – she needed sleep and she needed to speak to Darren. Until she achieved both of those, she was no good to anyone.

'Crack on finding out more, Bob. Gary, can you keep in touch with the hospital re Scotty? I'm off to freshen up.' They both nodded and she stood up.

As she got to the door, ACC Leon Mills and his staff officer appeared. Without acknowledging Jo, he looked over her shoulder and said, 'Gentlemen, could you give Mrs Howe and I a moment please?'

Jo tried to look him in the eye but, for once, he avoided her gaze and watched as Gary and Bob scurried out. 'Your phone please, Jo.'

'What?'

'Your phone,' he said again, this time with the tone of a parent reaching the end of his tether.

She picked up the handset and held it out. On taking it, he handed it back. 'Unlock it.' She looked again in disgust and disbelief and snatched the phone, prodding in the four-digit code. Thrusting it back, she said, 'Care to explain?'

He scrolled through the phone then showed the screen to his staff officer, who jotted something down.

He looked up at Jo, his face a visage of disappointment. 'Sit down, Jo. This is serious.'

41

Gary walked in silence towards Bob's office on the floor below. They needed to confer, and the privacy to do so.

They walked across the sparse open office where a few of Bob's staff were working away. It wasn't unusual to see the DI with the superintendent in tow. So much of today's policing, whether covert or overt, required a senior officer's say-so that Gary was often down here giving or declining an authority. None could have guessed that this was a crisis meeting to save the divisional commander from herself.

Bob took his usual seat behind the desk and, once he'd shut the door, Gary sat across from him.

'What the fuck was that about?' Bob asked rhetorically. They both knew the ACC but Bob, for one, had never seen him like that.

'Search me,' said Gary, 'but it didn't look good. He certainly picked his moment after what she'd been through all night – but one thing's for sure, she's on a slippery slope.'

After all they'd been through together, Bob's respect and protective streak for Jo had soared. She'd put her life on the line in the most perilous of ways and there was not a selfish gene in her body.

'She's not easily put off when she sets her mind to something, but with Darren and everything, she's heading for self-destruct.'

'I remember an old inspector of mine when I was a gobby sergeant in Cardiff telling me to keep the passion but pick my battles. I've learnt that there should be a third part to that: know when you're beaten.'

Bob nodded. 'Wise words, but how do you tell someone like Jo to back off when she'll only see that as giving in to bullies? The number she's faced down, she'd relish the challenge.'

'I'm not sure about that. Other than the burglary a couple of years ago, it's never got this personal for her and previously she'd known who the enemy was. Now, all she knows is that someone is hell-bent on a thriving drug trade and they'll stop anyone in their way.'

'I'm out of ideas then. She's not likely to back off on our say-so. And I can't imagine the ACC is having any more luck.'

'Unless he suspends her,' said Gary thoughtfully.

'Do you think he might?' Bob instinctively looked over his shoulder to the senior officers' car park to check her car was still there.

'I doubt it. He's got a soft spot for her. Whatever they're talking about, if he wanted rid of her he could have done that when Darren blabbed about the UC, or when he was charged. I reckon he's trying to save her.'

'How do we convince her to back off?'

Bob watched his boss as he mulled that over. 'She'll be thinking there are only two people in the world she can trust.'

'Us?'

'Yep. It's always one of us she comes to when she needs back-up or validation of some idea or other.'

'So?'

'It's not guaranteed to work. After all, we've disagreed with her before and she's carried on anyway, but if we tell her she can no longer count on our support, maybe she'll see sense.'

Bob couldn't believe what he was hearing. 'It'll kill her. We're all she's got.'

'It won't. She might think it will but, if she's got her head screwed on, it'll help her focus on what matters; Darren, the boys and getting the workforce back on duty.'

There was a silence. Bob racked his brain for an alternative that wouldn't smack of a Caesar–Brutus moment, but he was all out of ideas. The betrayal he knew was necessary brought back memories of when he'd come out to his wife and kids. He hoped now, like then, the expectation would be infinitely worse than the reality.

'All right, but let's be careful. She's vulnerable at the moment.'

ACC Leon Mills was always convivial and polite, and he had more emotional intelligence than all his peers combined. His stony face, therefore, told her that whatever she'd done was indefensible. His staff officer was glued to his notepad, indicating that he knew what was to come.

'Whose is that phone number?' Mills said, pointing out the missed calls from yesterday.

She looked at it, repeating the number in different rhythms over and over in her head. Defeated, she shook her head. 'I'm sorry, sir, I have no idea.'

'Think harder.'

'You can see I didn't answer them. It's not a number I've saved or recognised. I bet if you go back through the calls it's never called me before.' It was unusual for Jo not to pick up a call, any call, and once she discovered whose a number was, she'd save it under their name. 'They didn't leave a voicemail so I can't think who it might be. Perhaps a sales call.'

'Would you like me to tell you?'

Jo was confused and exhausted. 'That would be nice.'

Leon's face turned even darker. 'Last night, your husband Darren . . .'

'Darren? How's he . . .'

'Darren's cell was searched and they found a package of what is believed to be cocaine and a miniature mobile phone.'

'Drugs? A phone? There must be some mistake. I take it he's sharing a cell, right? It'll be the other person's. Darren just wouldn't . . .'

'Take a breath Jo. I can go through all the reasons the prison is sure they were Darren's if you like, or you can just trust me that they were not his cellmate's. That number on your phone is the one found in his cell, as you'll have guessed.'

Jo didn't know what to think. Was she learning about a whole new side to her husband or was he being set up yet again?

'Sir, this is all part of it. You must be able to see that.'

'Part of what? I'm prepared to accept one or two coincidences but I can't ignore what's plain to see.'

'We're agreed then.' The relief was overwhelming. She'd thought he was here to discipline her, but he'd been on her side all along.

'No, Jo, we're not.'

'What? But . . .'

'I don't dispute that you and your officers have been targeted, but you must agree that you could have done so much more to prevent that. You're losing focus.'

Jo was so furious that she had all but forgotten the staff officer scribbling away in the corner. 'How am I losing focus? Tell me.'

'If you insist. An under-resourced operation that led to the murder of a drugs worker. Redeploying an undercover officer on dubious intelligence who was then killed along with a major target. Your husband miraculously finding out that officer was, indeed, undercover just before he's charged with paying for corrupt information. Allowing an illegal informant to operate who has distributed drugs that have gone on to kill. Then, allowing one of your sergeants to tackle dangerous drug dealers single-handed and end up on life support. Finally this.' He held up her phone.

'That's not fair.'

'Which part?'

'All of it. I'm trying to save lives here and someone is out to stop me. All of what you've just said illustrates that, yet you put it down to me being a crap leader.'

Leon raised his hand. 'No one is saying that, it's just there have been a series of unfortunate events which arguably stem from your poor judgement.'

'I'm not having that. I thought you were the one chief officer who actually supported their staff. How wrong I was.' She leapt up.

Leon stood and stepped in her path. 'Sit down.' To her own disgust she did as she was told, knowing that she had the look of a chastened schoolgirl. 'That's better. You need to know that I spent a good hour and a half before I came here persuading the chief constable not to suspend you.' She was about to interrupt, but Leon's hand silenced her. 'What I am here to do though is to give you a formal order to close Operation Eradicate. The investigations that have fallen out of it will be taken on by the Major Crime Team, but so far as you are concerned, it's finished. Be under no illusion – you are lucky to still be at work, but take this as an opportunity to focus on more achievable goals and to restore the chief constable's faith in you.' He gathered his papers. 'I hope I made that clear.' He nodded to his staff officer, who seemed only too pleased to jump up and follow as the ACC left the room.

Mills had not been gone more than five minutes when Gary and Bob walked through the door.

'Thank God you're here. You will not believe what Mills has just done, or should I say tried to do?'

It was Gary who spoke. 'Jo, we need a word.'

'Me first. I thought that bloke was on our side, but he comes down here shouting the odds. Someone's stitching Darren up from inside—'

'Jo, please,' said Gary. It was then she noticed that both were still standing, looking edgy.

'What is it? Is it Scotty? Oh, God, I'm going up to the hospital.'

'It's not Scotty.'

'What then? You're scaring me.'

The two men sat down.

'You know how much we support you,' said Gary.

'Is there a but coming?'

'I think the time has come to rethink Op Eradicate. I, we' – he looked at Bob who nodded – 'we know you've only got the city's best interests at heart, but we aren't sure it's ready for what you're trying to do. Look at everything that's happened, the lives lost and ruined. We don't think we can just carry on as we are and accept the collateral damage.'

'How dare you. I've never used that term.'

'Jo, please. I know you haven't but that's what it's been. Bob and I have wrestled with this but we need to go back to basics. Treat anyone who breaks the law as a criminal and let others worry about whether they can be cured.'

'Surrender? That's not what we do here. You both need to grow a pair and accept that when things get tough, we do not give up and go back to our old ways.'

Gary left a silence. 'Read the writing. Eradicate's not working so we can't be any further part of it. We can't have blood on our hands. You're on your own.'

Jo struggled to find the words. This was treachery, plain and simple, but she needed to come up with something better than that to bring these two turncoats back in line. She breathed deeply. 'Did you know these bastards have planted drugs and a phone on Darren just to get at me? No, of course you didn't 'cos you didn't bother to ask what the ACC wanted.' Bob went to say something. 'Shut up, Bob. Did you also know that he's ordered me to drop Eradicate? Whether I do or not is another matter, but why should you cowards care? You're no better than the rest of them. Well you can both fuck off. I don't need you. I don't need the fucking ACC. I don't need anyone. I'll do this, with or without you.'

She stood up, grabbed her bag in a swish, and just as she was about to reach the door, turned round. 'And if you're not with me on this, find yourselves other jobs 'cos you're not welcome here.'

She just managed to get out before they had a chance to respond.

She sat in her car, aware of the eyes that would be watching her from the windows which surrounded three sides of the car park. She needed to pull herself together. God, she needed sleep. And food; she could murder a bacon sandwich. But sleep, preceded by a glass of wine – just to help her get off – must come first.

She pulled away, her bed and a large Pinot Grigio calling.

42

It wasn't unusual for Gary to take the helm. It was what deputies did. But Jo did pick her moments to storm out. He knew it was partly of his own making, and if he were in her shoes, he'd have done so months ago.

The next hint that the day was on a collision course was when the duty inspector called him and asked where they should take prisoners.

'Where do you think? Bit of a daft question.'

'Well, obviously, sir, but have we got permission to go out of county?'

'Why would you do that? If Brighton is full try Worthing, Crawley or Eastbourne.'

The inspector took on a patronising air. 'But they're all closed. Have you not read the email?'

Gary tapped the touchpad on his laptop and typed in the password.

Force-wide email.
To all officers and staff,
With immediate effect, due to a contractual issue, all custody centres

in Sussex Police area are closed. Prisoners already in custody have been transported to neighbouring force facilities, but until further notice only essential arrests are to be made until the situation is clarified.

Thank you for your cooperation and understanding.

Chief Constable

'What the hell . . . ? I'll get back to you ASAP.' He ended the call and immediately called ACC Mills.

'Gary, how can I help?' said Leon, sounding much more like his usual self.

'Have you seen this email about custody? What the hell are we supposed to do?'

'I know, it's a bit of a pickle. Just bear with us and we'll sort something.'

'With respect, sir, it's not as easy as "bear with". I've got officers attending calls as we speak and my money is on most of those ending in an arrest. We can't just ask people to pop back when we're open again.'

'Gary, we are dealing with this and, for your ears only, the force maintenance contract and vehicle recovery contract have been suspended too. It's hell up here so do what you can. Phone round other forces, voluntary interviews, you know the drill.' Gary pressed to end the call, if only to stop himself detonating his career with a reflex response.

He messaged all the inspectors and chief inspectors to attend an emergency meeting.

Ten minutes later, the three of them walked in.

'Right. We know that custody is closed, so the second this meeting is over I'm contacting Reigate and Portsmouth to let them know to expect our prisoners . . .'

'But boss,' said the chief inspector. 'That's a three-hour round trip to either. We've next to no one on duty anyway, so what are we going to do when they all bugger off to Surrey and Hampshire?'

Gary shrugged. 'Have you got a better suggestion?'

The inspector who'd called him earlier then spoke. 'I've got two units at

RTCs and no one is available to recover the cars. So that's the Mill Road roundabout and the Rottingdean traffic lights gridlocked.'

'Jesus,' said Gary. That was two of the busiest junctions blocked, effectively cutting off most of the city.

The second inspector chipped in. 'And undertakers too. I've had a PC at a sudden death for three hours and no one will come out. It's bad on us but worse for the families.'

This was a new one on Gary. 'Why won't they come out?'

The inspector shrugged. 'Comms say they can't get hold of anyone but they'll keep trying.'

'Good God. Is there anything else I don't know about?'

They shook their heads.

'Great. I need to make some calls,' said Gary, gathering his papers while trying to figure out where the hell this was heading.

43

At first Jo thought it was a lorry reversing. She rubbed her eyes, then swung her legs off the mattress and retched. Grabbing her phone from the bedside unit, she realised it had been her ringtone that woke her and the *Unknown Caller* had rung off.

She checked the time: 2.32 p.m. Three missed calls. God, how long had she slept?

Then she caught sight of the empty bottle of Pinot next to the fingerprint-smeared glass. Surely she hadn't drunk all that. On a school day. She fumbled the glass and staggered to the en suite. As she passed the mirrored wardrobe she had to double take then ran her hand through her matted hair.

She put the glass on the sink and sat on the toilet. Once she'd finished, she washed her hands and filled the wine glass with water, downing it in one go. She was about to repeat the exercise when she heard the phone ring again. She dashed back to the bedroom to grab it. Voicemail. She hit 'play'.

'Mrs Howe, it's Mrs Holmes, North Hove Primary School. I'm afraid we've had to call an ambulance for Ciaran and Liam. It seems they have some kind of food poisoning. I wonder if you could call me as soon as you can.'

The headteacher's even tone was at odds with her message. Food poisoning? Ambulance? What the hell?

Jo's fingers raced across the screen as she located the school's number. Hitting the call button, she paced the bedroom willing the pre-recorded messages explaining how to report an absence to fuck off. Eventually an equally insidious voice to Mrs Holmes's answered.

'North Hove Primary, how can I help you?'

'Put me through to Mrs Holmes,' Jo snapped with more panic than aggression.

'Can I ask what it's about and I'll see if she's free?'

'My two boys who've just been rushed to hospital. Put me through.'

With a fluster, the receptionist couldn't transfer the call fast enough and in two rings the West Country burr of Mrs Holmes came on the line. 'Mrs Howe?'

'Yes, what the hell has happened?'

'I'm afraid Ciaran and Liam have both been taken ill this afternoon. We did try to get through as soon as it happened but . . .'

'Both of them? How? I mean, what's wrong with them?'

'Well, they've both been fitting and vomiting quite violently and Liam was unconscious for a while.'

Jo's head span. 'Are you sure? They're OK now, yes?'

'They're on their way to hospital. The paramedics did what they could to stabilise them. They thought it was some kind of food poisoning. Can I ask, have either any allergies we weren't aware of?'

'No, of course not.'

'It's just if they have, you really should tell us.'

'I said they haven't. Which hospital are they going to?' As she asked this, Jo was racing downstairs to search for her keys, purse and warrant card.

'The Royal Alex,' said Mrs Holmes. 'But the paramedics said they'd go straight to trauma so you should call first.'

'Fuck that,' said Jo as she ended the call.

She dashed to the front door, leapt in her car and wheel-span it off the gravel driveway. She powered down the road, mentally planning the quickest route across Brighton to the children's hospital. It seemed every red light was conspiring against her, so she made up time by racing down the bus lane. If only she was in her police car. She prayed that all her officers would be too busy to pay any attention to her Brands Hatch driving, too preoccupied to put a tube in her mouth. That would be the final nail in her career's coffin.

Once she passed her own police station, she was logjammed in the Brighton College school traffic. She cursed the town planners who had decided to build one of the country's most prestigious public schools and the dual-sited Royal Sussex County Hospital and Royal Alexandra Children's Hospital within yards of each other on the same narrow road. Weaving between buses, taxis and white vans, she eventually arrived at Upper Abbey Road where she darted into a residents' bay. She was about to jump out of the car when the bottle of Pinot sprung to mind, so she grabbed a handful of mints and a face mask from the glovebox.

She stumbled as she stepped out of the car, then regaining her footing, sprinted to the Children's Accident and Emergency entrance. Her mind raced as to how she could let Darren know. She shoved that to the back of her mind as she ran through the doors to reception, fixing her face mask firmly around her ears.

'Mrs Howe. My sons have been brought in by' – she frowned – 'what do you call it, ambulance, from North Hove Primary.' She hoped her slurs weren't obvious.

The receptionist tapped a keyboard. Jo saw a frown flash across the young man's face before it returned to the corporately approved smile.

'Take a seat, Mrs Howe, and I'll ask one of the doctors to come and see you.'

Terror coursed through her. 'They are OK, aren't they?'

'The doctor will see you soon.'

Jo took the only vacant seat, next to a woman whose toddler seemed intent on coughing her lungs up onto the linoleum floor. Now she was grateful for the face mask for a second reason.

Each time the door to the treatment area opened, Jo went to stand – but each time the doctor, nurse, cleaner or whoever strode past on a mission that did not involve her.

God, her head ached.

After what seemed like an hour, but was only fifteen minutes, a young floppy-haired man in a check shirt and grey jeans ambled into the waiting area, looked around then, guided by the receptionist, headed grim-faced towards Jo.

'Mrs Howe?' Jo nodded. 'My name is Deepak. I'm one of the doctors, would you like to come through for a chat?'

'Are they OK? Can I see them?' she said, aware she'd given too many death messages in her time not to spot the preamble.

'We're helping them all we can at the moment, but we should talk in private.'

Jo followed the doctor as closely as she could without tripping into him, then waited while he used his ID card to unlock a door to the left.

As she stepped in, the room did little to salve Jo's terror. The soft chairs, gentle wallpaper and tissues on the table all screamed somewhere where hearts were broken.

'Please, take a seat,' said Deepak.

Jo perched on the edge of a floral two-seater settee, silently urging the doctor to get it over and done with. Her whole body shook.

'Mrs Howe, both of your boys are very unwell. They seem to have some kind of food poisoning and we have sedated them for now, but the next twenty-four hours are critical. I must ask you, is there anything you know that they might have eaten which could have brought this on? Any allergies, any food which might be out of date? I gather from the paramedics that they take packed lunches to school.'

'Yes to the packed lunches, but no to the allergies. My mum looked after them overnight but I'm not sure what she put in their boxes. Probably something like a cheese and pickle sandwich, cereal bar, a banana and a fruit drink. I can check but they can eat anything.'

'I understand.' By the age of him, Jo doubted that. 'Nothing else?'

'No. They'd both have had Coco Pops for breakfast, I think. She always gives them that. Do you think it's something they've eaten?'

'We don't know yet. As I say, we have sedated them both and they really are in the best place. The symptoms we are seeing, well, we don't see them every day, so we are trying to work out what they have taken so we can provide them with the right treatment.'

'Do you think they've been poisoned?'

The doctor looked taken aback. 'Well I'm not able to say. Is there any reason why they may have been?'

'I'm not sure, it's just some stuff's been happening to some of my colleagues and I just wondered.'

'Poison?'

'No.'

The doctor looked more relaxed, infuriatingly so in fact. 'I see. It's probably best not to overthink these things. Let us focus on what's causing their condition so we can make them better.'

'Can I see them now?'

'Briefly, but they are in isolation until we know what we are dealing with.'

Deepak stood and Jo followed him out of the door, up some stairs and through a maze of corridors. They reached a sign saying *High Dependency Unit*, and once again the doctor's card allowed them in. He guided Jo to a window. She was about to ask what she was supposed to be looking at when it dawned on her. The two mounds beneath the tangle of tubes and cables, surrounded by multicoloured flashing screens and what looked like bellows, were Ciaran and Liam.

'My babies, my babies,' she cried as she pounded against the glass. 'What have they done to you?'

The world blurred out.

She couldn't remember how she ended up in a different but identical family room, but as she looked up, she saw an older doctor who seemed to wear both a look of empathy and of wanting to get this over with.

'I'm sorry,' said Jo. 'Can you tell me what's going on?'

'Of course. I'm Rebecca, one of the consultants. I won't go over what Deepak told you, other than to say Ciaran and Liam are very sick but in the best hands. It's a matter of time but we really do need to know what's in them so we can give them the right treatment. You have no idea?'

'No, I told him that. I think they might have been poisoned deliberately though.' Jo could have punched Rebecca's patronising look right off her face. 'I mean it.'

'Of course, but that's most unusual and doesn't affect what we are trying to do. I'm afraid until we know, it's a waiting game.'

Jo stood up. 'Well, if you don't believe me, I'll speak to some people who will. You never know, it might just save their lives.'

Running down the stairs and out of the hospital, Jo had no idea of where she was going or what her next step should be. All she knew was that hanging around watching her boys fade away would only achieve just that.

As she reached her car, the flapping yellow fixed penalty notice mocked her from the windscreen. She ripped it off, opened the door and chucked it into the footwell. She needed to tell Darren so tapped on Belmarsh's number. Three times it rang out.

She sat in the driver's seat and gripped the steering wheel. People said that long, deep breaths were the key to a calm mind, so she gave it a go. After five, she concluded that was bollocks. What the hell could she do? Instinctively answering her own question, she called Bob.

'Ma'am, you OK?'

Just the sound of his voice broke the dam of tears and all she could do was sob.

'Jo. Where are you? What's happened?'

Even she couldn't understand her own words as she blurted out, 'Boys . . . poison . . . life support . . . Darren.'

'Tell me where to find you? I'll be there.'

'The Alex . . . west entrance . . . God . . .'

The line went dead and Jo howled so loud that a passing dog walker tapped the window and mouthed, 'You OK?' Jo ignored them.

Five minutes later, Bob wrenched open the passenger door, threw himself in and embraced her with the strength of a bear. Jo looked up and saw his car not so much parked but abandoned between two communal bins just down the road.

'I'm so sorry about earlier. Tell me what's going on,' he whispered. She couldn't get the words out so he said, 'Take your time.'

It took a full two minutes before Jo could compose herself enough to utter a comprehensible sentence. 'It's the boys. They're in there with machines keeping them alive. They say it's food poisoning.'

'Please. Tell me everything from the start. And slowly.'

Between her tears, she started from being woken up by the school's call and finished with seeing the boys hooked up to more contraptions than she'd ever seen in her life. 'They're saying it's food poisoning but it's not, Bob. They've got to them.'

Bob squeezed her tighter. 'You don't know that. These things happen you know. Kids get ill, doctors fix them and they carry on like nothing's happened. You'll see.'

Jo broke his grip and glared at him. 'Really? Two brothers, whose mum and everyone connected with her are targeted by God knows who, just happen to fall victim of "food poisoning", and you say it just happens?'

'How would anyone have got to them? At the same time? It's probably something they ate, like the doctors said.'

Jo shook him off. 'I thought you of all people would understand. Just go back to the nick and sort the other shit out. Find out about this Evans bloke and who attacked Scotty.'

'What are you going to do?'

'I've no idea, but I know what I'm not going to do. Sit on my fat arse and wait for the loves of my life to die through apathy.' She reached across Bob and opened his door. 'Go on, get out.' She shoved him. 'And get a message to Darren.'

He stood on the pavement, then stuck his head back in. 'You really shouldn't be driving you know.'

'Is that so?' she said, then started the engine and accelerated down the hill.

44

Bob was right. She was still over the limit which, added to the red lights she was jumping in her panic to get to the school, made this journey like a game of Russian roulette. However, despite her fuzzy brain, a plan started to form.

She checked the clock on her dashboard. 4.30 p.m. Had it really been only two hours since she'd woken from her daytime binge to have her world explode around her? She hoped that, despite school finishing over an hour ago, Mrs Holmes and enough of the staff would still be there for her to do what she needed.

Ten minutes later she dumped her car in a disabled bay and headed straight for the front door. Locked. She ran around the perimeter trying every door, without success. Then she glimpsed a meeting going on in the small hall she'd frequented on countless parents' evenings. A dozen adults looked ridiculous, perched on chairs made for under-elevens. Governors, she presumed. She banged on the window and the heads turned, some looking indignant, others terrified. She kept banging. After a few seconds, the headteacher stood up, came to the window and pointed to a door to Jo's right.

She glanced over and reached it before Mrs Holmes did. The head only had the door open an inch when Jo barged in. 'What happened to my boys?'

Mrs Holmes turned round and muttered an apology to the others. 'Come with me, Mrs Howe.' The headteacher led the way to her office where she pointed to a chair. 'Please, have a seat.'

'I'll stand. Now what the hell happened?'

Mrs Holmes sniffed the air then sat behind her desk. 'As I said on the phone, I was told it was food poisoning. That seems the most likely explanation. How are they?'

'Dying. How were they poisoned?'

'I'm so sorry. The paramedics assumed it was something in their lunch.'

A thought that should have flashed much earlier sparked in Jo. 'Where are their lunchboxes? Maybe we can get anything left tested.'

'I'm not sure. I presume in their bags. Lunchtime was finished by the time they fell ill.'

'Didn't you give them to the paramedics for the hospital?'

'No, they didn't ask.'

'Jesus. Well find them and get them preserved for forensics.'

Mrs Holmes went to leave the office when Jo called her back. 'Get someone to do it for you. I want to see the CCTV.'

The headteacher stopped in her tracks, suddenly subservient. She picked up her desk phone and instructed the person on the other end to find the bags and boxes and bring them to her. 'I'm not sure how seeing the CCTV will help,' she said to Jo.

'I'm the police officer here. Just bring it up on your screen and talk me through the lunchtime routines.'

Mrs Holmes obeyed once more, tapping on the keyboard as she spoke. 'The children put their lunchboxes on a trolley in the classroom when they arrive in the morning. At lunchtime, the midday meal supervisors take the trolleys to the hall and the children retrieve their boxes then sit down to eat. Afterwards, they put the boxes back on the trolley and it's taken back

288

to their class. That way, if they are elsewhere in the school before or after lunch, they don't have to carry them around nor return to the classroom.'

'The boxes are unattended for at least some of the morning then?'

'Well, yes I suppose so, but the school is very secure so it's not really a risk.'

Jo agreed. It certainly seemed that people couldn't just wander in or out without being checked.

'Where are the CCTV cameras?'

'We've got quite good coverage. The system was updated a year or so ago. It's in all the communal areas, everywhere really, apart from the classrooms themselves and the toilets and changing rooms obviously.'

Jo struggled to understand why the classrooms weren't covered, but that was for another time.

'Right, I want to see the cameras that cover the outside of both Ciaran and Liam's classrooms during the morning, and the lunch hall when they were eating.'

Jo grabbed a chair and sat next to Mrs Holmes so she could see for herself. Then she had a thought. 'Actually, to save time, find when the classrooms were empty but the boxes were in there. Then we can look at the lunchtime footage.'

'We had a whole school assembly today so that's probably the first place to start.' Mrs Holmes navigated the playback with surprising dexterity and homed in on the outside of both Ciaran's and Liam's classrooms. She allowed it to play out in 1.5 speed, from when the children left each room in single file to when they returned. No one had entered the rooms in that time.

'What about external doors?'

Mrs Holmes sighed. 'We can look but I promise you, it would only be staff with access by this time of the day.'

'Play it,' said Jo.

Again, it showed nothing and no one to raise Jo's suspicions.

'Were the classrooms occupied up until playtime?' said Jo.

Mrs Holmes changed screens and checked the timetable. 'Yes, both classes were in their rooms.'

'Right, go to playtime then.'

With a flick of the mouse, the timestamp moved forward to 10.30 a.m. and the footage played again. 'The children will have left via the external doors,' said Mrs Holmes, before Jo asked why no one had left through the one they were watching.

The corridors were practically deserted other than a few members of staff wandering along. Then, at 10.34 a.m. outside Ciaran's class, a man appeared to be about to walk past but then checked his step, looked behind and darted in.

'Stop. Play that back. Freeze it there. Who's that?' said Jo.

'That's Mr O'Leary. He's a casual speech and language assistant.'

'What does that even mean?'

'He comes in occasionally to help the speech and language therapist. He's only been with us a fortnight or so, but I don't know why he's going in there. They have their own room.'

Jo sobered up instantly. She was on to something. They watched, one eye on the footage, one on the timer. Ninety seconds later and Mr O'Leary was back out, as furtively as he'd entered. 'Follow him,' demanded Jo.

Mrs Holmes clicked from camera to camera as the SALT assistant moved out of shot of each. At 10.37 a.m., he again paused outside a classroom, glanced around and darted in.

'Liam's class?' said Jo.

Mrs Holmes nodded solemnly.

This time it was sixty seconds and O'Leary was back out, scurrying down the corridor.

'I want his file, photo, address, references, the whole nine yards,' said Jo. 'And I want to see a copy of his Disclosure and Barring Service certificate.' At that last point, Mrs Holmes flinched. 'He has got a DBS?'

'It's not come through yet.'

'What? So why's he even in here?'

'He's supposed to be supervised by one of the speech therapists until he's cleared. I've no idea what he's doing wandering around on his own.'

'I do, Mrs Holmes. Not as a mother but as a police officer, I'm telling you to get me everything you have on this man. You might just have employed a child killer.'

The switch from frantic mother to steely detective came as naturally to Jo as breathing. She was on a mission now and, other than the occasional flash of anguish demonstrated by her checking her phone for missed calls or messages, nothing was going to throw her off the scent.

In contrast, Mrs Holmes was in pieces – but Jo really didn't have the time, energy or inclination to reassure her. Without her though, the task of identifying who this mysterious staff member really was would be nigh on impossible.

O'Leary's personnel file, such as it was, was laid out on the desk in front of them.

'Are you telling me you've heard nothing back on these two reference requests? Also, you've accepted what was, in all likelihood, a fake passport, and as he was the only applicant for this job you had a cosy chat rather than a formal interview?'

Mrs Holmes wept. 'You make it sound like we were negligent.' Jo raised an eyebrow. 'It's not unusual to get just one applicant these days and we'd lose the funding if we didn't appoint. He should have been supervised at all times until the checks came back though.'

Jo swallowed back the rant. 'How you did or did not appoint him is for others to answer and for later. Now, if we have any hope of saving Ciaran and Liam's lives we have to focus on finding out who he really is and where we might find him, so I suggest you pull yourself together and help me do that.' Mrs Holmes nodded.

Jo slid the application form across the table and with the other hand opened her phone. She found Bob's number and tapped call. She thought it was going to ring out when he finally answered. 'Ma'am?'

'I need you to run someone through PNC for me.'

'Why? What are you up to?'

'Trying to ID the person who poisoned the boys.' She lowered her voice, turning away from the headteacher. 'Please help me out here.' She read from the application form and waited.

'No trace. Why do you . . .'

'Can you do a voters register check on this address?' She read out the Portslade house and road O'Leary had said he lived at.

'No trace again.'

Jo pictured the road, and something occurred to her. 'What number does that road go up to?'

'Jo, you really need to tell me what's going on.'

'What number Bob?'

'Forty-four.'

'Not forty-eight then?'

'Nope.'

'Right, listen. I'm looking into a man who's hoodwinked the school into giving him a job. He just happened to sneak into Ciaran and Liam's classrooms when no one was in there this morning.'

'And?'

'And he had the opportunity to tamper with their lunchboxes. I need to find out who he is.'

Jo could almost hear Bob's eyes lift to the ceiling. 'I'm not being funny but . . .'

'Oh, just drop it Bob. If you're not going to help, I'll do it myself.' She tapped the red button and slammed the handset on the desk. It buzzed almost immediately and seeing it was Bob, she rejected the call and pushed the phone away. 'Listen to me,' she said to Mrs Holmes. 'I need you to think. What else can you tell me about this man? Any car he uses? Friends? Anything he talks about that might give us a clue as to who he really is?'

'I'm so sorry, I don't really know much about the support staff. You see I'm so busy . . .'

'Who will know? Every school has its busybody.'

'Well, Mrs Brakespear, the receptionist, keeps her eyes and ears open. Shall I call her in?'

'Yes please.'

The headteacher left the room, then returned accompanied by a surly-looking forty-something woman whose look of disdain suggested that she either hated the police or parents in general. At any other time, Jo would have spent a moment or two trying to win her round. But at those times, her sons' lives wouldn't have been hanging from silk.

'I'm investigating the attempted murder of my two sons by someone who gave false details to get a job here, and I need you to tell me everything you know about him. He's using the name Dominic O'Leary.' Jo picked the photo up off the desk and thrust it at Mrs Brakespear. The shocked receptionist looked at Mrs Holmes as if asking for permission to speak.

The headteacher nodded. 'It's important, Janet. Tell Mrs Howe anything you know.'

Still standing, the receptionist spoke. 'Not much to say really. He's only been here a couple of weeks. There're only a few other men on the staff and they say there's something odd about him.'

'Odd?'

'He keeps himself to himself. Doesn't join in their chats, although I can't blame him as it's always football or the most recent Marvel movie.'

'What about the other staff? Does he mix with them?'

'Not as much as some would like.'

'Meaning?'

'Well, he's a bit of a looker, you'll have to agree.'

'Oh, spare me,' muttered Jo. 'Tell me though, which teachers, support staff, fancy him?'

'I don't know about fancying him but some would like to get to know him better, shall we say.'

'Write me a list. Meanwhile, how does he get to and from school? Car? Bike? Bus?'

'I'm not sure. I've never seen him park up or with cycling gear.' She paused again. 'Hold on, I think he gets the bus.'

It took every ounce of restraint for Jo not to bellow at the woman to just come out with it. 'Why's that?'

'It was something Miss Mitchell said the other day.'

Christ, this was worse than painful. 'Which was?'

'It was the day of the bus strike. She was crowing that Dominic had asked her for a lift home. I think she thought she was in with a chance if you know what I mean.'

Jo turned to Mrs Holmes. 'Where does Miss Mitchell live?'

'Er, I'm not entirely sure. The other side of Brighton, I think.'

'Not Portslade, as per this application form? Not on her way home then?' Mrs Holmes wisely kept quiet. 'Where can I find Miss Mitchell?' Jo continued.

'She's in the hall. She happens to be one of our staff governors so she's stayed back for the meeting. I'll fetch her.'

A couple of minutes later, Mrs Holmes returned with a teacher in Lycra leggings and a blue windcheater bearing the school's logo. *You know you're getting old when teachers look younger*, thought Jo.

'Miss Mitchell?'

'Anna.'

'Anna, this is really important but I haven't got time to go into details. You took Dominic O'Leary home the other day, yes?'

'Well, to his home, not mine.' She flicked a glance at her colleagues. 'It was just a lift.'

'Yes, yes, I know. Where was that?'

'Just off the seafront in Brighton. I live in Rottingdean so it was on the way.'

'Where on the seafront?'

The PE teacher gazed into the middle distance. 'Just before the Old West Pier I think. It's in a square but I can't remember the name. There are so many along there.'

'Could you show me?'

'Well, I suppose so. At least I could try.'

Jo took a picture of O'Leary's photo, grabbed her bag and pointed to both Mrs Holmes and Mrs Brakespear. 'You two wait here. I'll be back. Anna, come with me.'

Anna looked terrified and her eyes pleaded for support from her headteacher.

'It's OK, Anna,' said Mrs Holmes.

'Follow me,' said Jo and breathed a sigh of relief when she sensed Anna behind her.

Just as she was about to leave, Mrs Brakespear spoke. 'There was something else.'

Jo stopped in her tracks. 'Yes.'

'I saw Mr O'Leary dash out of school before playtime this morning. He came back a couple of minutes later. Now I think of it, it seemed odd.'

Jo glared at her and Mrs Holmes. 'I'm sure it does. Is the outside covered by CCTV?'

'Yes, it covers just outside the gate and a bit either side,' said Mrs Holmes.

'Check and send me what you find while we're gone. My number's on your files.'

As she dashed to the car, Jo checked her phone again for calls or messages from the hospital. Nothing. She called them as she fiddled with the ignition. It rang and rang. She was about to call again, but knew she didn't have time if she was going to save the boys. Anyway, she tried to convince herself, surely no news was good news.

Fifteen minutes later, and after firing questions at the terrified teacher which elicited not much more than O'Leary was 'hot but brusque', they joined the snail-paced traffic heading east along the seafront. 'Right, I need you to think back to the day you dropped him off and tell me exactly what you saw and did. Anything he said too. Don't filter, just tell me.' Thank goodness Jo remembered some of the more mystical elements of her cognitive interview course she'd attended as a young DC, when life was simpler.

Anna seemed to be buying into the exercise and, as they passed the Peace Statue that marked the boundary between Brighton and Hove, she said, 'Left here.'

Jo wasn't expecting the command so soon. 'What, Bedford Square?' Was this a coincidence? It was two streets from where Lizzie had been murdered and where the burner phone had pinged.

'Yes, up here,' said Anna, pointing to her left. The square of Regency town houses was one-way, so Jo had to take the east-most road and crawl up and round.

'Where did you drop him?'

'I think it was just as you loop round and come back down.' Jo did so. 'Yes, yes, it was just here,' said Anna. 'There was a bin lorry blocking the road, so he got out here and said he'd walk the rest. I remember he turned and waved as he headed towards the sea.'

'Did you see where he went?' said Jo, more in hope than expectation.

'Can you edge forward a bit?' Jo complied, then Anna said, 'There. He went into that door there.' Jo looked at the tattered blue panel door, which looked like it had been on the wrong end of a police battering ram on more than one occasion.

'Are you sure?'

'Yes. Certain. I remember wondering how could someone so good-looking live in a dump like that.'

'My thoughts exactly. Just a second.' Jo pulled into a parking space and took out her work phone, located the number she was looking for then typed out a brief message. The reply came back from Saira in seconds.

Yes, we do know it. It's a squat. An Op Eradicate target address. Tactical Enforcement raided it a few weeks ago but it's active again.

'Jesus,' said Jo, then messaged back. *Can you meet me here?*

On my way, came the reply.

'Anna, I'm going to pay for a taxi to get you back to the school but I need you to do two things. Firstly, tell Mrs Holmes and that receptionist to stay put. And, secondly, if anyone asks, we didn't find the address. OK?'

'Sure,' said Anna. Jo had no choice but to trust her.

45

This was not her first seizure but, to Sir Ben, it seemed the most severe. He'd become used to his mother's short, sharp 'absences' and didn't even bother timing those any more, much to the doctors' dismay. This was different though. He did his best to calm her and stop her falling, but something told him this was the start of a new phase and if he couldn't free up the cash to send her to the States soon, he'd lose her.

Once she'd settled, he called Dr Trevor Blaketon. This time he was taking none of his shit. He'd already amassed compromises against the medic to see him struck off, and this time the doctor would be in no doubt that helping him was his only other option.

The call went to voicemail but experience told him that he'd soon pick it up. The menacing message he left would secure the swiftest house call known to the medical world. When the gate buzzer sounded five minutes later though, even he was surprised.

He looked at the app and saw Tony Evans filling the video frame. He buzzed him in while walking to the front door.

Dispensing with any niceties, Evans said, 'All done.' For a moment, Sir

Ben mentally searched for what his lieutenant could be on about, and then it came to him.

'Oh, right. What did you use?'

Evans's brow creased. 'You sure you want to know? Deniability?'

'I'm curious. From a pharmaceutical perspective.'

'Spice.'

'Spice?'

'Yes, you know, synthetic cannabinoids.'

'I know what spice is. I just thought you'd go for something more sophisticated. Are they dead?'

'Not as far as I know, but it's only a matter of time.'

Sir Ben was about to demand why not but, with his inside knowledge of pharmaceuticals, he had to concede that different people responded in different ways.

'Where are they?'

'At the Royal Alex. High Dependency Unit I'd imagine, for now.'

'Have we any assets on the staff there?'

'We're working on that.'

'OK, well keep me updated. Does Jo Howe know yet?'

'I'd imagine so. We're trying to find out but the school would have told her straight away. Oh, and something else about her.'

'Go on.'

'A little bird tells me she's been ordered to drop Op Eradicate.' Evans looked like he was due a medal.

'How can we trust your little bird?'

Evans tapped the side of his nose.

Sir Ben allowed himself a second of optimism. Was this it? Had they finally won? Then he heard his mother scream out from the floor above.

'That changes nothing. We've come too far and, in any case, she needs teaching a fucking lesson. I'm not having jumped-up coppers thinking they can come up against me and get away with it. She still needs to be punished.'

'You're the boss,' said Evans.

Sir Ben wandered into the kitchen and knew Evans would be following. 'So, back to her brats. Even if they die, how will she know it was aimed at her? Won't she just think it's food poisoning?' He perched on a breakfast bar stool. Evans did likewise.

'She's not daft and the chances of both her sons falling to some dodgy sandwich at the same time won't escape her as suspicious.'

'Is that what your guy did? Poisoned their sandwich?'

'I just told him to spray something they'd eat in the lunchbox. Worked a treat.'

'And where is your bloke now? We need to deal with him.'

'Leave him to us.'

Just then the gate buzzer sounded again and, to his relief, Sir Ben saw Dr Blaketon's car waiting for access. 'It's my mum,' Sir Ben explained. 'She's in a bad way.' Then he headed for the door.

46

Jo had told PC Saira Bannerjee to meet her on the opposite side of the square, where she'd found a spot vacated by a BT Openreach van. It wasn't perfect, but it would have to do. If she leant back in her seat she could just about see the squat's front door, and hopefully the bushes in the way would act as a half-decent shield.

Saira appeared as if from nowhere at the passenger window, opened the door and slid in.

'Did you walk?' asked Jo.

'Jogged.'

'Christ, haven't you got an off button?'

Saira laughed. 'I've got a regional judo tournament at the weekend and I need to make the weight.'

Jo compared their midriffs. 'You look fine to me. Did anyone ask where you were going?'

'No. I'd just been visiting Scotty up the hospital.'

'You didn't run all the way from there, did you?'

Saira pinched her waist. 'There's a few pounds to go.'

'How is Scotty? He wasn't responsive this morning.'

'No change. I went more for me than him. He's still in an induced coma. The doctors won't tell me much but it seems they are taking it hour by hour. It's a good job he was an ugly bugger to start with, as his modelling career is over.'

Jo smiled. 'Thanks for coming. I need your help but first I'll bring you up to speed.' Jo explained everything that had happened that afternoon, reminding Saira of the previous attacks on police officers to explain why she was so convinced the boys had been poisoned.

The PC took in her boss's every word. 'Right. That's the blue door across there we're talking about, yes?'

'That's the one.'

'Grubby place, even by the usual standards. I reckon there are three flats on each of the three floors but to be honest, there are no more than a couple of doors in the whole building so it's just an open-plan hovel.' Surely O'Leary would have looked and smelt like he'd slept in a hedge when he had his rudimentary interview.

'When you raided it, did you record everyone's name who was in there?'

'As ever,' said Saira.

'Sorry. Was anyone by the name of Dominic O'Leary there?'

'Hold on, I'll look.' Saira tapped away on her work mobile phone, which served as her pocketbook. 'No, no one gave that name.'

Jo opened her own phone and showed Saira the snap she'd taken at the school earlier. 'Recognise him?'

'Oh, er. He's a bit of all right,' said the PC.

'Not you too.'

'My bad. Can I have a better look?' Jo handed her the phone and waited while Saira enlarged the image, then tilted it to catch the light. 'I can't be sure but, other than him having scrubbed up a bit, I reckon it's this bloke.' Saira returned to her own phone and pulled up a picture of a man called Terry Murphy, who seemed to have collected convictions like stamps. Immediately, Jo saw the likeness. The same rugged good looks set off by a roguish crooked nose. The only differences were, in the photo Saira had, that Murphy's nose appeared freshly broken and he still wore the washed-out complexion that defined most drug addicts.

'How long has he been around here?'

Saira thought about it. 'Scotty would know for sure but he's usually in the background. Doesn't give us any bother really, just one of the crowd.' She was still flicking through Murphy's record. 'Hold on, here we are. He was released to no fixed address from Dartmoor Prison four months ago.'

Jo's thoughts went to how anyone could be so alone in the world that they had nowhere to call home. She'd never allow her boys to be in that situation. That catapulted her back to why she was doing this and how she had no time to lose. 'Can we get in there to see if Murphy's in?'

'Not without a warrant and a dozen or so others to help,' said Saira. 'We'd have no chance. But I know someone who might.'

Jo saw the grin beam across Saira's face. 'Not Spanners?'

'Want me to try? Off the record of course.'

'You know he's on bail and supposed to be lying low?'

'Yep, but I can get hold of him.'

'Go on then, and if any shit comes your way, I ordered you. Got it?'

Saira nodded. 'As Scotty would say, rules are just guidelines. They never survive contact with the streets.'

'He says that?'

'Yep, tosser isn't he?'

'I'd be less polite. You get Spanners over here while I phone the hospital.'

Sir Ben had no sooner opened the door than he dragged the doctor in.

'No more pissing about Trevor. If we don't get Mum the help she needs now, she's going to die, and if that happens you'll be next.'

Sir Ben let go of his jacket and before the doctor could protest, said, 'Follow me.' He took the stairs two at a time and sensed Trevor and Tony Evans following him. 'You don't have to see this Tony.'

'It's OK. You might need me.'

The three men walked into the room to find Audrey Parsons sitting up in bed. 'Boys, I hope you've been playing nicely. Now go and wash your hands and you can have some of the Chelsea buns I've been baking.'

'It's OK, Mum, we're not hungry. Dr Blaketon's here. He's come to check you're OK.'

'Oh how kind. Is he going to carry out a pregnancy test?'

'Not today, Mum.'

Dr Blaketon flicked his head to Sir Ben and both men stepped into the en suite, leaving Tony hovering in the bedroom.

'What do you want me to do? She seems fine, in the circumstances.'

'She's far from fucking fine,' hissed Sir Ben. 'I thought she was going to die during her seizure earlier. She needs medical help and she needs it now.'

'I'm afraid with her condition, she is dying and these ups and downs are how it's likely to be for her. Can I suggest—'

'No you fucking can't suggest anything, unless it's certifying her fit to fly to the States and getting her ready for the air ambulance.'

Dr Blaketon looked over Sir Ben's shoulder back into the room, then said, 'That would go against just about every ethical principle I'm sworn to uphold. I have to act in the patient's best interest and do no harm. She's in no state to travel in a car let alone an aeroplane. It'll kill her.'

'I don't think you are grasping the situation – your situation – here. You're mistaking what I said as a question. They evacuate soldiers from battlefields with half their limbs hanging off. All I'm telling you to do is stabilise her so she can be taken to Gatwick Airport and loaded onto a private air ambulance.' At that moment, Tony stepped into Sir Ben's eyeline. The man only had to be in a room to fill it with menace, and Sir Ben could tell from the doctor's expression that he was having the desired effect. Even he was shocked though when Tony pulled an automatic pistol from a concealed holster under his jacket. It took all he could to retain his poker face as if it were part of the plan.

'What the hell is going on?' said Dr Blaketon, as a dark wet patch ballooned across the front of his trousers.

'I'm just trying to help you understand what your job here is. Sir Ben has made a couple of simple requests and it seems you need some encouragement grasping that.' Tony thrust the gun into Dr Blaketon's right kidney.

Sir Ben needed to get this back under his control, while keeping up the illusion that he and Tony were working in consort. 'It's really simple, Trevor. My mum is going to fly to the US today. You're going to sign the necessary papers and prepare her. In the meantime, I'm going to free up the funds, book the air ambulance and confirm the procedure with the doctors at the other end, then we give my mum her life back.'

'But . . .'

The gunshot silenced the doctor and Sir Ben was sure he'd lost his hearing for ever.

47

It had taken twenty minutes for Jo to get through to the hospital and another five to assure the ward clerk she was who she said she was. Only then did she learn that the boys were still critical but stable. She wasn't sure whether to take heart from that or be terrified it meant they weren't going to recover.

By the time she'd finished the call, Spanners had arrived and was talking to Saira up the road. Jo risked flashing her headlights and the two walked briskly to the car. Saira got in the front, and Spanners in the back.

'Hi. I'm Jo. We've met before,' she said over her shoulder.

'Yeah, I remember. I heard it was you who got me arrested, so this better be good.'

'No, you did that. Forget about it though. Can you help save two boys' lives?'

'Your boys. Sorry to hear that.'

Jo turned to Saira. 'I see you've brought him up to speed?'

'I thought it would save time.'

Jo nodded. 'Shown him the photo?'

'Yep.'

'And can we trust him?'

Spanners interrupted. 'I am here you know. Yes, you can. Despite you getting me nicked, I need help to get out of this shitstorm I'm in so, for now, I'm all yours.'

'Do you know the guy?' Jo showed him the picture.

'I've seen him about. Not sure I've ever spoken to him. Not properly like, but we are on nodding terms.'

'Good, good. So, do you think you can get in there and coax him out?'

'What, so you can nick him? I'm not happy about that. I'd be known as a grass for ever.'

'No, we're not going to nick him,' said Jo, leaving 'yet' off the end of the sentence.

'What are you going to do then?'

'We need to speak to him. Urgently.'

Spanners didn't reply, then, as if a lightbulb had appeared above his head, he smiled. 'I've got an idea.'

Jo and Saira exchanged glances. 'Go on.'

'Well, from what Saira told me, this bloke has come to Brighton on the same terms as the rest of us. He's completed his task, so now he should be looking over his shoulder as it won't be long until they deal with him like they have everyone else. I'm on borrowed time too, you know.'

'And not just from them,' added Jo. 'What's your idea?'

'He needs a reason to come with me. I'll make him think the time is up for both of us but that I've found someone to get us away.'

'What if he's not in there?' said Saira.

'Let's worry about that later,' said Jo. 'Off you go then and don't be long. We may not have much time.'

Spanners got out of the car and walked across the square. Jo could only see him standing at the door, not how he managed to get in, but in a second he was out of sight.

'You reckon he'll do it?' said Jo.

Saira shrugged. 'He's our best chance.'

Jo said nothing but bit her lip, watching the car clock tick over.

Eight minutes later, two figures darted from the squat door, and in thirty seconds were sat behind Jo and Saira.

'This is Terry,' said Spanners. 'I've told him you're going to save his life.'

As Dr Blaketon fell, Sir Ben glared at Tony then went to the medic, checking for wounds.

'Trevor, are you OK?'

'He's OK,' said Tony, 'which is more than I can say for your bathroom tiles.'

'Boys. Has one of you dropped something?' came Audrey's voice from the bedroom.

'It's OK, Mum, nothing to worry about.' Sir Ben turned to Tony. 'What the fuck are you playing at?'

'He just needed a reminder that he's not in charge.'

Sir Ben stood up, then dragged the quaking doctor to his feet. 'He's a nutter, a fucking nutter,' said Dr Blaketon, his eyes streaming and his whole body still shaking as he supported himself against the shower cubicle, rubbing his ears.

Sir Ben stared Tony down, then said to Blaketon, 'You need to learn to do as you're told, when you're told. Next time it'll be more than the decor with a hole in it. Now are you going to do what you're here to do or what?'

Not for the first time, Sir Ben could have punched Tony's lights out as he caught a glimpse of his smirk out of the corner of his eye.

'Do I have any choice?'

'That's the spirit. Now what do you need to do?'

The doctor ran his hands through his hair. 'Is there somewhere we can go?' he said as he scanned round the dust-covered bathroom.

Sir Ben led them into the bedroom and back out the door to the landing. 'Won't be long, Mum,' he said as they left.

Once they were downstairs, they assembled around the office table.

Dr Blaketon still looked as white as milk as he sat opposite Sir Ben, whose eardrums screamed still. Now was not the time to ask for a medical opinion. 'As I say, what do you need to do?'

'The first thing is to issue a fit to fly certificate?'

Tony piped up for the first time. 'Fit to fly? She's not going easyJet, you know.'

Trevor kept his sights on Sir Ben. 'Fit to fly is not a blanket declaration. I need to consider the facilities and support she will get in the air ambulance and certify her according to her health and their ability to look after her. You say you have an air ambulance on standby.'

'Yes, CareFly. They specialise in long-haul medical evacuations. The CEO is a chum of mine.'

'Of course he is,' muttered Tony.

Trevor and Sir Ben snapped their heads round. 'Tony, stick to what you're good at and keep quiet while we sort this out.' Sir Ben turned back to Trevor, who looked terrified. 'So, issue the certificate and get her ready, I'll put in the call to CareFly.'

'It's not as simple as that.'

Tony twitched but Sir Ben's reproachful glare settled him back down. 'What do you need?'

'I need to examine her, then speak with the lead physician who'll be accompanying her to discuss how they will care for her for, what, eight, nine hours in the sky? That really is the bare minimum for me to issue the certificate.'

'Great. Get on with it then.'

'I need to warn you of something first . . .'

Sir Ben stood up. 'No, no more warnings.'

Dr Blaketon remained seated, the only one of the three who did. 'I'm sorry, I do need to spell this out to you, and your mother too.'

Sir Ben sat back down. 'My mother? You have seen her this morning. She has no idea whether it's breakfast time or Christmas Day.'

'I'm sorry, Ben, but capacity fluctuates. If we can speak to her in a lucid moment, I have to find out how she is and whether she consents to the journey.'

'I've had enough of this,' said Tony as he pulled the gun out again, raising his aim to Trevor.

'Put it down and disappear,' said Sir Ben just as it looked like Trevor was about to empty his bowels.

Tony flounced out of the room.

'Just say she consents. We haven't got time.'

'I won't do that. I need to prepare her for the flight in any case and I can hardly do that without talking to her.'

Sir Ben realised that arguing would only prolong things. 'Just do what you have to but, whatever she says, you will certify her and you will make sure she's ready to go as soon as the road ambulance arrives. And, before you get any other ideas in your head, I will be there when you speak to her. Wait here while I put the call in.'

Sir Ben stepped outside and saw Tony pacing the hallway. 'Not everything has to be a fight, you know,' he said as he walked past.

'Maybe not, but my way does focus minds.'

Sir Ben ignored the backchat and headed for the kitchen.

The first call was to his director of finance. The tax-free threshold for a director's loan was £10,000, so the amount Sir Ben was demanding would require not only shrouding in labyrinthine accounting measures but a potentially eye-watering debt to His Majesty's Revenue and Customs. That was for the future and others to sort out. His only concern now was to get his mother on the plane and to doctors who had the skills and bottle to make her last few years worth living. This was in her best interests. Thankfully, the director was well used to Sir Ben's demands, and only too aware that he'd pulled so many financial strokes in the past that if Sir Ben went down, he went too.

The money sorted, he now had the leverage to mobilise the road and air ambulances. The end of his nightmares was on the horizon.

48

At least Terry Murphy had the decency to look shell-shocked as he sat bolt upright behind Saira. His film-star looks had vanished, in their place pale terror.

'Do you know why you're here?' said Jo, clicking a switch on the door.

'I, er, I think you're going to make me disappear before that lot catch up with me.' The soft Irish burr was incongruous for a man who'd tried to murder her children.

'Get you out of here?'

'That's what he said,' replied Murphy.

'Yeah, sorry about that. I might have told you a little white lie,' said Spanners, with an insincere shrug. 'Still, you're here now.'

'You fuckers,' Murphy shouted as he grabbed the door handle. Saira twisted round to seize an arm but Spanners already had the man in a headlock.

'You can let him go,' said Jo. 'Child locks. Now, listen to me. You're here because you defrauded your way into a school to poison two little boys. Correct?'

'Fuck you. Ouch, get the fuck off.'

Jo looked again at Spanners who was squeezing Murphy's testicles. 'Thanks, Spanners, but maybe you can leave the questioning to us.' She faced Murphy. 'Now, usually I'd want to find out a bit about you, establish any common ground, that sort of thing, but we don't have the time.'

'Who the fuck are you?'

'The combination of your worst fears. I am both the boys' mother, and my friend and I are police officers. No one else knows we are here, and it doesn't much matter as I'm the boss, so if I unleash Spanners on you again, who's to know?'

'You fucking grass,' Murphy yelled as he launched himself at Spanners but the ex-soldier was too strong.

'Pack that in,' said Jo. 'Tell me what you did to my boys, what you used and who paid you.' Murphy just glared at her. Jo pointed a finger between Murphy's eyes. 'Tell me now because if they die, what we'll do to you is far worse than whoever you're running from will.'

'I don't know,' he said. Spanners looked between Jo and Saira as if begging for permission to give Murphy a dig. Jo gave the faintest shake of her head.

'I know how you got in there and what you did. What you're going to tell me is what you used and who's the brains behind this, 'cos that certainly isn't you.'

'Fuck off.'

'Right, we're running out of time here. Saira and I are going to take a walk for a few minutes.'

The PC looked confused.

'Spanners, are you OK staying here with Mr Murphy?'

'My pleasure,' replied Spanners. 'Fancy attacking kids.'

Jo and Saira walked slowly down to the seafront.

'Is this wise, ma'am?'

'Eh? He's not under arrest and we've just left two like-minded chaps

312

to have a chat. That said, we'll only give them five minutes.'

Saira shrugged and they ambled along the promenade in silence.

Four minutes later, Saira took out her phone and read the message.

'What is it?' said Jo.

'Looks like they might not be playing nicely. Shall we go back?'

When she reached the car, even though the windows were shut, she could hear the screaming. She opened the door and got in as quickly as she could. Saira did likewise. If it wasn't Ciaran and Liam's tiny lives at stake, she'd never have risked this – but seeing the fingers on Murphy's right hand pointing in all the wrong directions, she had no regrets.

'Oh, that looks nasty. Ready to talk?' she said.

'Fucking yes, just keep this animal away.'

'Good. Leave nothing out.'

Murphy spoke full and fast, not least because Spanners kept a tight grip on his left hand should he have second thoughts. Jo remained twisted round so she could look this would-be killer in the eyes.

His route to Brighton had been the same as Spanners' and his way into the school was as Jo had already worked out, exploiting the school's impatient clause in the advert which declared *DBS check required in due course, but will not be a barrier to the right candidate starting early.* 'I just had to wait to be told what to do,' he added. It was obvious really but hearing it from his mouth made it all the more sinister.

'Who?' Jo demanded. 'Who put you up to it?'

Murphy glanced at Spanners. 'Gorby, we call him. Squat, bald fella with a huge birthmark on his head.'

'That's the same bloke who told me to distribute the smack,' Spanners said.

His openness in front of Murphy surprised Jo, but she pressed on. 'And how did you poison them? I'm guessing you tampered with their lunchboxes, but what did you put in them?'

'I don't know.' With this Spanners gripped Murphy's left thumb.

'Hold on,' said Jo. 'Why don't you know?'

"Cos the fella, he just gave me this spray bottle and told me to squirt four shots into whatever might absorb it in their lunchboxes. He didn't tell me what it was and I didn't ask.'

Spanners looked across at Jo. She shook her head and carried on. 'Where were you when he gave you the bottle?'

'He messaged me and told me to meet him outside the school this morning.' A surge of adrenaline washed through Jo. Just as Mrs Brakespear the receptionist had said. Where was that CCTV she'd asked for?

'Anything else?'

Murphy shook his head. 'No, I swear.'

'Where's the bottle?'

'Dumped.'

Jo could have pushed it but the clock was against her. 'Spanners, get him to the hospital. Stay with him until you hear from us.' She turned to Murphy. 'Listen to me. You tell the hospital you were jumped and these guys you've never seen before broke your fingers. You do not tell them why and, when the police arrive, which they will, you point-blank refuse to talk to them. They'll push it to a degree but not for long. When you're fixed, you stay with Spanners and we'll be in touch with the next steps. Understood?'

He nodded. Spanners added, 'If he needs reminding then I'm happy to help.'

'Just be careful. Now off, the pair of you.' She released the child locks and the two men exited the car.

When they were gone and out of sight, Jo called the hospital. More than once she bellowed at the unanswered ringtone to 'Fucking answer', and eventually she was put through to the HDU. After a hurried update it was clear that the doctors, like her, were none the wiser regarding the source of the symptoms. They were screening for everything imaginable but nothing was coming up positive. The vomiting was being held back by anti-emetics and their temperatures kept at bay by paracetamol, but both boys' condition seemed to be in stasis.

For now, she had to block it from her mind while she made a couple of calls. First to the school to find out where the external CCTV had got to. Next came a trickier call but one that she had to make.

When he answered, he still sounded offended.

'Bob, look I'm sorry but I'm terrified,' she said, 'and I need to update you.' She ran through everything, except the broken fingers, and tried her best to differentiate the certainties from the inferences, of which there were many. 'It's essential we locate this Gorby bloke – it has to be Evans – and find out what was in those bottles.'

'Finished?'

'For now.'

'Right,' said Bob. Jo could tell he was struggling to remain civil. 'It might surprise you but I've not been idle myself. My lot have been digging into Evans and he's been remarkably busy over the last few weeks. Usually he keeps out of the way but he's been getting his hands dirty, meeting with people he'd usually avoid like a month-old kofta.'

'Such as?'

'Few you'd know specifically, but loads of them have been linked to the anti-Op Eradicate activity and most have gone missing.'

'Well done.'

'Mmm. Anyway, here's the jackpot ball. Despite what he thought were Soviet-standard counter-surveillance techniques, guess who he's visited regularly?'

'I haven't got time for guessing games, just tell me,' she said as a dog walker allowed his mutt to cock a leg against her tyre. She couldn't help but bang on the window, which terrified the owner and set the terrier off into a cacophony of yelps.

'Sir Ben Parsons.'

'Say that again.'

'You heard me. Some of his phones and several of the cars linked to him have been tracked to Sir Ben's house, and on occasions both of

315

their phones have been together away from the address.'

The thrill of the chase, which was so rare in her current role, overwhelmed her. 'Let's find him and nick him then,' she said.

'Hold your horses. We might need a little more than that.'

'Usually, yes, but you're forgetting my two boys' lives are at stake. Until we know what these bastards have given them, they could die at any moment.' She choked the last words. 'We don't have time for a gilt-edged arrest plan. We need to find out what they know, like five hours ago. By force if necessary.'

'Their phones are both showing at Sir Ben's address now.'

'Which is?'

Bob gave it to her then said, 'But I need something to firmly link them before I can get a surveillance authority, let alone a warrant to search the place.'

'Oh, you crack on then. Let me know when you think you've got enough. Meanwhile, I've got a couple of funerals to arrange.' Jo hung up before Bob could reply. She knew she'd treated her most trusted colleague appallingly once again but she needed action.

She was about to call Bob back but before she could, a WhatsApp from a number she didn't recognise flashed on her screen.

CCTV from outside school. Mrs Holmes, read the message with a video attached.

'Watch this,' said Jo, angling the screen to Saira.

The frozen frame showed the school gate and the road beyond. The timestamp showed that day's date and 10.15 a.m. Jo pressed play. She watched intently as Murphy ran into shot and out of the gate, then stood at the side of the road directly outside. Almost immediately, a Brighthelm cab pulled up on the other side of the road. Murphy then peered at the car and hesitated. Next Tony Evans – his birthmark thankfully spotlit by the sun – got out of the car and seemed to shout towards Murphy, who ran over and got in the cab. For a full two minutes, nothing happened. Then Murphy got out, checked the traffic and ran back into the school, stopping only to pull something from his pocket, examine it, then stuff it back. He then disappeared from shot.

Jo started the car. 'Buckle up. We're off to pay someone a visit.'

49

'What's the plan, boss?' Saira said, as Jo accelerated away.

'Yes, good point. I don't actually have one yet but given the likelihood of us being stuck in traffic, we can cobble one together before we get there. But here's what we know. Tony Evans, and probably Sir Ben Parsons, are behind the boys' poisoning and most likely the whole campaign to undermine Op Eradicate.'

'What, including killing Lizzie and putting Scotty in hospital?'

'Yep, all of it. I need to find out from Evans what Murphy contaminated their food with so the hospital can treat them. For me, everything depends on that.'

'Right. Can't Mr Heaton pull some troops together?'

'Of course, and I'm sure he's on to that, but we're not blessed with a lot of time so we need to do what we can while he's getting sorted. There are risks, though. Are you OK with that?'

'If they've done what you said, to your kids and my mates, you bet your fucking life I am . . . ma'am.'

After all these years policing Brighton, it still amazed Jo how angry the languid traffic made her. Despite needing thinking time, she could have done with making more progress. As she tried the shortcuts, she realised that she wasn't alone in knowing the rat runs.

'We need to get in the house,' she said. 'Or at least strike lucky that Evans or Parsons come out.' Jo glanced at the dashboard clock. 'It's a bit late in the day for the old parcel delivery trick, so we need to think of something else. Can you bring the address up on Street View?' Saira fiddled with her phone, while Jo zipped into a bus lane to undertake a lorry which was, frankly, taking the piss.

'There's a huge set of gates which look like they're remote-controlled. That probably means a camera too, so we might struggle with the element of surprise.' Out of the corner of her eye, Jo saw Saira zoom in on the image. 'Same on the front door by the look of it. What are you like at climbing?'

Jo gave her a look that said *In your dreams.*

As she bullied her way towards Dyke Road where, God willing, the traffic would thin, Jo wrestled for ideas. 'It's going to have to be subterfuge. We have to trick our way in,' she said.

'With respect, you sound like Scotty, ma'am.'

'How so?'

'Mansplaining. I do know what subterfuge means.'

Jo laughed. 'Sorry, you must forgive me. I'm used to working with Superintendent Hedges.'

'Well, there are a host of things I could be. No one suspects a young Asian woman to be a cop. The only difficulty is, you're too well known. Unless of course . . .'

'What?'

'Can you pull over at that parade of shops?' said Saira. Jo obeyed and the PC got out of the car and ran into a chemist. Two minutes later, she was carrying what looked like a tissue box. Once she was back in the car, Jo was eager to learn what Saira had in mind.

'Face masks. Nowadays, people wear them without getting a second glance. At least they might not realise it's you. Well, until you want them to.'

'Mmm,' said Jo. 'It might buy us some time, but that's all. We still need a story.'

'And quickly. Looks like we are only a few minutes away.'

Jo's heart sank. She pulled off Dyke Road and weaved through the streets that served the heart of the most exclusive area of Brighton. Checking her satnav, she saw Sir Ben's road was next on the left. She gently coasted round and was struck by how quiet it was, and thus how exposed they were. They both knew the house was on the left, so kept their heads straight ahead, straining their eyes sidewards to scope out what obstacles or opportunities there might be. As Jo looked ahead again, she saw a red and white ambulance, with red roof-bar lights and *CareFly Medical Care* emblazoned on the side, crawling towards her.

Both the woman driver and the female passenger seemed to be searching for a house, their heads flicking right and left and the passenger pointing. 'Keep an eye on them,' said Jo as it passed at a snail's pace.

Saira crooked her neck to study the wing mirror. 'They've paused outside Sir Ben's, now they are heading to the end of the road. I reckon they're turning round.'

Jo threw caution to the wind and crunched her car into reverse, backed into a driveway two mansions down, then drove out at speed to catch the ambulance up. 'Got it,' she announced. 'Follow my lead and bring the masks.'

Just as the ambulance was about to complete the turn, and out of view of Sir Ben's, Jo blocked their path. She got out of the car and Saira followed. Ambling up to the driver's door, she took out her warrant card and flashed it just long enough for the other person to see the badge but not the name. The window glided down.

'Good morning. Are you here for the Parsons residence?'

'Yes,' came the reply in an accent Jo struggled to place. 'We are taking the patient to the airport.'

Jo managed to keep her expression neutral but a thousand questions erupted in her head. 'Yes, of course. My colleague and I just have to complete the security checks.'

'The security checks? What security checks?'

Jo looked at Saira for the ambulance crew's benefit, as if to say *Not again.* 'No one told you? I'm so sorry. Sir Ben has special status and we are his personal protection detail. We have to search you and scan your phones and the ambulance. It won't take long, then you're free to carry on. I'm so sorry your office didn't pass on the message. Would you mind stepping out?'

Both women obeyed and Saira went to the passenger while Jo attended to the driver. Loud enough for Saira to hear, Jo said, 'If you just slip your jacket off and pop it on the seat. I'll check that in a minute. Oh, and your phone.' The driver obeyed and Jo frisked her, aware that Saira was doing the same. When they completed the search, Jo said, 'We won't be a moment. We have to drive the van through the X-ray just inside the gate, then we'll be done. Just wait here.' She couldn't believe that, despite them looking so confused, the two women didn't question a thing. Before anything dawned on them, Jo got in the driver's side and Saira into the passenger's. 'Won't be a mo,' said Jo as she drove the short distance to the gate.

'We cannot get away with this,' said Saira.

'We have to,' said Jo. 'Now get that jacket and your face mask on.' Jo did the same as she was driving. 'What does that say on the clipboard?' she added.

Saira scanned it. 'Looks like we're taking an Audrey Parsons to Gatwick to catch an air ambulance to New York.'

'What?'

'Yep,' said Saira, just as Jo turned level with the intercom. She pressed the buzzer and it was answered instantly by a gruff male voice.

'Yes?'

'CareFly ambulance. We are here to collect Mrs Parsons.' Jo's heart pummelled her ribcage, certain she'd be rumbled.

As the voice said, 'Come to the front door,' the gates opened, and Jo paused, turning to Saira. 'Last chance. You sure you want to do this with me?'

'Got nothing else on,' she replied. Jo wished she still had the naive enthusiasm of the young rather than an overwhelming sense of doom.

As Jo pulled up to the door, it was already open. Emerging from it was the man who made it his life's goal to be in every charity event photo the local paper printed: Sir Ben Parsons. Aware that her own face was also no stranger to the *Argus* front page, she adjusted her face mask. 'Let's do this,' she whispered to Saira. 'Whatever "this" is,' she added, more to herself.

Just as she stepped out of the van, Sir Ben ran forward, followed by a shorter man who, while appearing sportier than Sir Ben, had a look of fluster and fear about him.

'Come quickly,' said Sir Ben. 'You're late and I'm told the slot time at Gatwick is tight.'

Jo grunted as she flicked her head for Saira to follow.

'I'm Dr Blaketon by the way,' said the other man. 'I've signed the FTF and the patient is ready for you. I just need to hand over, then you can be on your way.'

'Thank you,' said Jo in what she knew was a dreadful Eastern European accent. Hopefully the muffling effect of the face mask would have stifled it enough so as not to arouse suspicion. She was desperate to ask what an FTF was, but instinctively knew that would give the game away.

Jo scurried behind the two men with Saira in tow as they raced up the stairs. Halfway up she wondered whether she should have brought the stretcher. Then she remembered she was not actually going to take this patient anywhere – she just needed to be in the house so she could confront the men who'd tried to kill her sons. They reached the top and were soon in a huge bedroom with ornate furniture and knick-knacks from a bygone era. However, it was the wizened, confused-looking old lady in the ornate lime-ash bed at the centre of the back wall, and the faint whiff of a recent gunshot, that took her aback.

'Mum, these ladies are going to take you on the aeroplane Dr Blaketon was telling you about, so we can make you better.'

Jo heard a buzz coming from downstairs and prayed it was not who she thought it was.

'How kind,' said Audrey, then a vicious coughing fit consumed her. The panic that followed told Jo the woman was choking. Dr Blaketon rushed over. 'You, come and help,' he shouted to Jo. She faltered, then joined the medic, with no idea what she was expected to do. 'Sit her up and forward.' Jo hesitated again and she could tell the doctor noticed. She grabbed the woman by the shoulders, which made the doctor shout, 'Careful. She's incredibly frail.' The look he gave her could have frozen mercury.

'Get back,' came another voice from the door. Jo swivelled round to see a short, squat, bald man with the distinctive splatter of a birthmark on his head, aiming a pistol in one hand and pushing the two genuine ambulance crew into the room with the other. Jo did as she was told and noticed Saira step back and edge towards the door. Tony Evans saw it too and swung the gun in the PC's direction. 'Don't even try it,' he snarled.

'Tony, what the hell's going on?' said Sir Ben.

Tony shoved the terrified newcomers further into the room. 'These two just came to the gate asking whether security had finished with their ambulance yet. Seems your personal protection officers needed to scan it before they were allowed in.'

50

Sir Ben tilted his head as he looked at Jo. 'Get away from my mother and take your masks off,' he said to both Jo and Saira.

Saira made a bolt for Sir Ben but Tony pistol-whipped her, splitting her cheek under her right eye. As she fell, she made a grab for the gun but Evans's boot to her chest was too much and she crashed to the floor.

'Oh do play nicely children, or you'll all have to go home,' said Audrey.

No one took any notice. Sir Ben spun Jo round and ripped her mask off. 'Chief Superintendent Howe,' he said. 'Aren't you people supposed to have warrants before you trespass on private property? Take her mask off,' he said to Dr Blaketon.

Plainly not used to this, he pleaded with his eyes before Tony pointed the gun at him. 'You heard.' He stepped forward, knelt to where Saira was groaning on the floor and gently slipped off the mask.

'This is going to need stitches,' said the doctor, looking up at Sir Ben.

'You'll need a military field dressing if you don't shut the fuck up,' said Tony, still guarding the two terrified paramedics. 'Stand her up.' Dr Blaketon obeyed. Saira stumbled but the doctor held her tight. 'Turn her round.' As soon as Saira was face to face with Evans, she spat square in his eye which earned her another gun butt to the face. This time she ducked and the pistol caught her on the top of her head. Still the doctor held her, his horror plain in his expression. 'I know you,' said Evans. 'You're Sergeant Scott's bitch. What is it? That's it, Bannerjee. PC Bannerjee. You need to choose more carefully who you work with.'

'This has got nothing to do with her,' said Jo. 'I told her to come with me. We don't want any trouble.'

Sir Ben stepped up close. 'No trouble? You're the Old Bill. Of course you want trouble.'

Jo had so many horrors she wanted to spell out to this evil narcissist, but that would have to wait. 'I only want to know what your guy used to poison my little boys. If the hospital don't find out, they'll die.'

'I'm afraid I have no idea what you're talking about,' said Sir Ben, but his eyes told a different story. Jo could tell from the doctor's look, on the other hand, that he really was in the dark. Tony's smirk confirmed what she already knew.

'Your thug here was seen passing the bottle that Terry Murphy used to contaminate their lunches and now they are on life support, so you better start thinking if you want to avoid a life sentence.'

One of the captured paramedics whimpered in the corner but Jo needed to focus on what was happening in front of her. On cue, Evans stepped forward and thrust the pistol at Jo's face. 'You fucking reckon,' he said.

'That's it, I'm calling your mothers to come and collect you,' said Audrey.

'Shut her up,' said Evans.

'That's my mum,' said Sir Ben. 'Treat her with respect. Trevor, see what you can do to calm her down.'

'What have my boys done to you?' Jo said to Sir Ben, hoping to capitalise on his apparent soft spot for family. 'I don't care what else you've done, just don't let them die.'

She saw his steel falter, then Trevor said, 'I'm not sure she's fit to fly any more.' *Oh, that's what FTF stands for*, thought Jo.

'Think again,' said Sir Ben. 'And now we've got the real paramedics, we can get back to what we are all here for. Get her ready.'

Suddenly, Audrey Parsons shouted out, a strained, panicked moan. Everyone in the room whipped round to face her.

'What's happening?' said Sir Ben in a state of dread. Dr Blaketon ignored him and dashed to the old lady. All her muscles were as taut as anchor rope and her crimson face bore a look of sheer terror. Her body tremored and her legs and arms thrashed with a ferocity such a frail woman shouldn't have been able to manage.

'Do something, Trevor.'

'There's nothing to do. It has to work its course, I'm afraid.'

'There must be something you can do,' said Tony Evans.

Sir Ben glared at him. 'Let the doctor work.'

Blaketon watched on as the seizure showed no sign of abating. He appeared to busy himself as if to distract Sir Ben and Evans.

'Once she's stable, hand her over to these two,' said Sir Ben, pointing to the paramedics cowering in the corner.

'This has to stop,' said Jo, vaguely aware of movement over her right shoulder.

'That's not your call, said Evans, standing at the apex of a triangle with Jo and the doctor at the other corners.

Dr Blaketon looked up. 'She can't travel now. Look at the state of her. We'll be lucky to get her to hospital, let alone New York.'

'Nothing's changed, Trevor. You've signed the paperwork, so get her sorted or we're going to miss that bloody flight slot.'

Trevor faced Sir Ben. 'That was then. Look at her. How the hell will she survive a nine-hour flight? She'll barely see the night out here.'

'GET HER READY!' yelled Sir Ben.

'This has gone far enough,' said the doctor as he bolted for the door. Sir Ben went to grab him but a gunshot stopped him in his tracks.

51

Time stood still as the doctor crumpled in front of them all, blood obliterating the front of his white shirt. It took a second before Jo registered the paramedics' screams, then saw Tony raise his gun towards them. In a flash, Saira grabbed Tony's right arm, clamped it under her own and with a lightning swivel powered him to the ground, his screams suggesting that she'd dislocated his shoulder. In a second, she'd goosenecked his wrist and the gun dropped to the floor. She grabbed it, aimed it at Evans on the ground and stamped down on his clavicle. 'Stay where you fucking are,' she yelled.

Jo was momentarily taken aback by the PC's devastating martial arts skills, a millisecond too long as Sir Ben bolted from the room.

'Get back here,' she yelled, almost tripping over Dr Blaketon's body. 'See to him,' she shouted, hoping that the paramedics would know that was aimed at them. Confident that with the gun in Saira's hands, Evans was going nowhere and that, if she had misjudged Blaketon as being a reluctant conspirator, he was in no state to be a threat anyway, she headed off after Sir Ben.

He had a good five seconds on her which, in a house this size and with his forensic knowledge of it, might as well have been an hour.

As she sprinted along the landing, he could have taken any one of the doors that flanked its oak-panelled walls. Or none of them. Her instinct told her that he was running to get away, rather than hide, so she headed for the way he had brought her and Saira minutes before.

The pound of steps on stairs confirmed her theory and as she neared them, she glanced over the balustrade and saw Sir Ben stumble on the half-turn.

'Get back here,' she yelled, causing him to glance up. In that brief moment, fear flashed in his eyes. He regained his footing and she guessed he'd created enough distance to go where the hell he liked.

She grabbed the bannister as she reached the top step then, taking two at a time, seemed to fly down the stairs. As she reached where he had tripped, a tremendous crash came from below. On completing the turn she saw what it was. A huge Welsh dresser which, in her trepidation, she'd not spotted on the way up had been heaved on its side and blocked the bottom of the staircase.

It served to distract her attention but as she got to the bottom, with the downward momentum, she was able to leap it with relative ease. Thankfully her trainers provided good grip as she landed on the wooden hall floor, and whilst she had lost sight of Ben, a door slamming to the left gave his position away. As she took in where the noise had come from, she had the pick of three doors.

There was no logic to apply, so she went right to left. The first door swung open easily in her hand and she was able to discount it immediately. The small toilet had no room to hide and the window, some ten feet up, looked like it hadn't been opened in decades.

She spun round and tried the second. She should have guessed this would be the washroom. Equal in size and certainly Sir Ben had not been here.

That meant the left door must be the one. Jo was about to wrench it as she had the others – impetuously, now she thought about it. If he was in here, he could be waiting with God knows what ready to attack her. She took a breath, held it, wedged her ear against the wood and waited for any sound.

Silence.

She shuffled to the side of the door, inched the handle down and shoved it open, keeping to the edge. When the counter-attack did not come, she crouched down and peered in. Instead of a knight of the realm in front of her, there was a stone staircase descending into the darkness.

The chill wafted up, bringing with it a sharp tang of damp and chemicals, which Jo couldn't name. She thought about leaving it and calling for back-up.

She was tempted to reach for her phone and use its torch to guide her but knew that would be tantamount to putting a target on her head. Instead she glared into the darkness, waiting for her eyes to grow accustomed to the gloom. Then her little boys' faces flashed in her mind. It took a minute or two but soon she had as much night vision as she guessed she ever would, so step by oh-so-slow step, she made her way into the unknown.

She could just make out the bottom when, she estimated, she had half a dozen steps to go. Her strained eyes scoured the black, willing that she would spot Sir Ben before he saw her.

'Stay where you are,' came the shout from the near distance – about two o'clock. Jo squinted but could see nothing.

'Come out,' she said as she squeezed against the left-hand wall, tiptoeing down the last few stairs.

'You're not getting away with this,' Sir Ben said. 'Even if you survive, with everything you've done you're finished.'

Jo had no idea exactly where he was nor whether he had any weapons, so played it safe. Her foot touched the floor.

'Think about your mum. She needs you and we can sort this. Come out with your hands on your head and I'll take you to see her.' She took two more steps.

'I said stay still, or you'll get hurt,' he shouted.

She stopped, but every time he spoke, Jo was able to reassess where he was. But she had no idea whether he had the means to harm her. It was a risk she might have to take, but for now her mission was to keep him talking.

'No one needs to get hurt. I just need to know what's harmed my kids, then Saira and I will be out of your hair.'

She allowed her voice to mask more steps, but the last one clanked against something heavy. She leant down and, among the debris, her fingers brushed a cold metal object which she gauged was about two inches wide. When he next spoke, she would pick it up. If she could.

It was the scurry of a rodent to her left that made her jump first, then, true to form, Sir Ben couldn't resist what he thought might be the last word. 'You don't expect me to believe that, do you?'

She managed it and stood up. 'I'm serious. This has gone too far. Let's save my boys and your mum. What do you say?' She ran her hands over the heavy tool in the darkness. As her fingers explored the end, she worked out that it was the heftiest adjustable spanner she'd ever held, not that there were a whole lot of lighter ones. Its surface was cold to the touch and felt pitted with rust. Her right hand gripped the shaft and she rested the head in her left.

Jo suspected that, unless he had a gun, Sir Ben wouldn't have a tastier weapon than this. In any case, time was running out for her boys.

'OK, enough's enough,' said Jo. 'If you don't show yourself, I'm coming to get you.' She gave him no more than thirty seconds, then, 'Time's up.'

As she walked forward, she stumbled over a stack of paint pots. 'Get out here,' she shouted, intent on shielding her fear with anger.

'Don't come any closer,' yelled Sir Ben. She was about to ignore him when a hissing followed by a whoosh and a flash stopped her in her tracks. 'Stay back,' he ordered as the spear of blue flame from an oxyacetylene torch he was holding danced in front of him, lighting his face like a Halloween mask.

Jo worked out that he was only about two metres away but had no idea what damage his makeshift flamethrower could do.

'Put it down, you idiot, you'll kill us both.' Behind the fire she could make out his grimace.

'Then get the fuck out of here and let us go.'

Jo stepped forward and took a swipe at the torch with her wrench, but it missed and clattered onto a steel upright. She tried again on the backswing but Ben dodged out of the way. As she brought the wrench back, the flame caught her arm and it flared her sleeve.

'Ah, fuck.' She dropped the spanner as her hoodie caught fire. Instinctively she dropped to the floor and rolled, desperate to snuff the flames. The acrid smoke gagged in her throat but all she could focus on was not combusting. She managed it just in time but her arm hurt like the worst sunburn.

Sir Ben sprung forward, the lance of the flame roaring. Jo shuffled away to stop him igniting her hair, at the same time grabbing his ankle as he tried to kick her. Using the only weapon she had left, she sank her teeth into his calf. He screeched and stamped down, Jo using her whole body weight to keep his foot rooted to the ground.

'Get off me, you mad bitch,' he shouted as he tried to shake her off. Still he gripped the torch though, and now both his other leg and the gassy flame were homing in on her. She bit deeper into the flesh; her jaw cried out for her to let go but she knew that would be fatal.

He managed to lift the leg she was biting and swung it from side to side. Jo was sure she'd get whiplash but his screams told her that she was having effect. He flipped her, thrusting the flame towards her, and as she put her hand out to steady herself, she touched the wrench again. Gripping it, she managed to bring it back and brought it square against the shinbone of his standing leg, his screams drowning out the shatter of bone.

Sir Ben collapsed in front of her, still gripping the torch but wailing like a footballer. Jo sprung up, just in time to see the flame catch a mass of dust sheets to her right. They erupted with frightening speed and, for the first time, Jo could see the whole cellar by the light of the fire. It was rammed with a lifetime of crap, like her dad's garage but multiplied fivefold.

Sir Ben seemed to be inert on the ground and the flaming cloths were dangerously close to his head. She was about to leave him when she remembered why she was here in the first place.

Grabbing his smashed leg and straining every muscle, she heaved him along the concrete floor, away from danger. If his screams were deafening before, now they were ear-splitting. She blocked them out as she dragged him a good three metres away from the rapidly expanding inferno.

'Get me out, get me out!' he cried.

'Tell me what the boys have taken.'

'Get me out first.'

'No. It doesn't work like that. You tell me first, then I get you out. Otherwise you stay here and fry.'

'You wouldn't dare.'

'You called me a mad bitch. Do you want to see how mad I can be?' She stood up and backed towards the stairs. 'See you in hell.'

She was genuinely prepared to do it. After all, Tony Evans was being held at Saira's gunpoint upstairs. As a last resort, they could get it out of him.

'OK. OK. Spice. They gave them spice.'

Jo was dumbfounded. 'Spice, on kids? Have you seen what that stuff can do to grown adults? That's it – fucking stay here and burn, you fucking monster. It's too good for you.'

She took two more steps back, then saw a bank of five or so large plastic containers, close to the fire. *White Spirit*. She'd seen a demo of what one of those could do and, much as she would love to see Sir Ben cremate, she had to act.

Running back to him, she grabbed his arm. 'Stand up.' Her skin was exploding in blisters.

'I can't. My leg.'

'You've got one chance, you piece of shit, or I'm leaving you here. I've got what I want, remember? Now lean on me and get on your feet.' When she felt his weight bear down on her, she heaved him and, whilst she wasn't strong enough to carry him, now she could use adrenaline and momentum to pull him to relative safety.

She adjusted her position so his arm was across her shoulder. 'This is going to fucking hurt but we're not stopping.' She turned towards the stairs and, to her horror, saw their exit completely cut off by the fire. She glanced to where the spirit was and saw that as well as having no exit, she had about a minute, if that, to get out before the whole place went up.

'Another door?' she yelled in Sir Ben's ears in an effort to be heard over his screams.

He didn't answer.

'Get us out or we die,' she shouted. The flames advanced closer.

'Over there,' he said between sobs, his shift in body weight telling Jo which way to head. She dragged him in a straight line, shouting at him to walk so at least his goodish leg did some work. She clambered across a generation of clutter, ignoring Sir Ben's cries. There was only one way they were going to get out of here and it wasn't going to be pretty.

In a few seconds, having kicked God-knows-what obstructions clear, she found a doorway. She dropped Sir Ben like a sack, as she needed both hands to clear a stack of boxes away, then she worked the key so the door opened. She looked out and found she was in a courtyard with steps leading up to a lawn.

For the second time, she was tempted to run and leave Sir Ben, but she turned and grabbed him again, forcing him to lean on her so she could heave him out. As she got them both clear of the door and into the open, she slammed it shut, a second before what sounded like a bomb going off on the other side.

52

'Wait here, I'll get help,' she said to Sir Ben, as if he had any choice. Jo ran up the steps and looked up. To her horror, she saw the whole side of the house ablaze and she worked out that she was just below Audrey Parson's room, where she'd left Saira and the rest.

She fumbled for her phone and, one-handedly, found Bob's number. He answered before the second ring.

'Jo, where the hell are you?'

'It was spice, Bob. They poisoned the boys with spice, tell the hospital straight away.'

'Sure, but what's happening?'

'I'm at Sir Ben Parson's with Saira. Call the fire brigade, the house is in flames.'

'What the fuck?'

'Just do it Bob, but the hospital first. I'm going back in.'

She knew what he'd say next so she ended the call.

'I'm going to rescue your mum,' she shouted down to Sir Ben.

'No, help me!' he yelled exasperatedly. Jo pretended not to hear as she ran round the perimeter of the house, searching for a safe way back in. She found a set of French doors at the back. Thankfully, they were unlocked. She ran through what looked like a dining room and reached the door which led into the hallway. Opening it, she could already see the hell that faced her. They said it was the smoke that killed you in a fire, and there was enough of that to snuff out an army. She spotted a cabinet and willed what she needed to be in there. She flung open the cupboard door and snatched a folded tablecloth, grabbed a soda syphon from a tray and gave the handle a squeeze, soaking the material. Ramming her makeshift mask over her nose and mouth, she counted to three and ran out into the hallway.

The blaze, already devastating the ground floor and licking up the stairs, might as well have been an iron gate. There was no way she was getting up those alive. She thought fast. This was an old house. Surely, back in the day, the servants would not have been permitted to use the main staircase. There must be another way up, unless some floppy-haired interior designer had ripped it out.

Jo ran to the back of the house, using her free hand to navigate by touch as far as she could, the other crushing her mouth and nose through the tablecloth. Despite that, the fumes clogged her lungs and her eyes were screaming at her to get out.

She felt a door to her right and darted through it. The worst of the fire had spared this area so far, and she worked out it was the kitchen. At any other time she probably would have admired its grandeur, but her sole focus was to find a way up to rescue four innocent people and one killer, all probably screaming for their lives. Dr Blaketon was probably past saving. She ran to the back of the room, crying out as she caught her hip on the edge of a granite worktop.

In the far corner was a door, which at first she thought would lead out to the garden, but when she examined it, a narrow winding staircase presented itself on the other side. *This house is a maze*, she thought.

Despite knowing she'd soon be cut off up here, she ran up the stairs. When she reached the top, the door leading off wouldn't budge. *Holy fuck.*

She shoulder-charged it but given the locker-sized space, she couldn't get enough momentum to crash it open. In panic, she kicked and kicked it before she spotted the bolt at the top. Cursing herself, she slid it, then now driven by logic saw the one at the bottom and freed that too. Rushing through, she found herself on another landing.

She didn't break stride other than in a hopeless effort to gain some sense of direction. She gambled on turning left, but the smoke was billowing up from there. It wasn't much better the other way but she had to make a choice if she was going to find any of them alive, so she headed right. She glanced in all the open doors as she crawled along the landing, but it was like staring through ink.

Then one closed door on her right drew her attention. It dawned on her that you didn't get to become a paramedic without learning a little about self-preservation. She sized up the door, and learning from the last one, tried the handle. This time it opened.

Saira swung the gun at her, but dropped its aim back to Evans who was still writhing on the floor. 'Welcome back, ma'am. On your own?'

'Yep, we need to get everyone out of here.'

'Even this piece of shit?'

'I'm afraid so, even though he thinks it's OK to poison children with spice.' Evans looked up in horror. 'Yep, even your boss will grass in the right circumstances.'

'I'll fucking kill him,' he said. Saira stamped down on his injured shoulder. He wailed in pain.

'Whoops, I keep doing that. Sorry again,' she said.

'Be careful,' said Jo, nodding towards the two paramedics.

She was impressed that they'd already fashioned a smoke hood out of spare sheeting and were dousing the floor with water from the bathroom.

'How's he?' she said, looking at Dr Blaketon.

One of the paramedics shook her head.

'Let's get out of here,' said Jo.

The two women just stared at her. Hardly surprising, as it was her stealing their ambulance that had put them in this situation. They were doing all they could for now, so Jo dashed over to the remains of the window.

She'd not heard the cavalry arrive, but the sight of three gleaming fire engines chewing up the pristine lawn was like an oasis in the Sahara. The roar of their engines and pumps was deafening and she could see they'd just arrived, as not only were firefighters only starting to drag hoses from the back of each tender, but the gates they had crashed through were still swinging on their hinges.

'Up here,' she yelled. 'Up here.' But no one heard her amid the scream of machinery. There were plenty of helmeted firefighters staring at the burning building but none looking in her direction.

She looked around and saw a flat-screened TV on the wall. It was all she could think of. 'You two, give me a hand.' The paramedics stood and scowled. 'Now.'

They scurried over. 'Grab this.' They did as she said and after several tugs, the bracket gave way and Jo and one of the paramedics had the screen in their hands. 'To the window,' she said, then, when they were there, 'Help me throw this as far as we can.' The paramedic looked at her quizzically. 'Just do it. One, two, three.'

The screen seemed to fly in slow motion as it headed towards the largest fire tender. It crashed on the grass, not ten feet from a firefighter in a white hat who, for a second, looked down at it, then at the sky, then finally in Jo's direction. She waved her hands frantically above her head and then the penny dropped for him.

All she could see was him mouthing orders, but within thirty seconds the nearest engine was racing across the grass towards them.

Once the aerial ladder was at the window, Jo grabbed the equipment on the platform. She, the firefighter and the paramedics worked in unison to ease Mrs Parsons onto the stretcher and carry her to the window. Jo insisted the paramedics be taken down with her, before returning. Then Saira and her prisoner were next. Jo had put everyone in this position, so she owed it to all of them to get them out before she did.

She had no idea whether the building would hold out for the time it took for the ladder to come back up. The rumbling and crashes did not bode well but once it was back in position, she stumbled into the safety cage, moments before her world went black.

53

Two days later

For the second morning running, Jo woke to find herself hammering at the bedroom window, screaming for Ciaran and Liam. Her sweat-sodden nightshirt clung to her like a second skin and every frantic breath was like inhaling broken glass.

The same ringtone that had first alerted her to the boys being rushed to hospital mocked her from the bedside table. She grabbed at the phone but it fell to the floor and under the bed. She retrieved it, knocking her burnt arm on the way back up. 'FUCK.' She rubbed the bandage and looked at the screen, to see Bob's name displayed there.

'Yes?'

'We're outside, can you let us in?'

'What, now?'

'Yes, now. Don't leave us standing.'

Jo ended the call, checked herself in the mirror, sighed and threw on a robe. She stomped to the front door and flung it open. 'Why not ring the bell?' Then she had to double take.

'Darren?'

'Glad you recognise me,' Darren said.

'You didn't tell me you were bringing him home,' she said to Bob, who was wearing a grin more suited to Santa than a world-weary DI.

Darren grinned at Bob. 'Do you think she'll let us in or what?'

Jo stepped to one side as Darren and Bob passed. She knew she should be pleased to see her husband but she couldn't summon up any feelings.

Bob glanced down at the doorbell receiver plugged into the wall, and switched it on.

'You're shaking,' Darren said as she walked into the lounge.

'I'm just a little shocked, that's all. You know the boys are still in hospital?'

'Yes. Bob's brought me up to speed. I'll get myself cleaned up and we'll go and see them.'

Jo could see the sadness in Darren's eyes, but her emotions were all over the place. 'Have you got bail or something?' She dropped herself onto the settee and reached for a third-full bottle of Pinot Grigio. Bob slid it away. Jo looked at him, daggers.

Darren sat next to her.

'No, the CPS have discontinued. Finally they realised it was a massive stitch-up. I understand the Met are looking for Sam Parkin as we speak.'

'You know the boys are still in hospital?'

'You just said that, Jo,' said Bob.

'Yes, as I said, we'll see them,' said Darren.

Jo fidgeted with her fingers, then stood. 'I suppose I better tidy up.'

'Why change the habit of a lifetime? Sit down a mo.' Darren stood and guided her by the arm, lowering her back onto the settee.

'I'm so scared.' Jo started to tremble, then burst into tears.

Darren took her in his arms. 'It's OK. It's all going to be all right,' he said.

'I don't know if it is, though. I'm having these terrible nightmares.'

'Would it help to talk about it?' said Darren.

'I don't know,' she said, her voice muffled by his shoulder.

'Try.'

'I keep seeing the boys' room on fire and I need to get in and save them, but I trip over Saira Bannerjee's body, then you're there pointing a gun at Ciaran and you shoot it and Liam tries to get it off you, but you kick him away. Then I cough until I can't breathe. I wake up trying to escape from the window.'

Darren squeezed her. 'It's OK, it's just a dream. It'll pass.'

Jo sobbed, then a racking cough took her over. Once she'd recovered, she said, 'What happened? In prison. They said you had drugs. And a phone.'

'Later, but none of that's true.'

'I'm so sorry. I did all this to you. You must hate me.' She coughed again, this time from the seat of her lungs.

'Of course I don't, but you can't carry on like this. You're not well.'

'This will clear up soon enough.'

Bob chipped in. 'He's not talking about the cough, Jo. You've really been through it – emotionally, I mean. We've all seen it. Don't you think it might be good to see someone, talk it through? You know, with a counsellor maybe.'

'I'm not mad,' she said, looking at Darren for back-up.

'No, you're not. But you really do need some proper looking after,' he said.

Jo stood up and picked up the bottle of wine, sloshing a hefty measure into the glass. 'I don't deserve help. Not when my boys are being kept alive on fuck knows what machinery.'

'You do and it's out there for you. They're going to need you well.'

Jo gulped her drink. 'I'm such a selfish bitch.'

Bob walked over and gently took the glass from her hand, putting it back on the table. 'You saved them in that house. Even the bad guys. You've put your life on the line for others, yet again.'

'That's what I mean. I'm always putting others first. I never think about

Darren and the boys. And now because of me . . . well look at them.'

'You didn't do those things. Parsons and Evans did and they'll get their just deserts.'

'They better.'

Bob nodded. 'They're already charged. And Claire Jackson is rounding up their cronies as we speak.' Bob opened the BBC News app on his phone. 'Look.' Jo wiped her eyes and took it from him.

Policing Minister Edward Baker arrested in dawn raid.

She handed it back. 'Nothing about the fire then.'

Bob raised his eyebrows. 'Yes, plenty, but don't you see? This went to the highest level. Seems Baker's son's been nicked too.'

'Really?' said Darren.

Bob nodded. 'Sounds like he and his Cambridge mates took the posh-boy antics to sickening new depths.'

Jo turned away. 'I don't care any more. Nothing matters except my boys.'

'Let me get you a coffee,' Darren said, standing up.

'I don't drink that muck. Anyway, I've got a drink,' she said, reaching again for the glass.

'I'll tell you what's going to happen,' said Darren, taking the wine before she could. 'We're both going to make ourselves presentable, then I'm phoning your GP. After which we'll see the boys. And that's final.'

Jo was about to argue when her phone rang. She recognised the number immediately. 'The hospital,' she said. Fumbling, she pressed 'accept'.

'Jo Howe.' She listened intently, barely able to comprehend what the caller was saying. She could just about mumble that she understood, then dropped the phone, her wails erupting like a devil from within.

54

Three weeks later

Jo couldn't bear to wear uniform. The very thought of buttoning up her epaulettes triggered another wave of memories of all she'd been through these past few weeks – years even. In any case, her dark trouser suit seemed more appropriate.

Darren parked the car in their reserved space behind St Peter's Church and, seeing the dozens of mourners, she wiped her reddened eyes. Her heart raced. How the hell was she going to get through today?

The ranks of well-meaning cops, many of whom seemed so edgy they could barely look at her, reminded her of all the people she'd let down and the lives she'd ruined. Christ, none of them would be here if it wasn't for her single-mindedness. But she was starting to recognise how much of a toll it had taken on her too. Her sessions with the new therapist were helping her to see that. The stresses she worked under weren't something you could just keep shrugging off. She'd been telling others that for years but never thought to look in the mirror.

She held Darren's hand. The physical scars from his time in Belmarsh

Prison were healing but no one could predict what the psychological legacy would be. 'You OK?' he said as he squeezed her grip.

'As much as I can be. You?'

'Getting there.'

She pecked his cheek and opened the door. Bob and Gary spotted them and were over in a shot. She managed a weak smile and allowed each to give her a brief hug.

'How are you both?' said Bob.

'Yeah, getting there,' said Jo.

Gary nodded. 'I'm sorry we weren't there for you when you needed us.'

'Don't worry about it,' said Jo, with a smile which stopped short of her eyes.

'Do you want an update?' said Bob, just as Jo was about to lead Darren towards the church.

She shrugged.

Darren stopped, making Jo do likewise. 'I do,' he said.

Jo started to walk away but Darren held her back. 'Jo, this might help.'

'Claire Jackson has done a cracking job. What with Sir Ben Parsons and Tony Evans charged, her team have uncovered a huge conspiracy against us. Nicola Merrion, Arjun Sharma the prison bigwig, the policing minister, plus a dozen others, are all on remand.'

Jo nodded and gripped Darren's hand. 'I heard Sam Parkin topped himself.'

'Shame about that,' said Darren. 'I'd have loved to have faced him in court.'

'Yes, the one who got away. Claire's still looking for the gunman who shot Pete McElroy and Challenor, but I reckon it's only a matter of time,' said Bob.

'Is the ACC coming?'

'I doubt it,' said Gary. 'You have heard about his staff officer, I take it?' Jo and Darren looked at him blankly. 'Nicked for leaking info for drugs? No, not heard that? Christ, we need to work on the rumour mill.'

There was an uncomfortable silence. Then Jo whispered, 'Sorry.'

'Eh?' said Gary.

'I said sorry. Sorry for dragging you all into this. Sorry for everything.' On the last word, she burst into tears.

Darren wrapped his arms around her and whispered, 'It's OK. It's OK.'

'When will you be back?' said Bob. 'We're missing you.'

'I don't know. I need to be a bit stronger first and get better at looking after myself. I'm making progress, but I want to make sure I don't come back before I'm one hundred per cent ready. I need to get over this too.' She looked around her.

'Oh my God,' said Gary. 'Over there.'

They followed his gaze and took in the sight. Saira, with Spanners alongside, was pushing a wheelchair carrying a frail old lady, waving at the crowd like she was royalty. 'Audrey Parsons? What the hell's she doing here?' said Jo.

'Saira seems to have adopted her, and the old lady heard what happened and wanted to show her respects,' said Bob.

Darren managed a smile. 'Well, she's certainly in her element.'

Jo shook her head. 'Come on, let's go and give Scotty the hero's send-off he deserves – then we've an afternoon of soft play mayhem with Ciaran and Liam to brace ourselves for.'

Acknowledgements

Each of my novels has been inspired by my experiences in Sussex Police, more so the latter years when I was in Jo's role; the Divisional Commander for Brighton and Hove. However, *City on Fire* is probably the closest to a significant, and somewhat controversial, policy I and some courageous partners both in and outside the police created.

Operation Eradicate is unashamedly based on Operation Reduction, a strategy I jointly led from 2005 to 2013 when I retired. Jo's mantra of 'Users in Treatment, Dealers in Prison,' was mine and I know its repetition was as tedious as Jo's is to Gary and Bob! Brighton was the drug death capital of the UK, had the country's highest number of heroin addicts per capita and crime was through the roof. Op Reduction slashed crime, created hundreds of treatment places, reduced addicts' offending, saved three times its investment in criminal justice costs and, most importantly, saved lives. It won a prestigious award and was heralded nationally. I was privileged to present on it at the United Nations in Vienna and at international drugs conferences. Like so many long term initiatives though, it became the victim of government cuts and now cities across the UK are bearing the brunt of this myopia.

Thankfully I didn't have the likes of Sir Ben Parsons to contend with and my own chief officers were very supportive, but I did experience the media and political backlash Jo suffers over me apparently going soft on drugs and crime. Those who brought the concept to fruition are too numerous to mention, and some can't be named, but a few, such as Paul Furnell, Richard Siggs, Mike Pattison, Bec Davison, Linda Beanlands and Graham Stevens stand out as being true visionaries who beat down doors with me.

I suppose now I ought to thank my agent, David Headley! Seriously, I owe this book, the previous in the series and hopefully many more to David and his DHH Literacy Agency team. David's insight, wisdom and drive keep me wedged to my chair and my fingers flying across the keyboard, safe in the knowledge I am in strong hands.

Susie Dunlop, my publisher, had the courage to sign this series for Allison & Busby and through her I have had the honour to work alongside just the most committed and innovative team I could have wished for. Like David, Susie's and her colleagues' guidance and listening ears keep me motivated and excited with each book and around each publication.

My readers in chief, Julie, my wife, son Deaglan, Samantha Brownley and Peter James all read *City on Fire* in its raw state and their pinpoint observations, corrections and candid advice meant that the version Allison & Busby saw, and you've now read, was blush and plot-hole free.

I advise scores of authors on police procedure but need the same from experts in other fields. Drs Chris Merritt and Philippa East, both clinical psychologists and incredible crime writers, gently guide me in making Jo's character change given the atrocities I throw at her. They teach me how she'd be scarred by her trauma and how that would present itself to the world. I am incredibly grateful to them both in helping me avoid either a cliched or bullet-proof protagonist.

Support too was needed over the science and the brain that is Brian

Price stepped in. Not only did he help me understand the pharmaceuticals but also has an enchanting way of pointing out what he thinks are typos but are really examples of my ignorance. Then of course is former Assistant Chief Constable Di Roskilly who, like in *Bad for Good* and *Force of Hate*, helped me understand the world of a woman senior officer as opposed to my male perspective on Jo's world. She's also found herself as my sensitivity reader, and her questioning of passages I now want to forget is far more direct than Brian's tact. Thanks also to former undercover officer 'Dom Smith' who generously allowed me a peek into his world. Any variations from reality are either dramatic licence, to protect operational security or my errors.

As well as the Allison & Busby team, Anouche Newman, Dani Brown and Jas Sheridan work miracles to get my books out there through social media and my website. There are so many brilliant crime novels and writers vying for reader's hard-earned custom that without the magicians who actually understand the cyber-world I would be shouting about Jo Howe into an echo chamber.

A huge thanks to all the readers, bloggers, reviewers, even award judges, who've bought into Jo Howe's world. Writing is a lonely business so the incredible feedback I've received on *Bad for Good* and *Force of Hate* has been humbling and liberating. Your response has been beyond my wildest dreams and you make those solitary hours of typing and doubt worth every moment.

Finally, a massive thanks to my ever-suffering family: my amazing wife Julie and triplets Conall, Niamh and Deaglan, as well as Murphy whose rhythmic snores by my desk keep the keys tapping. The slack you cut when I am locked away concocting, then re-concocting, Jo's world and putting up with my being mentally absent while trying to find ways to escape from corners I've written myself into is more than I deserve. The love you have for me, my books and my second career drives me on. You are my world and make this crazy dream possible.

A second finally! The themes in this book are serious and real. If you or anyone you know suffers from any form of addiction, please seek out the wonderful services such as I worked with to help. Anyone can stumble into a frightening world of dependence but so many can't see a way out. Support is there. You deserve it so please find and call your local providers. You won't regret it.

GRAHAM BARTLETT was the chief superintendent of Brighton and Hove police. His first non-fiction book, *Death Comes Knocking*, was a *Sunday Times* bestseller, co-written with Peter James. He has since published *Bad for Good* and *Force of Hate* starring Chief Superintendent Jo Howe. Bartlett is also a crime writing advisor helping scores of authors and TV writers inject authenticity into their work.

policeadvisor.co.uk
@gbpoliceadvisor